# THE Dove
## AND THE
# Rose

# ETHEL HERR

## THE
# Dove
### AND THE
# Rose

# BETHANY HOUSE PUBLISHERS
## MINNEAPOLIS, MINNESOTA 55438

*The Dove and the Rose*
Copyright © 1996
Ethel Herr

Cover by Dan Thornberg,
Bethany House Publishers staff artist.

Published by Bethany House Publishers
A Ministry of Bethany Fellowship, Inc.
11300 Hampshire Avenue South
Minneapolis, Minnesota 55438

Printed in the United States of America.

**Library of Congress Cataloging-in-Publication Data**

Herr, Ethel L.
    The dove and the rose / Ethel Herr.
       p.   cm. — (The seekers ; #1)
     I. Title.  II. Series: Herr, Ethel L. Seekers ; #1.
PS3558.E713D68   1996
813'.54—dc20                         96–4437
ISBN 1–55661–746–1 (pbk.)           CIP

To Walter
Supportive husband
Inspiration
Willing assistant
Prayer partner
God's gift to this plodding writer
on a long literary journey!
Thank you, Dear!

ETHEL HERR is a writer/historian, writing instructor, women's speaker, and the founder/director of Literature Ministry Prayer Fellowship. She has six published books, including *Chosen Women of the Bible* and *An Introduction to Christian Writing*. She and her husband, Walt, live in California.

# CONTENTS

# LETTER TO THE READER

History books tell us much about William of Orange, his four successive wives, and his fine old family from Dillenburg. Count Brederode also marches across the pages of those books, along with his ragtag army of Beggars. So do Dirck Coornhert, William Tyndale, and the flock of Beguine sisters in Breda.

In the history books, however, you will not find the van den Gardes nor the Engelshofen family. Tante Lysbet, Yaap, Barthelemeus, and Meister Laurens are not there, nor Oma and her weaver-preacher son Hans with their mysterious origin protected in Emden, city of refuge.

But as you take up imaginative residence in the world of William of Orange and Philip II, you will meet these colorful friends coming at you from among the masses of nameless individuals that lend depth and perspective to the well-named and respected leaders.

Their thinking processes may perplex, even annoy you at times. When they do, simply recall that European society was just beginning to shake itself awake from the long sleep of the Middle or Dark Ages. The sixteenth century saw the first great flowering of an artistic and scientific Renaissance, a massive religious Reformation spawned in large measure by the availability of Scriptures at every level of society, and an unprecedented series of political revolts.

The characters in this book knew little about time constraints and historical perspective. Glass windows and garbage collection were new innovations, and life was expected to be a perpetual struggle for existence. Medicine was a mixture of primitive herbalism and cultic superstition. Life was both violent and religious, crude and mystical. As church leaders of all kinds wrestled to unlock the secrets of biblical hermeneutics, they still resorted to the old practices of casting horoscopes and pronouncing curses.

As you read, search between the lines and beneath the naive attitudes and sometimes strangely worded phrases and you will recognize in them an amazing brotherhood of souls. For they are all significant ancestors of our own struggles with life and freedom and faith in a sometimes violent, always dangerous world.

# HISTORICAL BACKGROUND

*(for those who don't know their way around
in sixteenth-century Netherlands)*

*I*n 1566, Breda (pronounced *braid AH*) was one of the oldest and foremost cities of the Dutch province of Brabant. The city sat on a slight rise in the ground, nestled in the arms of two ancient rivers—the Mark and the Aa. She took her name from the broad (*breed*) place in the Aa created by its juncture with the Mark.

"A good and pleasant garrison town," wrote sixteenth-century cartographer Ludovicco Guicciardini, "home of a sumptuous castle with a double ditch full of water."

In 1538, the popular German-born nobleman William of Orange inherited the castle of the House of Orange-Nassau from a cousin who died in battle without an heir. William brought his new bride to Breda to live in 1551. A handsome man with winsome wit and social charms, he transformed the old castle into a center of extravagant hospitality to rival that of the royal court of his former guardian, Emperor Charles V in Brussels.

But while their "Prince" William's popularity brought a train of prestigious people into the little city, Bredenaars had reasons more accessible to the common citizens and street folk to lift their heads high above the neighboring villages spread out in the fields and marshes around her. Located ten hours' journey north of Antwerp, golden capital of the commercial activity of Northern Europe, Breda's burgeoning economic status was a justifiable source of civic pride. And not to be overlooked by even the most casual visitor, on the market square stood her grand old Gothic "Great" Church with its wealth of paintings, statuary, wood carvings, and a coronet-spired tower that glimmered like a crown jewel. For centuries, townsfolk had gathered beneath her finely painted vaulted arches to worship, while pilgrims from faraway places had enriched her coffers with their gifts.

Most important of all, Breda cherished the quiet, peaceful atmosphere that pervaded her streets, homes, shops, and churches. These were precarious times when, all over Europe, like weathered marble icons, some of the traditionally recognized controlling forces in society were beginning to crumble. To an increasing number of people, the *church*, represented by pope and prelate, no longer held absolute authority to dictate what men and women were to believe and how they were to pray. The *government*, represented by king and nobles, met with increasing challenges when it gave orders and wielded a sword in an attempt to make submission the preferred response. Even the *weather*, mostly dreary, wet and hovering, was forced to yield to the pressure of human ingenuity. While for the most part it persisted in creating an atmosphere that made all else in life either more pleasant or more miserable, men and women and children of this century were beginning to find some shelter in windows and fireproof roof tiles.

In previous centuries, few men had tampered successfully with the established order of things. Everyone knew that all three forces had been set in place by a sovereign God. With the emergence of the printing press in the fifteenth century, these conceptions began to be challenged as never before. Increasingly, the explosion of scientific knowledge, a humanistic approach to the arts, and new ideas about God and faith found fertile ground in more and more hearts and minds. This was especially true in the Netherlands,[1] where almost everyone learned to read and printers and bookshops sprouted like mushrooms. To the native-born Lowlander, ideas of iconoclasm and revolution had always held a fascination. But never before had these ideas offered themselves so plausibly.

One man held the key to peace and security in the whole Netherlands. He seemed, however, unable to grasp the fact that times were changing and his power was eroding. Philip II had inherited from his father, Holy Roman Emperor Charles V, the thrones of Spain, Naples, Milan, Spanish America—and the Netherlands.

To the great distress of his Netherlands' subjects, he had inherited neither his father's Lowlands birth and culture nor his diplomatic style. Born of a Spanish mother and reared in a Spanish court, Philip held Dutch culture in low esteem and would not stoop even to learn their "boorish" language. A devout Roman Catholic, he considered it his divine mission to purge the Netherlands of every taint of Protestant heresy and to rule as an absolute, though absentee, monarch. ". . . His Majesty would rather

---

[1] Also called the Lowlands or Low Countries. This was territory consisting of the present-day countries of the Netherlands, Belgium, and Luxemborg.

the whole land should become an uninhabited wilderness than that a single Dissenter should exist within its territory."[2] His violent methods rooted him in a previous century when kings had still enjoyed recognition as indisputable icons and emissaries of an equally indisputable Church.

Philip's attitudes made him less than popular in the sixteenth century, which spawned a proliferation of seditious groups all over Europe. Most notably, dozens of "new faiths" arose. They ranged all the way from conservative, state-connected *magisterial* reform movements such as Lutheranism and Calvinism to the more *radical* churches of Sebastian Francke's wild spiritualists and Jan van Leyden and his ill-fated messianic experiment in Munster. In between lay the more *moderate* pacifistic Anabaptist groups led by men like Menno Simons who emphasized practical purity of life and social concern for those in need.

In the Lowlands, the *magisterial* "new faith" that attracted most of her noblemen was Calvinism. Always somewhat militant in nature, here it served as a rallying point for a wide assortment of zealous religious and political dissidents and individualistic rebels who challenged the old order with strong voices and powerful arms. All who would fight in protest against what they perceived as the tyrannies of an admittedly "Most Catholic Monarch" must join with the churches that were in revolt against Rome. Regardless of their motives—religious, political, or personal—the Lowland rebels fought side by side in the religious arena.

The most radical of all Lowland Calvinists called themselves Beggars. Defying the Inquisition, they deserted churches and attended secret religious meetings in private homes and open fields. Through the influence of their noble leaders, they urged William of Orange, who could never sympathize with the rigorous application of the Inquisition, to marshal the Lowlands into a massive revolt against their foreign monarch and to open the doors and windows to fresh new ideas.

Nowhere was the battle more unexpected than in the city of Breda. As everywhere else, her churches all belonged to Rome. Her kings—Hapsburgs and staunch Catholics for many generations—had never allowed any other. Worshipers had no choice, and even well into the sixteenth century, few had access to Scriptures to enlighten them. But church attendance was no indicator of heart allegiance. Every parish had its true believers who had managed to push beyond traditions to the reality of simple, godlike faith and holy living.

While other cities in the Lowlands were caught up in the throes of

---

[2]Motley, John Lothrop, *The Rise of the Dutch Republic*. David McKay, Publisher (Philadelphia), Volume II, Page 169.

political and religious chaos, with blood flowing in their streets and canals, the citizens of Breda enjoyed a remarkable commitment to keeping peace. They were confident that the unrest stirring in other cities would not enter their gates.

Most recognized that these were crucial times of transition from a black-and-white world ruled by a single religious tradition to a black-and-white-and-gray world filled with a plethora of Bible-based doctrinal creeds and codes of conduct. To talk about it openly, however, invited trouble. So citizens developed their own responses, practiced in private. One thing they agreed on. This model city, home of the peace-loving William of Orange, would show the world beyond her sturdy walls how to treat its new thinkers without inciting them to throw stones at time-honored traditions and hallowed treasures. None but the occasional foreign rabble and fanatical riffraff would ever feel the rod in Breda.

Most Bredenaars didn't even notice when a pack of Beggar leaders rode their horses to the castle across the moat from the market square. Almost unseen to the public eye, these militant nobles wormed their way, under cloak of the prince's dashing younger brother, Ludwig van Nassau, into the stately halls and shoved their feet under William's table. Only a few ever took notice, and they tried to disbelieve.

Breda felt secure in the knowledge that she had no cause to fear conflict.

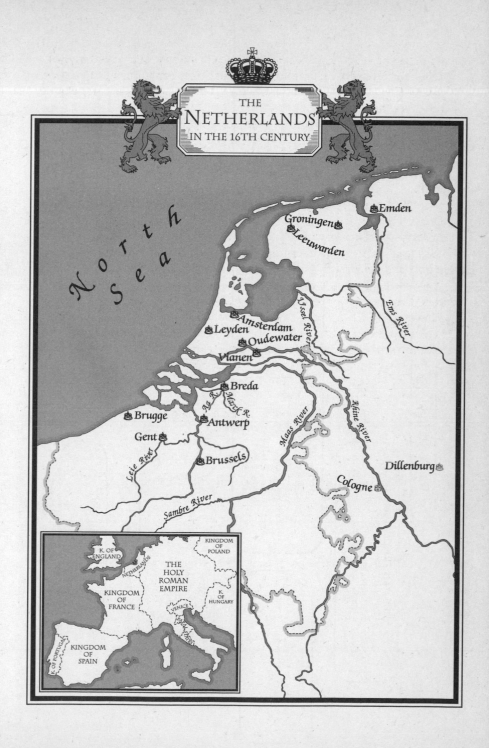

THE
NETHERLANDS
IN THE 16TH CENTURY

North Sea

Emden

Groningen
Leeuwarden

IJssel River

Ems River

Amsterdam
Leyden
Oudewater

Vianen

Breda

Aa R.
Mark R.

Maas River

Rhine River

Brugge

Antwerp

Gent

Brussels

Leie River

Sambre River

Cologne

Dillenburg

K. OF
ENGLAND

KINGDOM
OF POLAND

NETHERLANDS

THE
HOLY
ROMAN
EMPIRE

KINGDOM
OF
FRANCE

K. OF
HUNGARY

VENICE

K. OF PORTUGAL

KINGDOM
OF SPAIN

# Pieter-Lucas' Religious World

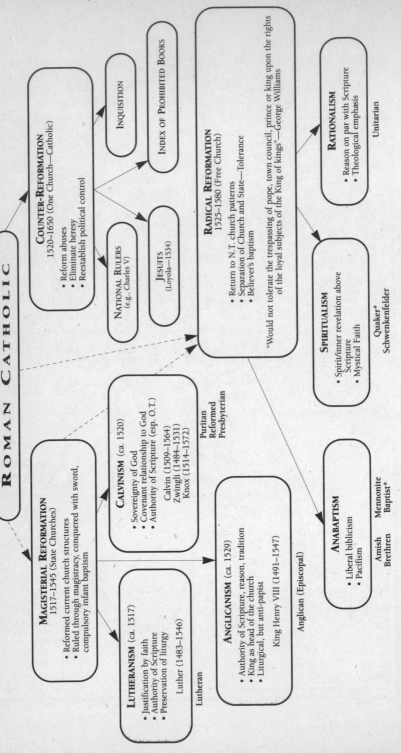

**ROMAN CATHOLIC**

**COUNTER-REFORMATION**
1520–1650 (One Church—Catholic)

- Reform abuses
- Eliminate heresy
- Reestablish political control

INQUISITION

INDEX OF PROHIBITED BOOKS

NATIONAL RULERS
(e.g., Charles V)

JESUITS
(Loyola—1534)

**RADICAL REFORMATION**
1525–1580 (Free Church)

- Return to N.T. church patterns
- Separation of Church and State—Tolerance
- Believer's baptism

"Would not tolerate the trespassing of pope, town council, prince or king upon the rights of the loyal subjects of the King of kings"—George Williams

**RATIONALISM**

- Reason on par with Scripture
- Theological emphasis

Unitarian

**SPIRITUALISM**

- Spirit/inner revelation above Scripture
- Mystical Faith

Quaker*
Schwenkenfelder

**MAGISTERIAL REFORMATION**
1517–1545 (State Churches)

- Reformed current church structures
- Ruled through magistracy, conquered with sword, compulsory infant baptism

**CALVINISM** (ca. 1520)

- Sovereignty of God
- Covenant relationship to God
- Authority of Scripture (esp. O.T.)

Calvin (1509–1564)
Zwingli (1484–1531)
Knox (1514–1572)

Puritan
Reformed
Presbyterian

**LUTHERANISM** (ca. 1517)

- Justification by faith
- Authority of Scripture
- Preservation of liturgy

Luther (1483–1546)

Lutheran

**ANGLICANISM** (ca. 1529)

- Authority of Scripture, reason, tradition
- King as head of the church
- Liturgical, but anti-papist

King Henry VIII (1491–1547)

Anglican (Episcopal)

**ANABAPTISM**

- Liberal biblicism
- Pacifism

Amish      Mennonite*
Brethren   Baptist*

* Organizationally broke off from Anglican Church but were influenced by Anabaptist ideas.

**Ach! & Och!:** Exclamations translated by "Oh" or "Ah." *Ach*, meaning *Alas*; *Och*, meaning *Oh, you don't say!*

**Anabaptists:** Group of Reformation churches who based their faith predominantly on the New Testament, practiced believer (as opposed to infant) baptism, refused to go to war or take an oath of allegiance, and supported complete separation of Church and State.

**Apothecary:** From Dutch word, *apotheek* [ah-po-take], meaning *pharmacy*.

**Beguinage:** [Bay-guee-noj] French word for local site of lay order of charitable sisters in late medieval church, mostly in France and Lowlands. They shared their wealth but didn't take religious vows and were free to leave. Many groups were suspected of heresy.

**Button leek:** Literal translation of Dutch word "Knoflook," which is garlic.

**Ciborium:** Covered receptacle for holding consecrated wafers of the Eucharist.

**Drukkerij:** [Drook-er-eye] Dutch for printshop, printery.

**Eyeblink:** Instant of time it takes to blink an eye. Literal translation of Dutch word, *ogenblijk*, which means *instant, second, jiffy.*

**Goed:** [Gud] Dutch for *good*, used in sense that we use *okay*.

| | |
|---|---|
| Gretta: | English translation of Dutch *Griet* [Greet], (short, common form of *Margriet*, which was most often used for nobility). *Mad Gretta* is translation of *Dulle Griet*. |
| Heer: | [Hayr] Dutch for *Lord, Sir, Mr.*, among burgher class. |
| Huisvrouw: | [House-frow] Dutch for *Housewife*. |
| Inquistion: | Tribunal and later a whole movement of Roman Catholic Church to erradicate heresy by means of arrests, interrogation, confiscation of property, and execution. Originating in medieval times, it targeted all faiths that would not hold to Catholic doctrines and traditions. |
| Ja: | [Yah] Dutch for *yes* (*Ja, Hoor* is common term which means *Yes, do you hear?*) |
| Jongen: | [Yong-un] Dutch for *boy, lad*. |
| Kaatje: | [Kot-yuh] Dutch for *Katie*. |
| Kasteel: | [Kos-tail] Dutch for *castle*. |
| Lowlands: | Area now encompassed in borders of Belgium, Luxemborg, and The Netherlands (Holland). |
| Mijn heer: | [Mine-hayr] Dutch for *My lord*. Used for nobility. |
| Mijn vrouw: | [Mine-frow] Dutch for *My lady*. Used for nobility. |
| Moeder: | [Mu-der] Dutch for *Mother* (Nobility might use Mama). |
| Munsterite: | Radical group of Anabaptists that had a Messianic Community in northern Germany (Munster), characterized by communal living, polygamy, and worship of their leader, Jan van Leyden. This ill-fated group gave Anabaptism a bad name, even as late as our twentieth century. |
| Nay: | *No.* |
| Oma, Opa: | [O-ma, O-pa] Dutch for *Grandma* and *Grandpa*. |
| Oom: | [Oam] Dutch for *Uncle*. |
| Papist: | A Roman Catholic, or one who practiced Roman Catholicism. |
| Physicke: | Old English word found in seventeenth-century herbal book, refers to medicine—profession or person practicing it. |
| Popish: | Describing anything that followed Roman Catholic ways. |
| Prima: | First rate, super. |

**Robustious:** Old English form of word, *robust*, used in seventeenth-century herbal book.

**Roza:** [Ro-sa] Dutch for *rose*.

**Straat:** [Strahtt] Dutch for *street*.

**Styver:** Dutch coin equivalent to our penny.

**Tante:** [Tahn-tuh] Dutch for *aunt*.

**Tot ziens:** [Tote scenes] Dutch for *See you later*.

**Vaarwel:** [Far-vell] Dutch for *farewell*.

**Vader:** [Fah-der] Dutch for *father*. Nobility of the sixteenth century might have used *Papa*.

**Verboden Boecken:** [Fair-bo-den Bu-ken] *Forbidden books*. The Roman Catholic Church kept a list of books that they forbade parishioners to read. Transgressors of this law could expect to be treated as victims of the Inquisition and be imprisoned or executed.

**Willem van Oranje:** [Vil-um fahn O-rahn-yuh] *William of Orange*.

# PROLOGUE

The Beguinage
Christmas Morning, 1548

*L*ong after the crowd of worshipers filed out of the Great Church following Christmas mass, one woman lingered on her knees in a quiet side chapel. Not until the bell in the ornate clock tower at the west end of the church had begun to ring out the hour did she rise to go. She picked up two large bundles and moved across the nave to the heavy wooden doors. Beneath her feet the uneven stone slabs vibrated with the bell's golden resonance.

"There's a reason why we call our bell Roland," she mused. "Gentle, friendly, faithful, almost a real person. It's as if he sees and feels my private joys and griefs."

Robed in a dark, hooded cloak, the young woman gripped one bundle in both arms. Over her left shoulder she'd slung the other, a large bulging sack. She shoved at the door until it opened out into the white and gray world of the wintry market square.

For a long moment she stood blinking in the brightness that glared up at her from an ankle-deep ground cover of snow. She inhaled the sharp icy air and, addressing no one but her own trembling heart, said aloud, "A new hour . . . a new day . . . a new life."

All her life she'd felt safe in this little garrisoned city of Breda with its strong walls and peaceful streets at the quiet confluence of the gentle rivers Mark and Aa. Certainly, this morning, everything in the scene before her looked peaceful enough. The old buildings that clustered around the market square pushed their heads up, silent, stately, almost enchanted, each wearing a glistening cape of freshly fallen snow.

Today, though, the peace of her surroundings did not reach her heart. She picked a set of freshly powdered tracks and moved toward her "new life." She trudged past the ancient castle that hugged its frozen moat on the north side of the market square. Often Breda's own Prince Willem van Oranje came to this, his ancestral castle, seeking peace from the affairs of state that did not run smoothly. Had he been touched by the tragic events that had forced her out of her safe nest in search of a new life? True, he was a prince, and she a simple commoner. Some would say he shouldn't care. But she knew better . . . or did she?

A rush of warm tears trickled down her cheeks, and she tasted their saltiness on her lips. "Nay, no more of this pity wasted on yourself, young woman," she chided herself, wiping her face on the blanket in her arms. "From now on, you give your life to others' woes."

Resolved, she pulled her mind toward the walled enclosure located only a stone's throw down Caterstraat. Behind the wall lay a dignified circle of identical brick houses with a tiny unpretentious chapel, all nestled up close to the castle grounds.

"The Beguinage, our new home, son." The woman whispered into the blankets that wrapped her infant against the chill of the morning. "We'll share it with a flock of simple lay sisters. Who would have dreamt such a thing as this last summer when a Beguine first laid you in my arms? Me, a Beguine? Now, that's what they're going to call your mama."

The woman sniffled in the damp cold and stopped before the rough wooden entrance gate. Amidst a flurry of ragged snowflakes wafting like feathers from a rent pillow, she set her bag at her feet. With a free hand, she tugged at the leather thong that rang a bell to announce her arrival.

She listened for the muffled, rhythmic crunching sound from the other side of the wall, followed by the rattling of the gate handle. The old gate groaned on its icy hinges, then opened, shoving back the drift of snow on the path at the woman's feet. Was it fancy, or did a strong current of warmth really reach out and gather her inward?

She looked up into a familiar face, framed by the equally familiar white kerchief-hood of the Beguine order. The blue-green eyes greeting her were gracious, though somber, and the lips did not move. With a sweep of her arm, the Beguine sister ushered her through the gate.

"Sister Lysbet." The newcomer bowed her greeting and pushed down the lump that begged to rise in her throat.

"Welcome, Kaatje."

"I have made my vows in the Church. I come to stay." She said the words too simply to belie the fear of an untried future that set her innards to quivering.

Sister Lysbet, tall, erect, as always a trifle aloof, looked at her with an expression Kaatje struggled to interpret. "I knew you would come," she said at last. She reached for the younger woman's bag and led her around the courtyard.

"Come along. We've just returned to our apartments from mass, and the sisters prepare to begin their Christmas day's work of feeding the hungry and administering herbs to the sick.

Sister Lysbet said no more. Kaatje followed in silence, past section after section of small-paned windows set in walls of neatly rowed bricks. She did not look through the openings between starched curtains but instinctively felt the penetrating gaze of dozens of eyes peering out at her. What were they thinking of her entrance into their exclusive world?

Sister Lysbet stopped abruptly before the last door on the east side of the complex. She grasped the door handle, dislodging a plump cushion of snow. Kaatje watched it fall to the ground with a muffled plop.

"Oh!" Sister Lysbet gasped. "A Christmas rose!"

Kaatje stared and held her breath. The tiny avalanche had indeed brushed aside a mound of soft white snow to expose a clump of exquisite, waxlike flowers. The tall Beguine sister dropped Kaatje's bag, then half knelt before the flowers as if at a shrine. She plucked the three white blossoms with dark purple veins, shaking what remained of the snow from their petals and dull green leaves.

"Black Hellebore, my mother's herbal book calls it," she mumbled. "Ugly name for so beautiful a blossom."

Slowly, dreamily, she rose, all the while gazing at her Christmas morning prize and speaking as if from a trance. "Precious, healing bloom. 'A purgation for mad and furious, melancholy, dull, and heavy persons.' So the herbal says. 'Its blossoms, when strewn across the floor, do drive out evil presences.'"

At the mention of evil presences, Kaatje backed away and shuddered a bit. The child in her arms began to stir, and she drew him tighter to herself. Blanketed sounds of discontent reached her ears.

Sister Lysbet carried on her detached soliloquy, only now to the faint strains of a sad melody Kaatje had never heard before:

"Lo, how a rose upspringing
On tender root has grown:
A Rose by prophet's singing
To all the world made known.
It came a flower bright
Amid the cold of winter,
When half-spent was the night."

As if suddenly reminded of Kaatje's presence, the Beguine smoothed out her skirts and adjusted her hood. "Forgive me," she said nervously. "I forgot myself. 'Tis an old tradition. My moeder—she was a *physicke*, a healer lady, you know—she prized this flower more than any other."

"But why? Did she encounter so very many evil presences needing to be driven out?"

Lysbet looked puzzled, then answered, "Evil presences are never far away. And because Christmas speaks of deep healing from all such, Moeder always celebrated whenever we spotted the first Christmas rose of the season. She taught us to celebrate, too, by singing about God's rose up-springing."

"Oh!" Kaatje decided that would take some thinking of the sort she was not eager to engage in on this already melancholy morning.

Lysbet continued to look at the delicate blossoms cupped in the palm of her hand and spoke almost absently. "Perfect gift for the melancholy soul God is sending me to serve this day."

Kaatje interrupted. "Lives this soul nearby?"

Sister Lysbet started, probing the woman's face like an inquisitor. "On yon corner." She nodded in the direction of *The Crane's Nest* bookshop.

Kaatje gasped.

"Your friend, Gretta Engelshofen," the Beguine said plainly, in the way she said nearly everything.

"Her illness is no secret, then, in this place?" The thought that Gretta's plight might be known to the Beguine sisters tore at Kaatje's heart, ripping away whatever feelings of security this, her new home, held for her.

"None know, but I alone. I was the one who attended her on the birth of her beautiful girl child. Even before her pains had begun, her strange and sudden madness was already plain to see. Her husband, Dirck, called me on that afternoon, and the child came not till after Roland had called out the midnight hour."

A fearsome chill swept over Kaatje, and warm tears trickled down her cheeks. What sort of omen might this be that Gretta's madness had begun on the same day God drew the dark, ugly curtains of tragedy over Kaatje's own world? It was only such a few short weeks ago. Perhaps time would heal all. But Lysbet and the Christmas rose. . . ? She pushed back another sudden rush of tears and forced herself to smile.

"Much too cold to stand here talking longer," Sister Lysbet said, picking up Kaatje's bag and opening the door. "Your new home," she said.

Kaatje followed. She found her cubicle chilly and damp, with a red tiled floor and high plastered walls. A bed, a table, a cupboard, a chair, a fireplace, and a painting or two furnished the room. "Thank you, kind friend."

Sister Lysbet nodded and went for the door.

The baby began to cry out, and Kaatje threw off her cloak, then lay her bundle on the square table beneath a wrought iron chandelier of unlit candles. Hastily she unwrapped the agitated child.

"Just one more thing," Sister Lysbet said. Kaatje looked up to see the Beguine standing with her hand on the door handle and glancing back over her shoulder. She spoke with a measuring of words so calculated that it made Kaatje's skin prickle. "Remember that Beguines never take a binding vow."

Without waiting for a response, Sister Lysbet let herself out into the iciness, a cold draft sweeping across the room in her wake.

"Never?" Kaatje asked, her cheeks once more dampened by a wash of unbidden tears. But she had all the rest of life to contemplate that question. For the moment, a hungry baby's cries for attention had grown into a heart-piercing howl.

Kaatje seated herself in the lone chair, opened her bodice, and offered her child a warm breast. Eagerly he suckled, nuzzling and punching with miniature fists. From round blue eyes, seeming to swim in their sockets, he stared up at her face. At length the sucking slackened, his little mouth formed a playful smile, and he gurgled his gratitude. He stretched an open palm toward her tear-streaked face.

She took the hand in her own and fondled it. In the glow of this sacred moment between mother and firstborn, all thoughts of unspeakable tragedies, Beguines' stares, evil presences, and binding vows melted away.

"My dear little Pieter-Lucas," she whispered, nearly overcome with awe. "We call you *Lucas* for your grandfather, Opa Lucas, who paints beautiful pictures and cannot wait to put a brush into your fingers and show you how to use it." She chuckled. "But your other name, *Pieter*, you will carry to remind you that your father and I prayed you will always be a follower of Christ."

From outside the window, a pair of doves filled the air with the gentle cooing music of mutual admiration.

Still holding the tiny hand firmly in her own, Kaatje crossed herself, and while tears of release trickled down her cheeks, she whispered, "A dove is for anointing, son—and for peace."

She wiped her face in the boy's straw-colored curls, then hugged him until he giggled.

---

## The Cranes' Nest

A rare moment of quiet hushed Dirck Engelshofen's house on the corner of Annastraat and Caterstraat. The young bookseller with clean-shaven chin and brown, trim mustache sat by the window with a big leather-bound book open in his lap. His wife, Gretta, slept, snoring lightly and tossing fitfully in her bed cupboard on the wall. For the first time today, she was free of the strange, howling madness that had been her companion so much of the time since she'd given birth to their firstborn. At Dirck's feet, swaddled in a warm blanket and lying in her wooden cradle, their baby daughter slept. The sweetness of an angel lighted her face. Who could ever have told him that this tiny infant would snare his heart as she had done?

"My Aletta," he whispered. Even her name, inherited from his own grandmother, stirred strong paternal feelings in him.

He turned to the book and read from its yellowing pages. A flurry of snow patted the windowpane and beckoned him. He looked out on the whiteness of Breda and the flock of Christmas Day worshipers streaming away from the Great Church. But his mind lingered over the mysteries of the well-known Christmas story he'd just been reading—mysteries of a virgin mother, angels, and a natal star.

He read it every Christmas day, usually with his wife. Today, though, he'd noticed something new. Joseph, the new father in the story, took special pains to protect both mother and infant entrusted to his care. Before Dirck's mind flashed a dozen paintings he had seen of the holy family fleeing on a donkey into Egypt. It seemed to be a favorite subject of painters.

Perhaps they, as he, were new fathers, he decided. Were they, too, seeing this third character in the sacred family as if for the first time? He looked intently at his sleeping daughter who was twisting her rosebud mouth into charming little grimaces and odd circles.

"My little Christmas rose," he murmured. "Beautiful, created for the healing of others, yet ever so fragile in a mad and violent world."

Something told him he should feel sad at not being able to take his family and join the others at the Great Church around the corner and across the market square. Instead, his heart felt warmed, more alive after these few moments of solitude with the big book than it did when he'd been to mass. Dangerous thoughts these, especially should he ever lose his presence of mind and voice them.

Ever since Martin Luther had nailed his "95 Theses" to the church door in Wittenburg, printing presses had been turning out new ideas that challenged the teaching of the Church. An unheard-of thing in Dirck's great-grandparents' time. The ideas were growing so great in number and spreading so far and wide that the whole of the world seemed to be tottering on the brink of a holy war. Many a man or woman had been burned at the stake for openly expressing the kinds of thoughts Dirck's mind was forming at this moment.

Not in Breda, of course. But in Antwerp, where he'd been born and reared and now made frequent trips to buy the books his customers required, such executions were still common. The thought sent a shudder through his body.

His memories of Antwerp would always be a mixture of joy and pain. A beautiful city on the wide and wonderful Scheldt River, it was filled with grand old buildings that reached up to the sky and people from all over the world who came to buy and sell their goods in its huge, colorful marketplaces. It was a great place for a boy to explore, to watch big ships and exciting processions, to listen to tales of adventure and church bells with booming voices.

But the memories that gripped his heart with icy fingers were the kind that still inspired terror—memories of angry soldiers and public executions, surpassed only by nighttime panics. Night after night, he lay in bed, afraid to go to sleep lest he miss the sound that would warn his family to run before inquisitors could arrive and take them all away to prison. He'd had friends who didn't seem to fear, but their families did safe, common things like selling waffles in the market, or shoeing horses, or running a tavern.

Instead, his mother's family—all devout people—were either printers or booksellers, eager to spread the "new faith" ideas that neither magistrates nor priests wanted the people to read about. Many times he'd heard the story of his mother's uncle who had been banished from the city simply for eating meat on Ash Wednesday.

In contrast, his father was a wild and irreligious English sailing merchant, who cursed and drank and never set foot in church. But even he had found it profitable to smuggle Bibles in his cargo of wheat, cotton, and animal hides, dodging the inquisitors who roamed the docks along the Scheldt River in search of banned books and the men who dared to traffick them.

One day they caught up with him at sea. He'd sailed away, with one of Dirck's brothers, serving as a deckhand and never came back. A bailiff came and told his mother that his ship had perished in a storm, but none of the family ever believed it.

In the printery and bookshop of his uncle, Oom Johannes, Dirck met dozens of men of all kinds, from merchants to scholars. Like all printshops, his uncle had explained, this local printery had become a center of unofficial "academic circles" that engaged in scholarly discussion. One always hoped that the men who gathered here at the sign of *The Christmas Rose* to exchange gossip, peer over editors' shoulders, and discuss important ideas for a new society could be trusted. But all the same, Dirck never trusted.

One old gentleman, William Tyndale, from England—the man who translated the Bibles that Dirck's father smuggled—trusted the wrong visitor just once, and he ended up being burned at the stake. That was when Dirck decided he would spend his life exercising caution so that he might have a long life to sell books.

Jan Davidszoon, a bookseller from Johannes' "academic circle," shared Dirck's goals. Growing weary of the danger in Antwerp, he searched until he found a haven in Breda. On several occasions, Dirck had come here to Breda to deliver books to the man. Eventually, he'd stayed to marry Jan's daughter, Gretta, and finally inherited *The Crane's Nest* from him.

A knock on the door at the front of the house by the bookshop brought him abruptly out of his thoughts. He closed the book, stowed it away in the back of the cabinet in the far corner of the room, then rushed to answer the persistent knock. As he expected, his two friends, Barthelemeus, the traveling cloth merchant, and Meister Laurens, stood on the stoop. They formed the heart of his "academic circle" that met in *The Crane's Nest*. Men of new ideas, seeking for a return to truth and a breath of fresh spirit in the Church, they'd spent many hours talking over the things that kept printers and booksellers in business. Dirck knew without an eyeblink's hesitation that he could trust either of them with his life.

With a finger pressed to his lips, he welcomed them into his shop. No one spoke until he'd securely closed the door and they'd taken their normal places in the circle of chairs beside the shelves of books.

"Well, friends," Dirck began, "so you both went to the mass in the church?"

"You should have been there," said Barthelemeus. He was a bit younger and slighter of frame than Dirck, had sharply formed features, and gestured when he spoke.

Meister Laurens shoved his way in front of the first speaker and carried on, "Take it from a schoolmaster, sprung from a long line of schoolmasters—and definitely the senior member of this 'academic circle,' I might add—that new parish priest is going to bring a wasp's nest about his ears in the days to come, and the whole city is going to get stung." His rotund middle, flabby cheeks, and goatee beard bounced as he talked.

"So, what did he say this time?" Dirck asked.

"He waxed really bold today, suggesting that confession and penance were not commanded in the Holy Scriptures. Didn't beat on the subject, just said it was the Christmas message, then dropped it and went on."

"Did no one dispute his words or call him to account?"

"The magistrates sat in their row, all nodding to one another and shaking their heads as if properly outraged," Meister Laurens answered soberly. "You can be sure they will not let those wasps go free."

Dirck cleared his throat. "Tell me," he threw them a challenge, "think you that God has sent this man to us with a word for our times and for our city?"

"Nothing he has said yet is new, not even in our city," Laurens said, stroking his beard.

"Indeed, everything I've heard from this priest so far, I have been distributing in my books for years and hope to teach to my children behind closed doors," Dirck said.

"But you don't preach it in the pulpits," Barthelemeus reminded them.

"Nor shall I ever do so. Have you noticed the sign that hangs outside my shop?" Dirck asked his younger friend.

"I guess it's been there so long, I haven't noticed in a while," Barthelemeus answered, looking thoughtful. "Now that you ask, I recall it is a crane. In literature that always symbolizes watchfulness."

"And so it does here as well," Dirck said.

Meister Laurens interrupted, "One foot, the lifted one, holds a stone to use as a weapon to frighten off intruders. This schoolmaster believes that the mother crane will never take her stone to the pulpit of the Great Church, but will always stand guard over her brood."

"Well said, Meister," Dirck said. "Her watchful eye is needed that the truth planted in the minds of the readers of the books we sell here might grow and flourish in their hearts. Breda is a peace-loving city, and the way of the crane is the way of a believer seeking peace in Breda."

"But evidently men like this new priest believe open speaking and the way of knowledge to be more important than the way of peace." Barthelemeus lifted his hands shoulder-high, palms skyward, and raised his eyebrows.

"He will soon learn if he stays long enough," Laurens said. "He is, after all, no Bredenaar. We've always had our share of rabble-rousers, but they have been outshouted by the quiet men and women, like Dirck's neighbor." He nodded toward the next house down Annastraat.

"You mean old Lucas van den Garde?"

"Ja, a more Christian man you'll never find, no matter what sort of church you search," Laurens answered. "I never meet with that man without feeling as if I've looked on God himself."

"How is it that his kind never cause their waves to swell or lap at the steps of the town hall, yet you can't forget what they say by their lives?" Barthelemeus asked.

"And they do far more for our cause than a dozen preachers," Dirck added. "Is it not enough that they influence all who know them and make people feel as if they've met God on the street—or in a book they purchased from *The Crane's Nest?*"

"Maybe," Barthelemeus said tentatively. "But I wonder if there ever comes a time to speak up and open the gates for blood to run in our streets so that all may know and pursue the truth."

"This schoolmaster would like you to remember who owns our churches and our Hapsburg kings."

"Why, Rome, of course," Barthelemeus answered.

"And how likely think you that Rome is to give us any choice in where or how we worship?"

"Not at all—at least not without a struggle."

"It appears to me to be the part of wisdom, at least in our lifetime, to content ourselves to practice our piety in the open but discuss our doctrines in private." Laurens rested his hands on ample hips and offered the others an authoritative stare.

Dirck knew this was Meister Laurens' signal that he had wrapped up the conversation, and there was nothing more to be said. But he had to add one more thing. "Let us take care, friends," he pleaded, "and make no haste."

From the rooms beyond the closed door, Dirck heard the cries of a baby. Where was Sister Lysbet? She should have come from the Beguinage by now. What would he do?

"Sorry, friends," he said. "My child cries and my wife . . ."

"We know, Dirck, we know," Meister Laurens said.

"We go. A blessed Christmas and *tot ziens.*" Barthelemeus was already guiding his older companion out the door.

Dirck hurried into the room where he'd left his family sleeping. Already Gretta was stirring. "Bring the little one to me," she called out.

"In an eyeblink," he answered her. He must have one more moment with his daughter, even if he had to steal it.

He picked up his crying infant, held her close to his heart and, ignoring her cries, whispered into the blanket covering her head, "Dear Aletta, I promise you this day that for all your life, as much as lies within my feeble powers as your father, I shall protect you from any persons, places, things, or ideas in this mad world that could ever do you harm."

Gently he moved her in his arms until he could see her face. She grew still, and for a long and miraculous moment, father and daughter looked into each other's eyes. The excited father watched his baby's little mouth offer up to him its first weak and crooked smile.

"Thank God, all will be well," he murmured. "All will be well."

# PART ONE

# The Anointing

"Lo, how a rose upspringing
On tender root has grown:
A Rose by prophet's singing
To all the world made known.
It came a flower bright,
Amid the cold of winter,
When half-spent was the night."

*Anonymous fifteenth-century German carol*

"A dove is for anointing."

—Kaatje

# CHAPTER ONE

*Breda*

Fallow Month (June), 1566

*P*ieter-Lucas watched Vader Hendrick wipe his mouth on his uniform sleeve, rise from the table, and stride across the single room the little family called home. The austere man, with broad shoulders and dark pointed beard, shoved a long sword into its sheath on his belt and fastened the leather strap of his metal helmet firmly under his chin. Pieter-Lucas, a lanky lad of seventeen with enormous hands, curly flaxen hair, and thoughtful blue eyes, sat at the table with his Moeder Kaatje and his grandfather, Opa Lucas. He felt fire from Vader's angry eyes glaring at him and stuffed the last chunk of bread into his mouth.

"Tomorrow we go to the field preaching," Vader ordered, his tone gruff, commanding.

"*Nay*, Vader," Pieter-Lucas protested, nearly choking on the bread. "Not tomorrow."

Vader took a step toward the boy and repeated his orders, this time his voice booming around the room. "I said, tomorrow we go to the field preaching—all of us."

"But, Vader"—Pieter-Lucas swallowed hard and felt the dry bread lodge somewhere between his mouth and his stomach—"for weeks now, we've gone with you to the fields to hear your 'new faith' preachers, but tomorrow is the Procession of the Holy Cross."

"Popish, idolatrous holiday!" Vader spat out the words. "We are not papists in this house and will not even think of it, do you hear?"

"Papists or no—that has nothing to do with it," Pieter-Lucas countered.

"It has everything to do with it!" Vader reached for the door handle.

Pieter-Lucas stepped forward and laid a hand on his arm. "Vader," he pleaded, "you know that Opa and I always celebrate the procession day by taking Aletta to inspect Breda's latest works of art. It is our Artists' Pilgrimage. . . ."

Vader pulled away and snarled, "Artists' Pilgrimage! Bah! Idolatry and nonsense!"

"*Nay*, it is not nonsense. Paint runs in the blood of our family. Surely it runs in yours, too. Why, then, do you not understand?"

"Don't talk to me about paint," Vader exploded. "We are van den Gardes in this house. Have you forgotten? Like our ancestors for generations before us, we are appointed to guard the castle of Prince Willem van Oranje, not to waste our lives painting pretty icons for false worshipers!"

Opa scraped his chair on the floor and shuffled to his feet. He pounded his gnarled cane on the smooth floor tile. With head held high and long gray beard bobbing to the rhythm of his words, he announced simply, "I go not with you to the field preaching."

"I said you all go!" Vader retorted.

"Not this time, son. For these long months, I've obeyed your orders in this your house. I've listened with care to your friends. In many ways, they speak of the things my heart has always held dear. In the beginning, I had hopes your cause might bring a much-needed breath of fresh new life into the Church. But you've carried it too far. I must retreat."

Vader shouted, "Coward!"

Opa wagged a finger at Vader but spoke calmly. "I am an old man with a bit of accumulated wisdom, which you would do well to respect. Have you forgotten that I answer not to you, but to the God that inhabits the altars at the Great Church on the market square?"

Vader's eyes narrowed. He moved closer and probed his father's chest with the point of his forefinger. " 'Tis demons that lurk in those altars. God never has acknowledged them." He screwed up his mouth till it puckered like a drawstring pouch, then spat on the floor at Opa's feet.

Opa gasped and held his breath while Vader continued his tirade. "So, you want to run to those heathen altars in the Great Church? You will parade down the streets after a lifeless, flower-decked replica of the holy cross? Then, go! But know this when you do. Never again will you shove your feet under my table or lay your head beneath my thatch. In this house, we worship a Savior who died on a real splintery cross to set us free from every act of wanton idolatry!"

Father and son glared at each other, unyielding and erect. At last, Vader spoke. "There are people who will take in the likes of you—fellow papists who will give you a table and a bed. You will need to go to them if you allow your feet to carry you into the Great Church tonight, tomorrow, or ever again, for you will find my door forever barred."

Pieter-Lucas grabbed at his father's arm once more. "Vader, Vader, have mercy on your own vader."

"The same goes for you, *jongen*."

Hendrick van den Garde pulled away from the boy's grip and stomped out into the long summer evening, shouting back over his shoulder, "You will all be ready to go to the field preaching when I return from my guard duty after sunrise."

Pieter-Lucas and Opa stared at each other in wounded silence for a long moment. Then Opa bowed his head, and moving it slowly from side to side, he said, "Hendrick has no paint in his blood."

Pieter-Lucas laid a hand on his grandfather's shoulder. He felt it tremble beneath his fingers. "We don't have to go to the church this time, Opa."

"What?" A look of incredulity spread across the wrinkled old face. A thin strand of white hair strayed across his balding head to a spot just above his left eye. "Of course we have to go."

"We cannot let Vader put you in the old men's house."

"Never fear for me," Opa said calmly. "Some things are worth going to the old men's house for—*ja*, even worth dying for, *jongen*. Learn it now." He started across the room toward his chair. Midway, he stopped, leaned with both hands against his cane, and announced, "I have a plan!"

"You always have a plan. What this time?" Pieter-Lucas asked.

"Tell me, what is our habit to do on this night before the Procession of the Holy Cross—you and I, with your little friend, Aletta?"

"We go out and inspect the procession decorations."

"See how simple it is, *jongen*? This night we leave the inspecting for someone else, and we go, instead, to the church. Your father busies himself guarding the prince's castle, and he will never know what we have done."

"You're sure it will work, Opa?" Pieter-Lucas felt a thrill run through his body.

"If not, so be it. This year of all years, we dare not miss our pilgrimage."

"Why this year more than any others?"

"A miracle awaits us in the church this year," Opa said. "You'll see." He sagged into his chair and breathed in great heaving gasps.

"Opa, are you all right?" Pieter-Lucas asked. "I fear you are not well enough to go out tonight. Only two days ago, you were lying in your bed too ill even to eat at the table. Our pilgrimage could wait for another day."

Opa straightened slightly, smiled a wide smile, and protested, "*Nay*,

*nay*, just let me sit a bit first." He let his chin fall against his chest and was soon breathing with the deep labored rhythm of an old man's hare-nap.

Pieter-Lucas heard sniffling sounds from the table behind him and looked back at his mother. She was gathering up the empty plates and cups and carrying them to the work shelf by the hearth, sobbing as she moved back and forth. He crossed the room and put his arm around her.

"O Moeder, Moeder. I'm sorry we made Vader angry and upset you so."

Her wrinkled face sagged below the white headdress that hugged her hairline. She sighed. "Hendrick is my husband, my protector, but I know he can be a difficult man."

"But, Moeder, must I forever go to his plain, dull meetings? For weeks he forced us to go with him to Antonis Backeler's house on Sundays. Then, when winter thawed and the fields burst into bloom, it was off to the field preachings. For months now, he's not allowed us to enter the Great Church on Sundays or any other time. Why can't he let us keep our own traditions just this once?"

"I know not, son, I know not." She did not look at him as she spoke.

"Besides, I'm nearly a man myself and too old to have Vader spoiling the festival by dragging me off to meetings of wild heretics!"

Moeder gasped and clapped her hand over her mouth. "Do not call them by that name! They mean well—to free us from empty traditions. But for some, their noble visions make them too restless for their own good."

"*Nay*, Moeder, they are heretics!"

She cringed. "Shh! When you talk that way, the inquisitors will hear you and come banging on our door. You can be sure when they carry your father to the stake, they will take us along." She clutched at her breast and anguish plowed fleshy furrows across her face.

"*Nay*, Moeder." Pieter-Lucas smiled at her and shook his head gently. "Breda has no inquisitors, and only a handful of people have ever died for heresy in our market square. Strangers, they all were—Munsterites or some such. Even Vader and his friends are not such as they—keepers of many wives, rebaptizers, naked prophets running through the streets . . ."

If only she were not with child again, perhaps she would not fear so much. Or would she? How could he know? It seemed to him that all his life he had known his mother to carry a child in her belly but never one in her arms. Always she was tired and pale and fearful.

Moeder sighed again and laid a hand on his arm. "Times are changing, son," she said. "Changing fast. You must learn patience!"

Pieter-Lucas ran strong fingers through the blond curls that bounced like coils atop his head. "Changes? Patience? *Nay*, Moeder, the hour is now. Tonight we take Aletta and make our Artist's Pilgrimage."

Moeder clung to him. "What if your father sees you there? You heard what he said."

"Moeder, fret not," he said. "Vader is occupied with guarding the castle. He will not be free to search us out in the Great Church." If only his pounding heart would quiet and allow him to follow his own advice!

From a hook by the door, Pieter-Lucas pulled down his wilted felt cap and brown street jacket. He crossed the room and stood over Opa, who had raised his head and was shaking away the sleep. Pieter-Lucas offered his arm. "Are you sure you're strong enough to go along, or do Aletta and I go alone?"

"Foolish *jongen*," Opa scolded, yet he allowed the boy to help him to his feet. "My illness is simply that of many years. I'm not quite at the end of my journey. Besides, you would miss the miracle if you went alone."

"What miracle?"

"*The* miracle. Come now, we go!"

Opa nudged Pieter-Lucas away from the corner where he had dozed. He felt a halting in his grandfather's steps as he helped him cross the room. He heard the old man mumble beneath his breath, "Never again will I go to one of those noisy field preachings. No more jostling fanatics, shouting preachers, power-lusty guards. Never, never, never . . ."

Moeder joined them near the door. She took them each by a hand, which she held beside her bulging belly. "Take care," she said. "Trouble comes to Breda, I fear. The magistrates have canceled the drama sections of the procession for tomorrow, you know."

"I know all about it, Moeder," Pieter-Lucas answered. Ever since he'd heard, he tried to imagine the procession without those magnificent street plays and characters. How could St. Barbara, patron saint of the Great Church, not come riding on her stunning white steed, accompanied by tap dancers? Or St. George with his dragon? And the host of kings and giants, clowns and soldiers, clerics and city magistrates?

"They say it has something to do with danger from too many bowmen." Moeder frowned, and her voice sounded pinched.

"I don't believe it," Opa said sourly.

"Nor do I," Pieter-Lucas agreed. "We've always had the bowmen and the dramas—and no trouble. 'Tis the work of Vader's fanatical friends. That's what it is."

Again, Moeder winced. She raised her hands as if to halt the boy's unbridled prattle. Though she would never call Vader a heretic or argue with him about his friends and their wild escapades, she could not hide the pain in her eyes.

Pieter-Lucas pulled free from Moeder's grip. Punching his right fist into the palm of his left hand, he vowed, "They may cancel the dramas for the procession, but nothing, *nay* absolutely nothing Hendrick van den Garde and his friends can do will destroy our traditions. We'll show them, won't we, Opa?"

Opa nodded and Pieter-Lucas continued, "We go, Moeder. Aletta awaits us."

"Are you sure it's safe?" Moeder's eyes pleaded with them.

"Naught will harm us, Kaatje," Opa said with a warm, gentle strength that put Pieter-Lucas momentarily at ease.

"And if Hendrick finds you in the church? *Ach*, but I cannot bear the thought of losing you to his anger."

"Moeder, Moeder, fret not!" Pieter-Lucas said. He brushed a kiss and a stubbly chin across his mother's forehead and hurried Opa out the door.

----

A rare warm sun dipped slowly toward the horizon of an equally rare cloudless sky. It smiled down on Pieter-Lucas and his two fellow pilgrims as they made their way to the Great Church.

On his left walked Aletta, the bookseller's daughter. As ever, she made the perfect picture of a miniature *huisvrouw* in her soft yellow dress, pleated blue apron, and gray cape. Her long honey-colored hair was braided and piled up under the white headdress worn by all women of Breda. On special days like today, she allowed several ringlets to hang freely around the edges. They framed her round face and bounced as she walked.

On his right, Opa shuffled over the cobblestones, stooped and looking a bit shriveled in his faded gray ballooned breeches, red coat, and ocher stockings. The costume had served as his castle guard uniform for more years than anybody else had been around to count. He clutched his shiny old cane with one hand and held his grandson with the other. Pieter-Lucas could feel him leaning while at the same time urging him forward.

"Take it easy, Opa," Pieter-Lucas cautioned. "No need to rush."

"Of course there is. Can't let Hendrick find us on our way to the church tonight."

Aletta spoke softly into Pieter-Lucas' ear, "Would your father really be angry with you for going to the church?"

"You know he hasn't let our family come here for months," Pieter-Lucas said, barely above a whisper.

"But on this special occasion?"

"Hush, Little One." He patted her arm and added, "He will not find us. No need to fret." Though Aletta was no longer little, it made him feel like her protector when he used the name.

The market square was jammed with people of every size and shape bustling about in preparation for tomorrow's festivities. Housewives in their voluminous aprons were scrubbing the cobblestones with big brushes. Young women were assembling a huge wreath of flowers to be hung from the church tower. Bowmen practiced marching in formation with long bows and brightly feathered arrows slung across their backs. Magistrates strolled amongst the others in black robes with shiny sashes of purple, yellow, red, and green.

About halfway across the market square, Opa began to sway first to the left, then to the right. Pieter-Lucas grabbed him in both arms and steadied him.

"Careful, Opa," Aletta reminded him. "Hasn't been that long since you were on your sickbed. Tante Lysbet says . . . ."

"Tante Lysbet, nothing!" Opa had regained his balance. He tugged at Pieter-Lucas and began moving again. "What does she know? I was already a seasoned castle guard before she could crawl across the market square, and she thinks she knows better than I?"

"Ja, ja, Opa." Pieter-Lucas tried to calm him. "But she is the healer lady, you know."

"Bah! And she has no idea of the medicine that comes from desire long barren when once it yields a miracle." He chuckled.

"Medicine from desire long what?"

"Never mind. You'll learn it soon enough. Just stop trying to hinder me with your advice. Now come along. A miracle awaits us!" Opa said, smiling with a mischievous grin and a jovial chuckle.

"What miracle?" Aletta looked at Pieter-Lucas and raised her eyebrows.

Pieter-Lucas looked sideways at her and shrugged. "You know Opa and his surprises."

"True." She nodded.

In many ways, each pilgrimage was predictable. Year after year, the two young people had followed Opa up and down the aisles of the grand old church, stopping at each painting, each sculpture, each stained-glass window. From his wise old lips they'd heard some wonderful stories about the artists—how they mixed their colors, carved the statues, leaded the glass, and the important ideas they tried to show with their work.

One story Opa repeated every year without fail.

"My uncle was the famous painter Lucas van Leyden," he told them, as if they'd never heard this astounding fact before. "He painted many pictures and even learned to etch his designs in copper." Next Opa would thump Pieter-Lucas on the chest and repeat, "You, grandson, are a true Lucas, born to be an artist. Someday, after you have turned eighteen, I will send you to Leyden to study with the men who learned from my uncle."

The moment both Pieter-Lucas and Aletta most looked forward to was when, in the midst of the familiar routines, Opa showed them something new and totally surprising. Sometimes it was a painting or a wood carving recently added to the collection on the seats of the choir stalls. But a miracle? He had never promised that before.

When Pieter-Lucas shoved open the huge door of the church, a strange mixture of excitement and trembling propelled him over the threshold. He closed the door against the frightening world where Vader Hendrick and his friends roamed about carrying swords. Then, taking a deep breath and spreading a wide smile across his face, he allowed the golden glow and waxy-sweet fragrance of the beloved sanctuary to sweep him into its warm, secure haven.

"Hush, be still," Opa said. "We enter God's sacred dwelling place." Then, nodding at the others, his eyebrows arched knowingly, he added, "Be careful that you always honor it."

"That we shall do, Opa," the two young companions said in unison. All three stood in silence for a space.

The ritual of the pilgrimage had begun.

For as long as Pieter-Lucas could remember, Opa had issued the same warning every time the three of them entered the church. And each time they had solemnly promised, partly because the old man's overpowering authority and thick silver beard commanded a respect they could not resist. But there was more. Something in the immensity of the high vaulted canopy ceiling, the soft warm colors smiling at them from walls and windows, the hallowed silence—something in the church itself led them instinctively to agree and want to protect this glorious spot.

Opa broke the silence with a cryptic: "Follow me."

He nudged Pieter-Lucas to the left, beneath the organ pipes, around the corner, and down the row of side chapels that lined the south wall of the church. Each chapel was named for the patron saint of one of Breda's trade guilds and displayed the symbols of that trade. On a normal pilgrimage, Opa would stop to expound upon the craftsmanship of at least one fascinating item in each chapel.

Today, though, he pushed on past all the chapels until they reached the Chapel of the Holy Ghost. Here, he turned out of the aisle and hobbled to the kneeling rail before the altar. He raised his head high and announced, "Behold!"

Pieter-Lucas and Aletta followed the direction of Opa's gaze upward. On the wall above the altar hung a grand painting in bright colors with a shadowlike frame painted directly on the wall around it. John the Baptizer, clad in coarse animal skins, knelt in the golden sand beside a green-blue Jordan River. He was worshiping Jesus, who had emerged from the river with water dripping from his white loin garments. A shimmering white dove hovered above Him, with its silver-tipped wings outspread, catching the light that radiated from Jesus' head.

"Your painting!" Pieter-Lucas cried.

"Beautiful!" Aletta added.

"It's more wonderful than I remembered!" Pieter-Lucas reached up and pulled the cap from his head, then stood dumb with awe. A thrill of excitement ran through his whole body.

Pieter-Lucas looked at his grandfather and saw a dignity he'd never seen before. Tears streamed down the wrinkled, smiling face and glistened in the flickering candlelight from the altar. "I've cherished this dream for a lifetime and worked and prayed and hoped and despaired."

Nobody knew better than Pieter-Lucas how long and hard his Opa had worked. All his life, the boy had watched the old man paint beautiful pictures. He'd helped him mix the paints and prepare the canvases—had even painted a few pieces of his own.

"One day," Opa had said over and over, "we shall create a masterpiece to hang in an honored spot in the Great Church on the market square."

Still, none of Opa's paintings had ever hung where people could see them. Vader would not even allow them to hang on the walls of their house on Annastraat. Only the walls of Opa's and Pieter-Lucas' bed cupboards were lined with them.

"Opa, I've watched you working on this grand painting for so long." Pieter-Lucas spoke hardly above a whisper. "You never told me we would see it here!"

"How did it happen?" Aletta begged.

"Did someone commission it?" Pieter-Lucas added.

Opa stood smiling and speechless.

"It is a miracle, right, Opa?"

"I told you it would be."

A sacred hush held the wonder-struck companions captive for a long moment. At length, in a tone of subdued excitement, Aletta broke the silence. "The dove! So perfect, so silvery-white, so peaceful, so pure!"

"The anointing of the Holy Ghost," Opa said. "A dove is for anointing."

Pieter-Lucas opened his mouth to ask him what he meant, but Opa was kneeling at the rail before the altar. Instinctively, the young man followed his example, Aletta close by his side. His eyes searched the painting, and his mind tried to count all the hours he'd spent in Opa's secret studio in the woods outside of Breda, watching him stroke the canvas with his brushes. "I can't believe it," he murmured to himself. At last, Opa's day to be recognized had come. Happy, happy day! So great, in fact, was his happiness, that he did not notice what transpired around him until a figure loomed between him and the painting.

Pieter-Lucas wrenched his gaze away from the painting to look full into the familiar face of the priest of the Great Church. He was the man who had baptized Pieter-Lucas as an infant. A friend of Opa, he always had a pat on the head and a warm greeting for the boy in his growing-up years.

Astonished, Pieter-Lucas watched the elderly cleric as he turned to face the altar and crossed himself. Then, dampening his fingers from the nearby baptismal font, he walked to the painting and sprinkled a gentle shower of drops on its vibrant colors. All the while he mumbled a string of Latin words.

Pieter-Lucas recognized the words. Many times Opa had recited them. It was a part of many of their pilgrimages. How often Opa had led them to stop at the foot of one of the huge pillars that held up the high, arched beams of the sanctuary.

"See the red cross painted here?" he had asked. And they always agreed and listened to his story. "Many years ago, when this church was new, the priests sprinkled each pillar with holy water and recited special words of blessing. 'Anointed for service in the name of the Father, Son, and Holy Ghost,' was what it meant."

"I think this is a holy moment," Pieter-Lucas whispered to Aletta.

"Indeed," she answered.

Next, the priest moved to where Opa knelt and repeated the process, this time anointing the wiry gray hairs of Opa's head with water, mumbling again the sacred words. Pieter-Lucas felt a chill of anticipation course through his body. Did this make Opa a holy man? Would he always be dedicated to the service of God as the church was?

While this latest thought was still jolting him, he realized that the priest had now come to stand over him. He was sprinkling cool drops of consecrated water on the startled young man's head. Again he recited the words: "Anointed for service in the name of the Father, Son, and Holy Ghost."

Confused, Pieter-Lucas looked up into the penetrating eyes of the smiling priest. A shimmering glow of pale candlelight played across his wrinkled face and sprinkled his gray beard with star pricks of sparkling light. He opened his mouth to speak, and his voice flowed over the young man like warm honey. "Anointing is reserved for sacred duties, devoted works of art, and for people with the call of God upon them. See to it that you never neglect your anointing, son."

As quickly and quietly as he had come, the priest exited behind the altar. Pieter-Lucas felt water trickling in all directions over his scalp, some making a pathway over his forehead and down his nose. What was this? Before he could put his scattered thoughts into words, he watched Opa rise from his knees and lean against his cane, the tears still streaming down his face. Dazed, Pieter-Lucas stood, too, and reached out a hand to help Aletta up. She clung to his arm.

He twisted the cap in his hands and wiped at a stray rivulet streaming down around his left ear. "But, Opa, why did the priest anoint me?"

"You heard him, Pieter-Lucas," Aletta interrupted. "The call of God is upon you." She spoke in a whisper that hung heavy with awe.

A glow crinkled Opa's eyes, and a wide grin revealed his snaggled teeth. "You and I both know that God created our hands to wield paint brushes and the carver's knife—not to tote swords, right?"

Pieter-Lucas nodded assent.

Opa rearranged himself around his cane and cleared his throat, as if preparing for a long dissertation. "Breda has never understood us. Nor could my . . . my son, Hendrick." He paused, head bowed. Then, looking up at the painting, he said, "Thanks to God, at last the work of my brushes has ventured out to tell our glorious secret to the world."

"You still have not answered my question," Pieter-Lucas protested. "Why my head as well? I have no painting to hang, no canvas worthy of the slightest honor."

The old man leaned both hands on his cane and looked up, startled. "And what of your little carved animals?" he demanded.

"Child's play, nothing more," Pieter-Lucas responded.

"I once thought that, too." Opa stared at the floor and spoke slowly. "When I was your age, nothing could convince me that I was a real artist until I had painted a masterpiece. So I threw away my carver's knife and my drawing pens and did not pick them up again for many years."

"See what a great painter that made of you?"

"See what a useless artist I have been most of my days—only to come to recognition at the end of a life filled with struggle. Had I but been content to draw and carve, I might have been freed sooner and even carried on the great tradition of my uncle Lucas. He was foremost among the engraver-artists of the Netherlands, you know. Think where I might have gone had I followed his lead."

Pieter-Lucas shook his head. "*Nay*, Opa, you and I both have paint running through our blood. I, too, will become a painter, nothing less."

"Then, accept the anointing without question. Just remember, a paintbrush may not always lie within your reach. When it does not, do not be so foolish as to discard the knife, the pen, or the sketcher's charcoal. And never let a day go by without painting, drawing, or carving something!"

Pieter-Lucas caught a glimpse of Aletta clasping her hands and looking at him with an adoration in her eyes that made his heart thump in an odd sort of way.

"Oh, can't you see it?" she asked. "Now that you have been anointed to be an artist, of whatever sort it may be, you will never have to tote the prince's swords. Instead, you can spend your life making pictures and carving beautiful figures in wood. And soon you will go to Leyden where you may even learn to engrave copper plates."

"Easy, easy, Little One," Opa said with raised hand. "No one can say how many swords—or how few—this young man must tote in his day. He is a van den Garde yet, and of sound mind and whole body, with no excuses not to march with the rest of the prince's guard. Ordinary men with naught but blood in their veins will forever attempt to pinch us artists into their drab and painful molds. But a true artist cannot be forever pinched."

"You shall break free, Pieter-Lucas!" Aletta exclaimed.

"Mark my word, someday it shall be," Opa assured her, nodding his head with decisive movements.

"How can you be so sure, Opa?" Pieter-Lucas asked.

"Can you have forgotten my plan?"

"You mean about sending me to Leyden to study with the great artists?"

"Believe in it, *jongen*," Opa answered, a smile covering his bearded face.

"But when and how shall your plan come about? Do you recall how near is my eighteenth birthday?"

"Trust me, Pieter-Lucas. That's all I can say. If the plan comes not quite as soon as we expected, do not lose heart."

Opa reached up his left hand and rested it on the young man's shoulder. He looked straight into his eyes and said, "In the meantime, you will have moments when you doubt."

"Like right now?"

"Like right now. When those moments come, simply rush to this spot and gaze on this painting. As long as 'The Anointing' hangs on the wall of the Chapel of the Holy Ghost, hope will be reborn for you and your sons after you. Whatever it takes, you must never let yourself forget." He paused, staring at the grave slab tiles that stretched across the big church.

"Oh!" He raised his body from leaning on his cane and moved out of the chapel. "One more shrine on our pilgrimage. Can't miss this old tradition."

Grabbing Pieter-Lucas with one hand and plying his cane with the other, Opa directed the young people's steps. Back down the south side aisle they trudged, across the transept, up the altar steps, and through the carved wooden lattice screen into the Choir. The old man dragged heavily and more slowly with each step. His breathing caused his upper body to heave and sag in a labored rhythm. But he would not hear of stopping to rest along the way.

"Did you bring your carving knife?" Opa asked, puffing and leaning hard against the young man as if to steady himself.

"*Ja*," Pieter-Lucas said hesitantly. He patted the little drawstring pouch that hung from his belt.

"And a block of wood for today's lesson?"

Pieter-Lucas nodded and reached for the leather bag tied to his belt with a long thong.

"*Goed!*" Opa looked radiant, though weary.

Each year, Opa picked a different carving on one of the wooden seats in the choir stall and taught Pieter-Lucas how to carve it from his own little block of wood. As he carved, Aletta always watched and "oohed" and "aahed" over his workmanship. Then he sent the carving home with her, and she'd line it up with all the others around the edge of her cupboard bed.

"Today," Opa began, "we go to a familiar spot—six seats from the end on the south side." He shoved Pieter-Lucas toward it. "But we have a most extraordinary lesson." His voice carried a combination of excitement and soberness.

"The Birdseller!" Pieter-Lucas exclaimed. "Always you lead us to look at it, but never have you let me carve it. Is this the day?"

"*Nay*, my grandson, I shall never let you carve it."

"Why not? You've often said it is your favorite of all the carvings."

Opa wrestled with his breathing for a long moment before he spoke. "In a manner of speaking, yes, 'tis my favorite. You see, it was carved by a van den Garde."

Pieter-Lucas gasped. "You never told me, Opa."

"*Nay*, nor would I say a word now, but you must hear it." He paused. "The young van den Garde of whom I speak—Kees was his Christian name—dreamed of a day when he'd use the carver's knife and not have to carry a sword. In fact, he never did march with the guard, only curried horses for the prince. Quite a remarkable story his . . . though tragically short-lived . . ." He sighed and wiped his sleeve across his eyes.

"How did his carving find its way here?" Pieter-Lucas asked.

"After he died . . . quite suddenly . . . and was buried, it was installed here."

"It was not commissioned, then. Who ordered it placed here?"

Opa stared at the carving. "It was a kind of memorial. But enough of that. What you need to know is that he carved it when he was about your age."

"Was he your brother, Opa?" Pieter-Lucas felt a strange sort of tight curiosity stirring inside.

"That matters not now, *jongen*. What does matter is that he carved the dove inside a latched cage, carried on the hawkster's back. When he did it, his mentor chided him, 'Let the dove fly free.'

"But he refused, protesting, '*Nay*, for van den Gardes are never free.' "

"He should have been here today to see your happy moment," Aletta said.

Opa looked at her and pain pinched his features and his voice. "If only God had willed it."

Resolutely, he pounded the head of his cane with his fist, then shifted his gaze toward Pieter-Lucas. "And you, my grandson, must carve only free-flying doves, like the one that hovers in 'The Anointing.' Never allow yourself to fancy your art in a cage." Tears were streaming down his cheeks again.

Pieter-Lucas laid an arm around the old man's trembling shoulders. "Opa, one day, we shall both be set loose from our cages, you as the Grand Master Painter of Breda, and I as your assistant. We shall fly and dip and soar over the horizon and all Breda shall take notice."

"*Nay*, not I, *jongen*, but you and all van den Gardes after you with the paint in your blood and the carver's knife in your fingers. To you shall belong the Master's honor. In fact . . ." He paused again and sagged against his cane. "In fact, I fear I shall never again walk in this Great Church. My duties have come to an end."

"*Nay, nay*, Opa. You have only begun," Pieter-Lucas protested.

Opa ignored him and went on. "On this day of our Artists' Pilgrimage, I appoint you, Pieter-Lucas van den Garde, to guard the miracle—my painting—well."

"In the church it is safe and needs no guard."

Opa shook his head. "Nothing precious is safe without a guard, it matters not where it hides."

"What mean you, Opa?"

"Have you forgotten Hendrick and his wild, image-breaking friends, who see not icons in artistic likenesses, but only as idols?"

"Icons?" Aletta asked.

"Icons aid us in the worship of the God they represent," Opa explained. "Idols are objects that we worship in place of God."

Something in the old man's gaze made Pieter-Lucas uneasy. "One thing more you must remember," Opa said. "God gives us our work to use, not simply for our own pleasure or to gain honor from men. That would be idolatry. Rather, He anoints us to create icons to serve as healing elixirs for the many wounds of this mad and violent world where the sword still rules."

Pieter-Lucas blinked, as if to clear the puzzlement from his brain. Healing elixir for a mad and violent world? Why was Opa speaking in such riddles?

"Protect the painting," Opa repeated, "and your anointing." With a nod and a wink in the direction of Aletta, he added, "And this little one as well."

Hope collided with mystery in the heart of Pieter-Lucas the man, while the heart of Pieter-Lucas the boy trembled. He looked at his weary grandfather's faint smile arching his mouth oddly to one side. With strong, noble feelings nearly overwhelming him, he promised, "I shall, Opa. I shall guard them all with my life."

He and Aletta exchanged smiles in a pool of colored light between the rows of seats in the Choir. She slid her arm into his, and he squeezed it with his elbow. Visions of a glorious future with this special friend and the paint pots and canvases and wood blocks he so dearly loved made him wonder what could ever bring doubt to him again.

He turned back toward Opa. To his horror, he watched the old man slump into a folded heap on the floor. The two young people fell to their knees beside him.

"Opa, Opa, Opa," they called out to him. He did not respond.

"Hurry," Pieter-Lucas said to Aletta, "go call Tante Lysbet."

The young woman sprang to her feet and ran across the tiles.

"Opa, speak to me. Opa, come back," he cried out as he turned the old man onto his back. The smile was gone from the beloved, bearded face; the eyes looked glazed and remote. The mouth pulled the beard crookedly to the right, and a thin line of drool ran away toward an ear.

A muffled groan came from somewhere deep in the uniformed chest.

Pieter-Lucas leaned close and patted the still warm cheeks. "Opa, please don't go. Leave me not alone with your brushes and my memories. Opa, Opa, Opaaa . . ."

With great effort, the old man raised his left hand and grabbed at his grandson, while his right arm lay helpless at his side. For an instant, the eyes flickered and the mouth twitched. Three words escaped, slurred and barely intelligible from stiff lips: "Studio . . . healing . . . Beguinage . . ."

"Studio? Healing? Beguinage? Tell me more, Opa, tell me more."

Opa had dropped his left arm to the floor and fallen silent once more. Frantic, Pieter-Lucas patted the cheeks again and again. He tugged at the arms, now heavy and less pliable, and continued his pathetic wail. "Opa, come back, Opa, Opa, Opaaa . . ."

He stared into eyes—always filled with tender care and lighted with mischievousness—now vacant, cold, unseeing.

"*Nay*, God," he screamed out into the cavernous church. His words mocked him from a dozen corners. "*Nay, nay, nay*, you cannot take my Opa yet. . . ." Then he threw himself across the lifeless body, buried his head in Opa's chest, and soaked the old guardsman's jacket with hot, angry tears.

------

### 10th Day of Hay Month (July), 1566

A soft, warm rain sprinkled jewels into the spider webs in the bushes beside the road. It drizzled onto Aletta's headdress and slickened the cobblestones beneath her feet. She inhaled the aroma of summer dust, welcoming a fresh baptism of life-giving moisture, and listened to the lively chatter and singing of a hundred birds in the linden trees that lined the narrow lane beyond the Guesthouse Gate and the city wall.

"Just enough sounds to cover my footsteps and keep Pieter-Lucas from hearing me," she said to herself. "How much farther can it be?"

Going places with Pieter-Lucas was a way of life for Aletta Engelshofen. All their lives they'd played together, explored Breda together, done almost everything together. Following him at a distance and ducking in and out between bushes so as not to be detected was quite another matter. This time, though, she could find no other way.

Ever since that fateful day in the Great Church when Opa had revealed his "miracle" to her and Pieter-Lucas, then fallen to the floor and died with apoplexy, she'd scarcely seen her special friend. "It's as if his spirit has taken a long journey away from me," the distressed young woman had complained to Moeder Kaatje when they met in the fish market one day.

"It has indeed," Moeder Kaatje agreed. "But not only has it taken leave of you, I, too, seem to have lost my son."

"Does he ever come back to your house since Vader Hendrick forbade it?" Aletta had asked.

The woman looked about her anxiously before answering, as if to be sure no one eavesdropped on their conversation. "Whenever Hendrick is on night guard duty, Pieter-Lucas will spend the night in his bed. Beyond that, *nay*."

"Where, then, does he stay?"

"Sometimes in the *Kasteel* stables. And for the rest . . ." She paused, once more looking about her. Then drawing up close and whispering into Aletta's ear, she confided, "Somewhere, I know not exactly where, lies a hidden studio where he and his Opa used to go to work on their paintings. I think he sleeps most often there."

"Aha," Aletta whispered her reply. "I've heard him speak of that place. Though I used to beg him to take me there, he always brushed me aside. 'It's our secret—Opa's and mine,' he'd say, and no amount of begging or asking could ever coax the truth from him."

Kaatje sighed, rubbed her pregnant belly, and smiled weakly at the girl. "Someday he will come back."

"Surely we can do something to hasten his return!"

"Wait, my Child," the woman answered. "Do not rush him. Sorrow has called him from us, for he loved his Opa perhaps more than any other." She smiled, squeezed Aletta's arm, and added, "There is just one thing you can do. Indeed, we must both do it."

"Tell me, please."

"Never, never stop loving him. Love alone brings people back."

"That I can promise with my whole heart."

Since that meeting, Aletta had watched each day until she saw Pieter-Lucas running toward the edge of the city. "That must be the way to his secret studio," she told herself. "Someday, I know not when or why, but someday I shall follow him."

Today was that "when." For last night, sister Gertrude at the Beguinage had given her a "why." Unbelievable as it seemed, she told Aletta that the Beguinage had commissioned Opa to do a painting, which he had not delivered to them before he died.

"Please, do all you can to find and retrieve it for us, child," the gentle woman had begged of her.

At a Y in the road, Aletta followed Pieter-Lucas' lead to the right, and the way narrowed even further to become a tunnel-like lane where weeds fringed the contours of the cobblestones. Then they turned off into a neglected pathway that led to a dark stand of oak trees. Without an eyeblink's hesitation, Pieter-Lucas left the path and shoved his way past overhanging branches, creeping berry vines, and healthy bushes of wild carrot, cow parsley, and liverwort. Cautiously she crept on behind him, thankful for the tall weeds where she could crouch quickly to hide when he turned her way, yet fearful lest she attract his attention when her full skirts rustled through them.

From the shelter of an ancient spreading oak with an enormous trunk, she watched his slowing steps. He stopped before a tall thorny hedge that loomed among the trees like a city wall. A profusion of wild pink roses covered it, blending their strong sweet fragrance with the damp dust. She held her breath and suppressed a sneeze.

"Still, still," she told herself. Her heart raced and pounded in the bosom of her dress. "He must not know I am here, else he will turn back. And I must get the painting. Sister Gertrude was insistent. Besides, Opa would will it so!"

Fascinated, eager, fearful, she stared, not daring to miss a move or to be caught by a stray glance. She watched him fumble in his pocket and pull out a large key. Then after a wary look in every direction, he turned to the hedge and thrust the key into it at a spot where the late morning sun cast a long bright shaft of light through the gloom. He tugged at the hedge until a section opened before her wondering eyes.

"A secret door!" She stifled a cry of amazement.

"This is the moment," she told herself. Holding her skirts off the ground, she dashed from her hiding place and came up behind him in the doorway just as he reached back to pull it shut. His jacketed elbow nudged her shoulder, causing him to turn and utter a short, sharp cry.

"Who's there?"

He looked into her eyes. "Aletta! How did you get here?"

She shoved him across the threshold. "Please let me in," she pleaded. But he stood firm, blocking her passage.

"You may not enter this place, Little One," he said, attempting to push her back out.

"I had to come, Pieter-Lucas." She planted her feet firmly in the damp, cold earth of what appeared to be a musty cellar. A single torch mounted on the wall burned fiercely, its flames reaching toward them and nearly blinding her for a moment. She reached behind her and pulled the door shut.

"Why did you have to come?" he demanded, still blocking her way.

"You know Opa never allowed me to bring you here. It is our secret hide-away—his and mine." A tear formed in his eye and glistened like molten gold in the torchlight.

"I know, I know," she replied softly, placing a hand on his arm. She wanted to remind him that Opa was gone now, that he had left Pieter-Lucas with a mission to take care of her. It was part of his anointing. Surely Opa intended that after he was gone, she should enter this part of Pieter-Lucas' world. But the pain and tears in his eyes and the rigid upward tilt of his stubbly chin stopped her.

Moeder Kaatje had been right. He was not yet ready to let her back into the place she'd always occupied in his heart. She looked at his face where aloofness mixed with a hint of tears, and struggled to follow Moeder Kaatje's advice. But the waiting felt like dying, and how could she know when it was time for her to coax him back?

She smiled and stroked his arm gently. He did not brush her away, and she imagined that he dropped his chin ever so slightly. With all the warmth she could summon, she said, "I've a message for you."

Pieter-Lucas' lips parted, and he mumbled, "For me?"

"For you."

"From whom?"

She saw a flicker of curiosity and went on. "From Sister Gertrude at the Beguinage."

"Beguinage?"

Hesitant, hopeful, she told him at last, "Yesterday, my moeder was having one of her bad howling spells. Tante Lysbet sent me to the Beguinage to fetch some soothing herbs. Before I left for home, Sister Gertrude instructed me to beg you to bring her one of Opa's paintings."

A tiny spark of interest appeared to ignite in the watering blue eyes. "Which painting?"

"She called it 'The Healing.' Said she had commissioned Opa to paint it to hang above the altar in the Beguinage Chapel." She held her breath and waited. Would this bring him back?

"Studio . . . healing . . . Beguinage . . ." He let each word hang momentarily before going on to the next. Then, without another word to her, he walked away into the strange cellar, saying under his breath so Aletta could just barely catch his words, "Opa, Opa, Opa. You tried to tell me."

Hesitant at first, then gaining confidence, she followed him through what proved to be a passageway with earthen ceiling, walls, and floor. At the far end they climbed a short flight of worn stairs, and she found herself in a broad room spread out beneath a low wood-beamed ceiling. The whitewashed walls shut out the world on three sides. The fourth side contained a window formed of multicolored leaded panes in various sizes and shapes arranged to create a large framed rosette. The floor was strewn with drawings and wood chips, and against the side wall a pile of logs propped up a pair of stretched canvases.

"Oh, Pieter-Lucas!" The words slipped out before she realized. Quickly she clapped a hand over her mouth.

"What do you think?" he asked, still not looking at her.

"It's a wonderful place!"

Mesmerized, she moved toward the window where one low table held an assortment of carving tools, small paint pots, brushes, varnish flasks, and a well-used palette. Beside the table sat a straight-backed chair and an easel with a canvas on which had been painted another of Opa's pictures, radiant with the same colors that adorned "The Anointing."

Aletta stepped back till she could see it all at once, yet focus on each detail. A crowd of people, all either lame with wrapped limbs and simple crutches or blind with eye patches or mad or simply clad in tattered rags, flocked around the central figure of Jesus. He reached out to those nearest Him, one hand cradling the leg of a lame girl, the other resting on her head. The look of compassion on the magnificently formed face sent a shiver down Aletta's back.

"How He loves them all," she whispered. "Surely, this is the painting, is it not?"

Pieter-Lucas stood perfectly still in the splotchy rainbow-hued sunlight that filtered through the window. He looked away from her.

"There is no other in the collection that could be called 'The Healing.'" The voice had none of the sparkle that belonged to her Pieter-Lucas.

"It will be just right in the place for which he created it—the chapel of the Beguinage, the healing place." If only she and the Beguines could have reached Opa soon enough with their peach kernel juice drawn with pennyroyal water! Tante Lysbet said it performed wonders against apoplexy. Vader Dirck always said God had a time for everyone to die, but why did He have to choose now to take Opa? Didn't He know Pieter-Lucas still needed him?

"It shall never hang in the Beguinage." Pieter-Lucas did not move from his spot by the window.

"But, of course it shall."

"*Nay*, it cannot!"

"And why not?"

"It's not finished!" A sigh escaped, followed by a series of nervous sniffles.

"Not finished?" Aletta retorted.

"Look for yourself." He pointed to the lower left corner. "Nay," he protested, "Opa would never let them hang it thus. . . ."

She looked as he instructed. Indeed a pair of figures had been sketched out in rough ghostlike form and never painted. But what did that matter? In an excited flush of discovery, Aletta swept across the room and grabbed Pieter-Lucas by the hand. "Oh, Pieter-Lucas! Opa left it for you to finish." She was triumphant with the wonder of the old man's cleverness.

For an instant he stared at her, expressionless, then pulled away and began pacing back and forth across the cracked, dirty tile floor, shuffling heedlessly through the clutter of creative debris scattered there. "Nay, nay, nay!" he shouted. "Opa was commissioned, not Opa's grandson. Only Opa can finish Opa's painting."

She stationed herself in his way in midroom and said in her firmest voice, "For what was your anointing in the church? Tell me that!"

Startled, he paused, then returned her challenge. "For what was anything that happened in the church?" Grabbing her by both arms, he removed her from his path and paced on. "When Vader Hendrick learned that I had accompanied Opa to the church on that dark day, he ordered me never to return to his house. Since then I am forced, when not on duty at the prince's stable, to sleep and eat in this studio. Once warm and filled with life and love and learning, 'tis now peopled with the ghosts of broken promises and mocking dreams. They scream at me in the night and taunt me in the day. Where, I beg of you, has the anointing gone in all of this?" He stopped at last, sat in the chair before the easel, held his head in his hands, and said nothing more.

Aletta walked to him. If only she could take him in her arms and soothe away his sorrow and fears. All her life she had watched her own vader do this for her moeder when Moeder Gretta's frequent headaches led to wild howling spells. Sometimes it worked for him. Could she make it work as well?

Gently, timidly at first, she laid a hand across the big shoulders and felt them shake. Ever so gently she rubbed them. With tears drenching her cheeks, she repeated Opa's words spoken in the church: " 'When moments of doubt come, simply rush to this spot and gaze on this painting and remember your anointing. . . . Whatever it takes, you must never forget. . . . Protect this painting and your anointing. . . .' "

Aletta paused, then in a whisper repeated Pieter-Lucas' own solemn answer: " 'I promise, Opa, I will protect them with my life.' "

Now she heard him cry. Deep, broken, agonizing sobs blended with her own freely flowing tears. He leaned back against her, and she let her tears anoint his curls with a common anguish. He grabbed both her hands in his and pressed them to his lips, covering them with damp caresses.

The sun's shifting rays no longer streamed directly through the eastern window. Pieter-Lucas' sobs came to an end, and he guided her around by the hand till she faced him. Then gathering her skirts beneath her into a cushion, Aletta sat before him by the canvas and watched the life creep back into his beloved face.

"I will protect the painting—and my anointing—with my life," he said. "And you, my Little One, as well." When he called her by this name, she felt closest to him.

He reached down to his belt and lifted out his wood-carving bag. Without speaking a word or looking up at her, he drew out the carving knife and then a small wooden object.

"The birdseller's cage!" Aletta exclaimed. "You imprisoned the dove. Oh, Pieter-Lucas! Please, set it free."

Still unspeaking, slowly, deliberately, he passed the knife blade through the bars, then ripped them away. With large, sure fingers he plucked at the tiny dove and placed it in Aletta's open palm. For a long moment he stared at her, until a sparkle began to light his eyes. He picked up a paintbrush from the table and turned it over in his hand. A smile began to form across his thoughtful face.

"It fits your hand most perfectly, new Master Painter of Breda," Aletta said, her mind astir with grand dreams.

She watched him continue to handle the brush, till at last he let it lie poised between his thumb and fingers as if ready for a painter's work. He raised his head and looked first at her, then up beyond the shaggy rafter beams of the ceiling above them. "Opa, tell me, what colors have you planned for these last two figures?"

"Whatever you wish, Master," Aletta said with a curtsy. "You are the artist now!" She stood smiling down on him, spread a hand toward him, and said, "Welcome home, my dearest friend. Please promise you will never leave me again."

Still holding firmly to the paintbrush, he rose to his feet and wrapped her in his arms. They gazed at each other in the multicolored glow beside the rosette window, and he said, "I promise. Never will I leave you again!"

Almost the voice belonged to her Pieter-Lucas!

# CHAPTER TWO

*Breda—The Crane's Nest*

Early morning of 21st day of Harvest Month (August), 1566

*D*irck Engelshofen's day always began as soon as the sun arose. He liked to straighten the books on his shelf before Aletta came in to dust and sweep. Then, he'd review the inventory of books left after the close of business on the day before, and finally, he'd spend a quiet hour or two reading from a new book or one of his favorite texts. During the summer months the days were long. The sun might rise before Roland had rung out five bells from the tower and not set again until after twenty-two bells at night.

This morning he'd started his routine sometime after five bells and was already settled into his chair with a thin, untitled pamphlet he had received just yesterday from a friend who lived in Antwerp. He'd hardly opened the decorative cover when a rapping at the door announced the arrival of his friends from the "academic circle."

"*Och, jongens!* You are up and out before the sun."

Meister Laurens jabbed his younger companion with his elbow and groused, "No more sleeping once this traveling messenger comes pounding on your door."

"I have news so big I would have come to you both the instant I arrived back from Antwerp last night." Barthelemeus was quick to jump to his own defense. "But, as you know, a curfew has been imposed by the magistrates, and unbelievable as it sounds, they made me pass the night outside the Prison Tower Port rather than let me in."

"You tried the other gates—the Harbor Port and the Guesthouse Port?" Dirck asked.

"*Ja,* but of course, and the Haagdike Port and Eynd Port—at every little opening in the wall, I banged and begged and shouted. None would lend me so much as half an ear." Barthelemeus gestured wildly as he spoke. "But you must hear my news—now!"

Dirck motioned his friends toward their chairs in the corner.

"There is trouble and image-breaking going on all over Flanders and South Brabant, and already agitators are on their way to Breda," Barthelemeus began.

Meister Laurens yawned, intertwined his fingers across his belly, and looked up drowsily from beneath drooping eyelids. "You saw it? Heard it? Felt it in your bones?"

"I was nearly trampled into the cobblestones by it yesterday morning."

"In Antwerp?" The words stirred old memories in Dirck's mind of the sort he'd wished never to remember.

"Ja, in Antwerp. For three days in a row, the most despicable class of riffraff has swarmed the Cathedral of Our Beloved Lady and staged massive riots."

"Riots?" Dirck gasped. Inquisition and executions, with fearful and sometimes angry responses—he'd known them in his life. Even protests of a sort. But riots were rare.

Barthelemeus sat forward in his chair, his whole body astir with a sense of urgency. "You act surprised. As if you didn't know that the whole south has been seething with religious and political unrest, on the verge of rioting for . . . months."

"Years!" Dirck corrected. "Nothing new about unrest."

"It's never been like this before. Since Brederode and his riotous bunch of noble Beggars started running around with fake Beggars' bowls dangling from their necks and Beggars' pennies from their caps, the whole country is about to go up in flames."

"So it was a Beggars' riot!" Dirck began to make some sense of this strange report.

"Probably they incited it. I did not go into the cathedral, so didn't see it all. But what I did see was a mass of angry people. They were shoving and shouting, 'Long live the Beggars!' and a host of obscenities against the Virgin image that was paraded through the streets three days ago. They were mostly riffraff—vagabonds, street urchins, prostitutes—no noblemen in Beggars' attire."

Laurens cleared his throat and began in that officious tone that amused, exasperated, and endeared him to his two companions. "Noblemen with golden tongues and wild swords are rarely seen fighting in popular riots. They simply parade through the streets and drink in all the adulations. Then they mount high platforms whence they can spectacularly deliver incendiary orations. When it comes to the action, they stand back and watch with lily palms and unbridled glee while the riffraff rushes in and bloodies hands and garments at their command."

Barthelemeus shot a questioning look at the older man. "How did you know? Were you there?"

Meister Laurens cleared his throat again and added, "Take it from a schoolmaster, it always works that way. And I might add, they will never lack for a following. Men with dilapidated fortunes, petty grievances, and a greed for plunder won at the point of a sword will always abound."

"You're telling us that not all who follow in the Beggars' train do so for religious reasons?" Barthelemeus asked, a combination of disbelief and the excitement of a fresh discovery tinging his voice.

Laurens laughed. "If the truth were known, we might find a mere fistful of truly devout men at the heart of this thing, no more."

"How then can they call it a holy war if what they really seek is wealth and power?" the younger man added.

"Have you forgotten, friend, that we are ruled by a king who calls himself our 'Most Catholic Monarch'?" Dirck asked and watched a light go on in Barthelemeus' eyes.

Laurens lifted a hand and leaned toward his listeners. "Our King Philip claims he has a mission from God to exterminate the last lingering shred of heresy and restore a pure Church in the whole of the Lowlands. In his mind, ruling what he considers these uncouth, impious, petulant lands on the fringes of his empire is a religious crusade."

"Which means," Dirck added, "that no matter how irreligious a rebel may be, if he would change his 'Very Catholic King's' mind, he must do so in the name of religion."

"Bah!" Laurens puffed. "Philip may be Catholic and religious, but if you ask me, he's far from Christian. He's one big-headed, small-hearted Hapsburg with a kingdom ten times the size of his sense. King of Naples, Milan, Spanish America, and the Lowlands, indeed! Bah!"

"Sh! Not so loud," Dirck said. "Mustn't let those words escape through these windowpanes, or we may all find ourselves tied to a stake with bales of hay and gunpowder at our feet."

Barthelemeus leaned forward, and they all followed his lead, creating a small circle of whispering heads. "I shall speak more quietly, but I have to know something. Why did Charles V put the Lowlands under his son's control when he divided up his Holy Roman Empire between successors? He knew better than we that Philip is a Spaniard, born and reared there, who refuses to learn any other language than Spanish, and is ruled by fanatical Spanish religious sentiments. He thinks like a Spaniard, lives only in Spain, and won't rest until he can turn all the rest of us into Spaniards."

"Only Charles V knows the answer to that question," Dirck suggested.

"If Philip would take the advice of this schoolmaster and read some of the old Latin records of our history, he'd discover what the ancient Roman conquerors discovered—that he's dealing with a fiercely independent people." Gradually the Meister's voice left off being a whisper and grew louder. "We will die first before we let him turn us into either loyal Spaniards or Catholics with a commitment to exterminate heresy."

"Ah," Barthelemeus said, a grin forming at the edges of his mouth, "but he could not read the records. They are not written in Spanish!"

All three men leaned back in their chairs and laughed.

"He wouldn't have to read Latin to listen to the messages his Lowland subjects send him," Dirck suggested. "As I see it, his problem is not language, but an arrogant spirit."

"You've touched the heart of it," Laurens said, nodding. "If he were willing to listen, he could learn many things from his father's example. Charles was as committed to keeping his subjects Catholic as Philip. In fact, he was the one who first put the Inquisition into force. But he was a Lowlander himself and would at least talk with us. That was his secret for keeping down a revolt."

"A pity he doesn't listen," Dirck shook his head. Would there always be a King Philip to run from and an army of Beggars to object in ways that hurt more people than they helped? How much longer could he continue to keep his family safe, with war crouching on their doorstoop?

Barthelemeus interrupted his thoughts. "Remember when Prince Willem's brother, Ludwig, gathered his noble friends around a table in Willem's *Kasteel* to seek a way to get the king's attention?"

"I do remember," Dirck said. "We sat in this very room discussing it and decided it was a grand idea."

Meister Laurens crossed his arms, dropped his double chin into his chest, and said, "On the surface it did appear that the men who met there were a respectable Confederacy of Nobles with one commendable goal. They were drawing up a reasonable petition to request that King Philip would restore all the rights and privileges written into our city charters by his long-ago predecessors—"

"Rights he had stolen from the citizens by the exercise of his oppressive ambitions," Barthelemeus interrupted.

"I still believe," Dirck added, "that all Ludwig and most of his friends ever wanted was to free us from Philip's unreasonable controls. How were we to know the Confederacy of Nobles would one day turn into these warmongering rebels with the unlikely tag of 'Beggars'?"

Meister Laurens tapped a finger on his knee and stared hard at his friends. "You may also remember," he began, "that I tried to warn you when that wild creature Hendrick van Brederode joined the group that there would be trouble. Just as I suspected, in no time, Brederode wormed his way in next to Ludwig and took over as the Great Beggar."

They exchanged bemused glances and sighs, then shrugged.

"We never argued with you," Barthelemeus said.

"Never!" Dirck agreed.

Laurens seemed to ignore them, continuing his speech with a slow deliberation that exasperated the other two. "Take it from a schoolmaster, descended from a long line of schoolmasters," he said, wagging his forefinger at first one, then the other of his friends, "Hendrick van Brederode is an outdated, savage, mutinous noble. He has delusions of heading up some fiendish restored fifteenth-century army and one day establishing and occupying a 'Throne of the Lowlands.' Mind my word, when once the going gets mired in a peat bog, the Great Beggar will be the first to flee in search of some new cause. . . ."

"Built, of course, upon utopian promises, wild orations, wine, and women," Dirk finished for him.

Barthelemeus sighed, tipped his head to one side, and gestured toward the others. "I think if I'd been Philip's regent, Margriet, sitting in her chair all propped up by cushions and receiving that petition from those rebel noblemen with Hendrick van Brederode at the head, I might have been tempted to shut them all up in a tower and throw away the key."

Laughter filled the room.

At length, Dirck spoke, "Think of all the grief that might have saved us."

"A pity I couldn't have done it," Barthelemeus added. "But no pity at all that I have not to sit in that woman's chair."

Laurens pushed himself to his feet and said, "Well, *jongens*, one word of caution. Beware, beware. Nothing good will come of this, I warn you."

"Thank God we live in Breda, not Flanders or Antwerp." Dirck pulled his shoulders tall and smiled, almost feeling as confident as he tried to sound. "In our city of peacelovers, the leaders of the Beggars may find a closet in which to write their rebellious petitions. But no wild armies will be allowed to unleash their fury against our churches."

Laurens shook his head and frowned. "Dirck, Dirck, be not so blind. For when the troublemakers come, you and I may be surprised to see which of our trusted friends and neighbors may join swords with them for the work. And when the battle is over, and King Philip plans his retribution, his broom will sweep wide and take in all who can be connected by the slightest association."

Without giving either of the other men a chance to speak, the Meister had started for the door. "And now, I take leave from you both, for I have a class of young men expecting me to expound to them of the classics and sums and earth science." He put his hat on his head and walked out the door with a final, "Good day, *jongens*, and be wary till the storms are passed."

Barthelemeus followed close on the older man's heels, stopping long enough to pat Dirck on the shoulder and say, "I wish I did not agree with Meister Laurens, but I fear you are living with your ear plugged against the falling of the crane's warning stone. Good day, take heed, for booksellers will always be more at risk than the rest."

Before Dirck had said his own final farewell, he caught sight of the familiar figure of Pieter-Lucas van den Garde rushing toward his door.

"Heer Engelshofen—" Pieter-Lucas was short of breath. He grabbed Dirck by the arm, and they hurried into the bookshop.

"What is it?"

"There are troops of Beggars on their way from Antwerp—one thousand of them—armed with swords and halberds, ropes and mallets. They've already smashed the whole cathedral of Antwerp to powder, and our own beautiful church is next."

"Where did you hear such a thing?" Dirck remained outwardly calm, but inside he thrashed about. What was this? First, Barthelemeus with his rumors, then Laurens with his warning, now the neighbor's son with word of an approaching army!

"A messenger, fresh from Antwerp, just arrived at the *Kasteel* stables. He rode all night to bring our magistrates word."

"What can they do in Breda? We are well fortified and alert. And we have no men living amongst us of the sort who would give them aid, have we?" Why did he sense a seed of doubt in his own mind?

"I . . . I know not." Pieter-Lucas winced as he spoke.

Without warning, Dirck saw a picture in his mind so terrifying he tried desperately to dislodge it. Why he'd never seen it before, he couldn't imagine, but it now seemed perfectly clear that his next-door neighbor might be just that sort of man. Hendrick van den Garde, always a restless and sometimes violent man, had of late associated himself with the Calvinists that met at the end of Boschstraat, in Antonis Backeler's home. Was it possible that these agitated new thinkers had plotted with the Beggars? Had they even joined the Beggars? Did the young man standing before him suspect his father's involvement, and was that the reason for the pain on his face?

If the threat went no further than this little group of rebels, it would not stand a chance against the city's defenders. But what if the rumors were true? *Nay*, but they could not be! A thousand armed Beggars? Impossible! There weren't that many of them in all the Lowlands—or were there? *Nay*, he decided, it had to be an idea born in some deranged imagination and spread abroad for the evil pleasure of terrorizing innocent people.

"I believe," he told Pieter-Lucas, "that the rumors you heard are only that. We must not be alarmed."

"But, Heer Engelshofen, the magistrates and clergymen believe they are more than rumors. Already they have locked the church doors, and word flies all around the city that they are busy hiding away her treasures against the madness of the intruders on their way."

"Be calm, *jongen*, be calm," he said, feeling anything but calm himself. He must do all he could to quiet the boy's fears. Otherwise, who knew what he might say to Aletta that would stir her up? Dirck was her father, her protector, and he must not let her hear the frightening rumors.

"Trust God to protect what is His own," he went on, as much to try to convince himself as Pieter-Lucas. "Remember that Breda is a fortified city, with a force of marksmen and city guards completely capable of bringing a prompt end to any fire that the Beggars could ignite in this place."

"You sound so certain, Heer Engelshofen. But if a thousand Beggars really do come, what then?"

"Rumors, *jongen*, rumors. A handful? Perhaps. And if that should happen, you hide yourself, do you hear me? Let no one see you near the scene or in company with any of the rioters. Just remember that any person seen with the perpetrators of violent acts in such an uproar, large or small, would be counted guilty by association. So flee if the need should arise, whether the threat comes from one man or a thousand."

Pieter-Lucas stood silently, and Dirck Engelshofen watched him stare first at the floor then into his own eyes. Gradually he saw the pain give way to a cajoled bravery. The boy extended his hand, and Dirck grasped it in his own.

"I go, Heer Engelshofen . . ." The young man left his voice hanging as if he intended to say more, but nothing more came. Then quickly he hurried toward the door.

"Good day," Dirck said. Clearly a warning came to him with a fatherly urge to pass it on, "and don't say a word of this to my daughter." But something held his tongue from speaking the words, and the idea echoed in his mind to the rhythm of the footsteps rushing down the cobblestones on Annastraat.

---

*Breda*
21st night of Harvest Month (August), 1566

In the gathering late summer dusk, Pieter-Lucas felt an eerie stillness hovering over all Breda. It followed him through the streets, casting its mantle across the harbor and nearly deserted market square. Instinctively he knew it seeped through old stone walls into the halls of the *Kasteel* of Prince Willem van Oranje, the vaults of the Great Church, and every shop and house that lined the city's cobbled streets and coursing river.

Beneath its suffocating cloud, he crept into the garden of the tiny brick house he had always called home on Annastraat and crouched behind a clump of bushes. His heart beat hard against his chest, and he fancied the breath was being sucked out of him.

All day he'd watched his friends and neighbors huddle into anxious clusters about the city, spreading the terrifying rumors about a thousand armed Beggars headed for the Great Church, intent on waging a holy war against her treasures. Unthinkable!

Breda's grand old Gothic Great Church boasted a wealth of paintings, statuary, wood carvings, and a coronet-spired tower that glimmered like a crown jewel. It made every Bredenaar hold his head high. For centuries, townsfolk had gathered beneath her finely painted vaulted arches to worship, while pilgrims from faraway places had enriched her coffers with their gifts. Nothing could be more inconceivable than the thought that all these works of art would fall into the hands of religious fanatics.

Shopkeepers and housewives, scholars and tailors, clergymen and dock hands—Bredenaars from every station in life shook their heads and protested the threatening news from abroad. "In Antwerp, *ja*, that we can believe. In Breda? Never!"

Still, they feared it would happen.

Pieter-Lucas sensed it too. A foreboding air hung over the constant train of people coming and going through the *Kasteel* stables. Even the horses he fed and watered and curried there were uneasy, hard to control.

For two weeks now, city magistrates had enforced a curfew, not allowing anyone without official duties to walk the streets after dark. The unprecedented announcement sent Moeder nearly into hysterics. "Come sit with me, my son," she'd begged him. "It's so lonely while your vader is on duty every night."

Pieter-Lucas' hidden vigil quickly became a ritual. Every night at sunset he came here, waited for Vader Hendrick to leave for guard duty, then went in to keep his moeder company and hoped his vader would never discover him there.

He stared at the door and waited. Had it ever taken Vader so long to leave? The gray of evening had turned into blackness before the door finally burst open. Vader dashed out with an uncharacteristic spring in his step and his big overcoat wrapped securely about him. At the gate, instead of taking the street to his left and the *Kasteel*, he glanced quickly in both directions, then slinked off to the right.

"He's not on guard duty," Pieter-Lucas muttered into the bushes. "No doubt, though, he expects the street watchmen to believe he is and wink at his defiance of the curfew. If only I could believe it too!"

There was a time when he could have believed, a time when he trusted in Vader Hendrick. Not that the man had ever been the genial, pious vader—all-strong, all-wise, all-wonderful—that Opa seemed to be. It was just that he never did anything so bad that Pieter-Lucas could point a finger or call him evil. Yet something dark and sinister brooded in the man's eyes. When he handled his sword, that something glinted with a strange delight that had always stricken Pieter-Lucas with a fear of some unknown future danger.

Then the Calvinists broke through the protective hedge, bringing their "new faith" and its passion to destroy all the icons and the ancient priesthood and the long-held traditions. Vader joined them immediately, and ever since, his dark side had shown itself more and more. Never again could Pieter-Lucas believe in his good intentions. Intuition told him that tonight Vader Hendrick was making a rendezvous with his fanatical friends at Antonis Backeler's house at the far end of Boschstraat to plan an image-breaking. The word sent a shudder through him. When Opa had suggested that his painting might need a protector, even in the church, Pieter-Lucas hadn't taken the old man seriously. If any place on earth was safe, it had to be a church. And yet. . . ? But what could he do about it?

Moving as stealthily as possible around the edges of the garden so as not to call attention to his movements, he came to the door, shoved it open, and called out softly, "Moeder?"

"Here, son." He heard her voice, thin and weak, coming from her bed cupboard on the south wall of the room. "Do not take off your shoes or coat. Come to me quickly."

He found her crying, her face pinched with obvious pain in the pale glow of a lighted candle flickering near to its end on the table. "What is it, Moeder?" He sat on the edge of her bed and took her hand in his. It felt warm, moist, limp.

"You must not stay here this night." She sniffled. "Your vader will be back soon, I fear."

"He didn't go to the *Kasteel* tonight. I saw him go in the other direction."

She stared at him. "It matters not where he went. You must stay out of his way, my son. Cross him not. For once his anger is aroused, it will know no limits. Your vader knows no mercy."

"Did he hurt you, Moeder?" Pieter-Lucas had never seen his vader strike his moeder. But many times he'd come into the room after Vader left, to find her weeping over a pot of soup or her sewing as she held her head with one hand and propped her sagging body against a wall with the other.

"Hendrick is no wife beater," she said.

"What then?"

"Ask me not, son. I only beg you to spare us all and flee now, while there is time."

"But, Moeder, I cannot leave you here to weep alone."

"I do not fear solitude tonight. Rather, to be forced to see what your vader might do if he finds you here would be more than I could endure. Flee now."

Her eyes searched his face with a tender pleading that made him yearn to gather her in his arms and shield her from a whole world of angry men. He kissed her forehead.

"I shall be back, Moeder. Hang a bunch of good luck purslane in the window when it is safe."

He had barely touched the floor when he heard a noise at the outside gate. Vader had returned. No time now to escape. He bounded into his own bed cupboard next to Moeder's and pulled the curtain shut behind him.

Once Vader entered the room, Pieter-Lucas strained his ears to pick up each sound. He decided the man had only removed his overcoat, blown out the candle, then climbed into Opa's bed on the north wall next to the fireplace. All fell so silent that Pieter-Lucas felt certain his heavy heartbeat must be audible throughout the whole house.

Having had no time before Vader arrived to settle into a comfortable position in his bed, Pieter-Lucas dared not to move now. The muscles in his legs and back tightened and cramped, and his mind began to race with disturbing thoughts.

What sort of image-breaking had Vader and his friends planned? Would "The Anointing" hang safely in its spot above the altar of the Holy Ghost?

His ears rang with his grandfather's words, "Protect my painting. . . ."

How simple it had been, kneeling in a pool of rose-colored sunlight at the Artists' Pilgrimage to promise, "I shall guard it with my life." And how terrifying it was lying here shut up in the dark, private world of a forbidden bed, wondering whether the painting had been removed by the priests or not. He knew they had removed some of the church's treasures throughout the day, but no one was allowed into the church to see or to help. So he could only wonder where Opa's grand masterpiece would spend this dreadful night, and if it remained in the church, whether Vader would spare it for the sake of Opa's memory or slash it to shreds.

He shuddered. Had the time come to make good on his promise to Opa? Just this morning Dirck Engelshofen had warned him to hide away lest he be seen and be held guilty by association. But Dirck Engelshofen knew nothing of his promise to Opa. Of what value was his own safety when he had a promise to keep? What would Opa say? Or do?

The sound of his own breathing echoed around his sleeping cell and threatened to smother him. Beads of sweat poured from his forehead. A loud creaking from the next bed startled him. Moeder Kaatje was turning and groaning in her bed. Would Vader come to her? Would he be suspicious enough to check Pieter-Lucas' bed, just in case it held a stowaway?

Roland began his tolling from the church tower. With each of the twenty-four strikes, Pieter-Lucas felt a fresh stab of fear. His stomach tightened into a stony knot. He compressed his head tightly between his hands and tried to control the panic. What could he do? Surely nothing as long as Vader was under the same thatch.

For the rest of the night, Pieter-Lucas lay fearing to move and yearning for sleep. "*Jongen*," he told himself with mounting passion and shrinking conviction, "there is nothing you can do now . . . so take your rest until Vader is gone."

Each persistent creak and sigh and thud of the old house jabbed at his conscience until they seemed to shriek audibly, "Take no rest, until you've done your duty. You promised . . ."

Yet, always in the background came that other voice, "Flee!" At times it grew louder, until the two voices clashed, and he felt his head would split with the pain.

Near daybreak he sat upright in his bed. The creaks and thuds had grown so loud they could only mean one thing—Vader was up and stirring about. Hardly daring to breathe, Pieter-Lucas stretched to the edge of the bed, fearful that the boards beneath his feather bag would give a telltale groan. He parted the curtains the tiniest crack and between stray curls, squinted out at the ghastly scene.

A freshly lit lamp sat on the table. Its flame rose and fell in frenzied leaps and silhouetted the grotesque specter of Vader Hendrick's burly, powerful form advancing like a thief across the tiled floor. He paused at the hearth, reached up to the mantelpiece, and grasped a long shiny knife by its carved handle.

*Nay, Vader.* Pieter-Lucas stifled a desperate cry. *Why that knife?* It never left the mantelpiece except on procession days when Vader marched down the city streets in formation with the rest of the castle guard. Today was no procession day. The boy shivered. *Stop! Stop! STOP!*

With jubilant gestures, Hendrick van den Garde thrust the menacing weapon into its sheath on his belt. All the while he grinned and laughed a low, repressive, growl-like chuckle. Then he shuffled to the far corner by the cellar, where he seized one more large object, shoved it under his brown cloak, blew out the candle, and stole through the door into the back entry room.

*Not the hatchet too!* Pieter-Lucas protested in silence. Fear, anger, and a sensation approaching hatred tumbled in his heart. A wave of shame washed over him. "He is your father still," he told himself.

"But he's gone mad!" From somewhere in his mind he heard the answer. Ach! He must do something . . . but what?

"Flee. . . ."

"Protect the painting. . . ."

"Flee. . . ."

"Protect the painting. . . ." Opa's voice gradually overpowered Dirck Engelshofen's until it tormented his memory. If only he could bring Opa back. . . .

"*Nay, jongen,*" he prodded himself. "*You* made the promise—*you* keep it."

Pieter-Lucas heard the latch lift and the outer door swing open on aging hinges. Then the latch clinked shut and a flurry of muffled steps scuttled down the cobblestone walkway. The boy sprang out of his cupboard bed and ran to the window, just in time to see Vader's brown overcoat flapping off through the somber mists of dawn toward the Great Church.

Pieter-Lucas paused, took a deep breath, then pounded his right fist into his left hand and told himself, "Nothing must destroy 'The Anointing.' Nothing!"

He lifted the latch to leave as quietly as possible. But Moeder Kaatje's thin voice called out from her sleeping cubicle. "Pieter-Lucas!"

"Oh, Moeder," he muttered to himself. Why couldn't she sleep through this? No time to stop and answer her now. He held his breath.

Maybe he had only imagined she called.

"Pieter," she called again. "What's all the commotion?"

"It's all right, Moeder," he answered, his hand still on the latch.

"*Nay*, it's not all right." Her voice sounded whiny, troubled. "With my husband and his wild friends headed for mischief in the church, and my only son set to prowl around the streets, how can I believe such nonsense?"

He drew her bed curtain to one side. "Calm, Moeder, calm." He tried to be gentle. "Worry not for me. I will take care."

She reached her hand toward him. "You're going to the church, aren't you, son? To save Opa's painting?"

He took her hand and squeezed it. "Just trust me, Moeder. I know what I'm doing. Remember, I'm eighteen now."

"Not quite," she corrected him.

"Next week I will be. Now, pray me Godspeed today."

He leaned into her cupboard bed, brushed a perfunctory kiss on her forehead, patted her warm hand, and then left her with a hasty, "I'll be back soon!"

He dashed out into the sleepy-eyed morning. Rain drizzled over his cap and splashed onto his nose. Never had the foreboding nature of life itself so clearly matched the normally nasty weather of the Lowlands. An invisible storm cloud seemed poised to bring destruction to everything he held dear.

Next door, he paused before the Engelshofens' bookshop.

"Should I take time to stop?" he muttered.

For an instant he stared up at the shop sign, hanging over the front door. The words, *The Crane's Nest*, stood out in bold letters above a well-shaped wrought-iron crane, balanced on one foot. In her other foot, the bird held a stone, and she spread her wings protectively over her egg-filled nest. The bird symbolized watchfulness, so Aletta's father had told him. "She sleeps with a stone in her claw to use as a weapon if surprised. And if the stone drops from her grasp, the shop she guards will hear and be alerted that she has fallen asleep."

Pieter-Lucas never understood what sort of watchfulness Dirck Engelshofen fancied that his books were responsible for. But in an eyeblink, he knew that he was Aletta's personal watchman—the crane guarding her nest. His lifelong friend mustn't go out while the image-breakers were at work. He had to drop the warning stone he held in the claw of his mind.

He dashed up the walkway to the side entrance and tapped on Aletta's window shutter—three short, brusque taps. He gave this signal each morning when he stopped on his way to the stables at the *Kasteel* where he groomed the horses and cleaned the stalls. Then he sprang onto the squat doorstoop and paced from corner to corner in cramped miniature diagonals. "Aletta, come quickly," he groaned. "Where are you?"

A second time he ran around to the shutter and tapped—three short, frantic taps. "Aletta, come. Can't wait any longer." Maybe he should go on. No, he had to warn her. Just one more signal.

Before he could spring off the step, he heard the latch lift. The solid oak door sighed and opened a wedge and Aletta's round face appeared. Her blond tresses hung loose, and her shy blue eyes squinted at the faint morning light. Pieter-Lucas leaned on the door, widening its gape. "May I come in?" he whispered.

"Ja, sure, but why so secretive? So hasty? Is the sun even up yet?"

"Almost." He squeezed himself into the back entry hall and grasped her shoulders with damp hands. Still whispering, he warned, "You stay here today with your brother Robbin and Tante Lysbet. Don't dare to go out—not for anything! Do you hear?"

She rubbed her eyes and stared blankly at him. "Not even to the market?"

"Not even to the market. You must go nowhere today."

"But why? What is this all about?"

He felt a strong, impulsive urge to gather her into his arms and hold her tight against all the evils of the world. "I want to keep you safe, Little One," he said, looking down into her eyes. Had they always been so blue? Maybe it was the dim light that made them look so soft, so beckoning. . . .

"Safe from what?" Aletta's question pulled him back to his mission.

"Troubles come!"

"To the Great Church?"

"To the Great Church!"

"You're sure, Pieter-Lucas?"

"I only wish it were not true."

"My father says the trouble is all rumors. 'Breda is no place for church looting and image-breaking.' Those were his very words."

Pieter-Lucas shook his head, dislodging a shower of morning mist. So that's what he had told her. How could this man who knew so much and had so much wisdom so stubbornly refuse to believe the rumors? He had to know how dangerous things were! He simply chose to disbelieve. But why? To enable him better to keep his precious daughter ignorant of the truth? What made him think she would be protected from a world of trouble by ignorance?

"Your father's words are beautiful, Little One, but comfortable-sounding nonsense."

"What makes you so sure it's nonsense?" Aletta was asking.

Pieter-Lucas hesitated, not wanting to be overheard. He lowered his voice once more and explained, "My father sneaked out already this morning with a hatchet and the long shiny parade knife and headed for the church. He and his wild friends are set for some sort of action." He could see she was trembling, and he smoothed her arm as he added, "So you stay inside. Believe me, Aletta, the streets are no safe place for this pretty girl today."

Aletta grabbed his arm and pleaded, "Please stay with me. Surely with you close by, nothing could ever be dangerous."

An involuntary smile lifted the corners of his mouth and offered her a flicker of security. "There's nothing I'd rather do."

"Then you'll stay?"

"I can't. I have to go to the church."

"Whatever for?"

"I have to rescue Opa's painting."

" 'The Anointing'? With the wonderful dove? Oh, Pieter-Lucas. They wouldn't dare touch that one. Surely your vader will stop them."

His jowls tightened. How he wished Aletta spoke the truth. He forced his tensing muscles to relax and spoke with more composure than he felt, "Ja, sure! Vader and his friends are lunatics these days. I've seen a strange fire in their eyes like you never dreamed. It's frightening. They've become rough and wild and dangerous."

"Then it's true what I heard in the marketplace."

"What did you hear?"

"That your father and his friends are Beggars."

For an instant he glared at her. "Calvinists—wild, violent, religious fanatics—ja. But Beggars? NEVER. Believe it not!"

For months, Pieter Lucas' mind had persisted in painting frightening portraits of his father dressed as a Beggar and hanging them on the walls of his heart. The horrible exhibition was sketched from a mass of ugly rumors that blew up and down the streets, whirled around the market stalls, and skittered into dead-end alleys all over Breda. The leaders of this fanatical band of militant Calvinists, who called themselves Beggars, tiptoed in and out of the *Kasteel* of Breda under the protection of the prince's brother, Ludwig van Nassau.

Pieter-Lucas had met some of them and groomed their horses in the stables. An odd mixture they were—lesser nobles (some of them highly respected gentlemen with long-honored pedigrees), malcontented burghers, and riffraff with dilapidated fortunes. To mock the familiar mendicant priests who went about begging, they shaved their beards close, leaving long trailing mustachios. They wore common felt hats, doublets, hose, and short cloaks of a drab ashen color. They hung wooden beggar's bowls from leather thongs around their necks and dangled beggar's pouches from their belts. They harassed churchmen, raided churches, urged civil disobedience, and stocked weapons.

Hendrick van den Garde did none of these things.

"*Nay, nay!* My father is no Beggar!"

Pieter-Lucas turned toward the door. "I must run *now* before the damage is done."

Aletta tugged at his sleeve. "Don't go, Pieter-Lucas. If anything happens to you . . ."

"Shh, Little One. I'll be back soon."

"On the day I found you in your hidden studio, you said you'd never leave me again."

He paused. Why did she look so defenseless and tug so at his heartstrings? "I'm not leaving you," he explained. "Only going to the Great Church. I will be right back."

"Promise me?"

"I promise!"

The old oak door closed heavily. Why did he feel as if he were leaving a part of himself behind?

Down the alley he clogged, an awkward combination of attempted speed and silence. He turned onto Annastraat, then cut through the alley behind the city hall and stopped at the market square opposite the Great Church.

He hesitated, scanning the empty cobbled square. All seemed quiet—too quiet. The rain sprinkles that had baptized the dawn were lifting and vanishing into a gray fog cover that held the sun aloof. Somebody ought to be stirring.

Pieter-Lucas raised his head, looked high up into the ornate tower that caged the clock and its huge bell, and whispered, "Even Roland hangs speechless!" He shivered.

He tried to take a step forward, but something held his body taut. Immobile, he lingered, an uncertain worshiper at the shrine of a carefree youth. Was it to be forever snatched away from him? Replaced with a dangerous manhood? His heart thumped wildly. He'd come to do a duty. Quiet or no, eerie or no, there was no time to waste.

With renewed urgency, he zigzagged across the square and around the apse, ending at the tiny side door of the church. Locked! *Now what?*

He was heading for the main entrance when the side door burst open. Pieter-Lucas drew back against the building. A bareheaded priest bolted past him, his robes flapping out at all angles. Under one arm, he lugged a wood carving of St. Barbara. On his heels came a stranger, brandishing a long club. The curate fled into the market, shouting, "Run for your lives!"

"What?" Pieter-Lucas exclaimed. "My anointing hangs in jeopardy, and he wants me to run?"

He jostled his way past three more fleeing clergymen and the sexton, through the side door, and into the sanctuary. There he stopped, too stunned to get his bearings. "It's like the hell of a Bosch painting," he exclaimed. Though Pieter-Lucas had never seen one of the master's strange paintings, Opa had described them to him many times—filled with ghouls and monsters, blood-red skies, dismembered bodies and infernal fires. *Ja*, surely they looked just like the scene before him.

Explosive dust clouds catapulted and swirled in the ghastly light of dozens of blazing torches mounted around the walls. Scrapings, thuds, crashes, crackles, and sounds of shattering windowpanes mingled with jubilant shouts of "Long live the Beggars!" and "Destroy their altars, break their images!"

Pieter-Lucas pressed his back against the wall, his own body as damp and cold as the rough stonework behind him. He groaned and cried aloud, "*Nay, nay, nay!* It can't be real." His bitter cry was so muffled by the shouts of madmen around him that he hardly heard it himself.

He stared unbelieving at the drama in this ruined place. The sacred hush had fled, the beauty was reduced to wreckage. Men he'd been taught to trust and respect moved about—Meister Joost the schoolmaster, Pierre Vlaming the weaver, and Antonis Backeler, leader of the "new church."

Like a pack of wolves attacking their prey, the crazed men swarmed over the unfortunate statues, monuments, and choir stalls. One group attached ropes to the images along the rood screen that fenced off the high altar. At a shout of "Smash the idols!" they pulled the images to the stone floor in a cloud of memories turned to dust. With shouts of triumphant glee, they hacked at the carved people with hammers and enormous hatchets. Pieter-Lucas' eyes burned, and he choked on the dust.

In the choir stalls behind the screen, he could see other men slashing at the wood carvings—madmen decapitating, slicing off faces, disfiguring Pieter-Lucas' childhood friends. Had they left "The Birdseller" with his cage untouched? Ironically, the wild men's voices rang out:

"Carve no graven image
Of whatever thing it be
If you give it honor or homage
You provoke God to jealousy."

"Stop it!" Pieter-Lucas shouted. "Stop!"

"Go home to your mother!" Pieter-Lucas heard the words close behind him and felt his right shoulder being shoved forward. He turned to find his face just inches from the heavy, blunt point of a medieval halberd. A group of strangers dressed in gray-brown doublets and trousers brushed past him, bumping him with the wooden beggar's bowls and bags that dangled from their belts.

"Beggar troops from Antwerp! They've come!"

Until this moment, he had managed to tear most of the strange mental paintings of Beggars and bloodshed from their threatening pegs in his mind. Never again! In the midst of the melee and unholy destruction, they leered at him with their gaudy colors and grotesque figures until he could no longer free himself from the fears they inspired.

If Vader had really joined the Beggars, Opa's painting would never be safe in this desecrated place. "So long as it hangs in the church . . . ." Pieter-Lucas heard Opa's voice and chilled, refusing to listen to the rest. It was all up to him now. The time had come to put his life on the line.

Dodging falling debris and heaps of clutter, he hurried down the side aisle. He passed men slapping at the gorgeous wall paintings with dripping whitewash brushes. He stumbled over a large chunk of busted statuary and fell on a bed of slivered glass. Picking himself up and cautiously brushing the slivers off his breeches, he nearly collided with a priest attempting to flee with a silver filigreed ciborium. A knot of attackers blocked the priest's way and snatched the sacred chest from his hands, yelling, "You papist, give us that."

The enraged men tore out the host wafers and threw both them and the ciborium to the floor. Two of the assailants trampled them beneath their feet, grinding them with shards of colored glass into the grave-slab tiles. What sacrilege! How ugly! Would they stop at nothing? Pieter-Lucas' mind screamed until he came at last, with tears streaming down his cheeks, to the Chapel of the Holy Ghost, ready to defend "The Anointing." He found it wrenched from its moorings and dashed to the floor. Vader Hendrick stood over the painting, wielding the huge parade knife. A dark wooden beggar's bowl dangled from a long leather thong around his neck.

"Stop, Vader, stop!" Pieter-Lucas screamed. "Tell me you are no Beggar, please, Vader, please!"

The man ignored him. With savage strokes and loud guttural shouts, he slashed at the beloved characters—John the Baptist, Jesus, the beautiful, pure white dove that Aletta loved so dearly.

Frantic, Pieter-Lucas lunged and tore at his father's arm. "*Nay*, Vader, not that one."

"Who sent you here?" Hendrick snarled, his dark beard trembling and his eyes blood red in the reflected torchlight. He swung his arm forward, carrying the boy along.

"How can you do this, Vader?" Pieter-Lucas groaned.

Hendrick van den Garde gave no sign of hearing his son's pleas. Instead he raised his arm once more, his knife glinting in the hot glowing light. Pieter-Lucas spun quickly around and covered the remainder of the painting with his body. His felt hat dropped to the floor.

Arms spread wide, head bare, feeling totally defenseless, he begged, "Please, Vader, no more, no more."

"Move away." The words sounded gruff, cold, detached.

Possessed by a stubborn determination, Pieter-Lucas pleaded, "Nay, Vader, *nay*. For the love of God, and your father, and your only son, STOP NOW!"

"Talk to me not about my father or my only son." The words came out in catapults of spray. "They have nothing to do with this, do you hear?"

Pieter-Lucas opened his mouth to protest. But a flash of murderous madness burning in the man's face left the terrified boy speechless. Then a curdling cry broke out of the harshly set lips: "Destroy their altars! Break their images! Long live the Beggars!"

Pieter-Lucas' legs grew faint, wobbly, like a toddling child's—but only for an instant. Thrashing out in panic, he grabbed his father's arm and grappled for the knife. He felt Vader's massive muscles tighten like iron under his fingers. The boy's young strength was no match for this seasoned soldier, but he had to try. Surely God would help him stop this ugly business.

In the scuffle that ensued, Pieter-Lucas felt the cold sharp point of the knife pierce his breeches and plunge into his right thigh. Then Vader wrenched his arm free and swung the deadly weapon in a wide arc, etching a thin line across Pieter-Lucas' left cheek just below his eye.

Instinctively the young victim covered his face and dragged at the injured limb. Did Vader hesitate for a flashing second, bending slightly toward him? Was that a hint of tenderness he detected brushing across the familiar face? Surely the man nurtured one drop of mercy for his own flesh and blood.

As quickly as the vision of warmth had appeared it vanished. Vader Hendrick shoved him to the floor and finished off the painting, shouting, "No young man raised under my thatch will defend his Opa's idol!" He spat on the floor.

"Idol?" Pieter-Lucas cried. " 'Tis an icon that once helped me to worship God. You know nothing of worship—only violence." A stream of warm blood filled up the gaping hole in his breeches and anointed him with pain.

Pieter-Lucas' words were swallowed up in the obscenities of the scene. Vader turned from him and stomped off in search of another "idol" victim, chanting, "Long live the Beggars!"

Pieter-Lucas closed his eyes and tried to pinch back the tears that smarted as they mixed with the blood trickling from his cheek. He had failed. What would he tell his moeder? And Aletta, who counted on him to come back soon and well? He remembered Opa's words. "As long as the painting still hangs in the church . . ." Words that until this moment had brought comfort now throbbed through his aching head.

Blood gushed from his leg. With a savage yank, he tore at his trousers, ripped off a strip of cloth, and wrapped the gaping wound. Then he tried to raise himself to his good leg. "Ouch!" he cried out.

He let his chin drop against his chest and cried, "God get me out of here! Give me strength to stand, to drag my useless body from this inferno!"

His head still drooping, his eyes scanned the floor for one last look at the broken promises in the shredded remains of the painting. Tears and blood dripped from his face, and he dragged himself toward the fragments, crawling on one knee. With frantic gestures, he reached out to smooth the once-gorgeous masterpiece together. It was no use.

Then he saw it—one tiny fragment of the painting still intact. "Aletta's dove!"

Pieter-Lucas snatched it up and pressed the blood-spattered treasure against his lips. He tucked it between the layers of his clothes. Struggling to his feet, he swayed dizzily and stumbled down the side aisle of the church. He staggered around the old organ, now rendered songless, its pipes hanging precariously in the cluttered aisles.

He pushed through the side door of the church, gasping for air, and then half ran, half stumbled out into the drizzle and gloom of the city square. Just once he stopped, turned back, and stared up into the sky past the bell tower.

"Oh, God," he screamed, "where are you now? And what of 'The Anointing,' lying sliced to shreds on the floor of your once beautiful house?" He could not stop the flood of choking sobs.

Where half an hour ago silence had wrapped the square and held it tight, now confusion and clamor clashed all around Pieter-Lucas. Like a half-drunken rowdy, he reeled about, dodging angry burghers, distressed churchmen, and frantic citizens. His shoes slipped on the cobblestones in the trail of his own blood that defied the makeshift bandage and increased its flow with each labored step. His cheek, now feverish and swollen, obstructed his vision.

Once across the square, he remembered "The Healing" hanging still unmutilated above the altar in the Beguine Chapel that raised its small, unimpressive spire just ahead of him. Unless—had the destructive mob already reached this chapel too? *Heaven prevent it!*

With determined energy, he dragged himself across the few remaining cobblestones to the Beguinage gateway and pounded on the huge wooden door. Each thrust of his fist increased his anxiety. His head throbbed. Then gradually the ripped pictures . . . the drizzle . . . the chilled street gave way to a golden-warm cavern, and Pieter-Lucas van den Garde felt no more pain.

# CHAPTER THREE

*Breda*

25th morning of Harvest Month (August), 1566

*A*letta Engelshofen loved Sunday mornings. On this one day every week, Vader Dirck left his bookstore deserted, the door locked, the books in neat, undisturbed rows. Visitors did not knock on the shop door, and Aletta did not dust the shelves or scrub the doorstoop or shine the amber-colored leaded windowpanes.

Instead, in their living quarters behind *The Crane's Nest*, the Engelshofen family bustled into preparedness to attend worship at the Great Church. There they would light candles, bow and kneel, and listen to the music of the huge old organ that filled the high-ceilinged sanctuary. A priest would recite the liturgy and the mass, and Aletta would go home wondering what he had said. Vader never talked about the things they saw or heard or did in church. Yet, never would he let them miss a service.

Today began very much like every other Sunday. Aletta fastened the faded brown jacket around her chubby five-year-old brother and smoothed the wrinkles over his wriggling body. "Are you ready, Robbin?" she asked, giving his padded bottom a gentle pat.

"Ready, Sissy!" he lisped.

She straightened herself, tucked the stray hairs up under her hood, and adjusted her side curls to hang in precise ringlets from her temples. Nothing felt right on this Sunday morning, though. The air hung heavy with fear and cold with loneliness. Three days had passed since Pieter-Lucas promised to come back "soon." He had neither returned nor sent a word to explain.

Stifling a desperate urge to run to her vader and ask about the horrible image-breaking she was sure must have taken place, she swallowed the lumps that rose in her throat. She looked down at Robbin, squeezed the small warm hand grasping her fingers, and coaxed a reluctant smile across her own face.

Just then, Tante Lysbet glided through the room toward the fireplace, her back rigid, her steps confident, her skirts faintly rustling across the tiles. In the months just before Robbin was born, this stern, efficient nursemaid had left her place in the Beguinage and come to stay in the Engelshofen household. Vader gave her a bed up in the attic room where he kept some of his books. "They are the books I have no room for on my shelves," he would tell her. "And a few I must save for the eyes of certain friends." Who those friends were or what made the books so secret, Aletta could only wonder.

Tante Lysbet shoveled fresh peat onto the fire that kept the dinner pot simmering, then whirled around. Her supervisory eye rested on Moeder Gretta, who smiled placidly at the children from her chair by the window.

Moeder was a short, plump lady with wide-set blue eyes, a broad nose, and a pointed chin that seemed a trifle small for the rest of her head. Her fine linen hood lay askew atop a tightly fitted cap that held her graying hair in a bun of coils. Tante Lysbet pinned the hood in place. "Come," she said. "It is time for church."

Moeder always seemed so pleased when Lysbet dressed her up for church. Not that either woman ever went there. It was only make-believe. In fact, Moeder never ventured out into the streets for any reason.

"Much too dangerous," Vader said.

No one had ever told Aletta what the danger was. She only knew that her moeder often suffered with headaches and melancholy spells that set her to howling. If she should begin to howl out in the streets or the church, where people could hear her, something would happen—something too dreadful to risk, or even to talk about. Aletta had been soundly instructed that if anyone asked about Moeder, she must simply answer, "She is too ill to be out of doors."

This morning Vader Dirck stood in the middle of the room, handsome as ever with his perfectly tailored garments in place. Aletta noticed, though, that his soft gray eyes didn't sparkle as usual. And when he clapped his hands and called out, "Let us go into the house of the Lord!" the jolliness in his voice sounded forced, flat.

Robbin seemed not to notice. In his usual childish way, he mimicked his vader, grinning to the perimeters of his moon-shaped face. He pulled his hand free from Aletta's to clap three times and echo a shrill, "Let us go into the house of the Lord!"

"Good boy, good boy." Vader strode into the back entry hall. It was the signal. Aletta and Robbin rushed behind him to the wall by the door

where they shoved their feet into the leather overshoes that sat in a measured line, from the largest to the smallest. Vader Dirck stood by the door
smiling a strange, sad smile, apparently ready to lead his two children to
the church.

He had not yet raised the door latch when a rapid pounding noise
came from the bookshop door. "Wait here," he instructed, then dashed
through the house and disappeared behind the heavy door that led into
his bookshop.

Moeder Gretta began to sob, and Lysbet laid a hand across her shoulders. "Don't cry, Gretta. Don't worry." For all her gruff efficiency, Tante
Lysbet could be surprisingly tender when Moeder grew upset.

"He's coming for me. I'm cursed! I'm cursed!" Moeder cried. Fear filled
her voice and bordered on panic. "What shall I do? Oh, Lysbet, my head,
my head. Hide me in the bushes. God be merciful to us!" The distraught
woman's sobs crescendoed into a loud wailing.

Robbin clung to Aletta's skirts and buried his face in their folds, as if
trying to make himself invisible. Aletta stooped down and took him in
her arms. She rumpled his silky blond curls and spoke quiet, cheerful
words she wished she could feel. "Fret not, Robbin, my big boy. You have
nothing to fear." She hugged him tightly, adding, "Vader simply has a visitor at the bookshop door."

If only she could calm her own heart! Over the years, she'd never quite
become accustomed to her moeder's strange outbreaks. Always the words
were the same. Yet, she wondered who the "he" was that Moeder imagined
was coming for her. And what of the curse? The bushes?

Today, everything about her moeder's distress had grown to double its
normal size. Could there be a connection between her curse and the trouble Aletta knew was brewing in Breda?

No matter that her vader insisted that the whole thing was nothing
but rumors. For weeks now, she had sensed uneasiness in the damp
morning fogs and summer sunsets. In the marketplaces she'd heard people whisper about rebellion and Beggar troops and image-breaking. Yes,
something was dreadfully wrong out there. Something that Pieter-Lucas
had finally told her about three days ago on that drizzly morning when
he knocked on her window shutter, then left her alone, promising to return "soon."

That was Thursday. Today was Sunday. His "soon" had not yet come.
Where could he be? Was he ill? Was Moeder Kaatje in trouble? Maybe
Pieter-Lucas had met with a sword in the church. Then, where was he
now?

*Great God, don't let him die!* The cry came up from the pit of her being like a wrenching prayer. Aletta often found herself praying. Not that she learned it in the Great Church. The priests there never taught her to pray, only to light candles and confess her sins to them so they could pray for her. Yet Vader Dirck often prayed aloud with the whole family and told her that God really wanted to hear her prayers. She found it so confusing. But when her heart hurt bad enough, confusion gave way to an urge to pray that she couldn't suppress no matter how much she wanted to or thought she should. She felt Vader must be right, because when she did pray, God seemed so close.

A tear slid over her cheek. She wiped it away with the back of her sleeve. No one must know how wildly her heart was beating.

Perhaps, she tried to convince herself, her Pieter-Lucas stood even now in *The Crane's Nest*. Such visits were common. Her young friend always listened with both ears open to the latest news from the prince's friends who came and went through the *Kasteel* stables. When he had important news, he often came to talk with Vader. If only she dared to tiptoe into the bookshop and see.

————

Against the backdrop of Gretta's terrified wailing, Dirck Engelshofen opened the bookshop door. He found Barthelemeus standing on his doorstoop and ushered him in.

"There is no service in the church today, is there?" Dirck asked.

"*Nay*, and there is something worse." The cloth merchant spoke just above a whisper, as if an unwanted stranger lurked in the corner or behind one of the books.

"What more?" Dirck heard Gretta's howls growing fainter from the other room and tried to put her from his mind. He would not stay here with Barthelemeus long this morning.

"The Calvinists are planning to march through the streets and are demanding to be allowed to meet in the Great Church."

"In the Great Church? Surely they don't expect to be granted such an enormous favor!"

"Too much success with the image-breaking has emboldened them beyond the measure of reason. It will be dreadful."

"Surely our magistrates will not let this one slip by as they did the image-breaking. I still don't believe they did nothing to stop the outrage." Dirck shook his head, as if to clear the fog and find he had not heard Barthelemeus' latest story quite right.

"Even if they did, and Prince Willem might be persuaded through Ludwig's intervention or some such . . ."

"Not too likely, I'd say."

"I agree. But suppose they did. Margriet and Philip would never let such permission stand."

"How can those rebels be so foolish as to think it will help their cause?"

Barthelemeus shrugged, then pointing a finger directly at Dirck, he added, "I've said it all along. Our streets and canals will yet run with blood."

"Not in Breda!"

"That's what you said about the image-breaking. Breda's citizens may be peace lovers, but what of the nest of rebels and the horde of outside Beggars they invited in? It only takes a handful to set a fire, but a whole brigade to stop the conflagration."

Dirck turned his palms toward the ceiling and opened his mouth to protest. Nothing came out. Never before had his own theories seemed so inadequate. What good to protest that peace would reign, when he was no longer certain? Instead, he asked the question most burning at the moment, "Are the Beggars among the marchers today?"

"You mean the men who did the slashing on Thursday?"

"Ja."

"It seems most of those men have moved on to carry their 'holy war' to other cities—Heusden, Helmond, Leiden—who knows where all they have gone?"

"Hendrik van den Garde and his son—are they in the number of traveling warriors?"

"I know only what I reported on the night of the rioting. Hendrick was one of the slashers, and I heard someone say they saw his son running down Caterstraat, leaving a trail of blood on the cobblestones. Have you not seen him at the house next door?"

"There has not been a sign of life in the little house since that fateful morning." Dirck sighed.

"Where has his wife gone, then?" Barthelemeus asked.

"Only God knows."

"Strange indeed! If I hear or see anything, I shall come directly to you."

"Goed." Dirck grabbed his friend by the hand. "I must go to my family."

They exchanged good-days, and Barthelemeus slipped out into the streets. Dirck Engelshofen lingered in the bookshop. He leaned his back against the door and sighed. The whole house seemed to be filled with a thundercloud so black he feared a storm would soon be upon them. Something in his bones told him that it would not only strike the churches, but *The Crane's Nest*, and maybe even his hearth as well. For what the Beggars had done was sure to bring vengeance and prying eyes into other suspicious places—places like his bookshelves.

"Dear God," he prayed, "I promised to protect my family, but I know not where else to run. If you show me not the way, we shall all be lost."

———

Dirck Engelshofen returned to his family to find Robbin, now jacketless, playing on the floor beside the hearth. Tante Lysbet sat holding a calm Gretta's hand and talking with the bird in his cage above the table. Only occasionally did Gretta reach to her head and cry out in pain.

"Who was it, Vader?" Aletta blurted.

"Only a friend," he answered, trying hard to show no feelings. "He tells me there will be no services in the Great Church this day."

Tante Lysbet gasped. "No services? Whatever has happened?"

Dirck shrugged. He rubbed his hands together briskly and forced a smile. "It looks as if we make our own service today," he said.

"Make our own service?" Robbin questioned, screwing up his nose and wrinkling his forehead. "How do we do that?"

"We will read from God's book, then pray, as we often do."

"But you never called that a service before," Robbin said. The tone of his voice made it a question, not a statement.

As pleasantly as he could, Dirck answered, "Perhaps because we never did it in place of going to the Great Church before."

"Oh!" said Robbin, content with his vader's explanation.

Dirck caught sight of Aletta staring at him with narrowed eyes. It would take far more to satisfy her probing mind. Poor child, she was in such confusion. How he wished he could tell her what was going on in that wild and crazy world outside the door and still take away all her worry. *Nay*, that was not the way. She was his daughter and so young— his duty was to shield her from it all.

He felt her persistent eyes follow him as he crossed the room to the corner cupboard, opened the lower right-hand door, and, reaching back into the far corner, pulled out the big old leather-bound Bible. Must he always keep it hidden in that spot and fear that someone would one day discover it and bring him to account for harboring the number one book on all lists of *Verboden Boeken*?

From its now yellowing pages he had learned to read at his uncle's knee. From those same pages he had taught his daughter to read and soon would do the same for Robbin. Never before had he realized just how precious this book was to him—probably his most precious possession.

"Let's gather round and read from the Book of God. Come, Robbin," he urged. "Vader will read a story."

Robbin rushed to his stool and clapped his pudgy hands. "A story, a story, a story!"

Try as he might, Dirck's attempt to recapture the gala mood of an hour ago seemed totally useless. He forced one more smile, but it stretched his face to the point of pain. His voice sounded flat and lifeless, even to his own ears.

"Today we read from Exodus," he began. "One of your favorite stories, Robbin."

"Which story, Vader?" If anything could inspire courage, it would be the light in those five-year-old eyes looking up at him. Almost Dirck's smile thawed into reality.

"About Moses. Listen well, do you hear?"

As he read the familiar words, he felt his voice grow steadier, firmer. "An Israelite man from the tribe of Levi wedded a Levite woman; she . . . bore a son. When they saw that he was handsome, they hid him for three months long. . . ."

"Why did they hide him, Vader?" Robbin always asked this question at this point in the story. It had become a ritual.

"There was, remember, a king in Egypt who did not know Joseph, son of Israel. He feared the growing people of Israel who were slaves in his land and tried to stop them from becoming too many and too strong for him to control. So . . ."

"*Ja*, Vader, I know. He made the soldiers kill the baby boys. What a pity! They were good boys."

"Just like you, Robbin." Dirck patted the little boy on the head, then turned back to his Bible. "But they could not keep him hidden longer; therefore . . ."

Dirck began to hear the sound of voices singing from the distance and read no further. Aletta and Robbin were already gazing toward the window, for the voices came steadily closer, and soon the singers were passing outside their window, a growing swell in enormous unison.

Robbin dashed to the window, calling out, "A *Processie*! A *Processie*! Look, Vader! Look, Sissy!" He pressed his blunt little nose hard against the leaded windowpane and waved at the people swarming past the bookshop.

Gretta was sobbing again, and Lysbet could not quiet her. Dirck closed the big Bible and replaced it in its hiding place. He sat close beside his wife and put his arm around her trembling shoulder. The moment their bodies touched, she ceased her howling and looked up at him, her eyes wide with watery pleading and a touch of terror.

He took her hand in his and drew her close with his other arm. "It's all right, Gretta," he mumbled. The terror began to drain from her stare and a smile flickered across her lips.

"The eternal God is your dwelling-place," he said, the familiar words pouring healing ointment over his own troubled spirit. "And under you are his eternal arms."

He felt her frail body yield to his embrace and caressed her disheveled hair with his lips. "Great God," he prayed, "support us in your arms, now, and forever more. Amen."

―――――――

Unnoticed, Aletta slipped through the entry hall and out into the courtyard garden. Beyond the fence, she could see the noisy crowd surging toward the church. Men, some of them in the strange garments Pieter-Lucas had described for her as Beggars' costumes, mingled with women and children. Some carried Bibles, others toted swords. All sang lustily and the words were clear, rousing:

> Who under guard of God Most High
> His dwelling and retreat will have,
> As in a sure and peaceful place,
> Beneath His shadow even will lie.
> Boldly will I say to my God:
> "Thou art my fortress and my hope;
> In Thee my confidence will lodge,
> Most surely will I rest in Thee."

"Rest?" Aletta asked. "Looks more like an angry rampage to me!"

She stared at the crowd marching steadily on toward the Great Church. Frequent shouts of "Long live the Beggars!" and "God is our help!" echoed through the neighborhood. So that was why there was no service this morning! Vader Hendrick's restless "new faith" army was on its way to the Great Church.

"Oh, God," she cried out, "protect my Pieter-Lucas. Don't let them hurt him, wherever he is!"

Absently, Aletta ventured out the back gate and down the alley until she stood with her hand resting on Pieter-Lucas' gate latch. Silence hung like a shroud over the little house. No smoke rose from the chimney. Only the chatter of sparrows in the linden trees and the distant shouting broke the spell.

She entered the van den Gardes' courtyard and advanced slowly. Each step revived old memories, images of playful hours spent romping with Pieter-Lucas over these cobbled paths. She couldn't remember a time when the curly headed boy was not there like a big brother, strong and loving and protective.

He delighted to tell her the things her mind was so eager to learn, the kinds of secrets her vader held from her in his bookstore. Vader had taught her to read Bible stories and fairy tales and showed her books of flowers and animals that even her imagination could not produce. He was kind and gentle and made her feel safe. But she hungered to learn the multitude of secrets that filled his mind and made him the important bookseller of Breda—the mysteries that lay bound up between those brown leather covers with their exquisite gold letters and tucked in his bookstore shelves or stowed away in the attic. For some unknown reason, he never let her browse unattended in those enticing volumes.

Pieter-Lucas seemed eager to tell her everything he knew. He talked about the men who rode fast horses into the *Kasteel* stables and bragged about their battles and feasts and hunting successes. He described their fine ladies and Prince Willem's second wife, Anna, from Germany, a strange and fearsome woman who screamed out in the night, wore wild costumes, and drank too much wine.

"Some say she's a mad woman," he explained. "Others that Prince Willem is too quick to give her all the extravagant things she asks, when what she really needs is a good lashing now and again."

Aletta crept around Pieter-Lucas' empty house trying all the door handles, peering through unshuttered windows. It looked and sounded and felt as if the family had gone to bed and forgotten to wake up.

At length, she sat on the back doorstoop, where she and Pieter-Lucas had so often sat while he carved wooden figures and told her his fantastic tales. She buried her head in her lap and let the tears flow.

"Aha, so here you are," a familiar deep voice startled her.

She wiped at her face with her skirts and looked up.

"Vader!"

His smile looked as if someone had painted it on with a stiff brush.

"What brings you here and turns your sunny face to tears?" he asked.

How tired he looked, Aletta decided, like a man who had skated a tough race on the canal from Breda to Antwerp—and lost. She lowered her head and tried to think how to answer him. Vader folded up his lanky limbs to sit beside her on the stoop. The feel of his strong, warm body encouraged her to speak. "I fear for Pieter-Lucas. So suddenly he went away. And his vader and moeder too. Something dreadful has happened to them. I feel it like the winter's cold in my bones."

Vader patted her hand. "I know, my child."

"Do you know where he is?" Her heart raced.

His words came out slowly. "I know not how to tell you."

"What is it, Vader? Is he hurt?"

He spoke softly, without looking at her. "The truth is, no one I have talked with has even seen Pieter-Lucas or his family since Thursday."

"Where can they be?"

"Only God knows."

"Did Vader Hendrick take them all away?"

He shrugged, his arms nudging her shoulder and rocking her frame gently.

"Then he must be in trouble somewhere. Oh, Vader, I cannot bear to think of it."

He put a finger to his lips. "My child, we must speak softly, lest we be overheard by the wrong ears. This is hard for you—and for me. I, too, have loved and trusted our dear Pieter-Lucas. It's difficult to explain, my child—difficult . . ."

Aletta tugged at his arm. "Tell me. I am no empty-headed procession doll. I can understand whatever you need to say to me."

The big man at Aletta's side stared at the cobblestones and worried a tiny pebble into a crack with the toe of his shoe. When he spoke, his voice was barely above a whisper. "Listen to me, child. Many things were destroyed in the church on Thursday—beautiful, irreplaceable things. Only mischievous men were in the church that awful morning. Hendrick van den Garde was one of the ringleaders and Pieter-Lucas was last seen fleeing from the Great Church at the height of the terrible riot."

At last he had admitted it was more than rumors. "I know he was there. But Pieter-Lucas is no image-breaker!"

"Where did you learn that word?"

"Pieter-Lucas told me about them the morning he went to the church. He feared his vader was involved with them. That's why he went to rescue Opa's painting, the one with the wonderful dove."

"I hope you are right." He did not look at her as he spoke.

"It's true, Vader, you must believe it." Surely Vader couldn't suspect Pieter-Lucas of such a monstrous thing.

He paused and cleared his throat, then began again, still not looking at her. "If Pieter-Lucas spoke the truth, then he will return."

Aletta stared into his face and fought to control the anger that threatened to carry her into a rage. "*If* Pieter-Lucas spoke the truth, indeed. Vader, how can you say such a thing? You know Pieter-Lucas nearly as well as I do, and we both know he does not lie."

Vader rested a moist, trembling hand on her arm. "Shh!" he cautioned. "I've no idea what has happened. I only know"—he paused, then squeezed her arm tightly and went on—"I fear that for the time we must both dry our tears and try to put him from our minds."

Aletta lifted her tear-stained face, her eyes wide with disbelief. "Forget Pieter-Lucas? Perhaps you can forget. I would never let him slip from my mind or my heart, not even if I could."

The weary man beside her sighed, and she felt his body shaking. "I too, will find it difficult . . . but we must try," he offered lamely and turned his face away.

Aletta began to sob. "Nay, Vader, nay! If ever Pieter-Lucas needed us to remember him, it is now."

"I, too, weep for him. But there is nothing that our thoughts can do at this moment except to make us sad. My dear child, I beg of you to try to trust my wisdom."

Between sobs, she blurted out, "How can I trust a wisdom which I have not heard? So long as you refuse to tell me what you know, my mind will never cease to feed me with fears, and I cannot forget the boy I love for one eyeblink!"

Vader Dirck cleared his throat noisily. "I shall try, my child. You know so little that you may not yet understand, but . . . well, the Brabant of today is a dangerous place."

Could he really believe she did not know this? True, he had seemed to take care not to let her see any dangers outside the bookshop door. But she had walked Breda's streets and shopped in her markets and spent hours with the young stableboy from Prince Willem's Kasteel. Vader would probably be distressed to learn how much she knew. She must wait patiently and hear him through.

"I cannot tell you all the reasons, but will say this much"—he went on with a halting manner such as she had never heard in his voice—"we dare not allow anyone to think for an eyeblink that we are the friends of an image-breaker, or friends of any member of an image-breaker's household, it matters not how innocent we know he is."

Aletta shook her head with short, violent movements. "Nay, Vader, nay! He is my friend, and he has done nothing amiss. I could never turn the back of my head or my heart to him—not even if his vader were the Great Beggar, Hendrick van Brederode himself."

Vader slipped his big arm around Aletta's shoulder and spoke softly, "Aletta, my daughter, there is so much you cannot yet know."

She bristled, pulling away from her vader's embrace. "I know far more than you have any idea, and I know my Pieter-Lucas. That is enough. He is in trouble, and I must help him."

"Aletta, I see I must be plain with you"—he hesitated before going on—"you may not go to him or see him again. The danger is too great."

Stunned, she shook her head, until at last she could find a firm, quiet voice to protest. Only one word came out. "Impossible!"

"I am your vader, child," he said, his voice quavering with pain. "Don't make me have to grow stern with you," he pleaded. He stood, stretching his legs until he loomed above her.

"Come, child, let us go home and fill our minds with other things." He offered her his hand.

Aletta shook her head, then buried it in her arms once more and wept with no attempt to control the outpouring of grief. She made no move to leave, and her vader did not try to force her, but slowly walked away. The sound of each receding footstep on the cobblestones fell like a mallet blow on her bleeding heart.

# CHAPTER FOUR

*Breda*

The 26th day of Harvest Month (August), 1566

When Pieter-Lucas emerged into consciousness, he tried to focus on his unfamiliar surroundings. But his vision blurred, and before his left eye, his cheek loomed like a fleshy hillock blocking his view. The room felt hot, yet something cool lay on his forehead. He stirred a bit and pain shot through his leg.

"Ouch!" he cried out. Vaguely, he realized his whole body hurt.

"Aha, you are awake at last." A woman's voice broke into the silence. Where was he? Who was this woman? Why was he so thirsty?

He blinked again and again until the scene began to clear. He found he was lying on an open bed which had neither curtains nor cupboard doors. A woman sat at his bedside wearing a black robe and a white hood and collar. She held a damp cloth to his head and said smoothly, "Now, lie quietly, *jongen*. Can I get you a drink of water?"

Pieter-Lucas pressed his words out through dried lips. "If you please." Why did talking tire him so?

He sipped the water, and the room once more grew hazy, then disappeared. He felt himself slipping back into another place, strange and far away. How long he was gone or how many times he slipped in and out of reality he had no idea. At times he felt a hand touching his body or a cup of water at his lips, which he managed somehow to sip. Sometimes he felt a piercing pain. Often he tossed on his bed. A time or two he thought he heard his moeder's voice. Once he was certain he saw her face. Others, too, came and went. But they never stayed long.

He fancied himself drifting again. The sickroom and pain faded, and he was walking into a huge painting. The scene was set on a broad expanse of lightly rolling sandy ground with a few low shrubs and one large grove of dark green trees. In the upper background, huge rocklike mountains cropped up from behind the grove. The landscape swarmed with people, grouped in families and parading in couples. Some ate and drank, others played games, still others danced or moved off into the grove.

In his dreamlike trance, Pieter-Lucas joined the scene. He could feel the jovial atmosphere, hear the music, smell the pungency of festival wines. Aletta held his hand and ran beside him across the landscape. Her dress flowed around her in the warm breeze, and in her hair she wore a garland of fragrant pink wild roses. Together, they ran toward a circle of couples, all shouting and dancing around a large image at the foot of the outcropping rocks. The image and its pedestal were of solid, shimmering gold.

A Golden Calf! So that's where he was, in one of Opa's favorite paintings by that name. Painted by his uncle, Lucas van Leyden, Opa had described it so often to Pieter-Lucas he always knew he would recognize it when he saw it.

Never in real life had Pieter-Lucas seen an image so expertly crafted, so translucent, so dazzling, so gorgeous. Nor had he ever felt so drawn to an object. Strange irresistible inner stirrings drove him on to stand at the foot of the Golden Calf where he clasped Aletta to his chest in a passionate embrace. He felt exhilarated, lightheaded, and frighteningly possessive of the girl in his arms.

Before they reached the dancing ring at the foot of the image, though, Moeder Kaatje appeared beside their pathway. She wore a gray peasant dress with an uneven, shredded hem. Her eyes were set deep in their hollow-looking sockets, and her hair hung in ungainly strings about stooped shoulders. She walked bent over, heavy with child, and leaning on a twisted cane.

With maternal authority in her unsmiling face and wagging finger, she beckoned to him. He had no idea how, but he knew her invitation was for him alone and excluded Aletta. His eyes followed as she continued to urge him away from the gaiety toward the far side of the hill directly behind the Golden Calf. He could see at the end of her footpath a dark cave hewn out of the side of the hill. From the inside shone the lurid light of three altarpiece tapers.

Panic mounted within him. Never had his moeder looked so haggard. He must help her. Perhaps her time for delivery had come and she needed him in her hillside cave. But why could not Aletta go along? And why the three candles? Everyone knew they spoke of approaching death.

Frustrated he looked first back at Aletta, then up to the golden image. Desire lured him away from the call of filial duty and, clinging to Aletta, he led her on toward the dancing couples at the foot of the image. Above the whirling and throbbing of the music, he heard Kaatje van den Garde begin to cry, with loud wailing sobs that grew until they seemed to shake the earth with a deafening rumble. The hills swayed and staggered, and leaden clouds billowed up to block the sun and hover over the Golden Calf.

Aletta leaned against Pieter-Lucas for protection. Just as he began to savor her warmth and feel her heart beating against him, a gigantic bolt of forked lightning struck the ground at the foot of the image. Pieter-Lucas watched unbelieving. The shape of the image changed into a figure of an old man dressed for guard duty, his helmet gleaming in the magical rays of a volley of lesser lightning flashes. In place of a sword, the man held two large paintings.

"Opa," Pieter-Lucas called out to him. "You've rescued your paintings." Then, to Aletta, "See, Little One, there is your lovely dove. Come, let us hurry on."

At that instant a second crash of thunder shook the earth with such ferocity that a huge crevice opened through the grove of trees. Up from its depths marched a massive army in tight formation. Seemingly without end they poured over the scene, wearing Beggars' brown garbs and bowls and carrying clubs and hatchets and ladders. Brandishing his long parade knife, Hendrick van den Garde led the regiment straight toward Pieter-Lucas and Aletta.

Desperate now, Pieter-Lucas pulled Aletta toward Opa. But the harder they ran, the farther away Opa seemed to move and the closer Vader and his Beggar troops came. All the while he heard Moeder Kaatje's voice nearby, calling, "Come away with me, my son, to the safety of my cave."

Then, from the far horizon, one man dressed in burgher's clothes dashed toward them through the ranks of Beggars, carrying a huge book in his hand.

"Dirck Engelshofen!" Pieter-Lucas shrieked.

The angry man grabbed Aletta by the hand, landed a blow on Pieter-Lucas' head with his big book, and absconded with his screaming daughter.

Pieter-Lucas tottered and fell on his knee. The horizon heaved around him. With great effort, he fixed his eyes again on Opa. He opened his mouth to cry out, and yet another enormous bolt of lightning rent the landscape. This time it struck the old man directly. Pieter-Lucas pushed himself to his feet and surged forward with one last spurt of superhuman strength.

Just as he reached the spot, one more thunderbolt rocked the earth before him and swallowed up the crumpled remains of Opa and his two paintings. Pieter-Lucas looked up to see Vader Hendrick leering over him, his shiny parade knife poised above the boy's head.

"Enough!" he screamed. "Enough!"

From a far distance, he heard Aletta calling, "I'm coming, I'm coming." Her voice faded away.

"Aletta, my love, where have you gone?" He thrashed about in the direction where he thought she was, only to hear her from behind him. He whirled about, but neither was she there.

Closer now came his moeder's insistent, "Pieter-Lucas, Pieter-Lucas."

Exhausted and sweating, he opened his eyes wide. A circle of white-hooded faces hovered over his bed. And by his side sat Moeder Kaatje, her hand holding his. She smiled. "Come back to us, my son. God wills it so. You cannot leave us now."

Pieter-Lucas stared wildly. "*Nay*, Moeder. Let me go, let me go!" But no matter how hard he tried, he could not free his hand.

" 'Tis good, son. God has brought you home. Just rest. Just rest. Quiet now."

He felt her soft, warm hand gently caressing his forehead. How she had changed! Her pale blue eyes brimmed with tenderness. Her hair protruded in carefree wisps from under a clean white hood.

"Oh, Moeder, you are all right?"

"Of course, son. You were the one in danger."

"*Nay*. We were all in grave trouble just now. It was so awful. You enticed me toward that dark cave with three tapers burning. And you looked so haggard. Have you delivered yet, Moeder?"

"Calm, calm. You have had an ugly dream. All is well now, and I go not to childbed for some few weeks yet."

Pieter-Lucas scanned the room. What could it all mean? "Where are we? Who are all these white-hooded women? Where is Aletta? And Opa?"

He felt an inexplicable urge to sob and turned his head into the pillow. His whole body protested the movement with racking pain. Why did he hurt so much?

Moeder Kaatje's voice spoke once more, "Hush, Pieter-Lucas, hush. Don't try to move. You are in the infirmary of the Beguinage. These are our friends, the Beguine sisters. They have nursed you through many long hours of fever and pain. Our God has been with us. Now, just rest quietly."

Beguinage? He blinked against the memory. Why was he here? There was a reason—a very important reason. His mind fought to bring it back.

At that moment the door of the room opened, and a young noble lady entered. Her face was warm and pleasant, projecting an aura of concern. In her hand she carried a small carved chest.

"Our patient is awake!"

The fine lady smiled and swept through the room toward him. Moeder Kaatje relinquished her station at his side, and the newcomer took her place, reaching out a pale, cool hand to touch his forehead.

"*Jongen*, how good to see the white of your eyes and feel the coolness of your forehead. Tell me, how do you feel?"

"I hardly know, Your Grace. What a strange sleep! What dreadful pain!"

"You have been gravely ill," she said gently.

Who was this woman? Where had he seen her before?

"Let me have a look at your wound." She lifted the cover and examined his right leg. "A pretty nasty gash it is."

A wound in the thigh? *Ja*, that was where it hurt.

Even with the intense pain, his body seemed other than his own. This place . . . this woman . . . these women . . . "What brought me here?" he mumbled.

"Shh," his nurse cautioned. "You will tire yourself with such disturbing questions. This wound looks much improved—Pieter-Lucas. They tell me that is your name."

He responded to the question in her eyes with a smile and a weak nod.

"Have we not met before?" he asked, his voice unsteady.

"At the *Kasteel* stables, I believe. If my memory plays no tricks on me, you are the young man who often cares for my horse."

So that was it. "You must be one of Prince Willem's sisters." Two of them had come to the *Kasteel* to live, and indeed he had cared for their horses many times.

"Which is precisely why I came here," she teased. "I cannot let my brother lose such an excellent stableboy, now can I?"

Pieter-Lucas grinned.

The lady opened her little carved chest and produced a tiny crock. Pieter-Lucas twisted slightly, raising himself to an elbow. "Countess Juliana," he said. "I've heard about your famed apothecary cabinet." He should have guessed it instantly.

The countess smiled. "Thank God He led me to the recipe for this wonder-working salve in one of Count Willem's books. I found it in a story written by a young French battle surgeon named Ambroise Paré. He had been taught to treat gunshot wounds by cauterizing them with oil of elders scalding hot, mingled with a little treacle."

Pieter-Lucas cringed.

"On his first occasion of treating such wounds on a battlefield, the injured were so many that he ran out of oil before he could complete the painful procedure. He was constrained to try what he called a *digestive*—a salve of egg yolks, oil of roses, and turpentine. To his great shock, in the morning he discovered that those to whom he had applied his experimental medicine felt little pain, their wounds were without inflammation or tumor, and they had rested well.

"On the other hand, the men who'd suffered the searing of the oil were feverish, with great pain and tumor. He never again used the burning oil. This selfsame salve has worked such wonders on your wounds, *jongen*. We shall apply more of it and give you some fortifying broth."

He winced as she spread the sticky, odorous salve on his leg, all the while thinking how grateful he should be that she had not used scalding oil. As she worked, she gave directions to the Beguine sisters clustered in little groups about the room. "Prepare a nourishing chicken broth with a bit of cow's milk and a dash or two of herbs. Bring me a fresh, clean cloth for dressing the wound. Dip more compresses in warm milk and apply them to the cheek."

Cheek? He reached for it, and his fingers ran across a warm, puffy little ridge just below his eye.

She worked gently, responding to Pieter-Lucas' involuntary flinches with soothing words and a velvet touch. At length the wound was wrapped, fresh compresses lay on the still-puffy cheek, and Pieter-Lucas had sipped his first meal in days. He found the broth tasty, and immediately felt new strength flowing into his body and brightening his mind.

When the noble nurse had gathered up her famed "apothecary cabinet," she promised to return soon and left the moeder and son alone in the quiet, whitewashed infirmary room.

"Moeder." The boy reached out to her. She took his hand. "How was my leg injured? And my cheek?"

She shook her head. "Have you no recollection?"

"Only that a knife pierced my flesh. Where or how or who. . . ?" He shook his head, too exhausted to say more.

"Then only God knows, and may he visit the evil man who did the deed with a curse!"

"Moeder, help me remember."

"Not now, Pieter-Lucas. This is time for resting, not for remembering."

"I must know now."

"*Nay*, my son. Healing blesses your broken body, at last. Let not your imagination destroy the holy work of Juliana's fine medicines." She said no more, but simply massaged his hand and looked at him with heaviness in her sad eyes.

He closed his eyes and tried to put the questions to rest. But it was no use. His stubborn memory refused to be ignored. He struggled to clear the fog from his befuddled mind. Slowly he turned his head toward the wall where a large golden crucifix hung above a tiny table. A half-spent candle rested on the table beside a large pewter pitcher and basin. Near the candlestick lay a flat whitish object. He stared at the rough edges, smudged and scraped and spattered with blood. With sudden recognition, he snatched it up and stared, unbelieving.

"Aletta's beloved dove! How did it come here?"

"I found it tucked away in your doublet. But let it lie for now. You must rest your thoughts."

Too late for that. Pieter-Lucas felt the sluice gates burst, and a torrent of memories gushed over his mind and flooded his emotions. The scene came to life as if it had happened five minutes ago. The confusion and desecration and dust of the church, the altercation with Vader Hendrick, the shreds of the painting strewn across the great stone slabs . . . *Great God, must I remember?*

Tears welled up and flowed, their salt smarting the wound on his cheek. He clasped the dove to his chest and wrestled with unwonted tears and visions of his nightmare in the church.

He heard Moeder Kaatje's sobs blending with his own and felt her hand stroking his back. But he could not look at her. She had been right. How he wished he had not sought the answers today. Better never to have found them at all. One thing was certain. He did not dare to share the tragic memories with his moeder. They would kill her and her unborn child!

Once awakened, his memory dredged up more—his unfinished mission. How could he have forgotten that he'd come to this place to protect "The Healing"? He remembered that out in Opa's forest studio Aletta had prodded him till he'd finished painting it. He remembered, too, how his hands had trembled with excitement and a sort of awesome fear. And where was it now? Had Vader Hendrick come here as well with his murderous knife, shredding the painting over the altar while Pieter-Lucas lay in the delirium that dulled his brain? Perhaps that was what he did even as Pieter-Lucas watched him come marching toward him with the knife in his dream.

A sudden jabbing pain shot through his leg, and he sensed a new urgency to find the second painting. Raising himself to an elbow, he demanded of his weeping moeder, "Tell me, what did the image-smashing madmen do to Opa's painting in this place?"

"All is safe, Pieter-Lucas. Our Great God has protected this haven. Not a Beggar entered it—with or without a sword."

Pieter-Lucas stared at her. Was he dreaming again? Too stunned to speak, his eyes probed her face for a flicker of uncertainty.

"Believe me, my son," she said. "It was a miracle from heaven."

" 'The Healing' hangs yet above the altar in the chapel?"

"Ja."

"I must see it." He tried to swing his leg out over the edge of the bed, but the pain stabbed at him, and the room grew fuzzy once more.

His moeder guided him back to the pillow. "Not now, son. Just believe me, and wait until you are healed enough to go see for yourself."

Too weak to resist further, he closed his eyes. "God, if you are there," he prayed in silence, "protect 'The Healing.' "

"The Anointing" may be gone, but so long as "The Healing" remained in one piece, there must be hope. He felt his moeder stroking his arm and surrendered himself to the quiet rhythm of restful sleep.

---

*Beguinage, Breda*
30th day of Harvest month (August), 1566

Total silence wrapped the candle-lighted darkness of the infirmary when Pieter-Lucas opened his eyes. A pale glow of moonlight filtered through the leaded panes of the one small window. No Beguine hoods surrounded his bed. The chair at his bedside sat empty. He forced his eyes to focus and surveyed the room. Moeder Kaatje slept on a bed in the far corner.

From somewhere deep in his consciousness, he fancied that he heard a familiar voice accusing him, "You failed to protect 'The Anointing' in the church. Nor have you done aught to insure 'The Healing' is safe in this place."

" 'The Healing' is safe," he retorted and closed his eyes once more to sleep.

But his conscience gave him no rest. "How can you know? You haven't seen it!" it seemed to taunt. Ever since the day he learned where he was and remembered the tragic mission that had brought him here, the haunting voice had not ceased to torment him.

At last, yielding to the frustration, he raised his body to a sitting position, defying the pain and blinking back the filmy haze that obscured the scene before him.

With his own eyes, he must look on the painting to silence the voice once for all. His heart raced with anticipation. Slowly, deliberately, he swung his good leg out over the edge of the bed, then dragged the injured one after it. Holding firmly to the bed frame, he lowered his body weight gently onto both legs and stood for the first time by himself since he'd staggered down the street in a trail of his own blood on the day of the image-breaking.

Pain and weakness assaulted him. Almost he turned back. "You have to do it, *jongen*," he told himself. He reached for the single crutch leaning against the end of the bed and fitted its crosspiece into the pit of his arm. Gingerly he put his bad leg forward and rested his weight on the crutch. His head swam, his arms trembled, and perspiration trickled down his forehead.

Painful, exacting, each laborious step dragged him a bit farther until he had crossed the room, shoved open the door, and hobbled out into the moonlit courtyard. A cool wind whipped at his shirt and tugged at the length of cloth he had wrapped around his waist. He inched his way down the gallery toward the chapel, stopping now and again to lean against the clammy stone walls and regain his strength and wipe his forehead on his shirt sleeve.

When, at length, he pushed open the door of the chapel, he felt instantly enveloped by a warm slumbering world of suffocating candle-and-incense fragrance and a pervading sense of Opa's presence that had filled this place since the day the painting was hung here. Awed, almost stunned by an ambiance that held him close yet unnerved him, he stopped struggling with the crutch and the pain, and stood still, searching the far wall behind the altar.

"It's there!" he whispered with what remained of breath at the end of his torturous pilgrimage.

Once more, he dragged his body forward across the floor, the stockinged foot of his good leg searching out each tiny crevice as a rooting place to steady himself. Just before he reached the tiny gate that shut him off from the altar, he leaned against a kneeling bench and stared at the treasured painting. Flanked by two long burning altar tapers, it rose up high above him, seeming to fill the room with its overpowering grandeur.

The canvas was splashed with crimsons, blues, and greens that mixed with variegated hues of gold, purple, pink, and brown, all muted in the flickering lights. From the mass of details of line and form that blurred together like a wild man's palette, the figure of Jesus, the Healer, rose, a sharp etching of perfectly shaped and proportioned lines. Each fold of his garment, each feature of the gentle weathered face emerged, seeming almost to move with a smooth and rhythmic rise and fall of the Healer's chest. The hands resting on the child's head and lamed limb sprang from the picture, precise and lifelike, down to the hairs that ran across the well-defined veins.

For the moment transported, Pieter-Lucas fancied that he felt the pressure and warmth of Jesus' hands laid on his own head.

"Thank God, you protected this icon," he murmured.

He bowed his head and wept. For how long, he had no idea. When at length he felt the flood stop, he shook himself, as if from a deep sleep, and lifted his head for one last look at the painting. Gone were the blurred images, replaced by smiling faces of men and women and children made whole.

Vader Hendrick may have destroyed Opa's "The Anointing" in the Great Church, but here in the Chapel of the Beguines, Pieter-Lucas sensed that he had found the beginning of a new kind of healing. Just what it was that was being healed, he didn't know—a part of him he'd never felt before. One thing seemed clear to him, though. Whatever the healing was, once it had occurred, nothing could ever take a paintbrush from his hands again.

---

### 5th Day of Peat Month (September), 1566

On the foggy morning that Pieter-Lucas decided to make good his promise to Aletta, he expected to cover the short distance with something approaching his accustomed ease and speed. But as he trekked through the Beguinage gate, across the Caterstraat, down the alley, and up the walkway, the pain and weariness that accompanied each labored step jabbed at him with sharp pangs of mental anguish.

For the tenth time, he probed the deep pocket of his worn doublet until his fingers moved across the battered dove he had rescued and was carrying to his special friend.

"Forgive me, Opa!" he mumbled aloud, feeling the presence of the old man close by. "I should have saved it all. If only I had had the courage to stop Vader before he left the house with that knife. But I didn't dare. It would have killed my moeder if we had fought there. Perhaps I could have reached the church faster. But *nay*, I had to stop and warn Aletta. You told me to protect her, too, Opa! I guess deep down inside, I still trusted Vader. How could he do it, Opa? How could he?"

After what seemed an unending tortuous journey, he stood at last before the familiar window shutters just outside Aletta's bed cupboard. His heart pounded with an unexpected quiver. He reached up and knocked, three short, brisk taps. Then he hobbled onto the worn doorstoop and waited and puzzled.

What could he say? He had promised to return to her "soon." When she had suggested "If anything happens to you . . ." he had cut her off, feeling so sure of his own strength. So easy to promise. How was he to know that his vader's knife would force him to break his word?

If he now told this girl who trusted him implicitly how badly he had failed, would she ever trust him again? Like Moeder Kaatje, Aletta always seemed to want to trust him, but never stopped questioning and worrying and trying to uncover hidden troubles. Were all women like that? At any rate, he must not let her know how badly he'd been hurt. Yet, how to explain his limp, the long ugly scar across his cheek, and the delay? If only he could have healed faster and come sooner.

His legs began to wobble, and his head swam gently. He reached for the doorframe and tried to steady himself. Why was she taking so long to come?

Just as he began to wonder how much longer he could continue to stand, the wooden door opened, and he felt his heart leap. Aletta, at last. Instead, her vader stood before him, a look of surprise spreading across his long, thin face.

"Oh, Heer Engelshofen!" He reached out to shake the older man's hand, and his knees trembled beneath him.

Dirck Engelshofen offered a limp handshake and spoke hesitantly, "Well, good day, Pieter-Lucas. I did not expect to see you here."

"I know. I have been away longer than I had thought. I ran into a bit of unexpected difficulty."

Why did he feel intimidated by this old familiar friend? Why was he not invited into the house?

"I see." Dirck Engelshofen's voice radiated uneasiness.

The world still swayed. Beads of perspiration were forming on Pieter-Lucas' neck and dampening his palms.

"I have come to see Aletta. I promised to return and have at last come—with a gift."

"Ja, but of course. She has been . . . uh . . . looking for you." The older man looked over his shoulder, then back again, as if unsure of his move. He stepped out into the courtyard, closed the door behind him, and without looking directly at Pieter-Lucas, went on. "But, I fear she cannot see you now."

"Why? Is she away? Or not well? Please tell me she is all right."

"Aletta is very well, thank you."

"Then she must be out at the market or walking with Robbin in the birch wood. Goed, I shall wait." If only brave words would increase his physical strength. He grabbed for the stairway railing to steady himself.

"You do not understand, Pieter-Lucas. I simply cannot allow Aletta to speak with you at this time."

"What? Why not?" Surely he did not hear correctly.

Dirck Engelshofen's words came slowly, from a painful distance—so unlike him. "I think I have not to tell you that there is trouble brewing on every street corner in Breda these days."

Had the man forgotten that he, Pieter-Lucas, had told him, Dirck Engelshofen, almost the same thing the last time they met in the bookshop on the morning before the image-breaking?

"You are more right than you know. I have no need for anyone to tell me about Breda's troubles. With my own eyes and body, I have encountered more of those troubles than you have any idea. But I do not see what that has to do with letting me talk with your daughter."

For the first time, Pieter-Lucas noticed the sharpness of his English friend's nose and the graying and receding of his hairline that revealed a looming smooth pale forehead.

"I do not know where you have hidden yourself away these past weeks since the disgraceful image-breaking, *jongen,*" the older man said, "but I have the word on good authority that you were last seen in the Great Church on that ugly morning."

Was he hearing what he thought he heard? Pieter-Lucas blinked, swallowed, shook his head slightly. He must awaken himself from this, another bad dream. But Dirck Engelshofen talked on.

"Not too wise a move, *jongen.* Only men of less than honorable intentions dared venture there that day. I seem to recall warning you to flee and hide, not run into the midst of the uproar."

"Did not Aletta tell you why I went there—to rescue Opa's painting from the madness?"

"She told me that indeed."

"I had a promise to fulfill, which, I decided after much agony of thought, was of more importance than the sparing of my life. If you deem my decision unwise, then I can only beg your forgiveness."

The older man paced the length of the small garden, his hands folded behind his back, his gaze never rising above the cobbled pathway. He did not speak. Too weary to follow, Pieter-Lucas seated himself awkwardly on the steps and leaned against the white slatted railing by the door. Through his mind flashed vivid snatches of his nightmare in the Beguinage—Dirck Engelshofen running toward him, hitting him on the head with the huge book in his hand, then absconding with Aletta.

Was it, after all, some sort of portent, as every other detail in that dream also appeared to be?

"Please, you must believe me. I loathed the whole ugly business. It tore at the pit of my stomach to see the ghastly butchery and desecration that roared through the church that morning. When I tried to save Opa's masterpiece, I encountered a madman's knife, which nearly took my life."

No one must ever know who that madman was.

"I only escaped death through the mercy and healing skills of my moeder's dear friends, the Beguine sisters and the lovely Countess Juliana with her wonder-working apothecary cabinet."

He looked at his older friend, hoping for a sympathetic expression. Dirck Engelshofen did not return his glance.

"You do believe me, do you not?" the boy asked.

Aletta's vader straightened, his head finally erect. His heavily browed eyes, though still a bit distant, had softened. Pieter-Lucas caught the deep pain that filled them as he looked guardedly in his direction and spoke in hushed tones.

"I have chosen to believe you, son, and grieve over your misfortune more than you can know."

"Then, you will allow me to see Aletta?"

"Not yet, my son. It is too perilous just now."

"Too perilous? How so?"

"You have frequented *The Crane's Nest* all these years. Surely you can understand, Pieter-Lucas. A bookseller must be more cautious than most men. He is never fully free. Mark my word, we are watched day and night. Every move is recorded in someone's reckoning book, ready to prepare an accusation for us in the day when our services are no longer considered to be in the public interest."

"This I do understand. But what has it to do with me? And with Aletta? Surely, my friendship with your daughter is not worthy of entry in anyone's reckoning books. I am neither Calvinist nor Beggar, even though I was often dragged to the Calvinist house meetings and hedge preachings against my will. My heart always lingered in the church on the market square. Since the day your daughter could toddle down your garden pathway, I have been her constant companion. Have I led her astray in any way?"

"Led her astray? Never! You reason well, Pieter-Lucas. As you know, I have long considered you just like a son. My dearest desire for Aletta has been that you and she might enjoy a long and pleasant life together. I could not pick for her a better man to protect and care for her when she is old enough to marry."

Pieter-Lucas warmed at the consoling words, for the moment off guard against the ruthless reality that seemed bent on destroying both him and his dreams.

"But things cannot always happen in the ways we plan them."

"What do you mean? What need is there to change our plans? What have I done amiss that you can no longer trust me even to talk to your daughter?"

"You have done nothing, Pieter-Lucas."

"What then?"

Dirck Engelshofen shifted with obvious discomfort, his eyes carefully averting the boy's pleading stare. " 'Tis association, son, association." He clipped his words off sharply.

"Whatever that can mean!"

"When I was about your age, I, too, had to learn the meaning of the word through much pain. I had a dear friend, a great man, William Tyndale. I was forced to watch as they burned his body at the stake. The whole tragedy could have been avoided had he not allowed his kindly heart to deceive him into befriending a worthless young man who betrayed him."

"You suspect me of treachery?" Pieter-Lucas' words exploded. "Surely you cannot mean it!" A rising indignation gave strength to each syllable and left his mouth gaping.

"Of course, I do not suspect you. Easy now, *jongen*. You jump too quickly. 'Tis not so simple. Just hear me through to the end of my story."

Pieter-Lucas prodded his aching, stiffening joints into action. He pushed his full weight onto his feet, steadied his swaying body, and advanced toward the older man. "Who cares about your stories?" he spit out the words. "I came to see Aletta, to bring her something precious, not to listen to morbid bits and pieces of your family history. Your friend, Tyndale, died due to a lack of caution. I can see that will never happen to you."

"Hear me out, son, hear me out. Mr. Tyndale's execution marked the beginning of an ugly and painful censorship of all the printers and booksellers of Antwerp, including my uncle. Long ago, I determined to spend my life pursuing caution, that I might have opportunity to live long in the peddling of books and ideas, to open men's minds and free them from the shackles of tradition."

"So, your life work is endangered by traitors. But if I am no traitor, just what kind of peril do I pose when I simply want to talk with your daughter?"

Looking down at the cobblestones, hands clasped behind his back, the man answered with measured phrases and great hesitancy.

" 'Tis only this . . . the company my daughter keeps affects my reputation, my family's livelihood . . ."

"And what is it that makes me such dangerous company?" Pieter-
Lucas was nearly beside himself.

" 'Tis not you."

"What then?"

" 'Tis Hendrick van den Garde. All Breda knows you as the son of this
wild man who wielded the destructor's knife in the church. We also know
the day comes soon when envoys of our very Catholic King, Philip, will
swarm over our city and eliminate every one of us whom he can link, in
any way whatever, to such rebellion."

Pieter-Lucas breathed in hard. So that was it. He pounded his right
fist into his left hand and screamed, "It's not fair! Not fair! Not fair!" He
glared at Dirck Engelshofen and felt the blood well up over his face. "How
could you reject me for something that my vader has done? Does my character not speak for itself? Where is my good friend who will stand up to
the suspicious crowds and help me clear my name?"

"I don't believe you understand what I am saying."

"Oh, don't I though? I only cannot believe what my ears have told me.
I thought it was only in a nightmare of my illness that you would turn
against me. You, who have treated me more like a vader than my own
vader all these years."

"Pieter-Lucas, calm yourself. Wait quietly. This time of trouble will
soon pass. Then we can pick up where we left off and go on. But, for now,
I cannot allow my daughter to associate with any member of an image-
breaker's household—no matter how innocent you are!"

Pieter-Lucas pointed a finger at his dumfounded companion.

"Someone will pay. Someone will pay! Aletta will one day be mine!"

Engelshofen raised a hand to the boy's shoulder and protested. "Wait,
Pieter-Lucas, wait. If God has willed it, it shall be . . . and in His time. If
not . . ."

"What sort of God do you make Him out to be, who forces me to suffer
such monstrous injustice for the rashness and violence of a vader gone
mad? And a friend turned coward?"

"Wait, son, be patient," Dirck Engelshofen's voice wavered, and he
reached out to arrest the boy who had already headed down the garden
pathway.

Pieter-Lucas dragged his body through the gate, then looked back at
the window beside Aletta's cupboard bed. Was that the vague features of
a familiar round face he detected staring at him through the obscurity of
the glass windowpanes?

"I'll be back, my Little One, I'll be back. You can count on me—I promised." He whispered the words into an open, upraised palm, then blew them toward her and, without so much as a further glance in Dirck Engelshofen's direction, hobbled out into the alley and back to the Beguinage.

# CHAPTER FIVE

*Breda*

12th day of Peat Month (September), 1566

Aletta loved the fish market on the harbor. It opened an exciting window for her on the rest of the world she so longed to see and touch and taste and hear. Shouts and laughter, creaking of coaches and horsehoof cloppings, all blended with harbor sounds, pungent smells, and a disordered array of colors and bustling movements. Each, in its own special way, tugged her into the picturebook scene, enticing her to think romantic thoughts.

She had dreamed of the day when Pieter-Lucas' Opa would send him off to Leyden to become a famous painter, and her vader would give her to him for a bride. In this very harbor, they would set down their feet in a broad riverboat and sail away midst a flurry of shouts from well-wishers, all promising to greet Pieter-Lucas on his return as the Great Master Painter of Breda. While he studied in Leyden, she would cook and clean and read piles of books purchased in a store where her vader could not say *nay*. She'd search out an herbal cure for Moeder's illness and bear Pieter-Lucas a dozen children, and they'd all fill the cup of life to the lip with marvelous new adventures.

Such lovely dreams had become a sort of ritual, relived every morning on her trip to buy the day's supply of food for the family. However, since the ugly events in the church and Vader's orders to "forget about Pieter-Lucas," her dreams had slipped farther and farther over the horizon of the harbor behind the fishmongers' stalls.

Today, Lysbet had instructed Aletta, "Go, purchase a fine codfish and a basket of the tastiest vegetables in the market. We shall have a rich soup tonight."

Aletta's heart dallied far from fine codfish and tasty vegetables. Her dreams had sailed out of the harbor so far she could no longer see their masts, and their lure was draped with a mourning cloak.

As usual, Robbin scampered at her side, bumping now and again into the oversized market basket she carried on her arm. But she did not chat with her brother as they walked, or enter into the games he so loved to play, or sing with him the songs he loved to have her sing with him. Only one thing claimed Aletta Engelshofen's attention today. Pieter-Lucas was gone!

"Chase me, Sissy," Robbin coaxed.

"Not today, Robbin." She patted his head and smiled wanly.

"What makes you so sad, Sissy?" He stared up at her through eyes enlarged with innocent concern.

"Why do you say I'm sad?"

"Otherwise you would play."

"I just don't feel like playing, Robbin. You run along now and wave your paper windmill in the wind. Only be careful of the carts and horses."

Robbin ran ahead, pumping his chubby legs across the cobblestones, swinging his arms and windmill wide into the free, fresh air of a sun-sprinkled day. Aletta stood finally at the fishmonger's stall and tried to think of fish. She had scarcely begun to pull her mind to the business at hand when Robbin let out a wild shriek.

"Sissy, Sissy, help me. He took my windmill."

Aletta looked up and saw a boy a year or two older than Robbin dashing through the marketplace. He waved the stolen toy high above his head and smiled an impish grin of satisfaction. A few yards away, he stopped, turned, and jeered, "Ha, ha, Sissy's boy. Come and get your baby toy."

Robbin hesitated a second, then ran toward his waiting assailant. He lunged for the arm that waved his windmill triumphantly. But the boy slipped just beyond his reach, leaving Robbin to sprawl face-down on the pavement.

Aletta was there at once. She lifted her sobbing brother to her arms and kissed his reddened cheeks.

"There, there now. You're not so badly hurt."

"I want my windmill."

"Never mind, sweetie. Sissy will make you a new one. Come, let's buy Tante Lysbet a fish and some vegetables, and maybe we'll even find a treat for the boy who lost his windmill."

Aletta was brushing the sand from her brother's doublet and trousers when she sensed a shadow falling across her. A gloved hand reached down to Robbin's level and held out to him his windmill. Startled, they both looked up.

Hovering over them stood a monk in a brown robe. He wore his cowl pulled up over his head. A large black leather patch covered his left eye. His right arm was secured in a sling of gray woolen fabric. With his left hand, he helped Aletta to her feet.

"Thank you," she mumbled. "My brother thanks you too," she added, nodding toward the boy now peering out from behind her skirts with one wide eye.

The monk neither spoke nor smiled nor lifted the gaze of his good eye. Instead, he thrust a tiny wad of paper into Aletta's hand, then turned and hobbled off behind the fish stall and out of sight.

"Who was it, Sissy?"

Who, indeed? Several times in recent days she'd noticed this stranger skirting the edge of the market. Always, it seemed to her that he watched her every move. The sight caused her to quicken her pace toward home.

Aletta fumbled with the surprise scrap of paper in her hand. If only he had spoken or looked at her. Instead he remained a mystical shade, like some ethereal messenger from the spirit world. She shivered and drew her arms closer to her body.

"I've no idea who he might be, Robbin."

By this time, Robbin was already playing once more with his windmill, swinging it into the breeze and humming one of his favorite melodies.

With nervous fingers, Aletta unfolded the wrinkled paper and found a hastily sketched picture. Beside a stream of water in a grove of trees sat a young woman. In the distance, the Great Church tower was cut away on one side to show a long line of bells ringing, all in one direction—she counted fourteen of them. The artist's signature in the lower right corner consisted of an exquisitely sketched dove. Worked into the feathers, tail, and beak of the remarkable bird, Aletta recognized an intricate design of the letters *P,L,v,d,G.*

Pieter-Lucas van den Garde!

How often through the years she had watched him play with all sorts of animal designs, inventing clever ways to intertwine the initials of their names—both his and hers—into the curves of all kinds of animal figures. It was his message all right, regardless of who the messenger may have been.

But what did it mean? Every time Pieter-Lucas drew a picture, he said it was to tell her something. What wonderful picture-mind and fingers he had.

Aletta carefully folded the note and tucked it away in the folds of her bodice. In a distracted daze, she went through the motions at the fish market first and then at the *Kasteel* market, making the purchases she'd been sent for, with little thought for the fineness of the codfish or the tastiness of the vegetables. Instead, her mind scrutinized the details of the picture in search of Pieter-Lucas' meaning.

The grove of trees must be their trysting place in the wood east of the *Kasteel* park. He'd drawn it like this before. The fact that she sat there alone must mean he intended her to meet him under their favorite trees, without Robbin. So far so good, except that Vader Dirck would forbid it. If she told him, that is.

Aletta stifled an audible gasp! Never before had she entertained thoughts of planning to deceive or disobey her vader outright. Disobedience was something one did almost without realizing it was going to happen—like staying out to play too late on a warm summer evening, or forgetting to scrub the doorstoop, or accidentally spilling the bucket of water. Or it happened when you couldn't help it—like sitting on Pieter-Lucas' doorstoop after Vader told you to go home with him, because you weren't through weeping yet.

How well she knew the consequences to young people who premeditated how they might outwit their parents. If they managed to escape their vader's notice, or his rod, they could be sure that one day God would catch up with them. He had terrible ways of settling the score with unruly children. Aletta thought of this every Sunday when she sat in the church and looked up at the gigantic "Eye of God" staring down upon her from the ceiling.

No, she didn't dare to go.

Yet, did she dare not to go? She unfolded the intricate drawing and scanned it for more messages, more clues about the intent of the meeting and the strange man who delivered the note.

The church tower bulging with bells—they must hold some sort of key or Pieter-Lucas would have left them out. He never wasted pictures in a drawing. Besides, he had cut away part of the tower to reveal the bells. And there were so many. What was their hidden meaning?

In Breda, church bells rang for festivals or processions or baptisms or to welcome Prince Willem or to announce a visit from the king. They also rang on sad occasions such as burials, or to warn the people of fire or some other danger.

Mostly, though, they simply rang to tell the hour of the day or night. Twenty-four times every day, from sunrise to sunrise, they spoke to the people of Breda. Pieter-Lucas had drawn fourteen bells. Could that mean he wanted her to meet him when the clock chimed fourteen times? Yes, of course, that was it.

But why had he lined up all the bells swinging to one side only? Aletta knew this, too, held some special significance. Every child in Breda learned the lines of the poem inscribed on the biggest bell in the tower:

> My name is Roland,
> If I ring on one side alone,
> A warning of alarm or fire I'm voicing.
> But if I swing from side to side
> Then all Breda is greatly rejoicing.

Pieter-Lucas must have words of warning for her. Perhaps he was in graver trouble than she had any idea. Yes, she must go. "Great God," she prayed, "help Vader Dirck to understand. This once, I simply must go against his wishes."

————

Aletta's conscience tormented her all the way down Boschstraat. She'd told Tante Lysbet that she was returning to the market for something she had forgotten to purchase. Happily, Vader was busy in his bookshop when she left the house. She never could have deceived him to his face. Poor dear Vader. If he had any idea where she was now and what her plans were, it would break his heart. He must never learn the truth.

Once out of sight of home, she slipped off her shoes and dropped them into her shopping basket. She could not bear the terror that their noisy heels created today. Each sound behind her—in the trees that lined the street, from the houses along the way, each voice, each distant city clang or clop or bang—brought her up short.

How painful it was to live a lie! But she was only doing what she must. Pieter-Lucas needed her, and . . .

"Oh, God . . ."

She couldn't finish. How dare she pray for protection? Only God could know how right was her cause. And if He decided it was wrong?

By the time she reached the birch wood, her feet were sore, her heart was trembling, and her mouth felt dry. The spot was deserted by all but a few sparrows twittering in the trees above her head. The river ran at its normal sluggish pace, carrying occasional twigs, bits of refuse, and a pair of plain brown ducks.

If only it were dark. In this glaring sunlight, she felt so naked, so exposed. When would Roland chime?

*Pieter-Lucas, where are you?*

She scanned the restricted tree-bordered horizon and peered into the underbrush, then seated herself on the large stone where she and Pieter-Lucas so often had sat together. Everything in this familiar scene taunted her. Nothing invited her to rest.

When at last Roland sounded fourteen times from his tower, Aletta's heart raced faster than ever and a sadness settled over her. "It's ringing on one side alone," she mused. "Oh, Pieter-Lucas, what is your danger? Come to me quickly."

The last chime had not yet faded when she heard a rustling among the leaves and branches of the underbrush across a clearing in the wood. Startled, she looked up, then took several cautious steps in the direction of the sound.

Was it Pieter-Lucas?

Fearful to make a sound, she crept silently across the carpet of warm, damp earth until she spied him. There, just ahead, at the bend in the river, stood the brown-robed monk who had given her Pieter-Lucas' note in the marketplace. He turned halfway toward her and beckoned with his un-bound hand.

"Dear God, is it safe to follow?" she whispered. Who was this strange cleric anyway? What sort of imposter might he be? What wicked designs lurked in his shrouded mind?

Frozen to the spot where she stood, Aletta watched as he moved slowly away from her and stopped every few steps to motion her to follow. "He walks with such a limp," she noted.

Mesmerized, Aletta defied the voices of caution and followed—down the pathway and finally into the underbrush that led away from the river and deeper into the wood than she and Pieter-Lucas had explored. From the former borders of their adventures, this had seemed like such a mys-terious, enchanted place. Today, though, the charm gave way to a sense of fatal attraction.

"Don't go farther!" So real was the sound of her vader's voice in her mind that she turned to see whether he was indeed behind her, calling out to her troubled conscience. But her stockinged feet moved on, as if helpless to resist the lure of the strange monk with the beckoning finger.

She followed on until the robed figure walked behind a crude peat shed at the far edge of the wood. Aletta stopped and listened to the creak of the old wooden door. He'd gone inside. Trembling, she took another step forward. "Stop!" her wary mind cautioned, but drawn irresistibly, she ignored the warning and followed until she stood at the doorway of the shed and peered into the faintly lit windowless room. She could scarcely make out the silhouette of the monk who was throwing back the cowl from his head. He stepped closer to the doorway, till the sun shone di-rectly on the carefree profusion of golden-brown curls that framed his face beneath an old brown felt cap.

"Pieter-Lucas!" she whispered, catching at her breath.

He tore the coarse woolen sling from his arm and reached out to her. "Come, Little One," he spoke softly.

"Is it really you?"

"Who else?"

Aletta gasped, then moved closer. "Oh, Pieter-Lucas, I cannot believe it!"

He raised his good arm and removed the black patch from his eye. The little-boy smile that spread across his face could belong to no other. Impulsively, she dashed into the building and reached up to touch the scar below his eye.

"Oh, Pieter-Lucas! Thank God you are here! I was so afraid."

He grasped her hand and held it to his chest. "I'm sorry I frightened you. I could think of no other way. No one must see Pieter-Lucas and Aletta together in Breda these days."

"I know. I heard all those harsh words Vader Dirck said to you outside my door. He also told me that I must not see you or speak to you again. 'Too dangerous,' he insisted."

"Just what he told me."

She heard his sigh and felt his chest heave. She stared up at him. Was this really her dearest playmate from next door? Ah, but he was so much more than a lifelong playmate. Whatever else may have happened to him since that morning three weeks ago when he stood in her entryway with the fuzz on his chin and the drops of mist on his nose and promised to return soon, she decided he had become a man.

Feeling a nervousness she'd never known in his presence before, she tugged at his hand and said, "I celebrated your birthday while you were away. Your eighteenth! I lined up all your woodcarvings around my bed and told them stories of birthdays past and prayed God to take care of you. Did you feel me with you that day?"

He grabbed her and hugged tightly. He'd never done that before, and she felt a strange giddiness that made her heart palpitate. How could she ever let this moment pass? If Vader Dirck knew how happy she was to be with Pieter-Lucas again, he could not be angry with her.

"I don't remember the birthday very well. I . . . I . . . ."

She pulled away and stared hard at him. "You were injured, Pieter-Lucas. I can see it in that dreadful line across your cheek. And when you walk, you limp."

He smiled reassuringly and squeezed her hand in his. "I'm nearly healed now."

"You were injured in the church. I knew it all along when you did not return the day you left so early in the morning. I've heard such dreadful stories of the things that happened there."

"It was a bad nightmare. . . ."

"Tell me about Opa's painting. Where have you hidden it?"

Pieter-Lucas stiffened and walked a bit away, turning his back to Aletta. He cleared his throat. " 'The Anointing' is no more," he said.

"*Nay,* that cannot be, Pieter-Lucas. It was so beautiful. Surely. . ."

"I tried to save it and nearly lost my life in the effort. I . . . I . . . just was no match for the destroyer's knife."

"Hendrick van den Garde was the one, was he not?" She stared at him and refused to look away.

He did not give her an answer with his lips, but the slump of his shoulders told her all she wanted to know—and more. His wounds were not all of the body. What could she say to make him feel better? She edged up close behind him, touched his elbow, and said gently, "If Opa were here, I think he would remind us both that the real anointing was not destroyed. It was poured out on your head and lives on in your heart."

He turned toward her, placed his hands on her shoulders, and looked so deeply into her eyes that it seemed he had entered her very soul. The intensity of his voice made her tremble. "Aletta, I did not bring you here today to talk about anointings. . . ."

"What then?"

"One thing I desperately wanted you to know."

"Tell me." She laid her hands on his chest and felt it heave with a warm and beckoning strength.

"Nothing," he said emphatically, "*nothing* can separate us—you and me—from each other. Not Vader Dirck's words, or my moeder Kaatje's words, or . . . not anything!"

"Of course not, Pieter-Lucas," she assured him. "I know my vader will one day change his mind, once I can convince him you are no rebel like your vader."

"And if he doesn't?" Pieter-Lucas let go of her shoulders, looked at the floor, and shifted from his good leg to his bad and back again.

"He will—in time. Beneath that brusque and growling knight in heavy armor lies a heart that still loves you as a son and longs to bring happiness to his daughter."

Pieter-Lucas smiled. "I wish I could know you were right."

"Trust me, Pieter-Lucas," she said. "I know he will one day welcome you back."

"And in the meantime, if my moeder or something else . . . I mean . . . what if . . ."

"Nothing, Pieter-Lucas. You said it yourself—*nothing* can separate us."

Why did he suddenly seem so stiff, so hesitant? What was this about Moeder Kaatje? Surely she had no intention of trying to put some obstacle between them.

"Just remember this one thing," he said, looking straight at her once more. "You will always be mine, Little One. Someday—no matter what or who or how or when—someday, we'll find a way."

"God will make a way for us, Pieter-Lucas."

Strange! While the thought of God usually frightened her, lest she offend Him and call down His wrath around her ears, yet it seemed so natural to trust that He would always care for her. Vader said that all the stories he read to her from the big Bible were written to help us believe that. Was she believing?

Pieter-Lucas' look turned pensive, then he raised his finger and his eyebrows. A sparkle lit his eyes and a smile appeared. "The day will come—*soon*. I will wrap you in my cloak, carry you away, and shelter you in a warm, dry haven filled with sunshine and brightly colored flowers."

He gestured with broad sweeps to emphasize his confident words. They clasped each other by the hand, intertwining their fingers, and both laughed. With his free hand, Pieter-Lucas smoothed the back of her hand from fingertips to wrist. Then slowly, gently, his fingers moved up along the contour of her arm, her shoulder, and her neck, ending with his pointer finger lifting her chin toward him. She felt a strange, wild thrill course through her entire body.

"If only I could take you now!" His whisper seemed weighted with a kind of longing Aletta hardly knew how to interpret. They stared into each other's souls. Pieter-Lucas the boy was never half so charming, so alluring, so overpowering.

Slowly, reluctantly, he dropped his finger from her chin and grabbed her other hand. His face grew sober. "First, however, I must go away for a time."

"Go away?"

He shut his eyes and nodded.

"Not far, I hope."

"God only knows how far."

"Pieter-Lucas, remember the day I found you in your Opa's secret studio, and you promised you would never leave me again?"

"I remember well, Little One." He spoke the words carefully, and she saw pain etched across his face. He squeezed her hands in his and went on, "When I uttered those words, I had no way of knowing that at this moment Moeder Kaatje would lie in urgent need of help. Her time grows near. She is my moeder, who gave me life, and I must care for her before I dare attend to my own dreams."

"Of course, Pieter-Lucas. So, it goes badly with her and her unborn child?"

"Things never go well with my moeder and her unborn children."

"That I understand. But what sort of help could she need that you cannot find in Breda?" Aletta asked. "The Beguine sisters will attend to her, and no better midwife than Tante Lysbet can be found anywhere."

"All that is true. One thing, though, they cannot do for her. She is calling for Vader Hendrick. I must bring him home to her."

"Pieter-Lucas, your vader is not a kind and loving man. Why does she want him with her, especially in her time of pain?"

"I know not what stirs within my moeder's mind. I only know that he is her husband, and she will cling to him until the day she dies. If I bring him not, or if he refuses to come to her, I fear she will not live. . . ." An intense hunger filled his eyes as he looked at her. "Neither she nor her unborn child," he added.

"Does she know what he did to you in the church?"

His voice quavered, and a deeply furrowed frown clouded his face as he answered, "*Nay*, she must never know. It would break her heart and take her life instantly."

"Oh, Pieter-Lucas. Where has your vader gone?"

"Only Vader Hendrick knows for sure where Hendrick van den Garde is."

"Then where will you search?"

"I have a plan."

"Is it safe? I can't bear to think of you running off around the country, with all those Beggars out there. You limp so, and . . ."

"Hush, Aletta. Don't fret."

"Please don't go."

"I've a friend, a messenger for Prince Willem, who will lead me to the only man in all the Lowlands who can help me find Hendrick—if he will."

"Who might that be?"

"Count Brederode."

"You mean that wild nobleman who came to Breda to stir up trouble?"

"That's the man. It seems he is gathering an army of volunteer soldiers near his home in Vianen."

"Do you think your vader may be among them?"

"I have heard there is a possibility."

Aletta sighed. It was as she'd feared all along. Hendrick van den Garde had indeed joined the Beggars. Poor Pieter-Lucas. He'd tried so hard to disbelieve it. If only she could give his aching heart some herbs, bind it up, and watch it heal. Did all dreams of healing belong only to childhood?

"How can you be so sure all will go well? Vianen is a long way off, and the Beggars . . . oh, Pieter-Lucas . . . ."

"Aletta, please trust me. I must save the child . . . and Moeder."

Why was it that every time he talked of his moeder and her child he seemed so ready to weep and looked at her with such pain-filled longing?

"If you can believe God hears such prayers, pray me Godspeed."

She took him by the arm and smiled up at him. "I shall say many prayers for you every day and shall wait for your three short knocks on the window shutter." Whether she fully believed or not, she must at least pray.

She watched as without a word he reached inside his robe and pulled out a small object, which he pressed into her hand, tenderly folding her fingers around it.

"Aletta, I leave with you this little treasure."

"What is it?"

"Look."

She curled her fingers away from the flat, hard object and moved closer to the light from the doorway.

"The dove! You rescued it! Oh, Pieter-Lucas. 'Tis the promise of your anointing! Saved at the price of your blood."

She let him enfold her in his arms again. Clasped against his chest, she struggled to control the tears that threatened to gush.

"Only promise me two things," he said, burying his face in her hair.

"Anything you ask, Pieter-Lucas."

"Please look after Moeder Kaatje while I am gone—and her baby, should it be born before I return." He added the latter nervously. "You are like a daughter to her, Aletta—the daughter she never had of her own."

"And she like a moeder to me. Worry not about her. I shall visit her each day."

"And if your vader objects?"

"I'll find a way, all the same, do you hear?"

"Only be careful"—he went on between awkward pauses—"that you do not believe everything my moeder tells you."

Before Aletta could decide how to frame the question that so strange a command prompted, he continued, "As you should know, an ill woman does not always remember things too well."

How well she knew indeed. But was his moeder ill in mind as well? A new, unidentifiable fear snatched at her, and she leaned harder against

Pieter-Lucas. Must she ever leave this warm, secure spot? Dear God, there was no other warm place left to go.

All too quickly he was moving her to arm's length. A light shone from his face, the likes of which she had never seen before.

"One more thing," he said, his voice smooth and inviting. "Promise you will wait for me."

"You know I'll be here when you return."

"*Nay*, more than that. I mean, you will wait for the storm to die, for your vader to change his mind, or . . . whatever. Promise you will never give your heart to anyone else."

"How could I, Pieter-Lucas? It is already yours . . . always has been . . . always will be."

He was embracing her again, and then suddenly his lips were pressing hard against hers. Her heart was beating nearly out of her breast. If Vader Dirck could see her now. But for one long, glorious moment, nothing he ever did or said or felt could possibly matter. Even the Eye of God rested far away in the church.

Too soon it came to an end. Pieter-Lucas was looking down into her moist eyes and speaking with a gentle quaver in his deepening voice.

"Now, before the clock strikes again, I must meet my friend Yaap at the stables."

Aletta opened her mouth to protest, but he sealed her lips with his finger and added, "I cannot say when, but never fear, I will return to the girl who holds Opa's dove in her hand—and my love in her heart."

# CHAPTER SIX

*Low Countryside from Breda to Vianen*

13th day of Peat Month (September), 1566

*P*ieter-Lucas knew all the horses in the *Kasteel* stables. He'd curried them, fed them, stroked them, talked to them, saddled them. Often he'd taken the horses on routine exercise maneuvers around the *Kasteel* grounds or in the streets of Breda. At one time, when there was no messenger available at the *Kasteel*, he'd ridden up to the prince's hunting lodge to carry an urgent message from Princess Anna. But not until the late afternoon he left Breda did he actually ride one of them on a long trip.

Today, his messenger friend, Yaap, had offered to take Pieter-Lucas along on his mission, and the stable-master had even decided to trust him with Blesje, the horse Pieter-Lucas knew best.

"Only be sure to bring him home in good shape, do you hear?" The crusty old man wagged a menacing finger in his face.

"I will." Pieter-Lucas suppressed the urge to laugh. The old soft-hearted horseman could not sound gruff no matter how badly he may have felt it was his duty to do so.

Together, he and Yaap rode out through the Harbor Port shortly after Roland had chimed fifteen times from his ancient tower. "My first trip out into the big world," he mumbled to Blesje.

All afternoon and through the night, the boys rode on. Pieter-Lucas tried to fit his body to the unfamiliar and unyielding contours of the saddle, but to no effect. He wished alternately for a shade from the sun and a cover from the brisk winds and drizzly mists. All the while, his still-sensitive leg craved the cozy cupboard bed on the south wall of the living room. His mind groped for a way to forget Moeder and her unborn baby, and his heart yearned for Aletta's soft blue eyes, dimpled smile, and the exhilarating feel of her warm, supple body in his arms and her soft rosy lips pressed against his.

At least he was riding with a friend. Of all the prince's messengers that came and went through the stables, Yaap was the one most likely to please him.

Pieter-Lucas quizzed every messenger that rode into the stables. Where had they been? What had they seen? What courts had they visited? What important personages had they met? In response to his curious inquiries, most of the men only gave him sketchy morsels to feed his hungry mind.

With Yaap, he could always expect a little more. Younger than the rest and a bit of a newcomer, the tall, pleasant-natured fellow with wide shoulders, long thin face, and a growth of adolescent down on his chin had won Pieter-Lucas' admiration from the beginning. His blue-gray eyes sparkled, and his lively conversation captured Pieter-Lucas' imagination, leading him into one realistic adventure after another. He knew when to stop, though, and what not to tell. More than once he had led Pieter-Lucas to the edge of some tantalizing confidential story, only to back off and leave him stranded with nowhere to lodge his thoughts.

"Someday, when Prince Willem appoints you a messenger, you'll learn the secrets, too," Yaap would tell him.

"*If*, not *when*," he always corrected. Such a life would be better than carrying swords around the *Kasteel* and the streets of Breda. But in spite of his recent disaster in the church, Pieter-Lucas still expected to be the first generation of van den Gardes to live by the paintbrush.

The boys headed their horses along the narrow road that stretched out across the wide, flat landscape. "Today," Yaap announced, "you find out what it's like to ride a horse across the pasturelands and dunes, through the forests, and along the riverbeds of our beautiful Netherlands. Must say, it's pretty special for me to have company for a change. None of Willem's horses have much to say in response to my running explanations."

"I've looked forward to this chance for a long time, Yaap," Pieter-Lucas said. But the unhappy circumstances stole his enthusiasm, and he found it next to impossible to make himself care about his eager guide's endless stories of farming methods, ancient floods, polders under construction, and strange encounters in wayside inns. Instead, his apprehensive mind chased dizzily from Aletta to Moeder Kaatje to Aletta to Vader Hendrick, to Aletta . . . to Moeder's unborn child and that dreadful vow Moeder had told him about from her sickbed. *Nay*, he must not think such thoughts. It was safer to try to give his mind to Yaap's unending chatter.

Soon the sun's last rays faded and ceased to make the waterways distinguishable. Far out on the horizon, one village skyline formed a dark silhouette against the dusking sky.

"It's a pity we have to pass so much of the way in the dark," Yaap said. "For your first long ride, we should have had daylight. Maybe another time."

"*Ja*, sure," Pieter-Lucas answered halfheartedly. He rearranged his aching body in the saddle for the hundredth time. "Once is quite enough, like this," he mumbled, more to himself than to his companion.

Through the rest of the night, Yaap let out a constant stream of stories gleaned from his messenger trips all over the Lowlands, France, and Germany. He had just returned from a quick trip to Antwerp and bubbled over with news of a city in ferment.

"I tell you, boy, we're on the verge of war—nasty, ugly, all-out war!"

As the night grew darker, Yaap's voice grew softer. Who knew what enemies lay hidden along the now obscure pathway? Pieter-Lucas only vaguely heard the soft-spoken words in the wind that whipped around them. His mind persisted in chasing a flock of memories that lay much closer to his heart than Yaap's latest news of Willem's exploits and threats of danger.

When at last Yaap fell silent, Pieter-Lucas realized they were passing through a dark forest where even the occasional sight of the moon moving from behind the clouds was obscured by a thick canopy of tree branches. The lantern Yaap carried cast frightful shadows all around. He felt a strange, almost suffocating sensation, as if unseen walls had hemmed them in. Above their heads, trees of indistinguishable identity were shaking hands and showering them with drops of mist. He listened in silent apprehension to the horses' hoofs creating sharp splatting noises on the slickened roadway.

When they emerged from the wood, the moon spread a luminous ribbon across the roadway, and Pieter-Lucas felt an uneasiness stirring like some angry dragon deep down in his innards. He thought he heard it asking, "When you find your vader, what are you going to do?"

What, indeed? He'd deliver Moeder Kaatje's message, of course. That was why he came on this journey.

In the gloom that pressed hard against his chest, the angry inner voice came once more. "Is that all?" it taunted in a rough, vibrating whisper that made the boy's ribs tremble. Then growing bolder and louder, it seemed to hiss at him, "Your vader almost sliced the life out of you, and he shredded your Opa's anointing before your very eyes." Pieter-Lucas shuddered and shook his head to dislodge the tormenting reminder.

Sharp pains jabbed at his leg, and he gasped for air.

The dragon roared, "Leave it not alone. Go for your revenge!" Never had Pieter-Lucas felt anything like this before. It frightened him. How he yearned for the old days when one of the boys in the market would steal his choice woodcarving and make fun of him, and he'd run home to Opa.

"You're a man now," the inner dragon scolded. "You have to settle this score on your own." Perhaps! But how?

As long as Moeder Kaatje lived, he had to move with caution. "Vengeance belongs to God," she told him often, not just when he grew angry with Vader Hendrick, but also as she stood crying over a pot of soup on the hearth and he asked her why.

Dirck Engelshofen talked that way too. "Never strike back," he'd told him many times. It was the way he lived. He'd run or hide if need be— or send away the dangerous young man from next door—but wait for God to do the judging.

Pious sentiments indeed! And foolish! God couldn't even protect "The Anointing" and all the other priceless, irreplaceable works of art in the church. A bitter taste filled his mouth as he remembered that nightmare morning. What good would it do to wait for God to take vengeance? Except that, just now, Moeder needed Vader, no matter how heinous his misdeeds. At least for this moment, Moeder and her baby—especially her baby—must live, and revenge would have to wait.

The sky blushed with newborn light and hinted at pale shades of blue, rose, and gold as the two boys rode down Vianen's short main street. Just beyond the church, they clattered across a narrow bridge and halted before the gate to Brederode's *Batestein Kasteel*. Pieter-Lucas' legs ached till he wondered whether he would ever be able to make them work again. Directly ahead, a pair of uniformed guards stood like statues, their halberds crossed to bar passage.

"Strange," Yaap mumbled. "Never met a guard here before."

"Maybe because the count hasn't prepared for war before," Pieter-Lucas suggested.

Yaap pulled his horse up closer and shouted at the immobile figures, "I come with an urgent message for Count Brederode."

Pieter-Lucas watched their helmets catch the rays of rising sun and reflect them back. Dressed in their metal breastplates and ballooning breeches, with shining swords at their belts, they looked like Vader Hendrick did when he stood guard at the *Kasteel* in Breda. Pieter-Lucas noticed, though, that each man wore a Beggar's bowl around his neck, a Beggar's pouch dangling from his belt, and a Beggar's penny mounted on his helmet. He shivered. Count Brederode had used his charms to turn

*Batestein Kasteel* into a den of Beggars.

Stiffly, one guard spoke his lines, "The Great Beggar is not here."

The Great Beggar? So, that's what they called Brederode. Pieter-Lucas shivered again. What had they gotten themselves into?

"Not here?" Yaap leaned forward. "But my message comes from Ludwig van Nassau. He dispatched it with haste. We have ridden all night to bring it."

"The Great Beggar is not here." The second guard repeated his well-rehearsed line.

"Then where is he?"

"He has not yet returned from Amsterdam."

"Amsterdam? When do you expect him?"

"He will return soon."

Yaap stirred and demanded shortly, "When is *soon*?"

Just then, from inside the courtyard, the loud cadenced clatter of armor and boots marching across cobblestones mixed with a cacophony of throaty voices.

"Stand clear," shouted one of the guards.

Pieter-Lucas pulled up Blesje's reins and prepared to steer him to the side of the bridge. Before he could maneuver the tired beast out of the way, the guards stepped aside, the huge gate swung open, and a pack of soldiers burst through the opening, headed straight toward them.

Pieter-Lucas felt the horse's massive body tense beneath him. "Easy, now, Blesje, boy," he said. The soldiers pressed forward, their hard bodies and bulky armor pushing at both boys and their mounts, finally pinning them to the wall of the bridge. Pieter-Lucas' bad leg scraped the wall, and he strained to relieve the pain by digging it into the horse's flank.

In an awkward meter, forced to fit the rhythm of their relentless march, the soldiers shouted in unison:

"Long live the Beggars!
Brederode's Beggars!
On to Culemborg!
Destroy their altars!
Break their images!
Long live the Beggars!
Hurrah! Hurrah!
Long live the Beggars!"

Pieter-Lucas scanned the files of look-alike Beggar troops. Could Vader Hendrick be among them? If only they'd stop!

When the last of the soldiers had passed, Pieter-Lucas reacted instinctively, loosing the reins on Blesje and nudging him gently. The young man hardly realized what he had done, much less notice what Yaap was doing. Whatever it was, both horses kicked up their legs and charged straight ahead, racing past the shouting guards. They tore across the courtyard, beyond the gate at the far end, and came to rest in the stable enclosure with the two boys barely clinging to their backs.

"What now?" Pieter-Lucas asked.

Before Yaap could answer, a dozen Beggars swarmed around them, flashing clanging weapons, shoving one another in frenzied disorder, and shouting an assortment of wild messages.

"Who sent you here?"

"Spies! Traitors!"

"Seize the intruders!"

Yaap raised his hand and shouted, "Silence!" But his gesture went unheeded, and his voice was muffled in the tumult. The horses, already nervous and sweating, pawed at the cobbled pavement, though unable to force their way beyond the barricade of armed bodies on all sides.

The soldiers reached up and yanked the boys off their horses, dragged them to the cobblestones below, and marched them unceremoniously into the castle. "Stop!" both boys screamed. "We're messengers of Ludwig van Nassau, from Prince Willem's *Kasteel* in Breda," Yaap yelled repeatedly.

"*Ja, ja!* Tell that to the Great Beggar when he arrives," their captors jeered. "Spies! Traitors! Royalists! Papists!"

They burst into spontaneous singing. From all sides, the chorus swelled now, echoing in huge hollow balls that bounced from wall to wall to floor to ceiling, around the clammy, stone halls of the ancient castle:

> "Who under guard of God Most High
> His dwelling and retreat will have,
> As in a sure and peaceful place,
> Beneath His shadow even will lie.
> Boldly will I say to my God:
> 'Thou art my fortress and my hope;
> In Thee my confidence will lodge,
> Most surely will I rest in Thee.'"

"So this is the way you Beggars mete out justice!" Pieter-Lucas bellowed. "Singing about peaceful places and hope and rest, all in the name of God!"

Soldiers on both sides tightened their grip on Pieter-Lucas' upper arms and shoved him forward. "Hold your mouth, *jongen*," one ordered, and the others joined in.

"Where did you learn that pious word, *justice*?" one sneered.

"At your pretty moeder's knee?" another suggested with unbridled sarcasm.

"If your moeder were a bit smarter, she would have kept you there at her knee, where she could protect you from the likes of us hypocritical Beggars!" The stone walls rang with their uproarious mocking laughter.

Indeed, at this moment, that idea made great sense to Pieter-Lucas. Little good it had done him to come here seeking help for her. If these were Vader Hendrick's friends . . . He closed his eyes and swallowed hard to keep down the revulsion he felt rising in his throat.

The noisy captors pressed more closely around the two boys and shoved them down a long, tightly curving flight of worn stone stairs.

"Too bad your moeder can't be here to rescue her darling," someone taunted, touching off another volley of raucous laughter.

In truth it was Moeder who needed the rescuing. Pieter-Lucas stifled the urge to say so. What could he say that would not simply infuriate his tormentors further? Unreasonable, despicable beasts all. In his heart he heard the strange dragon's voice once more, "Revenge . . . Revenge . . . REVENGE!" The word crescendoed into a deafening roar that reverberated through the chambers of his mind. The ugly, triumphant throb obliterated memories of Moeder Kaatje's thin face and sad eyes. Visions of Aletta's lovely image melted into a warm, faraway blur, and an enormous, faceless God hovered above, wielding a gigantic golden sword.

"Hypocrites!" Pieter-Lucas shouted into the confusion.

The stairwell was becoming narrower now, forcing the company to hobble single-file down into the damp bowels of the earth below the castle. Weapons scraped the lowering ceiling, stenches of sweating bodies and stale beer filled Pieter-Lucas' nostrils, and drops of icy water splashed on the steps, turning them to slime beneath his feet.

Then, just when the circumference of his shrinking world had closed in on him so tightly that he felt certain he was smothering, they stopped. The leader unlocked a door with a key from a ring filled with old large clanging keys. The boisterous soldiers shoved Pieter-Lucas and Yaap into a dingy, damp cell lighted only by one heavily barred window high above near the ceiling. Pieter-Lucas landed in a heap on his bad leg on a floor strewn with old straw and an unrecognizable assortment of refuse.

"When the Great Beggar arrives, we will send him in to receive your message from Count Ludwig," their gaoler said, his hand already on the door.

"But it's urgent," Yaap protested, grabbing the gaoler by the sleeve.

"Then, perhaps you'd like to deliver it to me?" the Beggar suggested, a sly smile painted on his face in the sinister light.

"*Nay*," Yaap protested. "I have sworn to Count Ludwig that I will place it in no other hands than Count Brederode's."

"But he is not here. It must wait, and so must you."

"Please let me go. I can reach him in Amsterdam sooner than he could come here."

The man laughed. "What sort of idiots do you make us out to be? Beggars do not open cages to foreign birds of prey."

"I demand to see the steward of this castle," Yaap retorted. "He'll tell you who I am—Yaap van Breda, personal messenger of Willem van Oranje."

The gaoler ignored his pleas, turning instead to call up the stairs to his companions. "Come back, you lazy fellows, and bring your hammers. Our young guests are a bit restless here."

The Beggars swarmed into the cell and fell upon the boys. With quick, rough movements, they dragged them, kicking in protest, to the wall. While Yaap persisted in defending his innocence and repeating his demand for a visit from the castle steward, the jubilant Beggars secured the boys' legs to the oozing stones in irons attached to long chains. Then they disappeared up the stairs, locking the rough oak door securely behind them.

"And these are the men Count Ludwig supports?" Pieter-Lucas mumbled. "The ones who shove their feet under Prince Willem's table while they talk of noble battles against Spanish tyranny? Hah! These Beggars could teach the Spaniards plenty about tyranny!"

Yaap twisted his body awkwardly on the slippery rods of straw and groaned. "What a diabolical predicament! First time I've ever landed in a hole like this. Those guys were pretty rough, weren't they?"

"Rough, nothing," Pieter-Lucas retorted. "Mean, ugly, vicious is more like it."

"*Nay*. They just don't know our faces. Can't be too cautious. They're in a war, you know."

"Cautious? They're a worthless bunch of villians! Just like their leader, the Great Beggar!"

"*Nay*, hear. Brederode may be rough. But he's fighting for God's grand and noble cause."

"Grand and noble!" Pieter-Lucas gagged on the preposterous words. "He's positively dangerous, like a great, wild nobleman resurrected from tales of Holland's primitive history."

Yaap laughed. "Rowdy, *ja*. That goes with being young and wealthy . . . and noble! But these men are the Netherlands' true patriots, defending the ancient privileges granted to us by King Philip's predecessors in city charters. Everybody cries about oppression. The Beggars are finally doing something about it."

"Doing what? Preparing the rest of us for a royal slaughter? They're dangerous, Yaap, I don't care what you say."

Yaap pulled up his knees and rested his head in his hands. For a long while he sat quietly on the long, low wooden platform that was to be their stool, table, and bed for as long as they stayed here.

Pieter-Lucas' stomach began to growl. How long had it been since he'd eaten? His legs ached in the irons. A draft blew up between the boards beneath him, and his body felt the kind of damp chill that creeps through the skin and muscles into the bone. "Cold to the bone," Opa would say.

"There has to be an explanation," Yaap said at last. Then his voice slipped into a tone of dreamy perplexity. "I'll never forget that wonderful night, the first time they called themselves Beggars. Did I ever tell you about it?"

"Yaap, you're a maddening idealist!" Pieter-Lucas shouted at him. "These monstrous characters have tied you to the wall in their cold, stinky dungeon, and you want to tell about their heroic exploits?"

Pieter-Lucas had no stomach for a story just now, especially not one extolling the virtues of his captors. But he was chained to the same wall with this persistent storyteller and could not get away. Yaap chuckled a soft reminiscing kind of chuckle. Irritated, Pieter-Lucas snapped, "Keep your memories to yourself, do you hear?"

He might as well have spoken to the unlighted lantern on the wall. Yaap, lost in the past, began the tale Pieter-Lucas wanted least to hear: "It happened on my first trip to Brussels." He launched into his tale. "I carried a message for Ludwig from his sister. Arriving early in the evening and not finding him at the prince's palace, I was directed to the mansion of Count Floris of Culemborg, where I found a luxurious banquet in progress."

"Who cares about mansions and banquets?" Pieter-Lucas groaned. "My ankles hurt, and who knows what these scoundrels may do to Blesje? If I ever get out of here, I'll probably spend the rest of my days in Breda's tower dungeon for not returning him to the stables."

Yaap chattered on, oblivious to Pieter-Lucas' pains, protests, even his presence. "Somewhere around three hundred nobles were there, the ones who'd presented their petition to the governess earlier that week. You knew about the petition?"

Pieter-Lucas didn't answer. Of course, he knew all about the petition.

Yaap went on, growing ever more animated. "Well, let me tell you, the *Love of Vaderland* ran high in Brussels during that week in April. Brederode and Ludwig and the others were so certain the governess was going to give them all they wanted that they decided to celebrate. When noblemen throw a party, it gets wild, believe me."

"Especially if Brederode is one of the noblemen," Pieter-Lucas groused. Who in the stables hadn't heard the line: "If Brederode has anything to do with it, the wine will flow and girls abound"?

Yaap ignored his interruption. "You can't imagine how Culemborg's palace dazzled that night. Torches and lanterns blazed all around, animating the whole scene with jabs of darting light and slippery shadows. Gold and silver vessels glittered on the tables. Three hundred noblemen guzzled wine as only a company of Lowland noblemen know how to guzzle wine. The room buzzed and exploded with shouts and periodic outbursts of song."

Pieter-Lucas groaned. His head throbbed and his tongue stuck to the roof of his dry mouth. "Yaap, that's enough!"

But Yaap was only getting started. "Of a sudden," he went on with increasing animation, as if savoring the sounds of his own words, "amid the roar and rumble, Brederode rose, swaying on his feet. The noise level fell to a hush and the bearded noble master proceeded to tell a story, adorned with many thick-tongued flourishes. Sure wish I could tell it like he did."

How much longer must this go on? Pieter-Lucas moved as far away from his companion as the lengths of chain would allow. He sat in the straw, his back turned and head down, and wrapped his arms tightly around his ears. Nothing could free him from the maddening prattle.

"Brederode looked positively heroic standing there relating how, when they'd presented their petition, the governess was visibly irritated, 'her face awash with unbecoming dampness.' I do remember those were his words. I think he took a special delight in her discomfort. He grinned and the crowd laughed. Then he said her loyal councilor asked her, 'What, madame! Is it possible Your Highness can entertain fears of these Beggars?'

"By this time the crowd was worked up to such a drunken pitch I thought a riot would break out. 'How dare he call us Beggars?' someone shouted in a drunken drawl. 'We in whose veins flows the best and highest blood of the Lowlands?'

"The hall rang with waves of huzzahs and wild curses, until at last Brederode waved and yelled them down. He raised his arm high and shouted in triumph, 'Think, fine gentlemen, how appropriate a title this is for our noble army! They call us Beggars. Let us accept the name. We will contend with the Inquisition, but remain loyal to the king, even till compelled to wear the beggar's sack.' "

Fine gentlemen? Pieter-Lucas felt anger stirring through all his limbs in frustrated waves. "Hold your mouth, Yaap," he shouted.

"*Nay*, not now," Yaap answered with unbridled glee. "This is the best part."

Pieter-Lucas sighed and leaned his head and body at last against the wall. Icy trickles of water seeped off the walls into his hair and ran down his scalp and onto his neck.

"Brederode called a page, who brought him a leather beggar's wallet and a large wooden beggar's bowl. He hung the wallet around his neck, filled the bowl with wine, lifted it with rough hands, and drained it in one draught. 'Long live the Beggars!' he shouted and wiped his beard with his coat sleeve. The entire company joined in with thunderous applause and shouts of 'Long live the Beggars!' "

Nightmares from the Great Church darted through Pieter-Lucas' mind. A razor-pointed chill pierced the entire length of his body. Impulsively he wrapped his arms around himself, grasping for warmth and protection. The iron shackles held him fast, drawing blood from swollen ankles as he struggled.

Yaap was still running on: "Brederode passed the wallet and bowl to his next neighbor, who repeated his performance, then passed them on to his next."

What strange spirit possessed this crazed storyteller? Pieter-Lucas shook his head. Could the man feel no pain or chill?

"And so they circulated the now sacred symbols around the entire room. Roars of laughter and fever-pitched shouts shook the walls of the old mansion."

How could he paint the ghastly picture with such relish?

"The wallet and bowl having completed their rounds, Brederode pinned them to a pillar. Each man threw salt into his goblet, then joined in the singing of an impromptu jingling rhyme:

'By this salt, by this bread,
By this wallet we do swear,
Beggars, we will never change,
Even though the whole world stare.' "

Pieter-Lucas felt sick all over. The air grew close and putrid. He heard a rustling in the straw beside him and was glad he couldn't see what ran there.

"You should have been with me on that memorable night, Pieter-Lucas," Yaap prodded him. "Then you would not doubt."

"Not doubt what?"

"That the Beggars are on our side. They will set us free, and they will win. Their mission is from God, and it cannot fail."

"And when will they get us out of this abominable hole?"

"Soon, when Brederode returns. Just trust me, friend."

He'd already done that one time too many.

"Nay, Yaap, hear me. As long as I limp when I walk and hold this inhuman dungeon in my memory, I shall expect no good thing to come from your barbarous Beggars."

Yaap's tone turned imploring. "If you'd been there you would understand—you'd feel it in your bones."

"All I feel in my bones is the cold!"

Yaap sat silently for a space, then sniffled from the end of his restraining chains. Sporadically, he called out with a detached and plaintive wistfulness. "Such a glorious beginning! Such a glorious beginning!"

Pieter-Lucas turned his head and vomited into the rotting straw. He held his nose against the intolerable stench and set his mind to plan for his revenge.

# CHAPTER SEVEN

*Kasteel Batestein, Vianen*

13th day of Peat Month (September), 1566

*F*or what seemed an interminable day, Pieter-Lucas and Yaap huddled in the filth and damp cold of the *Batestein Kasteel* dungeon, waiting. Pieter-Lucas watched the light and darkness filter through the barred window and tried to track the hours. All the while, his newly aroused inner monster grasped at each new discomfort as evidence of injustice and screamed with intensifying passion: "Revenge . . . revenge . . . REVENGE!"

By spells, Yaap sat brooding, then babbling, as if trying to reassure himself. "Brederode will soon come to our rescue," he repeated. "Great and noble man he is, not at all like this ragtag bunch of malcontents he calls his soldiers."

Occasionally he leaned over, patted the bosom of his doublet where he carried Brederode's message, and spoke with increasingly uneasy passion. "It's here! The message that will set us free! It's safe." He looked up toward the cobwebby ceiling and pleaded in pious tones, "Great God in heaven, come and deliver us. . . ."

Pieter-Lucas winced. Was Yaap losing his mind? There was no one to hear his thoughts, no powerful stranger to sever their bonds and let them go. If God would just pay attention, He might recall that he, Pieter-Lucas, had come here on an errand of mercy—an errand certain to be doomed if they weren't released any faster than the exasperating "soon" Yaap kept raving about. He glanced heavenward, then closed his eyes and tried to pretend he was not in this awful place. But it was no use.

Twice that day a greasy wench brought them food. Her stringy hair was tied back with a dark scarf and a soiled white apron pinched in her rotund waist, causing her low-necked dress to stretch scantily over her plump torso.

She never spoke, but wore a smooth, too-pleasant smile as she leaned over them and, with scaly, dirty hands, placed within reach of each boy a hunk of dry stale bread and a mugful of some sort of undefinable liquid. Yaap devoured the pitiful rations, smacking his lips loudly and shouting, "Good gracious, girlie. You are an angel of mercy."

Pieter-Lucas gulped hard. Hardly his idea of mercy—or an angel! He left his food and liquid untouched. The miserable servant hovered so close that the warm stench of her rancid breath removed whatever appetite his bone-weary body had managed to cling to. He turned his head to the wall to avoid her presence and the imploring invitation on her mute face.

By the time the girl returned to the cell for her second food-bearing errand, Pieter-Lucas' head was throbbing, and his ankles had swollen to gigantic dimensions. When she leaned over the boys to lay the food before them, he swallowed his nausea and begged, "Please, tell the gaoler to let me go. My moeder's dying, and I must go to her."

"And my message is urgent," Yaap added abruptly.

The girl grinned placidly, as if neither of her charges had said a word. Pieter-Lucas grabbed at her arm, missing it. She shook her head at him with a glaring rebuke. Then silently, she moved away, still smiling.

"Maybe you don't have a moeder," Pieter-Lucas said. "But if you do— or ever did—wouldn't you want somebody to let you out of the dungeon so you could go sit by her side when she was dying?"

The girl curtsied, backed away, unlocked the door with a huge key hanging from her belt, and let herself out of sight, locking the door once more behind her.

At length darkness engulfed the cell. Yaap fell quickly into a sleep punctuated all through the night by occasional grunts, sniffles, and sharp little whimpering cries.

Pieter-Lucas found the silence of night almost as oppressive as Yaap's worst chattering. Alone with his memories and his fears, he felt himself trapped in that wild Bosch painting once more. In his imagination he heard ghouls moaning in the corners and monsters hissing in his ears while bats slashed at the putrid air above him. At one point he felt certain some evil creature was trying to suffocate him with his mantle. He gasped for air and shouted, "Help me! Won't somebody hear? Aletta, oh, Aletta, come quickly."

Refusing to lie down on the crude straw-strewn platform intended for that purpose, he paced about, straining his manacles to their limit. When at length he sat down, he stooped over and pounded hard on the floor, digging a hole through the straw and filth and into the damp, hardened earth with his fists. "Why, why, WHY?" he cried out. Tears streamed down his cheeks, and he shuddered at the sounds of Yaap moaning beside him. For the rest of the night he wrestled with ominous visions and yearned for daylight, never certain whether he was awake or asleep.

His visions and nightmares were interrupted abruptly by the sound of Yaap shrieking out in pain. Pieter-Lucas opened his eyes and glanced around the cell. "I must have fallen asleep," he mumbled to himself. "There's daylight filtering through the cobwebs that join the bars over the window." He stretched his muscles involuntarily. "Oei, but I'm stiff!"

"Where am I?" Yaap demanded with a deep, groggy voice. "Let go of my legs. Let go, I say. Ouch!"

"We're the guests of your noble friend, the Great Beggar." Pieter-Lucas edged the words with sarcasm. "We're enjoying our own private room in Lord Brederode's fine castle. Don't you remember?"

"What? Where? Brederode?" the older boy stammered, looking about him with darting eyes.

Pieter-Lucas' emotions fluctuated between disgust and pity. Was this the same young man he had admired and trusted, the one who brought him here supposedly as a gesture of kindness?

If Moeder were here she would say, "He could use some cheering words."

But Moeder wasn't here. And from deep down inside, Pieter-Lucas heard the voice of his latest companion. "Ignore him! He's a Brederode sympathizer who spent all day ignoring your pain, prattling about the Beggars' glorious beginning. Leave him alone and let him fret now in his own predicament. It's a part of the revenge you owe your Beggar vader— the only part you can play for now. But there will be more. . . ." Pieter-Lucas squirmed. Who was this monster, anyway?

"Who's there?" Yaap cried out, turning toward the door.

"Who's where?" Pieter-Lucas responded. "Nobody's here but you and me."

"Nay, they're coming for us. Can't you hear them on the stairs? I told you they'd come. Thanks be to God!"

By now Pieter-Lucas did hear. Raucous voices echoed down the stairway outside the cell. Then the key clanged in the lock and the door heaved open with an ominous creak of old wood rubbing against old wood. Two or three men—it was still too dark to see for sure how many— tramped into the cell and stood before the prisoners. One man carried a lighted torch which he lowered to the level where they sat. He kicked at them, rousing them with his boot.

"Good morning, boys. Nice sleep?" Hypocritical politeness barbed his icy words. It was the gaoler who'd ordered them chained. Pieter-Lucas refused to look at him.

Yaap responded with enthusiasm. "You've come, I knew you would . . . Brederode? My message is urgent!" He began digging around in his doublet for the document.

The gaoler shone the torchlight full in their faces. Pieter-Lucas felt the heat and backed away toward the wall. The man spoke again, "Here they are, Hendrick. What think you?"

Hendrick! Pieter-Lucas felt his heart pounding and shrunk deeper into the shadows. Vader Hendrick?

"Do you know these upstarts who claim to be from Breda?" the gaoler asked.

"*Ja*, but of course I know who they are." Cold, aloof, gloating, it was Vader Hendrick indeed, looking just the way he did the last time they'd met. Flames of that same mad anger flashed from his eyes—hot with passion and at the same time cold with calculating, soul-piercing hatred.

"From Breda indeed," the man said. "A couple of knaves of notably questionable character, undoubtedly dangerous spies for King Philip."

Pieter-Lucas gasped and his muscles bounded, ready for action. Hendrick wasn't through.

"The young one there"—he nodded his head toward Pieter-Lucas— "he's the deluded, devoted son of a woman who stubbornly persists in her papist ways. Her husband, the boy's supposed vader, is a pious warrior for the new faith, forced to flee for his life, so vicious was her gossip about him."

Pieter-Lucas screamed out, "Lies! Lies! My moeder has never uttered so much as an unkind word either to or about her despicable, unworthy husband. What's happened to your memory, Vader Hendrick? Did you crush it beneath your trampling feet in the Great Church, where you hacked the life out of so many other precious treasures, including my anointing?" The long-familiar name felt like slime sliding off his tongue. He spat in the straw and wiped his mouth with the cuff of his doublet.

Yaap stood and moved toward the visitors, protesting loudly, "Heer van den Garde, surely you cannot be so confused! You know I'm Yaap, loyal messenger to Willem van Oranje and Ludwig van Nassau! I've brought an urgent message for Brederode from Count Ludwig. And this"—he gestured toward his companion—"he is your own flesh and blood, your only son."

Hendrick van den Garde laughed. His forked beard bobbed in the other-worldly torchlight like the demons of Pieter-Lucas' dreams. "Didn't I tell you they were knaves? Such fantastic stories and fiery accusations they can create. Tell me, friend, does this wild one look like a respectable messenger of the Nassau family?"

"If he did, do you think we would have shut him up in this place?" the gaoler replied.

Yaap retorted again, "Heer van den Garde, I cannot believe . . ." He shook his head and stared in amazement. "Surely you know your own son? Look at him. . . ."

Pieter-Lucas searched the shadowed face of his vader. But the man refused to look directly at him. "*Nay*, Yaap," he spit out the words, "this man is not my vader."

For one long moment, Hendrick looked at him, his eyes wild, uncertain, almost frightened.

"I would not own his likes." Pieter-Lucas spoke with a strength that he didn't know he possessed.

He swallowed hard the great lumps of agony that multiplied in his throat and brought with them a whole army of unwelcome tears dredged from the depths of a broken soul. He cursed the tears, lifted his head high, and spoke with renewed composure, "My moeder lies near the time to be delivered in childbirth. Neither she nor her unborn child will live through the ordeal, lacking this one thing—her husband's presence at her side. If you know where he may be found, please tell him that his faithful Kaatje calls for him." He paused, searching for a glimpse of warmth in the hard face.

The man's square jaw was set, the heavy eyebrows never moved, and the eyes avoided his pleading gaze. He spoke as if condescending to the whim of a weak child. "If I see your moeder's husband, I'll send him home—if he is so disposed, that is . . . and has time to spare after we've finished off the idols in a few more dens of iniquity."

"If he is so disposed? If he has time? What sort of traitorous husband is that?" Pieter-Lucas shouted. With energy born of rage, he pursed his lips and spat in the man's direction. His lips tingled.

Yaap strained forward in his chains and spoke in an urgent tone, "Can you not find at least one tiny speck of kindness in your hardened soldier heart and let this loyal son go free to sit by his moeder's side and watch her die?"

The cell vibrated with silence, broken only by the crackling of the torch flame and the melancholy ringing of a distant church bell. Hendrick van den Garde said flatly, "Let him go, then, to his moeder. Rebellious child, he should have stayed there in the first place."

The men started for the door, but Yaap shouted after them, "Aren't you going to free him?"

"Hold your mouth, you troublemaker, spy," the gaoler snapped. "We'll let him go when the Great Beggar says to let him go, and not a day sooner."

"But when. . . ?" Yaap begged.

The gaoler looked back over his shoulder, a derisive grin drawn across his face. "Soon," he said with mock sweetness.

"By then it will be too late," Yaap protested.

The two Beggars ignored him. They climbed up out of the hovel, their heavy, clumping steps and rattling armor echoing off into the distance. Yaap howled and pleaded, hurling desperate words at the locked door. "Let us go, let us go. Our missions cannot wait!"

He broke into loud, heartrending howls of pain, interrupted by wails of "Where are all the brave and noble men? Great God, send Brederode!"

Pieter-Lucas felt his head swim and his stomach churn. Once more he vomited into the straw. No more tears threatened to flow. His mouth felt hot, dry, and sour.

"God, just let me die," he mumbled. "It's no use anymore. Moeder's dying. Her child is dying. Even Aletta won't have me once Moeder tells her about her vow. Where are you, God?"

Shivering in the damp, he waited for an answer. None came. No voice, human or divine, no return of Hendrick van den Garde, no fluttering wings of angels, no peace or joy or hope—nothing but a miserable, noisy cellmate howling at an ancient locked door.

In desperation, he screamed out, "God of the Beggars, begone. I want no part of you. Go. . . !"

His last word echoed around the cell and pounded in Pieter-Lucas' numbed brain.

"GO . . . Go . . . go . . ."

# CHAPTER EIGHT

*Breda*

22nd day of Peat Month (September), 1566

*I*n the household of Dirck Engelshofen, life went on almost as if nothing had happened. Tante Lysbet cooked the meals and attended to Moeder Gretta's daily needs. If anything, Gretta Engelshofen seemed more quiet and amiable, less deranged these days. Robbin—cheerful, full of curiosity and boundless energy—begged less for Aletta's constant attention when Moeder played with him more.

Vader Dirck welcomed the usual stream of visitors into *The Crane's Nest* at the front of their sandy brick house on Annastraat. Teachers who needed books came to order them. Men who loved books came to buy. Scholars and men who thought important thoughts came to exchange them with each other. Burghers came to learn the latest news from the Antwerp printers who came to sell their wares and fill orders.

For Aletta, though, everything had changed. Tante Lysbet seemed more severe than ever and more anxious for Aletta to assist her in caring for her moeder. Vader Dirck stayed such long hours in his bookshop that there were days when she did not see his face. It was as if every member of the household had become an actor in a festival drama scene—saying their lines and acting their parts well, but always leaving Aletta to wonder what they really thought and felt.

Worst of all, Pieter-Lucas did not return. Each afternoon Aletta listened for Roland to chime fourteen times. Then she counted the days and asked a series of questions that never brought answers. Was he safe in Vianen? Did he roam around the countryside in search of his vader? When would he return? What would become of their vow? Life grew grayer and more desolate with each passing day.

No one else in the house seemed to care where Pieter-Lucas was or what had befallen him. Since the day Vader had found Aletta weeping on

Pieter-Lucas' doorstoop, no one—not even Robbin—had so much as mentioned the boy's name.

Nor did anyone register alarm when every afternoon Aletta slipped out of the house without explaining her destination. True, she often went at Tante Lysbet's bidding to fetch herbs. Most days, however, she went for her own secret reason, stopping first at the empty house of the van den Gardes next door to pick a bouquet of asters, chrysanthemums, and late roses. These she carried down the street to the Beguinage and gave them to Moeder Kaatje.

Each day, Aletta found Pieter-Lucas' moeder weaker than the day before and more anxious about her coming ordeal. "The boy we both love will be home soon," the girl consoled with as much conviction as she could muster. "He'll bring your husband, and they'll take good care of you."

In her heart, Aletta couldn't quite believe the words her lips had formed. Comfort gave way to a nagging conscience. "You're disobeying your vader to come here," it screamed at her. "Nothing will come out right." She felt the fire of his wounded eyes, unseen and silent, piercing through the walls of the old Beguinage. She both feared and yearned for him to find her out, to scold her, at least to ask her where she went on the days when Lysbet had not sent her. Just anything would do to break the awful silence.

But her vader might as well have moved out of the house and into his own world, so seldom did she see him anymore. Even Sunday mornings had changed. Until now, he had never worked in his bookshop on Sundays. Now that the Great Church was closed while they repaired the damage done during the image-breaking, Vader retreated into the shop on Sundays the same as any other day. Did he have customers? Or did he just read the books? From early in the morning till late at night, he stayed hidden away.

On the second Sunday morning after Pieter-Lucas had gone away, the family arose to find Vader waiting to greet them. "Hurry and get ready. Church services are about to begin," he announced.

"We go to the church?" Robbin asked, his blue eyes pleading.

"Ja, my son, we go." Vader smiled a tight, distant smile that belonged not at all to the vader Aletta knew so well.

"Oh! Whee!" Robbin danced around the room chanting, "We go, we go, we go to the Great Church!"

Stunned, excited, fearful all at once, Aletta dressed herself and patted Opa's scarred, blood-spattered dove with the ragged edges, hidden away in the bosom of her dress. She had carried it there, close to her heart, ever since that magical moment when Pieter-Lucas gave it to her in the birch wood. Having readied herself, she turned her attention to Robbin.

Moeder Gretta, controlled by the caprice of some strange inner master, sat in her chair this morning by the window, holding her head in her hands and howling uncontrollably. "He's coming for me. I'm cursed!" She shrieked the familiar, mysterious words her family had come to expect, but never to understand. "Husband, protect me! Great God, have mercy!"

By turns, Vader Dirck and Lysbet sat beside the distraught woman, stroking her shoulders, seeking to reassure her. "All is well, Gretta." How like an old sweet tune Vader's voice sounded once more. "Rest easy. God is our refuge. He will protect us."

At length, Tante Lysbet said to him, "Heer Engelshofen, it is time for you to take the children to church. I shall give your wife the herbs I have brewed. Then, when the house is still, she can sleep and begin to mend."

"First let me put her in the bed," Vader offered, sounding weary.

Aletta watched the ritual she'd seen so many times over the years. First he took her hand in his and spoke in soft tones, "Gretta, your body is weary. Come now, let's go back to bed and sleep. You'll feel better."

"*Nay*," she screamed. "He'll lock me up in there, and I'll die of starvation. Take me away from this dreadful place." She held out her arms to him. Vader's aloofness of the past weeks seemed momentarily to have vanished, replaced with the tenderness he always showed when he looked at Moeder. An instantaneous reassurance soothed Aletta, and she watched him lift her moeder gently from the chair and carry her across the room, down the hall, through the bookshop door and back, finally wrapping her in a feather bag and laying her on a low bench opposite the hearth. The poor woman looked at him with blank staring eyes. Her loud wails changed to soft sobs.

"Thank God, she's calmer. She'll be better soon," Lysbet offered. "Go now, and give us a spot of silence."

As if reluctant to leave, Vader picked up Moeder's shriveled hand in both his big hands and pressed it with his lips. Roland, from his perch in the tower, was calling the city of Breda to worship, and Robbin was tugging at his vader's arm, coaxing, "Vader, Roland calls us. Let us go into the house of the Lord."

Dirck Engelshofen turned his attention to the boy and clapped the customary response. The three healthy family members rushed to the door, donned their street shoes, picked up their little wooden folded sermon chairs, and hurried off to fill their places in the old church on the market square.

Breda's worshipers came by the dozens. Aletta noted how somber their faces were and how uncommonly hushed and stealthy their steps as they walked through the grand old doors now scarred from the recent battle.

"Vader," Robbin whispered when they had settled into their chairs. "The stone people. They're gone!"

Aletta watched the boy turn his head slowly, his eyes big with fearful wonder as he surveyed the damage around them in the wounded sanctuary. He scooted his chair up closer to his vader, who looked down at the boy with an expression that supported his calm answer. "It's all right now, son."

Aletta hugged her elbows and cringed. What was all right now? How could he close his eyes to the rubble and try to give Robbin false assurances? Would he forever treat them both like fragile procession dolls with empty heads?

Vader Dirck wasn't the only one playing childish games this morning in the church, Aletta decided. The priest, too, ignored the destruction and chanted his mass, as if to reassure his trembling flock that everything was as it had been for always. But she was not fooled by the drama, and her senses coaxed her mind in other directions. No organ music swelled through the massive stone-bordered expanse. In its place she caught the eerie background sounds of wind whistling through paneless windows and across the jagged points of shattered images in colored glass. Gone was the rood screen, leaving the choir and altar open and exposed. The nakedness of this hallowed spot where Opa had died revealed that dozens of treasured creatures carved into the old wooden choir stalls had been mutilated by the image-breakers' swords.

Vaguely aware that the priest droned on, Aletta allowed her eyes to roam as far as they would without moving her head and betraying the improper wandering of her mind. The walls, once adorned with richly hued paintings, glared down at her, now streaked with coats of blatant whitewash. Straining her eyes upward to see the ceiling without actually tipping her head, she searched for the Eye of God. Only whitewash cast its silent, ominous blankness down on her.

Engulfed in her private painful struggle and conscience, she felt her heart cry out, "Great God, where have you gone? Is it possible I chased you away with my disobedient ways? Please, hold it not against me. If Vader had any idea how much Pieter-Lucas' moeder needs me, surely he would not say *nay*. Yet, now that I come to your house and see and feel that you have disappeared, I know not what to think."

Frantically, she tried to push from her mind all thoughts of Pieter-Lucas and Moeder Kaatje to concentrate on the service in progress. But irresistibly, her imagination carried her, instead, up and down the aisles and into the side chapels of this place she knew so well. Every nook and cranny of the old sanctuary was haunted by the spirit of Pieter-Lucas. She envisioned him running through the melee and the rubble, rescuing the dove, staggering out in a pool of his own blood, lying at death's door in the Beguinage, and now traipsing across pastures, bogs, and forests in search of an elusive vader gone mad.

Regardless of what her vader said, all was not well. Not in this once holy but now godforsaken place, not in the bookshop, not in the big wide world of men and swords and strange religious quarrels.

"Come, Sissy." Robbin's miniature voice and chubby hand tugged Aletta back to the present. "Worship has come to an end, and we go to home."

---

### The Crane's Nest

Dirck Engelshofen expected to spend the afternoon alone in the bookshop. Gretta was sleeping after her fearsome outbreak of the morning. Robbin had begged permission to go walking in the woods with a friend and his family from down Annastraat. And Aletta? Dirck shook his head as he opened the door that led from the hallway into his shop. Something had gotten wedged between them these days.

"I should have known," he told himself, "when I had to send Pieter-Lucas away and then tell her she couldn't see him again. But I thought she'd understand. Never thought either of them was old enough to have amorous ideas. How could I forget what it's like to be almost eighteen years old?"

He stood just inside the window, looking out, pounding his right fist rhythmically into his left palm. "Gone to the Beguinage again. I know she thinks I believe she is collecting herbs for Lysbet to use with her moeder. I wish she'd come and tell me the truth. She fears I would forbid her to visit Vrouw Kaatje. And maybe I would if she told me. But I simply can't bring myself to forbid something I have not seen nor has she told me. Besides, Kaatje van den Garde, in the Beguinage? What could be safer? Poor woman, with such a rogue for a husband. She probably needs my daughter. In many ways she's been like another moeder to Aletta all her life. Dear God, I fear I'm not doing too well as protector of my family. But what more can I do?"

If only God would speak to him with a voice from heaven, the way He did in the Bible to Moses or Gideon or Nehemiah or Paul. Why was it that the more a man wanted to do what was right, the more difficult it became to know what "right" was?

Dirck crossed the little shop toward the shelves. "Wonder if there's an answer of some kind in one of these books."

Before he could even look, a knocking on the door announced the arrival of his friends Barthelemeus and Meister Laurens. Glad to see them and at the same time irritated to be disturbed, he let them in, and they took their places.

"What is the news, *jongens*?" he asked, eager to get to the point.

"News?" Barthelemeus threw the question back at him.

Laurens looked from one to the other, then said, "We all know what the news is. There was a service in the Great Church this morning. But since we were all there to see it, it is not news."

"Then why have you come on a Sunday afternoon?" Dirck prodded them.

"We have a question," Barthelemeus answered.

"A question?"

"*Ja*, a question." Meister Laurens cleared his throat. "Tell us, Dirck, have you had a visitor here yesterday or today?"

"A visitor? You mean a customer?"

The men looked at each other, both nodded, and Barthelemeus answered, "Of sorts. A young man come to show you a pamphlet and discuss its contents with you?"

"Perhaps to solicit your help in distributing the work?" Laurens added.

"*Ja*, last night, just such a person did come to the shop after I had closed my doors and was putting the books in order."

"And you let him in?" Barthelemeus asked.

"Why, *ja*, I did." Dirck felt his friends' eyes directed at him with unusual keenness. "As you know, it is my practice to open the door as long as I linger in the shop."

"Did you know the man?" asked Barthelemeus.

"*Nay*."

"Had you seen him before?" Laurens added.

"Not that I remember. He said he lives here in Breda."

"You did not take his pamphlet and consent to sell it, did you?"

"*Nay*, that I did not do."

"What did you tell him, then?"

"Simply that I do not buy and sell such sectarian materials."

"How did he react?"

"He seemed disappointed and continued to urge me until I'd told him *nay* at least three times."

"What, may we ask, was the subject of his work?" Barthelemeus asked.

Why were Dirck's friends asking so many questions? It was not like them. "Do you ask because you want to find out," he said, "or do you try to trap me?"

"I cannot believe you suspect us of such a thing," Barthelemeus reprimanded him.

"Nor can I believe you are putting me through such an inquisition. If I did not know better, I would suspect you were strange wolves in the skins of Barthelemeus de Koopman and Meister Laurens. Now, just tell me what is amiss and what is the real reason for your visit here today."

Laurens leaned toward him, hands on his knees, and said plainly, "We are not certain, but we fear this young man may have been sent to entrap you. Was the pamphlet a Lutheran tract of some sort, perhaps in support of images?"

"Exactly so," Dirck agreed. "An anonymous work with a title something like, *Strong Evidence That People May Have Commemorative Images, But None That They Can Pray To.* Filled with biblical texts, it was a clever, almost convincing defense for the position that while Scripture forbade all idolatry, it had entrusted the responsibility for rooting out the evil practice, not to individual citizens, but to governments."

Laurens nodded, tapping a finger on his knee. "Just what I suspected. We have a Lutheran in our city desirous of felling two hawks with one arrow—the Calvinists and the Catholics."

Dirck smiled. "No doubt about it. The real sting of the booklet lies in its tail, where the author boldly insinuates that the motives of the image-breakers lie in disregard for authority, not in noble indignation over religious misdeeds."

"Fiery words! I'd love to get ahold of that one myself and plant it in some Beggars' knapsacks just to see them rage." Barthelemeus raised his hands and laughed.

"He has one line absolutely certain to enrage even the Great Beggar," Dirck recalled. "He said the image-breakers were so void of piety that they could not so much as recite the 'Our Father.'"

Meister Laurens had been leaning gradually farther forward in his chair as Dirck talked. His mouth opened as if in concert with his ears, until at last he raised his head and shouted, "Prima! Prima!"

"Just imagine what Brederode will do with that one!" Barthelemeus clapped his hands, and all three burst into laughter.

"Did you read it all?" Barthelemeus asked.

"The young man read it to me. I think he was enamored with his own voice. Sounded like a member of one of our Chambers of Rhetoric."

"We think that's what he is," Laurens interrupted, "a showman chosen for his theatrical abilities and not necessarily for his sympathies with the cause which the tract promotes."

"How came you two to know all these things?" Dirck searched both men's faces. "Were you hiding in the bushes beneath my window? Or was the man a friend of yours?"

Barthelemeus and Meister Laurens looked at each other once more and hesitated before the younger man finally spoke. "*Ja*, how did it happen, Meister? You were the one who heard. And you were hiding in some bushes, but not Dirck's, eh?"

Laurens laughed. "You might say. My wife and I were walking through the woods on our way home from church. There is one spot—you may know it—where the pathway is bordered by a rather high shrub of wild berry bushes."

Dirck nodded. "I know it well, just beyond where the river curves to the west?"

"That is the place. 'Twas there we began to hear voices coming from the river. It sounded as if two men were rowing in a boat, and they were imprudent enough to forget how voices are carried over the water."

"Not the kind of men I'd want to entrust with my secrets," Barthelemeus said, gesturing with his right hand.

"They were talking about my visitor?" Dirck asked.

"Evidently they were the plotters behind the whole thing. They talked about hiring the dramatic speaker from the Vreugdendal Rhetoric Chamber and how he told them he'd found you in lamplight and showed you the paper and you'd sent him away empty. Said something about your having Munsterite views that barred the use of all images in churches. Still they'd hoped you'd be so eager to dispute the popish use of icons that you'd fall into their trap. 'We'll find a way yet,' I heard one of the men say. Then they evidently beached the boat and went out of earshot."

Dirck had sat dumbfounded through the whole story. He shook his head and stared at his friends for a long moment before he could speak.

"Are you certain you heard right?"

"You've already corroborated all the details," Barthelemeus reminded him. "They fit your experience."

"But why?" He couldn't believe it yet.

"They have a reason. May not be a very good one, but they have one, and they considered that image paper a choice morsel of bait for the trap your enemies have set for you," Laurens said.

"Enemies? But I have no enemies."

Meister Laurens looked him straight in the eye and said, "Dirck, every man that traffics in ideas has enemies. Can it be you did not know?"

"But I have exercised such caution," he protested. "You both know how carefully I screen the books. Every contestable message must be veiled and subtle, or it does not pass across this counter."

"And what of the books with clearly stated antipopish messages? The ones you dispense from your attic?" Laurens asked.

"I screen my customers fully as well as I do the books. The few books that go through my attic are put into the hands of close and trusted friends, of the sort I know from long association to be of one mind with us."

"Aha," Barthelemeus slapped his thighs, "I have it!"

"What have you?"

"An answer. Have you on any occasion refused a Calvinist nobleman when he asked to place one of his tracts in your shop?"

"More than once," Dirck answered quickly. "Just last week, in fact. Calvinists, Beggars, Lutherans, even some of our own persuasions I've turned them all away at some time or another. If I have a reputation to arouse anyone's ire, it is at this point."

"Then, my friend," Laurens began, "why are you so overcome with surprise at this turn of events? If you will not give the Calvinists aid, they are prepared to bait their trap with sectarian materials of one kind or another until you agree to sell one of them. Then they can run off to the inquisitors and report that you are selling seditious books. The swordsmen will be the very next strangers to knock on you door."

Dirck shook his head once more and mumbled over and over, "Not in Breda, not in Breda, not . . . Great and merciful God, what will happen to us all?"

"Breda is changing, Dirck," Barthelemeus said, his voice pleading for belief. "If you would protect *The Crane's Nest* and your family in the days to come, you must act now."

"Act? How?" Dirck was sitting in a heavy fog, his brain numb, his eyes unseeing, and his ears hearing one line over and over, "Not in Breda, not in Breda . . ."

Barthelemeus was shaking him, nearly shouting into his face. "Open this door to no more strangers, do you hear me?"

"Especially at night," Laurens added.

Dirck nodded.

"And the books up in your attic, the ones you reserve for select friends," Barthelemeus went on, "you must gather up every suspicious one, and we will find a way to hide them for you."

"And take it from a schoolmaster, you'd best be prepared to flee when the crane drops one more stone."

"Flee this place?" It was more than he could take in. "Where would I go?"

"Any place would be better than the one where they know they can find you," Barthelemeus said. "I make a trip this week to the south. I could take you in my wagonload of fine cloth to the cloth market in Antwerp, and none would ever know."

"Antwerp?" Dirck shuddered.

"Haven't you family there?"

"*Ja*, but we are all in danger in that place." The world spun in little circles in Dirck's head.

"Then, perhaps you might all move on," Laurens suggested. "There are a few safe havens yet in this world for our people."

Dirck shook his head slowly and tapped a finger on his knee. "I cannot leave Breda," he said. "Surely. . ." But, *nay*, nothing could be sure in these times. When the inquisitors pounded on his front door he must flee through the back window. Or when the witch-hunters roamed the streets in search of women reported to be mad . . . What was he thinking? The shivers that ran up and down the length of his spine were already forming little gooseflesh on his arms.

"We will serve as eyes and ears for your crane," Laurens said, his voice authoritative, commanding. "When we come again, it will be through the side door into your living quarters. You must answer no more inquiries at your shop door, do you hear?"

Dirck nodded.

"Gather up the books," Barthelemeus added, "and be ready to flee in an eyeblink."

"In the meantime," Laurens said in his calm manner, "I seem to recall that the Sweet Singer of Israel once said,

'The God who girds me with strength,
Trains my hands for battle,
So that my arms can bend a bow of bronze,
And my feet have not slipped.'

You can find it in the eighteenth psalm, I believe. And now, *jongens* . . ."

The schoolmaster stood to his feet, and Barthelemeus followed. When they'd left, Dirck lingered with his precious books. Never had he felt so fearful and so alone. If only his wife could be the way she was when he married her.

There were days even now when she was free of those headaches and howling spells. On those days he would bring her into the sanctuary of this bookshop and let her look at the books she loved. He found courage just watching her smooth the covers with her fingers, as if tracing each detail of the intricate embossed designs and letters. Then she'd open them with all the reverence one would give to an old handwritten, illuminated volume chained to a table in a monastery library. Sometimes she'd read for a time, her lips swishing in a gentle whisper. Other times, she just looked, often calling him to share in the excitement of some new discovery she'd made.

In this literary woman, he saw hopeful glimmers of the wife she was so long ago—a woman so industrious, cheerful, and full of love for the books that on the days he had to travel, he could leave *The Crane's Nest* in her charge.

Dirck sighed, closed the door on his shop, and headed down the hall. "Great, merciful God," his heart cried out, "if only you could let me have my wife again, at least for what remains of this melancholy day."

In the big room, he found Tante Lysbet stirring the great pot of soup on the fire and Gretta sitting peacefully in her seat by the window. She looked up when he entered the room and smiled.

"Dear husband," she pleaded in a calm and pleasant voice, "please come sit here and read from God's big book."

He pulled out the old volume, seated himself beside his wife, and turned to Psalm eighteen. "I love Thee, O Lord, my Strength, O Lord, my Rock and my Fortress and my Rescuer . . ,"

He would read on and not stop so long as Gretta listened. For as he read, the noise and clamor of a Breda gone mad began to fade from his troubled mind.

---

At the Beguinage, Aletta found Moeder Kaatje in a highly agitated state.

"Sit down, my child," she urged, then sighed deeply and rubbed her bulging belly. "There is something I must tell you—now, before . . . before I give birth to this child."

Aletta obeyed, seating herself on the plain wooden stool beside the bed. She reached out a hand and laid it on the woman's arms. "What is it, Moeder Kaatje?" Then, as the woman winced with pain and beads of perspiration glistened in the subdued light, Aletta added, "Easy, easy now. Perhaps you should rest first."

"*Nay*, you must hear it now." Moeder Kaatje fought to control the quivering of her lips.

Aletta's heart wept with her. What must she tell that could be so urgent and so painful?

"Many years ago," she began, "I came here to this Beguinage to live and work."

"You were once a Beguine? You never told me."

"It was after the death of the last of my family," she explained, each word the obvious product of deliberate, thoughtful choice. "My vader and moeder had both died in the pestilence. I gave my inheritance to the Beguinage and promised God I would spend my life here, serving the needs of the sick and the poor."

She lay quietly, her breathing heavy, her gaze turned toward the far wall. Aletta stroked her arm while trying to make room in her mind for this strange new image of "Sister Kaatje."

"But," she resumed her story, "I was young, and Hendrick van den Garde was handsome and persistent. We'd known each other since we played in the streets. He was amorous and made such promises—warm hearth, loving care, the kindness of his congenial family, a flock of beautiful children." She stopped abruptly, then looking Aletta full in the eye, asked, "You know the tale of Beatrice?"

"Beatrice, the errant nun who allowed herself to be wooed away from the convent by an enchanting paramour?"

Moeder Kaatje nodded.

"Why, but of course. My moeder read it to me from one of Vader's books. It always made me cry."

"Like all other girls before and beside you. We grow up with it almost in our moeder's milk." She reached a hand out from beneath the bed covers and wiped tears from her cheek. "Sad that so many of us do not heed the warning it contains. If only I had not listened to Hendrick's tender wooings . . ."

Scenes of Beatrice's sad fate flashed through Aletta's mind. According to the tale, the young nun allowed herself to be carried away by her persistent childhood sweetheart to a faraway land where he treated her like a queen until his money ran out. Then he deserted her and their twin sons. The similarities of the two stories sent a shiver up Aletta's spine.

"But, Moeder Kaatje," Aletta said, remembering something Tante Lysbet had taught her, "you were no nun, as Beatrice. Beguines take no binding vows before God and the people in the church. You did not sin by marrying."

"*Ja*, I know. In the eyes of the church, I was free to go whenever I wished. All Beguines are so free. But in the eyes of God—that was another matter."

"What do you mean?"

"I did make a vow. Only God heard it. I made it in secret in the Great

Church on Christmas morning, when the last of my family lay freshly buried."

Aletta picked up a cloth and wiped the moisture from the woman's forehead.

"But, Moeder Kaatje, God has given you a wonderful son."

The woman stared at her, a wildness in her eyes, and then she began to sob. Wondering what she had said amiss, Aletta gathered her in her arms and soothed her till she stopped shaking.

Kaatje resumed her story. "One wonderful son! But, at what a price!"

"At what a price?"

"When Pieter-Lucas was not yet three years old, he became so ill we nearly lost him. I knew it was a punishment from the God who would not release me from my vows. So I promised to dedicate the boy's life, if God would spare him, to take the place I'd left vacant in His service."

Aletta started, "You mean. . . ?" She could not finish the question.

"I mean, I gave Pieter-Lucas to God for the priesthood. God willed it so. . . ." She stumbled over her words.

"Pieter-Lucas never told me these things." Aletta felt her legs go weak, and she fought to hold back the flood of tears now threatening to overwhelm her.

"He did not know," Kaatje whispered between sobs.

"You did not tell him?"

"I saw no urgency to tell the boy too soon. As the years passed by, I thought little about my vow. But God never let me quite forget. I've carried many more children in my lifetime, yet one by one, God took them from me before they had a chance to see the light of the sun. Each time, I would renew my resolve. But . . ."

She lay silent for a time, biting her lip, not looking at Aletta. "But by then, I had grown to love you, Aletta . . . to dream of the day when you would marry my son . . . become the daughter God would not give me from my womb. I could not bear to give you up. Always I've begged God for one more child, that I might give it back to Him . . . to take Pieter-Lucas' place in my vows." Soft sobs filled the room.

"Moeder Kaatje," Aletta spoke, "remember how, when Beatrice repented of her sin and returned to the convent, she discovered that all through her long absence the Virgin Mary had fulfilled her daily duties so that she was not missed by the sisters there?"

A smile played at the corners of Kaatje's mouth. "Like Beatrice, I, too, have one last hope."

"You think the Virgin has done your duties here these years?"

"Nay, child. But God is giving me one more child to fulfill my vows.

My repentance comes late, and this old Kaatje is broken and used up. I shall not live to raise this last child."

"Say not such things," Aletta reprimanded.

"I am ready to go . . . and you, child, must promise that this child of my brokenness will be dedicated from the day it is born. Nothing must hinder. For if it does, then Pieter-Lucas must fulfill my vows."

"Does he know it yet?" Aletta felt her grip tighten on Moeder's arm.

"At last I told him, just before he left in search of Hendrick." She let the words out one at a time.

Aletta looked down on the woman's pinched face while her own heart screamed out, "God, have mercy! Have mercy!"

"You are young yet, Aletta. I fear it takes a lifetime of pain to learn that God is cruel and harsh. If we would escape His fury, we must bow to His whims."

"Hush, Moeder Kaatje, no more now." Aletta tried to stop what was growing into a tirade from the lips that had always before spoken only kind words.

"I cannot hush. You must know it now, before you are trapped by the mistakes I have made and must suffer the grave consequences." She grimaced with pain and gripped Aletta's hand tightly, relaxing at last to go on. "God writes all our vows in His book—whether uttered in secret places of the mind or before His holy altar of gold and candles. We may fight Him if we choose, but in the end He will win. He always wins. . . ."

Kaatje closed her eyes and lay limp on the pillow. Only the steady rhythmic heaving of her round belly and raspy breathing assured the girl that she still lived.

Aletta kissed the wrinkled brow, then lay her own cheek against Kaatje's and wept, washing the beloved face with her tears. How long she hovered there, she never knew. For her stunned mind had turned into a vast hollow space where no thoughts moved about.

She felt a hand on her shoulder and sat instantly erect to face Sister Gertrude, who motioned toward the door. "Time for you to go, young friend." The voice was kind but firm.

"She will be all right?"

"As God wills it." Sister Gertrude's face, framed tightly by her white hood, showed tenderness. "We are but the caretakers, not the healers here."

"Please let me stay longer," Aletta pleaded.

"Nay, child. Vrouw Kaatje needs all the rest she can get before her childbirth."

"I will sit quietly and not disturb her. And when her time comes, perhaps I can be of some help. She has no family here, dear abandoned soul."

Sister Gertrude laid a hand on Aletta's shoulder and said with a tone of finality in her voice, "I have a whole flock of experienced Beguines and the help of God himself. Go now, and you may return tomorrow." She lowered her head slightly and gave Aletta a commanding stare accompanied by a crooked half-smile.

Aletta planted one more kiss on Moeder Kaatje's forehead. The woman opened her eyes wide, drew up her legs beneath the covers, and let out a curdling scream. Frantically, she grabbed Aletta's hand and held tightly to it while her wild eyes pleaded with the girl for pity. Then as suddenly as the outburst had come, it subsided. She dropped Aletta's hand and closed her eyes once more in sleep.

"Go now," the Beguine ordered. But Aletta stood rooted, her hand resting on the beaded brow. How could she leave now? Hadn't she been charged with the well-being of this child soon to be born?

"I must stay to help," she cried out.

Sister Gertrude took her by the arm and led her forcibly across the room, out into the crisp autumn air, over the cobbles of the courtyard, and out through the heavy wooden gate. Aletta heard the gate latch shut with a cruel thud.

Tears of anger washed over her face, and she leaned against the Beguinage wall, unable for a time to remove herself farther from the suffering woman she loved so dearly. She fingered the dove in her bodice and, in the descending twilight, stared into the confused jumble of multicolored giant oaks and lindens tossed by the wind against a background of gray clouds. What did it all mean? If only Pieter-Lucas were here.

"I need him so," she said aloud, unsure of whom she was addressing. "His moeder needs him so. His unborn sibling needs him even more."

Aimlessly, Aletta wandered up and down the blustery streets amidst a flurry of skittering leaves, searching, hoping, waiting for the sudden appearance of the brown-cowled monk, the familiar stableboy, the aspiring painter, in whatever guise he might stride back into her life and restore order to the chaos. With a growing sense of direction, she walked down to the water and gazed as far out through the Harbor Gate as possible. She stopped to peer into the *Kasteel* stables. Back on Annastraat, she put her ear once more to the little house of the van den Garde's in search of life.

At last she crept into the devastated church and knelt and wept before the remains of the altar of the Holy Ghost where "The Anointing" had once hung. "Great God in the heaven," she prayed, "I know it is presumptuous of me to come so freely and about matters other than forgiveness for my many transgressions." She paused to shift her position and think on what she'd just prayed. "Yet my vader has shoved me from his bosom by giving commands which I cannot obey. Moeder Kaatje has told me strange and fearful things this day. Sister Gertrude has put me out of her room in the infirmary. And Pieter-Lucas! How desperately I long to have him here beside me. Please keep him safe in that big frightening world where he roams about looking for his vader. Bring him back now. And heal Moeder Kaatje that she may see his face and raise her baby to fulfill her vow."

---

### 22nd and 23rd of Peat Month (September), 1566

That night Aletta fell asleep with tears wetting her feather bed and Opa's dove clasped in her hand. She had a desolate feeling that the prayer she had prayed that afternoon rose no farther than the lips that uttered it. A heavy cloud of foreboding hung over her, filling her dreamworld with goblins, ghouls, and winged evil presences. All night she tossed in her bed and came awake often. Finally, she awoke with a start to the sound of an old familiar signal—three short brisk taps on her window shutter.

"Pieter-Lucas!" She clambered out of bed, hurried to the door, unbolted, and tugged it open, her mind alive with a vivid image of the full face, long blond curls, and deep blue eyes that had a way of making her heart melt.

But Pieter-Lucas did not stand at the door to welcome her. Instead, a pair of doves cooed from the fence and a noisy cart rambled down the street, its horse snorting and prancing hoofs across the rain-slicked cobblestones in the faint light of dawn.

*Where is he?* Frantic with haste, she wrapped her cape around her head and shoulders and escaped out into the early morning.

With a hurried glance over the fence at Pieter-Lucas' home, she satisfied herself that he was not there and dashed on to the Beguinage. Sister Gertrude met her at the door and led her into the semidarkness of Moeder Kaatje's sickroom where one tall taper flickered faintly on the bedside table.

Aletta looked about the room for Pieter-Lucas. Not seeing him, she stood before the Beguine and demanded, "Where is her son?"

"Her son?" she responded, perplexed. "He has not come yet."

"B-but, he called me. . . ." Aletta shook her head, as if to clear away the clouds gathering there. "I heard him knocking on my window shutter."

"Methinks it was God sent His angel to summon you, child," Sister Gertrude said with warmth. "All through the long night hours, the woman has been calling your name."

"And her child—has it been born?"

"It was a girl."

"It was? But it is not?"

"The poor child never breathed. But at least the moeder lives." She moved toward the door. "I go and leave you two alone."

Aletta felt sick. A hard lump filled up the pit of her stomach. In a fog, she moved toward the bed where Moeder Kaatje lay unstirring, her wispy hair straggling about the pinched features. Aletta leaned over the silent form and kissed her forehead. The haggard woman opened her eyes with a flutter of eyelids and gave her a contented smile. She spoke so faintly Aletta had to lean toward her to catch the words.

"God has been merciful, my child."

"*Ja*, Moeder Kaatje." She fought to keep her voice even. She forced a smile across her face and a lie from her lips. "Pieter-Lucas is on his way, and all will be well." She patted the wrinkled hand. "He will care for you soon."

"*Nay*, but his care must be for you," Kaatje corrected, smiling faintly. She strained to raise herself on her elbow.

Aletta laid a hand on her shoulder. "Moeder Kaatje, rest please."

She smiled, tilting her head slightly toward the far corner of the room. "God is merciful," she repeated. "He gave me one more healthy child. Hear my newborn daughter cry?"

Aletta listened to the silence and swallowed the tears that rose with the lump in her throat. Never had she so wished to hear a baby cry. Oh, for an herbal elixir to bring back the child.

"Pieter-Lucas will yet come with his Vader Hendrick," Aletta said unsteadily.

Kaatje shook her head. "*Nay*, child. My husband comes never again."

"But Pieter-Lucas promised. . . ."

"I tarry not . . . I go. . . ."

"Do not say such an awful thing," Aletta felt herself approaching hysteria. Pieter-Lucas must come first. His moeder dare not leave her alone.

"See to it my daughter keeps my vow. . . ." Kaatje van den Garde closed her eyes and sank back into herself.

Make sure her daughter keeps her vow? Aletta was the only daughter she had left! "Great God, what is the meaning. . . ?"

Kaatje opened her eyes and grabbed Aletta by the hand. She squeezed limply, smiled wanly, and whispered, "Tell my son that God will always win. *Vaarwel!*" Slowly, methodically, she pressed Aletta's hand to her dried lips. Then she let her own hands fall to the bed. Her eyes closed once more, and the rhythm of her breathing grew heavy, irregular, and rattly.

Aletta dropped to her knees beside the bed. She lay her cheek one more time against the dying woman's and let the tears flow until at last Moeder Kaatje's breathing ceased, and her cheek no longer moved.

Silence hovered over the death chamber and held Aletta in a smothering grip. Looking up, she caught sight of yesterday's bouquet of asters. Their heads drooped. Dead like the embers of Moeder Kaatje's hearth, like the child that would never cry, like all her own hopes for the future.

"Great God," she screamed out, "this cannot be. Ask me not to keep Moeder Kaatje's vow. There has to be another way. Pieter-Lucas and I have made a vow of our own. Did you not write it in your book?"

Instinctively, she fumbled for the dove in her bosom and caressed it with sweating fingers. The feel of its jagged edges worn nearly smooth and the ridges of paint creating beak and wings caught her away for one last fanciful moment with the man she would always love. In her imagination, he who had risked his life to save this dove and left it with her as a surety of his love knelt beside her in the heavy gloom!

The tears ran in streamlets over Aletta's warm cheeks. She fancied she was yielding her trembling body to the embrace of her beloved. She pressed her ears into his strong arms to shut out the daunting question pelting her from every corner of the room: "Which vow will you keep? Which vow. . . ? Which vow. . . ?"

Only when the Beguine sisters had arrived to prepare Kaatje van den Garde's body for burial did the girl let her warm dream recede into the shadows.

"If only you had let me stay," she railed at the white-hooded women who prodded her toward the door. "Perhaps I could have saved the child."

In a calm, methodical, almost detached voice, Sister Gertrude said, "No one can save a life that God has ordained to take to himself."

---

### 23rd and 24th of Peat Month (September), 1566

Aletta walked through the rest of that day in a low-lying, spirit-chilling fog that neither Tante Lysbet's constant instructions nor her own studied efforts could dispel. Her heart ached for someone to listen to her pain, to offer her a soft shoulder for crying. Robbin's cheerful prattle seemed only to deepen her gloom.

Eagerly, she crawled into her cupboard bed that night. But sleep did not come easily at her coaxing. Nor did it hold her fast when it came. How often she awoke during the night, she did not count, nor how many times Roland sounded, reminding her of the fourteen bells, all ringing to one side. "God wins, God wins, God wins," they seemed to say.

Sometime after four bells, she heard muffled stirrings in the attic chamber above her bed. Terrified, she sat upright. "Great God," she whispered, "is it Moeder Kaatje's ghost?"

Frantically, she gathered up all Pieter-Lucas' little carved wooden animals in her arms and hugged them. The world swirled in big blurry circles around her. Images of Moeder Kaatje and the mythical Beatrice spun round and round in her head. The dying woman's voice sounded in her ear, repeating the same line over and over, crescendoing into a deafening shout: "Tell Pieter-Lucas GOD WILL ALWAYS WIN!"

The noises from the attic stopped, and she heard a rustling of the curtain that sealed off her bed cupboard. A presence, unseen in the dark, pressed through the curtain, and a soft whisper sounded in the dazed girl's ear.

"Come quickly."

"*Nay*, go away," she said, clutching Pieter-Lucas' animals more tightly than ever.

"Come quickly." The voice came a second time with an audible urgency.

"Who are you?" Aletta demanded.

"Tante Lysbet. Shh. Come."

Tante Lysbet? Aletta struggled to clear the mental fog. Her heart thumping wildly, she laid down the armload of her treasures and crept out of bed. Tentatively, she followed the woman across the room and up the ladder into the attic apartment which Tante Lysbet shared with drying herbs and Vader Dirck's extra books. A single candle burned on a small table, casting elongated shadows up the big beams and across the slanted ceiling tiles. The bed looked as if it had not been disturbed for sleep, and about the room stood several bags stuffed as if for travel.

"What is it?" Aletta whispered.

The woman motioned her to sit on the bed, then sat beside her. Without looking directly at the girl, she started to speak. "Your vader . . ." She cleared her throat, then started again. "Your moeder . . ."

Aletta looked quizzically at the woman by her side. "*Ja?*" she asked.

The longtime midwife, housekeeper, and nursemaid sighed and began once more, in the short, studied syllables most typical of her speech. "When the sun comes up again, soon now, I go away. . . ." She paused, then added a hurried phrase, "And you must begin to care for your moeder."

"Wh-what do you mean?" Aletta stammered. She pinched the loose skin on the back of her arm. Surely she must be dreaming. All her life, Aletta had rested in the comfort of knowing Tante Lysbet was nearby to help. At first she'd lived in the Beguinage. Whenever Moeder Gretta howled too much, she would come with her herbs and sometimes stay for a few days. In the months before Robbin was born, she had brought her bags and moved them into this attic room. Since then, she'd been one more member of the household.

Tante Lysbet was still talking, as if Aletta had not interrupted. "She is your moeder, you know. You are seventeen, almost eighteen. Time you learned."

Aletta thought she heard a sniffling sound and turned to see a glistening tear slide down the tall woman's well-chiseled face. She'd never seen her cry before and felt a rush of pity for the woman who had always been like a firm rock to her. No, this was no dream.

"But I don't know where to begin, Tante Lysbet. 'Tis you who chooses all the best herbs to calm her wild melancholy fits. She is used to your soothing touch, your voice, the healing herbal brews you make for her. *Nay*, Tante Lysbet, you must not go away."

"Hush, child! Your time has come. You've helped me all these years. Do what you've seen me do, pray each day for wisdom, and beware of strangers."

"Strangers?" Aletta tried to think what strangers she would meet. For Moeder never left their little house on Annastraat, and all the people who came here went only into *The Crane's Nest*. "What strangers?"

Tante Lysbet didn't answer for a long space. Then, with a painful air, she proceeded as if choosing each word carefully. "I've no idea what strangers. Only, because you will be responsible, you need to be warned."

An uneasiness crept over Aletta, almost as foreboding as that she'd felt this morning in Kaatje's death chamber.

"Your moeder's illness springs from strong melancholy humors in her body," Lysbet was saying. "Many people insist that all such illnesses come from the presence of demons."

"My moeder has no demons!"

"I know," she retorted defensively. "Only some people who do not know her will suspect she is a witch who harbors demons."

"A witch?" Aletta had heard wild tales about witches. They flew on broomsticks through the night to evil meetings in the sky called Witches' Sabbaths. If city guardsmen caught them, they were tied to a stake and burned in the city marketplace. Nothing in such stories could ever possibly happen to Moeder. "Nay, Tante Lysbet. Not Moeder."

"The state of her mind is quite enough evidence for some people to accuse her. Beware especially of devout and faithful pious souls."

"Devout and faithful pious souls?"

"They are the ones most quick to see in your moeder the figure of an evil witch . . . most eager to purge the world of all evil presences." The nursemaid's shoulders sagged, her voice quavered.

"Oh, Tante Lysbet." Aletta trembled. Oh to be a little girl once more, sitting on Vader Dirck's lap in the evening, listening to his deep voice reading from the pages of a beautiful book. Or to be seated behind Pieter-Lucas on a white steed riding into their dreams. . . .

Tante Lysbet turned to face Aletta. For the first time, she looked straight at the frightened girl and spoke barely above a whisper, with an urgent sort of vigor. "Watch especially for folks who gape at her or give you advice on how to treat her. If ever you discover sprigs of betony beneath her night cap or bunches of button leek hanging before the door, beware, beware!"

"Betony . . . button leek?"

"Pious witch-hunters use them to frighten demons away. If ever you see them, beg your vader to flee to Oudewater!"

"Why Oudewater?"

"Never mind why. He will know. Just make sure he gets her there."

Aletta shook her head in tiny, jiggling movements, as if to dislodge the confused tangle of grievous torments about death and vows and unanswered questions about her new duties as Moeder's nursemaid.

The attic room fell uncomfortably silent. Tante Lysbet stood and walked the two paces to the other side of the room. From one of her bulging packed bags, she lifted a wooden chest about the size of three of Vader Dirck's books stacked together. Her worn hands caressed the little treasure box, and she neither spoke a word nor cast a glance in Aletta's direction. She set the box on the table next to the lighted candle.

"How beautiful!" Aletta exclaimed.

Fingers of dancing candlelight played with the shiny black box and offered tantalizing glimpses of brilliant decorations on all its sides. Still unspeaking, Lysbet reached behind her neck and pulled a long leather cord over her head. At the end dangled a crude, square-cut key which she inserted into a lock Aletta could not see. Then she lifted the lid, and for one incredible moment Aletta saw the fantastic design clearly. An ornate spray of simple-petaled flowers in variegated shades of pink, blue, red, and gold was set off sharply by recurring clumps of tiny white starry blossoms.

"Here," Tante Lysbet said. "Take this with you." She'd pulled a little tattered book from the box and handed it to Aletta. Quickly, she snapped the lid back on the box and gave the startled girl a cryptic explanation. "My moeder's herbal. Use it often, learn its pages."

"Nay, Tante, I can't," Aletta protested. "It's your book. You'll need it."

"I know it by heart. Guard it always, and let no one take it from you." Coming closer, she whispered into Aletta's ear, "Not your vader, not another soul on earth, do you hear? It tells you all the secrets you will need to help you care for your moeder."

"Thank you," Aletta stammered and looked at the woman with a longing she never thought she'd feel for her.

"*Vaarwel*," Tante Lysbet said. Aletta knew from the cracking in her voice that tears streamed down those stern cheeks once again.

Tante Lysbet's voice regained its commandeering tone. "Now, back to your bed, before . . . before Roland calls you to begin the day." With her usual brusqueness, she escorted Aletta toward the ladder, where she held the light to show the way down in safety.

At the bottom of the ladder, Vader Dirck met her with another light.

"Vader, what is it?" she pleaded, grasping his arm.

"Shh." He frowned. "Make haste to tie your clothes into a bundle. We must leave this place, now!"

"Leave?" Was there no end to the uprooting torments of this awful night?

"Ask no questions. Pack your bundle." Never had she heard him so impatient.

"And where is Moeder?" Hadn't Lysbet told her she was in charge?

"I have her already settled in the wagon."

"Wagon?"

"Hurry, child, there is no time to dally," he rushed her.

With her mind a dizzy blur of questions and with feelings too deep to touch in the rush of hurried preparations, Aletta scooped Pieter-Lucas' carved animals into her feather bag along with whatever clothes she could grab in the lamplight. She tied them into a bundle, slipped into her street shoes, and headed down the hallway toward the bookshop door where Vader stood waiting.

Vader ushered her out into the night with the cryptic instructions: "Say not one more word until I give you notice. Not one word."

"*Ja*, Vader," she replied.

He picked her up, bundle and all, and put her down in a waiting wagon, where Moeder and Robbin already slept. He crawled in beside her. Someone else she could not see piled trunks and barrels between them and the door where they had entered, and soon the wheels were creaking and moving unevenly beneath them, and the hoofs of what sounded like a herd of horses were clopping over the misty slickness of the cobbles.

What could she do? She'd promised Pieter-Lucas she would wait for him. And when he returned to find she had indeed not waited? She imagined she felt the warmth of his breath on her forehead and his close embrace. But how could she have known when she made that promise back in the birch wood that her vader was possibly plotting even then to take her suddenly away in the night before Pieter-Lucas had returned?

Roland chimed again, "God wins . . . God wins . . ." Six times he repeated his taunting message. What did it mean?

The wagon rattled over the cobblestones, conjuring up one more image in her already tormented mind. An executioner's stake loomed before her at the foot of Roland's tower. It was piled high with hay and ringed with men bearing spears and pikes and carrying torches. Tied fast to it, she made out the figure of Moeder Gretta's body and heard her terrifying scream. "Aletta, my child, save me, save me!"

"Great God, who indeed will always win," she prayed with a bursting heart and sealed lips, "I must go now to care for Moeder Gretta. Later, when you preserve my life and bring me back, I will take Moeder Kaatje's place in the Beguinage of Breda—unless there is another way. For, whatever it costs, Pieter-Lucas must be free from his moeder's vow. He's been anointed to heal the world with his paintbrushes, not to be an unmarried priest."

She shut her eyes tight, trying to block out the face of Pieter-Lucas, and wept into her bundle in the strange wagon that was wrenching her away from hearth and childhood, vows and dreams.

# PART TWO

# The Wilderness

He whom God anoints to paint His masterpieces
Must first be wounded,
Then driven, limping, into life's bleak Wilderness.
"Take heart," he cries through healing touch
Of transparent angel wings,
And sends him forth at last,
With brushes tied by pierced hands,
To spread fresh healing colors on the canvases
Of other men's desert lives.

Opa Lucas

Miserable thou art, wheresoever thou be,
or whithersoever thou turnest, unless thou
turn thyself to God.

—Thomas à Kempis
*Imitation of Christ*

# CHAPTER NINE

*Kasteel Batestein, Vianen*

27th day of Peat Month (September), 1566

*H*ours, days, nights ran into each other and formed a blurred portrait of anguish in Pieter-Lucas' dulled brain. The colors clashed, the paints dripped in ugly, globby streaks across the canvas of the straw-covered dungeon floor soiled with human waste and crawling with nondescript vermin.

At times he felt so numb from his long confinement that he had to cajole his memory into telling him why he'd come to this wretched hole in the first place. On one such day, the tomblike silence of the underground world was shattered by sounds of a wild party descending the stairs.

"We have guests," Pieter-Lucas said, while visions of tipsy Beggars come to make fun of their plight splashed fear and disgust across the canvas.

"Brederode?" Yaap asked.

"*Ja*, sure, Brederode indeed. You don't think he's ever going to come, do you?" Pieter-Lucas laughed, but without gaiety. During their stay they'd seen a good many Beggar soldiers and cell keepers of one sort or another. And every day the silent, greasy wench paid her regular visits with unappetizing victuals. Yaap never missed an opportunity to remind them all why he was here and that his message was urgent. But Brederode? Indeed it did begin to appear as if he were a phantom from some old nightmare.

The door creaked open, and a small group of men practically fell through. The gaoler led the way. Behind him came a refined-looking white-bearded gentlemen wearing a dark suit, long cloak, and a wide, floppy-brimmed hat, followed by a big staggering man in the plain drab costume the Beggars had adopted as their hallmark. A short stocky soldier in an oversized Beggar's cap came in last and stood dutifully at attention.

"As drunk as he is, that tall one must be your Great Beggar come to call, after all," Pieter-Lucas said out of the side of his mouth and jabbed at Yaap with his elbow. The older boy started, then sat rigid, staring.

"Some hero!" Pieter-Lucas chuckled derisively.

The odor of liquor surrounded the group, and the two "noblemen" moved unsteadily, as if to signal the fact they'd just come from the castle wine cellar. Brederode, the more drunken of the two, stumbled through the doorway laughing raucously. With one arm he swung at his companion, barely managing to sling around his neck a long heavy chain with a large undefinable medallion hanging askew.

"Long live the Beggars!" Brederode drawled. "Long live Dirck Volckertszoon Coornhert, secretary of Haarlem!"

The full-bearded man ducked and nearly tumbled. "God have mercy on us when Dirck Coornhert dons a Beggar's penny," he retorted, pulling the chain off over his head and tossing it to the floor just beyond Pieter-Lucas' reach.

Pieter-Lucas felt a surge of anger awaken an energy in him he thought he'd lost. If only he could reach it, he'd trample that Beggar's penny beneath his feet and finish off the man who dreamed up this whole ghastly idea.

Brederode turned his attention to the two boys and nearly stumbled into the straw beside them. "So, these are the two prisoners you tell me you've had here for a day or two?" His tongue slurred the words.

Pieter-Lucas looked at Yaap. They exchanged glances of incredulity. In a barely audible whisper, Pieter-Lucas exclaimed to his companion, "A day or two?"

Yaap shrugged and rolled his eyes.

"*Ja*, Mijnheer," the gaoler answered.

"Which one of you has the message from Count Ludwig in your pocket?" He looked back and forth between the boys, his bleary eyes moving slowly in rhythm with his head as it jerked from side to side.

"I do, Mijnheer," Yaap responded. With fumbling excitement, he thrust his hand into the inner fold of his doublet and pulled out a smooth, well-pressed piece of folded paper with a heavy wax seal on one side and the name Hendrick Count van Brederode scratched across the other.

"Bring the torch closer," the man ordered. In the flickering light, he examined the seal. "It's Ludwig's all right."

Then, with clumsy fingers, he tore the letter open and scanned its contents. All the while his huge body swayed, his head nodded, and he gave off occasional great echoing belches.

"When did Ludwig give you this letter?" the man stormed, his voice sounding like a cannon. He looked at Yaap, his eyes throwing daggers.

"I . . . I remember not the exact date," the boy stammered, "but it was on the day he wrote it."

"The very day he wrote it?" Brederode roared. "Did you see him write it?"

"I did."

"Did Count Ludwig not tell you that this message required haste?"

"He did, indeed."

"Then why did it take you fifteen days to deliver it?"

"Fifteen days?" Yaap sat up straighter and shook his head vigorously. "*Nay*, but before Roland had chimed one more time after Ludwig sealed it up, my friend and I were on the road. We drove our horses hard all night and arrived here with the next daybreak."

Brederode rested his hands on his hips and glared hard at both boys. Pieter-Lucas hardly knew whether to fear the man's loud voice and stormy disposition or to laugh at the ridiculous sight he posed, still swaying under the influence of the drink he had such a reputation for being enslaved to.

"Then why did you not tell the guards at my gate that you carried an urgent message?"

"I did that, but . . ."

"Well, finish. But what?"

"They refused to believe my story . . . accused me of being a spy . . . threw me here . . . insisting I must wait until you came."

"And you have spent fifteen days here holding my message while I lived in my rooms above, oblivious to it all?" His voice crescendoed till it filled the cell.

For once, Yaap seemed speechless. Brederode turned to his gaoler. "What is the meaning of this, Jacobus?"

"You were not back from Amsterdam yet when the boys arrived, Mijnheer." The gaoler's words tumbled out in awkward haste.

"But I've been back from Amsterdam for over a week now. And you've kept these boys locked up all this time without telling me about their message?" The Great Beggar stood feet apart, hands spread, mouth gaping.

"Uh . . . Oh . . . please, Mijnheer, I can explain," the gaoler stammered.

Brederode yanked the man's belt off and with it the ring of jangling keys. He grabbed him roughly and shoved him to the floor, nearly toppling his own tipsy body in the process. "Explain, indeed!" he bellowed, his words still slurred. "Beg, rather. Beg for your life! It's time you sat on this floor in irons for fifteen days."

He motioned to the silent soldier in the doorway. "You, there, dumb man with the hat over your ears, you fasten him to the wall—ankles and arms—and if he gives you trouble, I'll finish him off here and now."

The soldier followed orders, and the big man zigzagged across the cell until he stood over the quavering gaoler.

"And when this revolt suffers a defeat because I did not follow Ludwig's instructions in timely fashion," he roared, "I'll be back to hang you from the gallows."

Brederode stumbled toward the door, beckoning to his companion and mumbling curses into his helter-skelter beard. Before they'd reached the door, the man he called Coornhert hung back.

"Pardon me, Great Beggar," he said, motioning toward the boys on the floor.

"For what?" Brederode drawled.

"Perhaps 'tis no account of mine, but methinks these boys have served their time and all unworthily no doubt as well."

"Ah, *ja*, but sure. You, there, with the hefty hammer"—he motioned to the soldier standing once more by the door—"loosen their chains . . . give them decent lodging for the night . . . prepare their horses . . . bring them to my council chamber at dawn." Turning to nod toward Yaap, he nearly stumbled once more. "I'll have a letter ready for you to take to Ludwig by morning."

The stout little soldier pried the irons from the boys' arms and freed them for the climb, on wobbly legs, up beyond the haunted stench to a terrifying new beginning. Tomorrow Yaap would ride off on one more mission, while Pieter-Lucas would head for home and Moeder Kaatje and Aletta—provided Blesje waited to carry him!

He stumbled up the stairs on legs so stiff and painful they all but refused to move. How would he ever be able to ride a horse? But with each step that dragged him closer to the inevitable, he felt increased energy. Once at the top, he stopped, inhaled deeply, and told himself, "Your time has come, *jongen*, to face life alone, to be a man!"

---

29th day of Peat Month (September), 1566

Arriving home in Breda in a rousing late afternoon thunderstorm could hardly be called a warm welcome. Leaden skies poured out their contents in an angry torrent and sent currents swirling over the city's cobblestones and around Blesje's ankles like a renegade river. Across the old bridge, through the fish market, past the church whose tower was swallowed up in the heavy clouds, Pieter-Lucas urged his horse onward.

"Just a few more steps, Blesje."

Visions of Aletta's pink cheeks and inviting smile pumped fresh energy into his limbs. He looked longingly in the direction of *The Crane's Nest* and felt his legs turn to porridge while his heart beat wild rhythms against his ribs. If only he could go straight to her. He sighed, then directed Blesje toward the *Kasteel* stables.

Just as he reined in the horse, a bolt of lightning split through the sheets of rain and cast an eerie luminescence across the little cityscape so full of beckoning memories. Fleeting, uneasy thoughts darted undefined through his mind.

Pieter-Lucas dismounted from Blesje, returning him to the care of the stableboy on duty. With nothing more than a hasty, "I'll be back later," he bounded back out into the sloshing rain and wild thunder, headed for the Beguinage. At the corner of Annastraat, he let himself be enticed by the sight of the bookstore again, and his steps slowed in their path down Caterstraat. "*Nay, jongen,*" he admonished himself. "First things first. Moeder, then Aletta."

But his eyes searched for the light of the lamp that always gleamed from Aletta's window. "Strange," he mused, "where is it? Tante Lysbet always keeps a light burning there. Maybe the storm is hiding it. But even the shutters are closed!" A loud crash of thunder spoke like an alarm bell, and he had to drag his unwilling body on to the Beguinage.

"Maybe she'll be with Moeder—and her newborn child." A chill gripped him, and he felt his body twitch. At least Dirck Engelshofen could not chase him from Aletta's side if he found her there. The Beguinage was the one safe haven left in Breda, a place for healing, not for pain.

He rang the bell, and the black-robed lady with the white starched hood that answered his call invited him to come in, remove his soaking wraps, and be warmed by the little stove in the corner of the simple room.

"Please be seated," the woman said, neither unkindly nor with reassurance. "Sister Gertrude has been expecting you." She disappeared and left Pieter-Lucas with his mouth gaping, trying to ask the questions about the only things that mattered to him. The air had an unexpected chill that matched the weather, and the uneasy thoughts he had so easily dismissed out in the streets were growing into threatening clouds.

When Sister Gertrude entered the room, her face wore a planned-looking smile. "I am glad you have come," she said. "God has smiled upon your travels?"

Pieter-Lucas shuffled his feet and looked down at the cracked red tiles of the floor beneath them. He cleared his throat, then spoke with a dry mouth. "My journey was filled with disappointments and not a few hazards, I fear. But tell me, how fares my moeder and her newborn child? She has given birth by now, has she not?"

"That she has. . . ." The woman's flat voice hung suspended between them.

"Well?" Pieter-Lucas prodded. "And is it well? A girl or another boy?"

"It was a girl. Right beautiful she was."

Pieter-Lucas' heart seemed to stop. He knew it already. "How long did she live?"

"Not past her difficult journey into daylight. The angels delivered her to her Heavenly Father's bosom quietly and without suffering."

The rumble of thunder and cascading of raindrops played a dreary funeral dirge on the roof of the Beguinage as Pieter-Lucas sat swallowing the pains that rose up to choke him. Sister Gertrude did not speak, but in a way he could not explain, he almost welcomed her presence. At last he asked the inevitable question. "And my moeder . . . is she . . . with . . . my sister?"

"Your moeder rests in peace beside your sister. She never knew the child did not live. To the end, she believed she heard her cries, and that belief gave her great comfort."

Tears were welling, more and more difficult to suppress. "And Aletta, my friend from next door, was she with her when she died?"

"She stayed with her to the end and bathed your moeder's cheeks with her own tears. No daughter ever loved more dearly." The Beguine's voice flowed through the room like warm milk sweetened with honey yet spiced with a bitter herb.

Pieter-Lucas stood and made for the door. "I must go to her," he started.

"Your moeder?"

"*Nay*, to Aletta. She will take me to Moeder Kaatje's burial place. . . ." His voice trailed off, and he reached for the door latch, vaguely aware that his hostess went on talking, yet not hearing a word. Midway across the threshold, he felt the woman grip his arm and heard her shout,

"*Jongen*, hear me." Annoyed, he paused, not looking back at her. "You will not find your friend," she went on, her words more forceful than he dreamed she was capable of.

"What do you mean, I will not find her? She did not die too?" He wheeled about and stared into the somber white-framed face.

"*Nay, jongen*, but she is no longer in Breda."

"What?"

"Sometime during the night following Kaatje's death, the wagon of Abarth de Koopman slipped out of the gates of Breda, and rumors have it that it was carrying Dirck Engelshofen and his family."

"How can this be?" He glared at her. "Aletta promised she would be here when I returned—and she does not lie!"

Sister Gertrude spoke with an unconvincing calm. "A young woman does not always have the power to keep her promises. As I said, her whole family is gone."

"Where did they take her?" he demanded.

"Not a soul in Breda seems to know. It was a secret operation."

"And Tante Lysbet? Surely she must know. Or did she go along?"

"*Ach*, I fear I have no answers for you—only more rumors."

"*Ja*, and what do the rumors report?"

"I've heard it said that a person thought to be the housekeeper was seen running toward the birch wood shortly before daybreak. Beyond that, silence."

"Someone must know!" Pieter-Lucas shouted.

"God only can know such things."

God indeed! Pieter-Lucas wanted to scream or stomp his feet or shake a fist toward the skies.

Sister Gertrude touched him gently on the shoulder. "Come with me," she said. "I shall take you to your moeder's burial spot. Only, first, you must know that the Beguinage holds some secrets rarely exposed to anyone from the outside world. The place I am about to take you is one of these. But first you must promise me that you will never betray this secret to another soul."

"Why should I promise?" Dark thoughts furrowed his brow and narrowed his eyes to a squint.

"Because I asked you to."

"But why?"

Sister Gertrude hesitated. "Beguines do not normally meet such challenges to our authority here. But, if you must know, in some people's minds your moeder will always be associated with her husband, the image-breaker. It could go very ill with her remains, and with those who guard those remains, should their whereabouts be revealed."

"Curses on the memory of that wicked Hendrick van den Garde!" Pieter-Lucas muttered.

The Beguine drew in her breath sharply, straightened her body, and rebuked him, her voice heavy with clerical aloofness, "Leave the vengeance to Almighty God. Just give me your word."

"All right, you have my word. Now, take me to her." He followed out into the courtyard and through the herb garden, past the last apartment to a tall thicket of briar bushes with a scanty fall leaf cover. In the far corner, up against the brick wall that separated the Beguinage from the prince's Valkenburg Park, a low, narrow opening let them into the thicket. Bushes spread out over most of the enclosure, with only a small open patch letting in the daylight and the rain. The ground was covered with a wild coarse plant, and a path ran through the middle.

"Here, beneath this spot, we buried your moeder, her infant folded in her arms," Sister Gertrude said.

Pieter-Lucas looked at the place she indicated. "But there is no marker, nothing to assure me that this is even a true burial place. How can I be sure of what I do not see?"

"*Jongen*," she spoke with indignant pride, "I am a woman of honor, a Beguine sister. Like your friend, Aletta, I do not lie. Your moeder and I have known each other well over the years. I could tell you more, but, as I say, the Beguinage has its secrets."

Vaguely aware that the woman had moved away and left him alone, Pieter-Lucas stooped down and ran his fingers through the ground cover till he felt a break cutting a straight line that squared off into a corner. Satisfied that indeed the ground had been broken here, he fell to his knees and tried to picture Moeder Kaatje lying beneath him in the heather. He saw her as she had looked when she told him of her vow and bade him Godspeed on his trip in search of Hendrick. Her eyes were hollow, sunken, her skin wrinkled and grayish. Her hands were twiglike as they grasped his and she spoke her final warning, "God will always win!"

God will always win, indeed!

"Cold, unmerciful God," he screamed out into the abating storm. "Cruel God of the Beggars, who claims victories over weak and innocent bereaved women and young men with long lives before them. I need you not!"

Great sobs broke out, then, tearing loose from his very heart. For a long while he lay his face on the ground and let his tears mingle with the drops still falling from the briar bushes. Then the tears stopped, and he curled his big hands into hard fists. Fueled by all the pent-up anger of what now seemed like a lifetime of frustration, he pounded a hollowed-out hole in the heather.

"Oh, Moeder, Moeder, my moeder!"

A surprising shaft of sunshine, slanting low from the direction of the *Kasteel* market square, fell across his shoulders and warmed the dampness of his curls. Looking up, he saw above the rim of the thicket a wide, perfectly curved rainbow. The huge transparent palette of intense hues of violet, blue, green, yellow, orange, and red glowed at him against a backdrop of the dark clouds. From long ago and far away, Moeder Kaatje's voice rang in his ears. "A bow in the cloud is God's promise in the heart." She used to say it to him every time she saw a rainbow.

Again he pounded the heather and cried out, "Nay, Moeder, the God you talk about only breaks His promises. 'Tis in my hands now. This time I shall win! You shall see!"

He shoved the voice from his heart, stood to his feet, and hurried out of the strange burial ground. Through the herb garden and on to the Beguinage gate he went. "Time now to find Aletta," he told himself. He nodded to Sister Gertrude, who waited to let him out.

Crossing the threshold, he grunted a perfunctory "Thank you" and walked out into the street. He hung his head and knotted his hands into angry fists. With each step, he stomped in fury and demanded of the stones beneath his feet, "Where is she? In all of Breda, you alone may hold the secret of the disappearance of my beloved."

Their answers came like taunts—maddening visions of a series of happy scenes played out here. Finally, he envisioned himself with Opa and Aletta on that memorable last Artists' Pilgrimage. All the lovely dreams he had shared with Aletta in this place now lay scattered in shreds across the cobbles.

He looked up once more. This time, *The Crane's Nest* stood before him, completely painted with the now fading bow of colors. He took a step forward, and as he walked, the rainbow grew fainter until it dissolved altogether. A shaft of sunlight rested on the window shutter which was indeed pulled to and tethered against the brick wall. Unable to resist the lure of one sunny ray of hope, Pieter-Lucas bounded forward and tapped three short taps. As from habit, he jumped up on the doorstoop and waited. The sunlight followed him and held him for a long heart-thumping moment in its warmth. He pressed his ear against the big door of the house. Just one sound, one little movement, one of Gretta Engelshofen's mad whimpers . . . Nothing stirred. He pulled back and noticed a large bolt hanging on the door.

"Never have I seen a lock secured from the outside of this door," he gasped.

The sun had vanished. A blast of wind shrieked around the corner of the house, driving a fresh pelting of rain into Pieter-Lucas' face and whipping at the protective cape he raised above his head. Madly, he dashed around the entire house, checking all the windows, looking for a sign of life in the bookstore or a curl of smoke from the chimney. All he found were more tethered window shutters, another foreboding exterior bolt, and a soggy booklet, rolled up and stuffed in the handle of the door that led into the bookshop.

Newborn hope leapt in his heart. "A note from Aletta?" It had to be. Why else would anyone leave a wad of papers in this place?

With clumsy haste, he yanked at the pamphlet, dislodging it. Then, pressing his body up as close to the door as possible in order to gain protection from the rain afforded by the tiny roof above the doorstoop, he opened the pamphlet with the sort of eagerness that propels a dying man to grasp at a floating plank. "She had to leave a message here somewhere," he murmured. "She wouldn't go without it."

He examined every inch of the pages and both covers for some hand-scribbled words, a picture, or some note tucked in between the now sticky sheets. But he found nothing but words printed in solid blocks across the pages, and on the front an odd title, *Strong Proofs That Men May Have Commemorative Images, But None That They Can Pray To.*

"Strong Proofs! Rubbish and flapdoodle!" he fumed. Throwing the pages to the ground, he dashed back out to the alley and on to his own house. "She wouldn't just disappear without leaving me a clue . . . unless . . . oh, *nay*, it could not be! She could not fear Moeder Kaatje's long-ago vow. . . . *Nay*, I will not believe it. God, what have you done? *Nay . . . nay . . . nay!*"

He tore around his house again and again, searching every chink in the bricks, every unsecured piece of woodwork, shaking the rain-soaked bushes, and prying up every loose cobblestone on the walk. The whole place resounded with the maddening patter of raindrops whipped about by a moaning wind. Not a word from the beloved girl who had promised to wait for him. . . .

Exhausted, empty of all thoughts but the vague consciousness of a wrenching pain buried so deep he could not even tell of what sort it was, he dropped at last to the doorstoop of his own home, made sacred by Aletta's often presence. He sat staring out into the storm and gathering darkness, half hoping for a flood of water to sweep him away into some ocean of oblivion.

Not until a strong hand patted him on the head did Pieter-Lucas realize he was no longer alone. Hardly remembering who he was, much less where or under what circumstances, he looked up, startled. The rain had stopped, and in the darkness of a starless night, he could barely make out a human figure towering over him, covered with a dark hooded robe and carrying a small lantern in one hand. With the other hand, the strange guest motioned for him to stand.

Pieter-Lucas grabbed at his cape, wrapped himself in its protective skin, and demanded, "What do you want?"

"I bring you a message from your beloved," came the answer in a hoarse whisper.

He sprang to his feet and strained to see the eyes that glistened in the occasional flicker of the lamp's wan light. "Who are you?"

Still whispering, the stranger said, "A familiar friend, whose name I beg you not to ask. Just let me give you the message your heart longs to hear, and I shall be gone into the night."

Pieter-Lucas' heart raced, and his palms grew warm and moist. A message from Aletta? What perfect timing! At the same time, a warning sounded deep within. What if this were a Beggar in disguise, come to cart him off to Hendrick van den Garde and some sort of sporting adventure?

Fifteen days in Brederode's dungeon followed by an uncomfortable encounter with Beggars enroute home from Vianen made him wary of the timing. The trip home from Vianen had turned into a slow torture. His legs pained him so from the long confinement that he'd not been able to move nearly as fast. Then somehow he'd taken a wrong turn in the road and ended up just at nightfall in a drizzly, ominous, owl-infested woods. Too tired to press on farther, he'd taken refuge in a deserted animal shelter.

To his dismay, a nest of Beggars had trooped into a nearby clearing and camped for the night. For hours they sat around a roaring fire, drinking, telling wild tales of image-breaking conquests, laughing, and singing the sort of militant songs Beggars gloat over.

Alerted by fresh memories, Pieter-Lucas eyed the robed figure with more than ordinary suspicion and asked, "How do I know you are not some enemy come to do me harm?"

"Shh, not so loud," the voice cautioned. "You don't. Just trust me. If I should reveal my identity, 'twould endanger Aletta and her whole family. Please, heed my instructions, and you will once more be reunited with your lovely young lady."

"What instructions?" He searched what little could be seen of the stranger's face for clues. Who could it be? And why must he persist in using that unnerving whisper of a voice?

The stranger drew close enough to whisper directly into Pieter-Lucas' ear. "No one must hear me say these words . . . or know I said them. No one, do you hear?"

Pieter-Lucas nodded and a chill tingled the length of his back.

"You will find Dirck Engelshofen and his family in Antwerp."

"Antwerp? But . . ."

"Hush, now listen. You must take with you two things if you want to find favor with Aletta's father. Take some cartoons you have drawn that show the Beggars for the fools you have found them to be, and a drawing of the *helleborus niger* with the words on this paper written beneath."

Pieter-Lucas felt a strong hand shoving a wad of paper into his own. Reluctantly, dazed, he took the sheet. What sort of fateful message did it hold?

The stranger continued, "And one other thing. Retrieve the booklet about 'Strong Proofs' that you discarded on the doorstoop of *The Crane's Nest* this afternoon."

"Where were you when I discarded it?" the startled boy demanded to know.

"In the rainbow, shall we say?"

"What must I do with the booklet?"

"Read it, burn it, carry it with you. It matters not, only do not leave it here. Now, do as I have said and all will go well. But waste no time. Set off on your journey before the rising of the new day's sun."

He turned to go, but Pieter-Lucas stopped him. "You didn't tell me where in Antwerp."

"Just inside the Red Gate where you enter the city, you will find the Beguinage. Behind it, toward the setting of the sun, lies *The Plucked Goose Inn*. Inquire of a stableboy with one eye and a hump on his back."

"He knows Dirck Engelshofen?"

"You must mention no names. Ask him only for directions to *The Sign of the Christmas Rose*."

"And if he does not trust me to bring me there?"

"Tell him the Wilderness Angel has sent you."

Wilderness Angel? Pieter-Lucas peered, straining into the night. What sort of spirit could this be? The dark, shadowy figure reached out a hand to Pieter-Lucas' arm with a touch too warm and heavy to be a spirit. Then it drew up close to his ear again and whispered, "One thing more. When all else fails, try Oudewater."

# CHAPTER TEN

*Antwerp*

30th day of Peat Month (September), 1566

The South Brabant countryside shivered under its silvery gray canopy. From Blesje's sweaty high back, Pieter-Lucas wrapped himself tightly against a brisk breeze springing up from the pasturelands about him. He squinted hard in the direction of the far horizon.

"I see a hazy row of needle-shaped towers out there," he mused. "Too many for another village, wouldn't you agree, Blesje? Has to be Antwerp!" Involuntarily, he nudged the horse's flank and bent forward over its heavy mane.

All his life he'd heard amazing tales of the Golden City a good day's ride to the south of Breda. What boy in Brabant hadn't dreamed of one day running across her time-polished cobbles, craning his neck upward at her towering facades, joining her boldly colorful processions?

"You know, Blesje, I've spent my whole life dreaming of some grand and glorious day when I'd ride into Antwerp and gaze on her endless galleries of famous paintings. I'd visit all her magical printshops—those wonderful little workhouses where they heat up lumps of dingy metals and form them into letters and flat thin plates that turn out books with pictures for Dirck Engelshofen to sell. . . ."

Books with pictures! The words enticed his mind with delightful visions . . . but only for an instant.

"Instead," he said, stroking his horse's neck alongside the mane, "I come in search of a prisoner—Aletta. And the ransom I bear in my knapsack? Two cartoons I sketched late into the night. Brederode with a huge head, two enormous horns, and a long skinny tail, holding a wine glass to his snoutlike lips, a Beggar's cruse in his other hand. How I've longed to draw him like this!" Pieter-Lucas laughed.

"And the other? Vader Hendrick in Beggar's garb. He's just broken into a house and killed a woman and her newborn child and is making off with the family inheritance he found hidden in a jar on the mantelpiece. Outside the door, I drew myself waiting with upraised knife for the thief to fall into my trap." He sat up straight and let the feeling of smug satisfaction tilt his head high into the moist air. "If this doesn't show Dirck Engelshofen what sort of 'Beggar lover' I am, nothing will!"

His mind wandered, and he chattered on and on. It felt good to say all this somehow. "Nay, I didn't draw the *helleborus niger*. Don't even know what it is or what all the nonsense was in the words scrawled on that wrinkled paper I was supposed to use. Something about a rose blooming in winter on a half-spent night. And who was that odd visitor that gave me those instructions, anyway? Whatever does the name Wilderness Angel mean?" Pieter-Lucas fell silent and spurred his horse on to cover the remaining distance with renewed haste.

"Glad they let me bring you along on this one more trip," he said to Blesje, giving him a solid pat on the back.

Gradually the hazy row of roofs and spires grew into an impressive skyline. Shortly, the horse and his rider clattered up over the bridge and passed through the impenetrable-looking fortified walls at the Red Gate. The gate broke through the wall in a brick-framed opening in the middle of an enormous square archway nestled up close to a jutting bulkhead topped by a high tower.

At the foot of the bridge, they were met by a team of slow-moving horses pulling a wagon with bulging sides. The driver guided his horses toward the Red Gate with an awkward, labored gait. The wagon creaked and swayed from side to side.

"Could that be the way Aletta and her family traveled to this place?" Pieter-Lucas asked. He paused, almost expecting an answer, and watched the wagon's slow, laborious progress. How easily he could picture his friends in flight!

In flight? Preposterous! A sense of urgency was growing within him.

Pieter-Lucas turned from the groaning wagon to look at the city of his dreams under a gloomy cover of hovery clouds. "Bigger and grander than I ever imagined!" He said, then let a low whistle escape slowly through his teeth.

Buildings crowded each other into tight corners, towers rose like a sparse woods from the bright red tile roof horizon before him. The cobbled streets swarmed with people and an assortment of carts such as he'd never seen. Everywhere dogs and chickens darted about, children played on doorstoops, and the air hung heavy with odors of sweating horses, city refuse, and evening soup pots.

Just as his strange visitor had indicated, he found the Beguinage immediately inside the gate and, close behind it, a rather unkempt old building with a thick thatch roof and a crude sign hanging out over the street that read, *The Plucked Goose.* He dismounted his horse and led him into the stable, where he found a boy of probably fourteen or fifteen stuffing hay into the mangers of the three horses in his care.

"Good afternoon." Pieter-Lucas offered his greeting abruptly. The boy straightened to his short full height and looked at him. He had both a humped left shoulder and one shrunken eye socket. A shiver of something akin both to delight and terror ran down Pieter-Lucas' back. What connection could this maimed creature have with the mysterious Wilderness Angel who had given him such cryptic instructions just at sunset yesterday?

"*Ja?* How can I serve you?" The boy spoke with a voice that fluctuated between boyhood and manhood. His one eye peered up with a look that could have been either friendly, angry, or wary. Pieter-Lucas couldn't decide which.

Without introducing himself, Pieter-Lucas went directly to his purpose. "Please, can you take me to *The Sign of the Christmas Rose?*" he begged.

"Now?" the boy spoke, scarcely looking at Pieter-Lucas. "Are you sure . . . I mean . . ." he stammered.

"My business is urgent." Pieter-Lucas shifted nervously from one foot to the other and tugged at Blesje's reins.

The deformed boy stood beside Pieter-Lucas, scrutinizing him from head to foot. "From whence do you come, and what is it you seek?"

Pieter-Lucas felt uneasy. How much did he dare divulge? Was this creature friend or adversary? And what sort of people were those he sought, where Dirck Engelshofen had taken his family? "I am in search of a friend, who supposedly has fled here. We—my horse and I—come from a distance."

"That I see by the heat and sweat of your horse." He stood silent for a long space before he spoke again. "Who, may I ask, sent you to me?" Doubt and caution glared at him from the stableboy's face and tone of voice.

Fear beat against Pieter-Lucas' chest like the thundering of the regiment of Beggars' feet on the bridge that led to Brederode's castle. Hardly able to breathe, he whispered, "The Wilderness Angel."

The boy looked into his face with an expression that penetrated too deep for comfort. "The Wilderness Angel is a friend of yours?"

Pieter-Lucas paused for a long moment before he gave the short, but tentative answer, "*Ja.*" The visitor had said he was "a familiar friend," even though he had refused to reveal his name.

The boy blinked as if taking second thought. "These are dangerous times in Antwerp," he said finally, still staring at Pieter-Lucas, as if searching for a telltale flinch or casting down of the eyelids. "You surely must know that."

"So I have heard." He held his breath and tried to appear calm.

"Then you must understand that I cannot easily throw caution to the currents . . . and that things are not always as they appear. . . ."

"But you do know the Wilderness Angel, do you not? And you will take me to *The Sign of the Christmas Rose?*"

In the silence that hung between them, Pieter-Lucas heard each straw-munching chomp and each airy breath of the horses in their stalls. At last the boy spoke. "You look to be an honest man, and unless you have gained this information by sly means, there is none but an honorable source from which you could have been led to me."

"May we go quickly?" Pieter-Lucas fought to mask his eagerness.

"*Ja, jongen,* we go. . . . Only . . ."

"Only what?" Why all the hesitation?

"Only . . ." He paused again. "First, we must give straw to your hungry horse."

Pieter-Lucas shifted uneasily. What sort of trap awaited him? Should he leave now, before it was too late? How then would he find Aletta before she should escape once more? His mind made up, he led Blesje to a stall where the manger flowed over with food.

On foot, the boy led Pieter-Lucas up one side street and down another alley, past markets and churches, shops and homes—hundreds of them, it seemed. At last the two young men entered a long narrow street, where late afternoon shadows were already creeping in between the towering buildings.

"Whew!" Pieter-Lucas whistled. "These buildings are so close that you and I could shake hands through open windows across this street."

"Believe me, much more than hands have passed between these buildings."

Pieter-Lucas followed his guide into a short alleyway containing only a handful of houses from which fragrances of evening fires and cooking stews wafted to them from all sides. Halfway down the alley, a woman stood in a doorway, and two children played knucklebones at her side. Pieter-Lucas' guide stopped abruptly and gestured across the street toward a low, two-storied building sandwiched between two higher structures. The bricks of red and graying yellow were arranged in a plain warehouse fashion, and the facade rose in a series of unadorned stepped gables.

"This is it?" Pieter-Lucas asked.

"This is it."

"But how can it be?" he protested. "There's no sign."

"No sign has ever hung out in the street here. That's why you needed a guide."

"But what of *The Sign of the Christmas Rose*? How can you know what sign it is, if there is no sign?"

"Dangerous times in Antwerp, remember? Only those who know what goes on inside know the sign."

"It's plain to see that nothing goes on inside here. Look, the windows are boarded shut, and no smoke curls from the chimney." Fear gnawed at Pieter-Lucas' stomach and sent fresh energies surging through his limbs. Into what ghastly fate had this supposed guide betrayed him?

"Calm, *jongen*," his companion said without a trace of panic.

"Calm, you say? Easy enough for you. You search not for an elusive love. . . ." He must say no more. Pieter-Lucas bounded forward and pounded on the door—three thunderous raps—and waited. "If she's here, I'll find her," he muttered to himself, "no matter how ingenious the means to keep her hidden from view."

"They were all here the last time I came this way." The stranger's hasty explanation sounded lame, contrived.

"Traitor!" Pieter-Lucas spit the word at his companion.

He repeated his knock, this time louder than the first, then tugged at the door. His throat tightened, the skin all over his body stretched till it seemed to squeeze against his ribs. A pain shot through his temples. *Aletta, where have you gone? Aletta, Aletta!*

From across the street, Pieter-Lucas heard a child's voice. "Nobody's home," the voice taunted.

"What does a child know?" he grunted.

He rushed to the windows and pried at the shutters around the edges. Everything was fastened as securely as at Dirck Engelshofen's house in Breda. She had to be here! He turned to go back and try the door one more time. Instead, his elbow nudged his guide in the middle.

"Move out of my way," Pieter-Lucas snarled.

The boy backed off. As he did, a tiny piece of paper floated from his hand and landed on the cobbles by Pieter-Lucas' great toe on his left foot. He stooped down and retrieved it. "Where'd you get this?" he demanded.

"It fell from the shutter when you pried at it," the younger boy answered simply.

With trembling fingers, Pieter-Lucas unfolded the little scrap of paper and smoothed it in his palm. Soiled, rain-spattered, its edges curling and its surface bubbly, it opened one more door into his memory. On a day that seemed so very far away—the last day he saw his beloved, the day they sealed their vows in the birch wood. . . . Disguised as the brown-cowled monk in Breda's fish market square, he had thrust this same piece of paper with its special message into Aletta's hand.

He ran his fingers over the rumpled surface of the note. Had she worn it in her bodice next to her heart, along with Opa's dove? He folded it tenderly and prepared to put it in his doublet, where he would carry it next to his own heart. He touched it to his lips, his eyes caressing the tiny folded object on its way. What was that writing in the corner? So faintly inscribed, it was, he could scarcely make it out in the deepening dusk. Like a ravenous man, he scrutinized it till at last the letters came clear— "WE MADE A VOW. I'LL WAIT."

"She's been here," he said aloud. "But she's gone again!"

"You shouldn't be surprised." The guide sounded frightened.

Pieter-Lucas wheeled around and grasped him by the shoulders. With panic he held the stranger in his grip.

"You knew all along that they were gone," he accused, "and yet you led me here? You nurtured my hopes!"

"*Nay, nay*, do you hear? I swear it," he protested. "I knew not when or whether they were leaving."

"What then did you know?" Pieter-Lucas roared.

"Only that peace-loving citizens are fleeing Antwerp in droves these days. And these were peace-loving folks, if ever I knew any."

"If you know so much about them, tell me, then, where they have gone, and who they might be . . . these peace-loving citizens who have taken my love captive!"

Like a mouse caught in the jaws of a cat, the stableboy squirmed in Pieter-Lucas' grip. "That I cannot tell. Such folk go to many different places and never do their friends divulge their names. I honestly cannot say."

"Places such as?" he demanded.

"*Nay, nay*, I cannot."

Pieter-Lucas towered over his guide and searched his face for some slight flinching, some shifting of the eye . . . anything that would bring him the truth he sought. But the boy was stoic, and his one good eye held a gentleness that reminded him of Opa.

Suddenly, from across the street the children shouted once more. "Mad Gretta's gone! They put her in a wagon and carried her away!" The raucous, naughty laughter of mocking children filled the empty street and echoed, bouncing off the closely placed walls.

Mad Gretta, indeed! Who but Gretta Engelshofen? What strange things had she done while they were here to reveal to the neighbors that she was mad?

He loosed his hold on the boy and turned to face the children.

"When did they go?" he demanded.

Still smiling, they looked at one another, shrugged their shoulders, and replied, "In the middle of a night, not so very long ago."

"Where did they take Mad Gretta?"

"To Oudewater!" The children exploded with more laughter. "Where else would you take a Mad Gretta?" they taunted in sarcastic unison.

What was it the Wilderness Angel had said? "When all else fails, try Oudewater." Ah, now it was making sense. Everybody knew that when mad women were suspected of being witches, Oudewater was the one place where they could flee and be sure to get a fair trial.

Pieter-Lucas tucked Aletta's note away in his doublet.

"Tell me the way to Oudewater," he demanded of his guide.

" 'Tis a very long and difficult trip, by the Yssel River, beyond Vianen, and . . ."

"I didn't ask you whether it was near or far, easy or difficult. Can't you see, I must go there? Lead me to my horse," he said, grabbing his guide by the collar.

"*Ja, ja*, follow me."

"And you will show me the way to begin my journey!"

"Whatever you say, *jongen*. Whatever you say."

---

*Oudewater*
15th day of Wine Month (October), 1566

If Antwerp was the Golden City, grand in size and bustling with enterprise, Oudewater was the Proud Village, perched behind the tiny circumference of its strong walls on the banks of the Yssel River. Within two days, Pieter-Lucas had explored every inch of the town.

He'd persuaded the stable master of the town's only hostel to let him sleep in a corner of the stables and give him one meal a day in exchange for his care of the horses.

"Blesje," he confided to his horse as he curried, fed, and watered the animals, "we could fit this whole village inside the walls of Breda three times and still have room to spare.

"Oudewater has five town gates, a town hall, one hostel, one church with a high tower, four monastic houses, a tower jail, two windmills, five hundred seventeen houses, thirty-four barns, and one weigh-house for which it has gained worldwide fame." Pieter-Lucas sighed and scratched Blesje under his chin. "Among all these rather ordinary buildings, I have counted one rope and thread manufacturer, two draperies, three breweries, two grain mills, four bakeries, three oil mills, an armament smithy, a health master who does tooth extractions and barbering, and even a brothel not open to housewives, transients, and Jews, I'm told. What I have not found is the one thing we came here looking for—Dirck Engelshofen and his family. Nor have I seen one witch being weighed for her life. For all I know, that may be nothing but a myth."

Pieter-Lucas' knowledge about the witch weighing of Oudewater had been garnered from bits of gossip that ran like lightning through the *Kasteel* stables back in Breda. Supposedly, witches were supernatural creatures and weightless. Suspects who could produce a certificate to prove that their weight was normal could never be tried as witches on any other basis. Since no standard procedure existed for determining what was a normal weight, justice was hard to come by. But in Oudewater, reputation had it, anyone could receive an honest weight, and no one was ever turned away without the coveted certificate.

"Stories have a way of not always being true." Pieter-Lucas slapped his horse on the rump. "Maybe tomorrow, old boy."

He trudged off to his corner, where he pulled his cloak over his lanky body and tried to sleep.

Sleep stayed frustratingly far, far away, avoiding him like Aletta and her family. Why was it taking them so long to get here? And since they had come this way ahead of him, why did he not pass them on the road? He remembered the plodding horse and its intolerably heavy wagon load creaking across the Red Gate Bridge in Antwerp. Slow, yes, that he understood. But this slow? *Nay*, they should be here by now. Unless they had come and gone again.

Both the hostel owner and the weigh-master had assured him that nobody matching Engelshofen's description had been here in recent days—or even weeks. They must still be on the road—broken down under the weight of the wagon, perhaps? Or hiding out in a thicket someplace? Unless, of course, those children by *The Sign of the Christmas Rose* were mistaken. But the Wilderness Angel had said it too. Besides, where else could one go with a mad woman? Knowing Gretta Engelshofen's mad ways, it could not be that the children had made that idea up. It all fit too well.

Where then could they be?

The rest of the night he argued with himself. Should he return to Antwerp taking a different route? If they had encountered trouble along the way, he might find them. Or was it better to stay here until they came?

The Wilderness Angel . . . But who was the Wilderness Angel? What did he know? What if they had gone somewhere else? But where? And if the stories about Oudewater were nothing but silly myths. . . ?

Round and round in ever tightening circles his mind twirled, until just at daybreak, on the other side of the stable wall, he heard horses' hoofs clopping across the cobblestones to the accompaniment of creaking wagon sounds. He bounded to his feet, ran out the stable door, across the courtyard gate, and into the street.

The wagon looked so like the one he'd seen leaving Antwerp, it took his breath away. Padding along the cobbles in stockinged feet, Pieter-Lucas followed behind the lumbering coach until it stopped before the weigh-house, where the driver descended from his seat and began pounding on the door.

"Good heavens!" the excited young man exclaimed, "I can't let them see me." He ducked into the doorway of the nearest house and watched.

Was this the wagon he had sought with such diligence? Could it be possible that his Aletta huddled in the corner even now? Had she passed as sleepless a night as he? Was she fearful? As lonely for him as he for her? Confused? Oh, when could he go to her? In his fancy, he saw those long blond curls framing her smooth, round face. His arms ached to enfold her in a strong embrace to protect her from the evil that lurked about. His lips felt hot and dry. His ears strained for the faintest sound from the wagon. But all he heard was the steady breathing and occasional pawing of the horses, the incessant pounding of the driver on the weigh-house door, and the beating of his own heart, which grew so loud he feared it would frighten the horses.

Silence hung with maddening weight over the wagon. For all he knew, it might contain nothing more than some farmer's grain headed for a distant village. But so early in the morning?

After what seemed half a day, the weigh-master appeared in the doorway. Pieter-Lucas listened in vain to decipher the lively conversation in the damp morning air. At length the men stopped talking and the driver returned to his wagon. Pieter-Lucas stood, hardly daring to breathe, not allowing his eyes to leave the wagon even for a blink.

The awkward old coach began to rock gently, and he was certain he heard muffled voices mixed with the increased squeaks. Then the driver helped a passenger down to the ground—a merchant-looking man in brown trousers and short cape and wearing a flat-brimmed tam on his head.

Dirck Engelshofen? Pieter-Lucas swallowed a wishful gasp.

He, in turn, helped a cape-shrouded woman into the weigh-house.

Gretta Engelshofen?

But the driver remained and at last ushered another cape-covered woman and a small boy down and across the threshold.

Aletta? Robbin? Could it be? It must be!

"Ale . . ." He started to call after her, then cut it short. They were already running for their lives. The last thing they needed was for someone to expose them in this place they trusted for protection. Besides, what would Dirck Engelshofen do if he confronted him head on in the street?

"Hold yourself under your cap, *jongen*," he told himself. He'd have to watch through the weigh-house window and wait until they came out. Then what? Then . . . do what seemed right at the moment. What else?

Pieter-Lucas sighed. Why did life seem to be so filled with waiting and wondering? He dashed from his hiding place and stood peering in through the window beside the big double doors. He knew the room well. In the past few days he'd come here more times than he could recount, always searching, waiting, hoping. . . .

But the room didn't matter this morning. He had eyes only for the little family being herded like a flock of trembling animals into the far corner. They stopped by a tall, cumbersome wardrobe looming like a room within a room next to the narrow stairway that ascended in two short flights—one doubled back over the other—up through the ceiling.

What if they carried them up those stairs and they were never seen again? Fear drew a tight tether around his mind and created wild and dreadful fantasies.

"*Nay, jongen*," he chided himself, mumbling softly into his almost-beard. "This is Oudewater, safe haven where the hunted find justice. No one has ever left this weigh-house without the coveted certificate."

"So the story goes," an inner voice tormented. "But how do you know? Or what if the woman weighs not enough to satisfy the judges—or the weigh-master?"

"No one has ever left this place condemned," he retorted. "No one ever will. No one. NO ONE!" His mumble rose to a pitch he could scarcely stifle. Yet, in this tense moment of wishing, hoping, he was not entirely certain he could believe the words his lips repeated.

Pieter-Lucas moved from windowpane to windowpane, frantic to see clearly. But each glass seemed equally clouded with a film that did not yield to his most persistent rubbing with the tail of his doublet.

"If I could only see their faces," he muttered.

"*Jongen*, what do you here?" A rough voice intruded on his private frustration, and a hand snatched him by the shoulder, spinning him around to face a group of town officials in their pretentious black suits with feathered hats and bright scarlet sashes.

Before the boy could answer, he heard another command. "Begone! You've no business here at this hour of the morning!"

When he did not move, a chorus of voices repeated the order. "Begone, at once!" They shoved him with such force he had to fight to keep his balance.

Reluctantly he moved, walking backward toward the hostel and the warm stable he'd been roused from, waiting till he heard the weigh-house door open and thud close and the voices cease. Then, looking anxiously about to satisfy himself there were no straggling officials, he returned, stooping to pass under the windows. He crept around the corner and along the wall of windows that lined the far side of the building until he found one pane sufficiently clear to afford him enough of a view to at least keep the balance scales in sight.

Already, the older woman was emerging from the wardrobe, stripped of all her garments but her nightshirt. Her gray hair hung in long, loose wisps around bony shoulders. The weigh-master's wife, whom Pieter-Lucas had learned was also the village midwife, was draping a trailing black veil over the suspect's head. With the weigh-master's help, she lifted the little woman onto one wooden platform of the huge balance scales that hung suspended by strong black chains from the ceiling in the center of the room.

"She's built just like Gretta Engelshofen—small, sharp nose . . ." Pieter-Lucas sucked in his breath and held it. "But she is so old."

Between swipes at the windowpane to clear it of the mist from his breath, he watched a servant pile weights onto the second platform. The town officials sat behind a long judges' bench under the watchful eye of an enormous painting of the crucifixion that nearly filled the far wall. At a smaller bench, placed in front of the windows to Pieter-Lucas' left, sat a clerk, quill in hand, preparing to write the verdict in a fat book. The weigh-master stood next to the judges, obviously staring hard at the tilt of the huge arm that held the two balance platforms.

"Where is Aletta? And her vader . . . and Robbin?" Vaguely Pieter-Lucas could see a knot of people huddled next to the wardrobe, but the clerk's bench blocked his view, and the next windowpane over was as useless as oiled paper.

Suddenly the whole scene moved into action. Evidently a judgment had been announced. The clerk began dipping and scribbling with his pen. The three people Pieter-Lucas had so longed to see moved forward, now, and with tender gestures assisted the old lady off the balance. For one breathtaking moment, the younger woman seemed to face Pieter-Lucas directly. With her cape thrown back from her head, he could easily see now that her hair was as dark as Aletta's was fair. Her features looked as unlike Aletta's as any woman he had ever seen. Thin, gaunt, and bony, they appeared to be covered with wrinkled skin on a face obviously old enough to belong to Aletta's moeder.

"*Nay, nay, nay*. It cannot be!" Pieter-Lucas pressed his nose against the cold, hard pane and wished for his eyes to tell him the truth he so wanted to know. Then he saw the man's face, and the boy's. When they'd dressed the old lady and prepared to help her hobble from the place, he had to admit that truth lay not where he sought it. Through increasing mistiness he watched the man place a coin in the hand of each of the officials: the clerk, the weigh-master, and the midwife. In return, the burgomaster handed him a document, signed, rolled, and tied by the clerk.

"The certificate," Pieter-Lucas said wistfully. "None leaves without it . . . except those who never arrive."

When the family emerged from the building, Pieter-Lucas heard shouts of "Glory be to the God of justice!"

"God of justice?" The words set his inner monster once more to growling, then roaring. Pieter-Lucas jumped to his feet and bounded down the alleyway between the weigh-house and the town bakery, back to the hostel stables. He yanked Blesje free from his moorings, mounted him, and prodded him into a furious trot across cobblestone streets and out through the gate at the southwest corner of the old diked village.

"Slow not, Blesje, slow not," he shouted. Faster and faster they sped along the high dike roadway that followed the twists and curves of the wide, muddy Yssel River. A mist-spattered wind whipped around Pieter-Lucas' face and ears.

"No God for me," he spat into the wind. "If this is the best He can do for justice, then let me go free! There has to be another way. . . ." The words fit into the rhythm of the horse's hoofs pounding and splatting across the oozy roadway.

"There has to be another way. . . . I'll make another way . . . 'nother way . . . 'nother way . . ."

All day they rode on—to Gouda and back. The wind had died, and a dense fog had settled over the river and flowed into the sleeping streets of Oudewater when they slipped back into the stable under cover of darkness. In total silence, Pieter-Lucas fed and blanketed Blesje, then curled up in his corner. Hoping for another day, another wagon, another certificate—and justice, he drifted off to a restless, dream-filled sleep.

# CHAPTER ELEVEN

*East Frisia (Friesland), near border of Lowlands and Germany*

Late in Wine Month (October), 1566

*A* fierce wind howled and drove the sleety rain in relentless sheets against the rickety horse-drawn coach. How many days Aletta's family had shared this journey with Oom Johannes and Tante Neetlje, Cousin Anneke, and Giles, their orphan servant boy, a weary Aletta could only guess. It seemed like forever and ever. . . .

She shivered at the sound of the angry pricks of ice pelting the side of the coach and sank back deeper into the tiny space allotted to her on the huge chest of books. She wrapped her woolen cape closer to her body, pulled its fur-lined hood tighter under her chin, and snuggled closer to her moeder.

If only she had cared better for Moeder Gretta, the way Tante Lysbet always did, they never would have had to leave Antwerp. No matter that Vader insisted they were part of a whole train of refugees fleeing the Golden City on the Scheldt River for "other reasons"—reasons which he refused to explain. She knew they had something to do with the fact that Prince Willem's men and the papists were at each other's throats.

But why would that uproot her family? Vader and Oom Johannes had nothing to do with all the hubbub. Good and faithful Christians they were, both of them—and respected businessmen. They had no enemies.

More important, it was no mere coincidence that the night before Vader announced they were going to leave, Moeder had somehow escaped out into the alley. She traipsed off in her nightdress, barefooted and bareheaded. Aletta had been aware, in her dreams, of the familiar sounds of her moeder wailing and crying out as she always did when the headaches possessed her. The woman had nearly reached the Kammerstraat before Vader found her and brought her back to Oom Johannes' printshop.

"Vader," the anxious daughter pleaded with her vader the next morning, "Tante Lysbet said that if Moeder ever wailed out in a public place, we must take her to Oudewater immediately."

"*Nay*, my child," he said with an aloofness that neither invited nor allowed for discussion. "Your moeder will be more than safe in Emden, far from here and far from Oudewater."

Once more, her vader treated her as the empty-headed procession doll. Aletta knew better. Her moeder's escapade had to be the real reason for this endless journey into the wilderness of Friesland. A barrage of accusing inner voices filled her guilt-ridden heart with torments:

"You disobeyed your vader!"

"You let Moeder Kaatje's baby die!"

"You didn't keep your own moeder safe!"

"God's eye is watching, and you must pay!"

She closed her eyes and longed for sleep. Instead, she heard Oom Johannes shouting from up ahead.

"Our destination, at last," his piping voice sounded like a thin reed, barely audible through the wind and sleet. "We'll reach the city before dark." He raised a cloaked arm and pointed ahead. Aletta peered out through the peephole between Oom Johannes and Vader Dirck, where they sat in the front of the coach. Straining her eyes and imagination, she could see nothing but whirling whiteness. The sleet had turned to snow.

"Those shadows between the snow are Emden?" Vader asked.

"Emden, indeed, wrapped in an early wintry shawl!" Oom Johannes laughed.

"Emden! Hurrah! Emden!" Robbin's enthusiastic shouts exploded in Aletta's ears. He jumped up and down, tromping near the toes of Tante Neeltje's street shoes and rocking the coach.

"Watch out, *jongen*," his aunt protested, her normally laughing blue eyes snapping. "You'll topple us all into the snowdrifts."

"Or into the water," Vader Dirck warned, shouting back over his shoulder, competing with the increasing winds.

"What water, Vader?" Robbin asked. "Another lake? Oh-ee!"

"Den Dullart," Oom Johannes shouted back.

"Den what?" Robbin screwed up his nose and jerked his head backward at the neck.

"Den Dullart is the estuary of the Ems River," Cousin Anneke answered, always ready with an instantaneous recitation. "It is very narrow from the point most opposite the city."

Robbin seemed to be unimpressed. Clambering toward the front, he cried out, "Let me see, Vader. Let me see!"

"There is nothing to see, my son. Nothing but snow, more snow, and still more snow. Now sit down, we'll soon be there."

Giles, who shared the metal trunk with Aletta's little brother, wrestled Robbin back onto his seat. "*Ja, jongen.* Sit down like your vader says," he ordered. With a broad, bare hand Giles grasped Robbin by his swiveling head until he held him firm at last. But the little boy's feet tapped on.

Only Moeder Gretta ignored the scuffling antics of the boys nearby. Poor Moeder! Swathed like a corpse in her cape and blankets, she let the coach jostle her along in utter silence, her eyes staring straight ahead. Ever since they'd left Tante Lysbet behind in Breda, she had lived constantly somewhere beyond them all, in a daze. Once they left Antwerp, nothing made her cry, nothing made her laugh. Aletta had all she could do just to coax her to eat. She did not act as if she knew her own brother, Johannes, or his wife. Even Vader could not rouse her from the dreadful, faraway trance that glazed her eyes and tethered the corners of her mouth in a tight, unquavering, puckery line.

Aletta gathered her moeder in her arms and whispered in her ear, "Take heart, Moeder. We're almost there." The gentle words fell on a sleeping mind, and the wind shrieked so loudly Aletta could not hear them herself. Nor did they do a thing to dispel the monstrous fear that mocked her feigned confidence. How could she be so sure Emden was a safe haven? Just because Vader said so? That should be enough. Why, then, did it not reassure her?

Outside the coach, the storm had escalated into a blizzard. All unannounced, the wind caught them in a vicious gust that snatched at the coach with giant iron fingers. The fabric cover was sucked to one side, and the long willow ribs of the frame bent so far Aletta feared they would snap. The violent movement sent the boys toppling from their seats. Boxes and trunks slid across the floor, slamming into the frightened passengers.

Robbin shrieked, threw himself onto Aletta's lap, and entwined his arms about her neck.

"Help, Sissy," he screamed. "I didn't do it! I didn't jump too hard! I didn't, I didn't!"

"Of course you didn't do it. It's just the wind," Aletta said, prying the tight little arms from her neck.

One more gust of wind grabbed the coach and shook it with a fierceness that nearly knocked them all from their seats. Aletta heard a loud ripping sound from above and looked up through a tiny, three-cornered window into the snow-pelted heavens.

"Quiet, quiet," she told her racing heart. Whatever happened to her, she must not arouse her moeder.

But the jostling and the noise had already caused Moeder Gretta to panic. She broke her long silence with one of those heartrending wails: "He's coming for me! I'm cursed! Hide me. . . ." In a flash, Vader Dirck had hurled himself into the coach and enfolded his wife in his arms.

Aletta heard the horses whinnying with excitement and Oom Johannes shouting words at them she could not understand. The coach jerked wildly from side to side, then came to a sudden halt with a screeching, scraping sound from under the floor. There was a straining, lunging sensation from up front, and the coach settled backward with a jarring thud. Boxes and trunks shifted so far back and to one side that the shaken passengers could scarcely manage to sit upright on their cargo perches. Snow swirled in, not only through the gaping hole in the roof, but through the open doorway now tilted upward toward the spot where Aletta assumed the sky must be.

Robbin clung to her, and she held him close, too stunned herself to find words to console the boy who shivered so violently she could feel his body quivering through the layers of wool that separated them.

"Johannes, my husband," Tante Neeltje screamed and began to pry and shove her way over and around trunks and boxes toward the doorway. Looking up, Aletta noticed the seat where Oom Johannes and Vader Dirck had sat all these days. It stood empty and the tongue of the coach rose into the air, broken into a shape that reminded her of a letter *L* she'd seen at the printshop in Antwerp.

Anneke reached for Tante Neeltje and pulled her back to her seat with a sharp reprimand. "Moeder Neeltje, you cannot go out there in this storm."

"*Nay*, God forgive me," she said, sitting on the edge of her trunk. Wisps of graying blond hair swirled around her pretty face. "I must not fear so." She lowered her head to her wool-padded bosom and held it in mittened hands.

"Johannes must have been dragged by the horses at the reins," Vader Dirck said. Then, extricating himself from his wife's wild grasp, he added, "I'll go find him. You, Giles, take care of the women and Robbin." He made his way up and over the driver's seat and disappeared out into the massive expanse of rushing, whirling whiteness.

"Here, Robbin," Aletta coaxed, giving the boy a gentle nudge. "Go with Giles. Moeder Gretta needs me, and you're a big boy, remember?"

Robbin hung still on her arm, wide-eyed and dazed, until Giles dragged him away. "Sissy, is everything all right?"

"Of course everything's all right," Giles announced, "and you and I are the men here now. We have to take care of all these women."

"Ja," Robbin said, the promise of a smile altering his mood.

"Nay, nay," Moeder Gretta sobbed. "He's coming for me! I'm cursed! He's taken my husband away. Dear God, what shall I ever do? Oh, oh . . ."

The woman's howl pitched itself against the wind and flapping coach cover till it hurt Aletta's ears. Thank God they were out in this forsaken wilderness where no one could hear her demented ravings. Aletta caressed the woman's cheeks and spoke soothing words, "It's okay, Moeder. God will protect us. He will keep us safe."

Did she really believe what she had just said? There was a time when she had believed it. But that was before the image-breaking, before she'd disobeyed Vader and lied to Tante Lysbet and made her vow with Pieter-Lucas, before she'd failed to save Moeder Kaatje's baby and keep Moeder Gretta from roaming through the streets in Antwerp. . . .

Now, it seemed God had deserted them all. What had made it suddenly so wrong for her to love Pieter-Lucas that God must tear her from her friend and wrench her whole family from the home where all was so quiet and beautiful?

"Great God," she cried from the depths of her heart, "will you dump us all in the Frisian wildlands? Will you punish us all for a love I cannot deny?"

Giles and Robbin had taken up guard duty in the doorway now. Between them they held a blanket across the opening, keeping out most of the snow that continued to pelt them. Robbin stood teetering on the edge of the driving seat, his hands stretched high to the frame on one side of the coach, holding up, as best he could, his end of the makeshift door.

"Any sign of the men yet?" Tante Neeltje asked.

Robbin peeked his head outside and back again. "Not yet, Tante," he shouted back, wiping snow from his face with his free hand. "But it's okay. God is protecting them. Right, Sissy?"

Aletta put on her best smile and nodded, wanting very much to be convinced. Indeed, the wind no longer howled quite so loudly or rocked the upended coach so violently. Perhaps there was hope.

"He will take care of our men," Tante Neeltje said in a calm voice. "In fact, He is watching over us all." Then her speaking voice turned to the clear, melodic strains of a song Aletta had never heard before. It filled the precarious tent that enveloped them in the midst of the storm.

"Those who in God do trust
And nev'r in shame do stand,
Both young and old, men and women,
God strengthens with His hand."

Aletta felt hugged by a strange warmth that did not come from woolen blankets or huddled bodies, and she imagined that the "Eye of God" in the Great Church actually smiled down on them. If only this feeling could last for always.

"Sing it again, Tante Neeltje," she begged.

"Sing with me along," the woman urged. "All of you."

For a long and beautiful moment, they did sing together—Anneke in her precise, bell-like tones, Giles adding accents of young masculine depth, Aletta catching on to the new words and melody with an ease that amazed her, Robbin punctuating the concert with an occasional exuberant phrase between peeks at the outside world. Even Moeder Gretta's melancholy wail edged close to song, though she sang no words. The song concluded, Tante Neeltje said, "And now we pray."

Tante Neeltje bowed her head, and one by one the others followed suit. It seemed odd to Aletta that no one spoke a word. Something about the way this family prayed made her uncomfortable. It seemed they stopped wherever and whenever they felt the urge and prayed. Yet, no one ever prayed aloud.

What could Tante Neeltje be saying to God when she prayed? Was she angry with Him for snatching her husband away on the brink of the estuary, so near to their destination? No, not Tante Neeltje. Never had Aletta known anyone so gentle and devout—not even the Beguines in the Beguinage who spent their lives praying and helping others in need. She felt irresistibly drawn to this unusual woman who displayed an amazing combination of pleasant liveliness and deep piety.

"Great God," Aletta found herself putting words to a petition that rose from somewhere deep down inside, "is it possible that you can forgive me my great errors and sins, and give me one more chance to protect Moeder Gretta?" For one long and beautiful moment, a settling, soothing calm came over her, and she knew everything would come out right. Even Pieter-Lucas would one day be hers, without her having to disobey Vader.

With Robbin amongst them, the silence could not last. From his wobbly guard post on the seat at the coach's mouth, he announced, "They come, they come! Vader Dirck and Oom Johannes. Hurrah!"

In an instant, Robbin and Giles had dropped the makeshift door, and the older boy struggled to keep the younger one from dashing headlong into the snow. "The snow's quit falling! Hurrah!" Robbin shouted. "Vader, Vader!"

Tante Neeltje raised her head, clasped her mittened hands, and exclaimed, "May our Great God be praised!" Then, to the boys, "Are they well?"

"They both walk," Giles offered. "Each one leads a horse."

The wind had nearly subsided, and only a few flakes of snow flurried into the coach through the gaping doorway and the hole in the cover. The sky, still clad in heavy grayish wool, yielded no secrets, but the fabric cover of the coach had stopped flapping, and the willow ribs, once more erect, held it in their precise graceful curves. Aletta felt a spurt of jubilance bubbling up inside. Impulsively she gave her moeder a squeeze.

"Moeder Gretta! Vader and Oom Johannes are back. God has heard Tante Neeltje's prayers." And her own? Time would tell.

Moeder's body began to quiver, and Aletta saw fresh tears flowing and heard soft sobs—the sort that signaled relief. "Thank you, God," she murmured.

"Can you see the city?" Anneke asked the boys.

"Ja, ja," Robbin squealed. "The city, the city! It's there! Emden!"

"Like a sugar-frosted fairyland," Giles added.

Robbin's continuing shouts of "Vader, Vader, Vader!" soon gave way to heavy men's voices, the jangling of bridles and reins, and the horses' loud snortings.

"The women all comfortable?" Oom Johannes sounded close and his snow-laden cap appeared just above the bottom rim of the doorway.

"Everything is good," Giles shouted.

"Then jump down here and help us," Vader said.

"Me too, Vader." Robbin scrambled after Giles over the coach seat horizon. Together the men tugged at the wagon tongue, trying to coax it down from its heavenward tilt. The wagon jiggled a bit, but to right it from its seated position in the snowdrifts was evidently beyond their strength. The wind stirred once more, though not so wildly as before. Between its shrieking blasts, Aletta caught the sound of the men's voices out in the snow.

"What . . . do? Night will overtake us . . . no spot to camp."

" . . . empty out the coach . . . to budge it . . . set it aright . . ."

Then from Giles, "Pardon, have you seen this tongue? . . . pretty badly broken . . . will it connect. . . ?"

"Vader, Vader," Robbin's little voice sounded from the low side of the coach, just behind where the women sat. "Look here, Vader! The wheel is broken!"

A flurry of feet crunched through the snow below Aletta and Moeder Gretta to the spot where the wheel joined the coach. Aletta felt fear rise once more as a mumble of excited voices accompanied mild shakings and proddings that jilted the wagon.

"I'll ride into the city for help." Oom Johannes spoke with authoritative finality.

Vader Dirck retorted quickly, "No time for that . . . heavy gray clouds—more snow on the way. . . . Get these women to shelter before nightfall."

The horseback ride into Emden began as an almost pleasant diversion once they had coaxed and lifted Gretta Engelshofen out of the coach with its precarious slanting floor. Too terrified to trust even her husband's strong arms, she insisted on clinging to Aletta. Every time her husband approached, she screamed out to her daughter, "Save me! Hide me! Great God, save me! Help, help, help!"

In the end it took Oom Johannes and Vader and Giles, all three, to lift her writhing body from the coach and mount her on the horse's long, broad back, with a warm sheepskin cover for a saddle. But once Aletta was mounted behind her and had wrapped her moeder securely in her arms, the woman yielded to her daughter's protective embrace. Giles led the horse by its reins with one hand and tethered Robbin by the other. At length, Moeder even allowed Vader to walk alongside.

In no time Aletta discovered how different riding on the back of the horse was from sitting wedged between her moeder and Anneke on a box of books through the jogging unevenness of the coach's movements. She had to teach her body the strange rhythms of the animal's undulating gait that tossed her first forward, then backward, then forward again. With Vader's help from the side, she managed to keep her own balance and hold Moeder Gretta in place.

All proceeded smoothly for a while. Tante Neeltje and Anneke rode atop the other horse led by Oom Johannes. Robbin's voice wafted across the frozen landscape, singing the songs he and Aletta so often sang together as they walked to the market back home in Breda. Aletta even allowed herself to enjoy the fairyland city before them: its row of overgrown tree branches, pitched roofs, and tower spires coated with white. From its chimneys, puffy columns of smoke curled up to vanish into the lowering clouds.

Then, just as they approached the bridge that led across the Ems River and to the city gate, a heavy cloud overhead descended and a combination of snow and sleet dumped on them in blinding, wet, white torrents. The horses whinnied and shifted sideways, caught in the current of whipping winds. Aletta heard Robbin crying somewhere in the thick moving cloud, and she felt Moeder Gretta scrambling to get off the horse.

"Quiet, Gretta, still now. We're almost there," Vader soothed with his voice while his arms tried to restrain her wild movements.

Aletta tightened her grip on Moeder Gretta and was adjusting her body to the new posture imposed by an almost horizontal wind when the horse stepped onto the bridge and stumbled beneath them both. She felt his hoofs slip on the icy-wet planks and his forelegs buckle. Moeder slid to the left, tumbling out of Aletta's grip toward Vader. Aletta reached out for her, then lost her balance and fell to the right. She slipped feet first into the icy water, striking her head on the side of the bridge as she went down.

The water was not waist deep, but the slime beneath her feet, the increased weight of her now saturated layers of woolen skirts, and the relentless wind threatened to drag her out into the channel where the ever-present currents could sweep her away. Frantically, she grabbed at the snowy-wet bushes that lined the shore and prayed they would not come out at their roots.

"Vader," she screamed. "Vader! Help! Help! Help!"

The wind threw her voice back into her face. Her eyes stung, and the snow and ice that filled her mouth tasted of bloody salt. Was this the way God took care of her when she'd asked His forgiveness? What more could He want of her? Pieter-Lucas to keep Moeder Kaatje's vows? *Nay,* never! She'd drown in Den Dullart first.

"Vader! Vader!"

Just as the spindly willow tree she clung to began to pull away from the shore and the river bottom turned to porridge, Aletta heard a voice. She looked up and through a snowy shroud saw the figure of a man bending over the bank with both hands extended to her.

"Vader?" She felt two strong hands grip her arms. She pawed at the elusive river bottom until she managed to get a precarious foothold. Then, working with her rescuer, she gradually climbed her way up the bank and onto shore. Exhausted, she collapsed into the arms that had dragged her from the threatening waters and scooped her up from the snow and ice.

"Oh, Vader," she whispered. Then, "Where is Moeder?"

"I'm not your vader." The voice did not belong to Dirck Engelshofen. "Your moeder is well and so are you."

"But who . . . where is my moeder? My vader. . . ?"

"Hush, child. We'll soon reach safety. God has given our family a house nearby for rescuing many in trouble."

She blinked again and again, pushing back the snow that piled onto her eyelids, weighting them into blindness. If only she could get a good look at this stranger's face! Who was he? How could she be sure he meant her no harm? Yet, she sensed a kindness in his voice and felt something akin to warmth in his arms and his big padded chest.

Too tired to fight any longer, she yielded her shivering body to his care and struggled to believe that she would indeed be warm and dry again. Then reality slipped away, and she no longer knew whether she dreamed or did indeed feel and hear her rescuer stomping his feet and carrying her across a threshold. Did she really hear a woman's voice and feel her wet clothes being stripped and replaced with fresh warm dry ones?

When at last she opened her eyes, they smarted in the warmth of a faintly lighted room with a low ceiling and shaggy beams. She lay on a simple bed near an enormous porcelain box that radiated heat. And beside her, a rotund little lady in a plain wool dress and a neatly starched white headdress was laying hot cloths on the side of her head.

"You have an ugly, bleeding scrape there," the woman said. "This goldenrod salve is just the cure. Thanks be to God you were so close when the blizzard began." Her Middle-Dutch words were precise, as if made of square chiseled letters. "I'm Oma Roza. They call me Oma."

Aletta smiled. With those rosy cheeks and a face that needed not to smile in order to show how much she cared, what else but Oma, grandmother? "I thank you for your kindness, Oma," she offered as politely as she could manage from her daze.

The storm still roared in her ears. Her head throbbed, occasional chills shook her frame, and it suddenly mattered very much that she hadn't the slightest idea where she was.

Looking up at her *physicke*, she begged, "When can I see my vader?"

Oma did not answer but stepped aside, and in her place Vader Dirck himself appeared. "God be praised, our family is all safe again," he announced, his voice deep with concern.

"Vader!" She grabbed his hand, and it brought him to his knees beside her. "And Moeder?"

"No worse than before, except a bit wet like all the rest of us," he said. "She landed softly in her blankets on the bridge. I picked her up and carried her so swiftly I doubt she ever knew a thing had gone amiss. Our hostess offered her a cupboard bed on the far wall, and I haven't seen her sleep so peacefully since we left Breda."

For the first time in months, vader and daughter looked into each other's eyes, the space between them heavy with uncertain wonder. Then Vader Dirck smiled that warm, welcoming smile he used to reserve just for her, back in the days before they'd quarreled on Pieter-Lucas' doorstoop. Aletta felt a surge of excitement, and before she realized what she was doing, she held up both arms to him. He leaned over, and she threw them around his neck and kissed him on the cheek.

"Oh, Vader, Vader!" she whispered, rubbing her nose in his prickly beard. It seemed so natural and yet so strange.

When he gathered her in his arms and squeezed, Aletta held him close and wept.

"How long it's been, Vader. How very, very long."

# CHAPTER TWELVE

*Emden, East Frisia (Friesland)*

Early Tallow Month (November), 1566

*T*he gray of the predawn morning dragged Dirck Engelshofen's steps as he carried a lighted candle across the main room in Hans the weaver's house. Carefully balancing the candle in one hand, he climbed the ladder. In one of the tiny attic rooms above, he lingered a moment, listening to the gentle pattering of raindrops on the heavy thatch of the roof. Softly, he approached the bed where his daughter slept.

"She still looks like an angel when she sleeps," he thought, smiling. "Just like she did as an infant."

If only he could leave her there. He knew how she would love to go on dozing in her warm feather bag. But life seldom let him do for her what his heart urged him to do. How could it be that God had never allowed him to protect this girl, now growing into a young woman, in the way he had so wanted?

He set the candle on the table near her bed and knelt beside her.

"Aletta, Aletta, wake up," he called, shaking her gently by the shoulder.

He watched the eyes open a crack then close again. "Sorry to disturb you, child, but it is time I go to the printery." He paused before adding, "Do you hear me?"

Her hand reached out to him and squeezed his arm.

"Vader," she ventured, giving the impression that she struggled to bring her mind back from the night's dreamworld. "How long must we be guests in this little house on the harbor of this wild and faraway Frisian town?"

"What a big question to be asking before the sun is even up," he answered playfully.

"I awaken with it on my lips every morning," she said, obviously ignoring his lighthearted spirit. "We've already been here with these strangers for five days. . . ."

She was wide awake now, and her eyes pleaded with him in the flickering candlelight.

"*Ja* . . ." he said, "that I know. . . ." It was not the way he had planned it. They should have gone straight to the printer friends of Johannes. But with the snowstorm, and Gretta awakening with that dreadful fever in the head and the hindrances to her breathing, the lady of this house—Oma they called her—had refused to let them move her.

"You will not take this woman out into the cold once more," she had insisted. She clearly ruled this house and would allow for no arguments. Besides, Dirck had to admit he was grateful enough to have her expert advice and care.

"I still don't understand who these people are," Aletta was saying, "or where they come from with those odd-sounding ways of saying their words. Oh, Vader, I am so frightened."

"Frightened? Of what? Can you not see they are devout, faithful souls, all of them? Out of obvious compassion, they rescued us from who knows what terrible fate in that vicious storm and opened their home to us. Is it then so necessary to know more?"

"But what happens when they learn the truth about Moeder?"

"So that's it!" he whispered. Dirck sighed, rose from his knees, and sat on the edge of his daughter's low bed. What did this child—no, she was no longer a child, yet she must always be one to him—what did she know? What did she think? Through the years, he'd managed never to talk openly with her about the awful facts of her moeder's strange illness or madness or whatever it was. When she was little and asked pointed questions, he always gave her half-answers. He'd always told himself his actions were a part of protecting her. Today he had to admit they went deeper than that. He never allowed her, or anyone else, to discuss it because he didn't know what to think himself and always harbored a bit of secret fear about it.

Meister Laurens was the one person who wouldn't allow him to wander away from it. In his authoritative way, he pointed a finger at Dirck and said repeatedly, "It sounds to me like a curse."

Dirck always denied it and refused to talk more. But he could never quite erase the nagging fear that the old schoolmaster could be right, and his friend's words returned to taunt him every time he thought about his wife. But what was that Aletta was saying now?

"Tante Lysbet warned me, in taking care of Moeder, to be most wary of devout and faithful pious souls."

"Why did she say that?" he asked and felt his heart beat faster.

" 'They are the ones most quick to see in a woman like your moeder the figure of an evil witch and most anxious to purge the world of all her kind.' Those were her words. Have you no fear of pious strangers, Vader?"

He smiled down on her and tried to dismiss the warning. Lysbet was a good and kind woman, a capable healer lady. But he knew she would no doubt be fearful if she knew their hosts and some of their plans for Gretta. Thank God she was not here to undo all that Oma and her son Hans were doing for Gretta. How much dare he say to the daughter tugging on his arm and begging for answers? With all his usual caution and smooth edging around the point, he said, "Tante Lysbet has planted worrisome ideas in your head, fair child. Believe me, she's never met the likes of Oma and her family. Oom Johannes knows them well. He assures me we can trust them. Besides, see how kindly they care for Moeder."

"I know, Vader. I know. I am not ungrateful."

He sat on the edge of the little bed and stroked her head with his big hand the way he used to do whenever bad things happened to make her weep.

"Rest, child, rest," he said softly. "Moeder Gretta is safer here with these people than in any other place on earth. Can you trust my word?"

"But what makes you so sure, Vader?"

"I have not time to explain it all now. Just trust me, and you will see. There are no witch-hunters in this house, nor friends of witch-hunters. Believe me."

He watched her young face relax. A smile appeared, and she wiped a stray tear from her cheek.

"*Ja*, Vader, I shall try to trust your words."

"*Goed!* Come now. I promise we won't stay in this place for a lifetime." He stood to his feet. "And for now, you must crawl down from this garret and assume your nursing duties. Your moeder sleeps for the time, but who knows for how long? She may need your help very soon. I go."

He kissed her forehead, then strode across the room, ducking his head to avoid the shaggy old ceiling beams. He waved in her direction, shouted, "*Tot ziens!*" and descended the ladder.

---

Aletta yawned, stretched, and gazed at the dried herbs hanging in hairy rows from the rafters of the steeply sloping roof. For some reason she could not fully grasp, Vader Dirck's words had soothed her anxious heart this morning, the way they used to long ago. She felt as if a pair of warm, strong arms were protecting her in this strange wild north country of Frisia. While the strangeness and uncertainty had not vanished into the unseen distance, they had been shoved into a far corner where they could not crush her.

All the same, a longing for home and Pieter-Lucas and life the way she'd always known it tugged at her heart. Even if she could trust these suspicious, pious strangers that gave them refuge, they could never replace the things and people she loved and understood. The house was dark and gloomy. She missed Robbin's daily chatter, since he'd gone on with Oom Johannes' family to make it more quiet for Moeder. No printing presses clanked in the other room. No fascinating people moved through with big piles of paper under their arms or spouted forth stories and ideas for her enjoyment as they had in Oom Johannes' printery in Antwerp.

Instead, from the far corner of the large room which housed the family came the soft clicking, swishing sounds made by a huge wooden-frame loom. Every day, Oma's son, Hans, the man who had carried her in from the storm, perched on a bench before the loom, surrounded with baskets of wool yarn. He worked the pedals and threw the shuttles and turned out large pieces of coarse dark woolen fabric. Several times during the day he stopped his work, came over to where Aletta sat beside her moeder, and asked, "How is she doing?"

The man was younger than Vader but older than Pieter-Lucas, with a sparse brown beard, large blue eyes, and rough, hairy hands. Something in the way he smiled at her and looked in on Moeder made her uneasy. He seemed to have no wife, but two daughters. Rietje, the younger of the two, was probably a year or two older than Robbin. Maartje must be at least ten years old. Lively little miniatures of their Oma in dark woolen dresses with white starched aprons and head scarves, they took turns spinning big mounds of died wool into balls of yarn.

All day long Oma and the two girls bustled through the house shaking feather beds, sweeping floors, polishing the pots and pans, scrubbing down furniture, spreading fresh rushes across the floors. Aletta had never seen such an obsession with scrubbing and polishing.

Several times during the day, young women appeared at the door bringing a variety of foodstuffs. They piled garden vegetables, eggs, freshly caught fish, chickens, or loaves of crusty, fragrant bread on Oma's table. In return, Oma went to a pantry room behind the kitchen corner and brought out little bottles of medicinal liquid and salves and powders and sent the women on their way.

She kept an assortment of herbal brews constantly boiling over her open fire. They lent a pungent odor to the cooking smells in the stuffy little house with its closed windows and enormous ceramic stove in the corner of the room. Each time a brew was finished, she brought a tiny steaming pot of the aromatic liquid to Aletta and identified the concoction by name.

Aletta wished for the courage to ask where and when Oma had harvested each herb, and how she preserved and concocted it. But fear always checked her urge to learn. This kind woman was a very pious stranger—never to be totally trusted according to Tante Lysbet. If pious strangers knew which herbs would keep witches and demons at bay, who could tell how many they brewed to tell them who was a witch and who was not?

Intuitively, Aletta knew Oma's wisdom could be mostly trusted. Her moeder moaned as if her head were aching, her breathing seemed to grow more and more plugged, and a deep, gasping cough rattled up from her chest.

"Juice of the hogs fennel root mixed with oil of roses to make her sweat out the heat," the elderly lady had explained with an air of experienced confidence that Aletta couldn't help but admire.

With a combination of trust and anxiety, Aletta pressed the hot herbal brews between her moeder's parched lips, held damp cloths to her feverish head, and lay on her chest the strong-smelling poultices that Oma prepared for her. But before she would administer the cures, she sniffed at each one and tried to recall what Tante Lysbet's Herbal said about it—if anything. If she only knew the book better. She could only hope she'd never given her moeder anything she would have known was dangerous.

At day's end when she climbed to her attic room, she held her flickering candle high to investigate the long rows of dried flowers and herbs that hung from the beams just beyond her bed. Then she climbed into her bed, pulled out Tante Lysbet's tattered treasure, and searched its pages to learn the secrets of each new herbal potion Oma had introduced her to during the day. She fell asleep probing her brain for clues, feeding her imagination, urging it to tell her what Oma's brews really were and what they could do to make her moeder well—or bring her to condemnation.

In the mornings, fascination changed to fresh apprehension as she arose to begin each new day. This morning, though, she descended the ladder with one new thing to make her glad. Her vader had opened his heart to her a wee crack. How or why it had come to pass, she could not be certain. Enough that it was no dream! She rolled the thoughts around in her mind and basked in the fires they lit in her heart. In their glowing light all good things looked possible.

At the bottom of the ladder, she discovered that Moeder Gretta did indeed appear to be much better.

"Her breathing comes easier," Aletta noted, leaning her ear toward the cupboard bed where she lay still sleeping. "Nor is she coughing or moaning so."

"The goldenrod has begun to do its work," Oma said from beside the gigantic soup pot she stirred over the fire. "I tried it yesterday at last."

"The goldenrod?" She tugged at the name trying to recall what she'd seen in Tante Lysbet's herbal about goldenrod. Good for wounds and coughs and asthma and sugar sickness and bed wetting. . . . Surely if there were anything dangerous besides, she would have remembered.

"*Ja*, the very same herb I used to make the salve that is healing your wound." The woman seemed eager to share a bit of knowledge. "Marvelous gift of the Great Physician for ever so many things!"

Spurred on by growing fascination and still encouraged by Vader Dirck's words, Aletta ventured a question. "Does it grow in your herb garden, Oma?"

"*Nay*, Child, no need to plant this wild and flourishing herb."

"Where, then, do you collect it?"

"It spreads beyond control at the edges of the woods behind the city. My granddaughters and I gather it by the armload on a sunny afternoon in August, then spread it out to dry in the attic where you sleep."

"I have seen it hanging in little bunches from the attic beams, then?"

"That along with tens of other fine and fragrant herbs—borage for dispelling melancholies, crow's foot to blister the skin and draw out pain from grievous sores, wild thymes of several sorts to promote urine and relieve shortness of breath, agrimony to purify the blood, horseradish for arthritis in the bones, and it makes a great good sauce to spice up meats and fish, the lovely calendula for adding to soups and mixing with other herbs that soothe the stomach and calm old coughs, and of course button leek to keep the demons at bay."

Aletta shivered a bit. Of course, there would be button leek. Every home must be protected. She shoved the negative feelings away. Her mind whirred in excited little spinnings. "Oh," she exclaimed in sudden abandon to the wonder of this magical moment. "All those names and the lovely pictures that go with them—I've seen them in . . . in an herbal from a friend."

"What sort of herbal was this?" Oma joined the excitement.

"It tells about a world full of herbs and what they do. A truly wonderful little book." Her breathing came quickly, causing the book to rise and fall next to her heart. If only she dared to bring it out, to show it to this woman.

"Did you bring it with you on your journey?" Oma's voice combined apprehension with a twinge of hopefulness. "I am always eager to see other herbals. There is so much to learn."

Above the pounding of her heart, Aletta heard Tante Lysbet's firm voice, "Give it to no one . . . not to another soul on earth. Do you hear?"

"I hear you," she'd answered. Now, how to answer Oma's direct question and still not lie?

"I had so little time or room to pack my things," she said at last. "Many of my treasures I had to leave behind."

"A great pity!"

"Great pity indeed. I loved it so and always knew it held some healing secrets—" She stopped short. "Oma is a stranger," a faint voice prodded from within. "Trust her not."

"What kind of secrets do you seek?"

Aletta did not answer. She'd already said too much.

"Secrets for your moeder who is often ill?" Oma was looking at her now, her eyes penetrating the heavy air between them. Aletta looked away.

"Who has told you such a thing?" she finally managed. "Moeder simply caught a bad cough and headache in the nasty weather. That means not that she is always sick." Aletta felt the panic take over once more, and all the possibilities born in this morning's intimate encounter with Vader lay in crumbs strewn among the rushes at her feet.

"Your moeder's body tells me, without a word. Her eyes lack light, her muscles sag, and when she moans, I hear the melancholy humors sighing in her breast."

"Moeder is not mad." Aletta fought to keep hysteria from her voice.

"I did not say she was mad." A smile softened Oma's wrinkled face, and her eyes probed Aletta's once more, this time with a look the girl did not know how to interpret. "She is only weak, the dear soul. I am quite certain that with time the herbs can bring her back to robustious health."

From behind them, an unexpected masculine voice intruded. "You may thank God in heaven He brought you by our way, young lady. My moeder, here, is the foremost expert on herbal healing in all of East Friesland."

Startled, Aletta swallowed, then turned to face Hans, with his dark beard and warm smile. Her hands felt sticky, her face burned then chilled. "I do give Him thanks."

"It appears to me that you, too, have a deep interest to learn the many secrets that she holds in her mind. Am I not right?"

What could she say? To admit it was to open the door too wide. To refuse was to offend them and to lie as well. Oma, always efficient, always in control, did not leave the choice to her.

"You will make a wonderful student, my child. I have long asked our

Heavenly Father that He would send the likes of you to us. A bright young woman who would love to learn my art and one day carry it on when I am gone. But enough for now. There is time to think of all these things later."

"*Ja*, there is much time." Aletta sighed, her legs suddenly drained of strength, her heart palpitating vigorously. Moeder Gretta's ruffled voice called from her bed, and Aletta turned to her with especial eagerness. As she did so, she caught a fleeting glimpse of the man of the house staring at her with a beckoning sort of expression that sent fresh terrors to her heart.

She must persuade Vader to take them away from here, now. He had no idea in how grave a state of danger they all lay. How could she convince him? She had not a shred of clear, obvious evidence. Only this recurring uneasiness that refused to let her rest long in the warmth of Vader's confidence.

She tugged at the bed curtains, eager to free herself from the stranger's gaze. Nothing in her wildest dreams prepared her for what she saw there. Her moeder lay with her arms reaching out toward her. Something more than a hint of recognition glistened in the puffy eyes, her lips spread into a thin smile. She spoke just above an awed whisper. "Aletta, my child, praise be to God, you are alive."

At least she recognized her. Jubilant, Aletta clambered into the outstretched arms. Moeder and daughter held each other in a rare embrace. The heat was gone. Her breath came more softly, not so rattly.

"*Ja, ja*, Moeder, and you too." She pulled free and sat up. With her hand she smoothed the wisps of graying hair away from the familiar face and kissed the furrowed forehead now cool, dry to the touch of her lips.

Oma's herbs had brought her nearly back from the coughing sickness. If only she would return, too, to her right mind!

"You were away so long, child." Moeder's voice grew stronger with each word. "I despaired of ever seeing you again."

"*Nay*, but God would never separate us. His eye smiles on us today."

Would she come all the way back? A tinge of uncertainty edged into her heart. Somehow she must convince Oma that this delirium was something extraordinary, not a common occurrence.

"You look so lovely, my daughter," Moeder said, her face crinkled with smiles. "Are you as well as you look after your long ordeal?"

Pain jabbed at Aletta's mind. Her long ordeal? What did she think? Where was her mind?

"I am very well, Moeder." Aletta smiled down at the woman lying at rest, placidness spread across her pale, wrinkled face. "And how do you feel on this cheerful morning?"

"Now that you have come home, I feel ever so fine." She looked at her a bit quizzically, then raised herself to one elbow and stared over Aletta's head out into the room beyond her bed. "But I must get out of this bed and put on the kettle so that Dirck can have his soup when the men are finished with him in the bookshop."

She grabbed the feather bag to fling it off her body.

"Wait!" Aletta cautioned. She reached for her moeder to steady her. But the woman shoved past her with amazing strength in her arms, dislodging the night cap from her head and knocking it to her shoulder.

In an eyeblink, Oma was there. "Here now, Gretta," she reassured the agitated woman. Then over her shoulder, "Hans, come help us, please. Our sister knows not where she is nor the limits of her strength."

"I can take care of her," Aletta protested. "I've done it. . . ." Enough! She must be still.

"I'm sure you've done it many times before. Today, though, 'tis best if you help me bring her another herbal preparation to soothe the humors that drive her so. Hans will hold her down. She is too strong for you."

"Then let Hans or one of the girls go for Vader Dirck. He knows how best to make her calm."

But Hans was already at her side, his massive body pushing against Aletta's. At the warmth of his closeness, she recoiled. Something in this man threatened her even more than his moeder. She must protect Moeder. Tante Lysbet was trusting her—and Vader Dirck. She grabbed for the flailing arms. They eluded her. With one strong pass of his muscular arms, Hans subdued Moeder Gretta. Helpless and frantic, Aletta looked on as Moeder glared at him with wild eyes. Undeterred, the persistent stranger held her crazed moeder and spoke gentle, soothing words, until at last she began to sob.

How like the way Vader quieted her!

Disarmed, Aletta watched him take Moeder's head in his arms and gently stroke her hair, all the while letting his warm, comforting voice pour over her. "Hear the words of our Master, 'Peace I leave you, my peace I give you. Let not your heart be troubled, neither let it be afraid.'" Then his voice turned into melody, and he hummed a soft, mellow tune. Aletta knew she'd heard it once before but wasn't quite sure where, until he added the words:

"Those who in God do trust
And nev'r in shame do stand,
Both young and old, men and women,

God strengthens with His hand."

Tante Neeltje's song! A man who sang such hymns and spoke the words of God to comfort a woman in such deep distress could not intend great danger to either of them.

Hans looked up at Aletta. "You see, she's nearly fine already. Just another drink from Oma's kitchen, and she will be like new." The smile that raised the contour of his beard beckoned her once more. Must he always look at her in that way? She looked away, at first seeing nothing, then noticing several sprigs of dried, purplish-eared flowers tangled in the night cap that had slid from Moeder's head.

Aletta stared. No goldenrod this. She snatched up the cap with its cache of blossoms and bounded off the bed and across the room, coming to a stop before Oma and her steaming kettle. "Betony!" she gasped.

"Laid beneath the cap, it checks a bad headache," Oma explained in her calm "teacher" manner.

Aletta thrust the herbs toward the older woman and shrieked, "Headache indeed! Think you that I do not know the rest? The part of the herbal book that says, 'Betony to dispel visions of horror and strengthen the weak head lest it wander away into strange worlds of devilish enchantment'? Rest assured, I know it well." Too angry to cry, she threw the night cap and the betony on the table, then clenched her hands into hard, round fists.

What more evidence could she need? For her own heart? To convince Vader Dirck? Oma did indeed know their secret, just as Aletta had feared from the first moment she'd handed her a bowl of steaming herbs to help her moeder "sweat it out." So did Hans, probably his daughters as well, and God only knew how many of their friends in this awful foreign land. For all she knew, they had already called the bailiff, and he stood outside the door just waiting for strong man, Hans, to pick up her dear moeder and deliver her into their accusing hands.

Oma stood with her mouth gaping, a bowl of brew held askew in her hand. "My child, calm yourself. . . ."

"I am no child, and I have been calm too long already. Please, I beg of you, if you are as pious as my vader says you are, do not deliver my poor moeder into the hands of the bailiff. She may be wild and say strange things, but she is no witch!"

Oma gasped. "A witch? *Nay*, never!"

Aletta raved on, her words tumbling out like a wild bull let free from a fenced-in pasture. "Vader Dirck and I will take her to Oudewater if we must to prove it. Only give us a chance. Tante Lysbet's herbal will yet yield the clues to bring her back to health."

Oma handed the bowl to Maartje, who carried it to her vader seated on the edge of Moeder Gretta's bed. Then Oma stepped carefully toward Aletta and laid a hand on her forearm.

"My dear young lady, I see you know not what sort of home this is where God has brought you."

"Indeed, I do not. Only that all is strange and frightening so far from home and Tante Lysbet and Pieter-Lucas. . . ." Careful! Oma, for all her disarming ways, was still a stranger.

"Sit please and let me explain." Oma motioned her to the bench beside the long table that separated the kitchen from the rest of the house. Covered with a white starched cloth, the table was already laden at one end with the day's first offerings of produce and fish. Aletta did not sit at once. She glanced first at Moeder. Hans held her still while his ten-year-old fed her the bowl of herbal brew Oma had just given her. Then she looked back at Oma. The elderly lady held herself erect, just like Tante Lysbet. But the lines in her face were drawn with a softer, warmer pen. Something in her expression made Aletta expect the kindly grandmother to embrace her to her breast and brush away all the tears, like a true moeder.

In her mind, Aletta heard her vader's words from this morning, "Moeder is safer here than in any other place . . . no witch-hunters here. . . . Trust me. . . ." Fear and reassurance fought for control of her mind as she sat on the end of the bench and waited.

"In these dangerous times," Oma said at last, "we do not talk about the places from whence we come, nor do we give our real names. I know not whence you and your vader's people came, nor do I know him by any other name than Dirck."

Aletta started. "But I do not understand."

" 'Tis better so."

"Why?"

"Most of the people who have thronged into the walls of Emden, and many whose homes snuggle up to the edges, have come here in search of peace and a last chance to live. We worship God in ways that in most other places would be cause enough for us to be led away to prison and thence to the stake or the scaffold."

"You are Calvinists, then?" Such an awful thought had never occurred to her. Oma and her family were so unlike Count Brederode and Hendrick van den Garde and the wild pseudo-soldiers she had seen patrolling the streets of Antwerp. *Nay,* they could not be Calvinists.

"You will find Calvinists in Emden. In our borders lodges the Mother Church of all Lowland Calvinism. Some truly fine and neighborly folks among them. But in this house, we are not Calvinists."

"Not Papists either, else why would you have to flee from arrest?" Aletta was amazed at how the isolated snatches of information she had garnered in the past months were beginning to blend together like the assortment of unrelated lines in one of Pieter-Lucas' drawings.

"You are so right." Oma did not go on.

"Lutherans, then?"

"*Nay,* nor Lutherans either."

"I can tell you are not Munsterites!" Aletta knew nothing of what those strange people believed. She only knew she'd heard that they did wild, violent, and fearsome things such as running naked through the streets of Amsterdam and locking up the city of Munster.

Oma's expression was half smile, half wince. "*Nay,* my child, never, never!"

"Dare I ask, what then?" Aletta ventured, not having the slightest idea what other options there were.

"The name matters not. We are a group of simple Children of God, who strive to live holy lives according to the Bible. We believe all it says about salvation through faith in the finished work of Jesus Christ, without the help of infant baptism and the other sacraments of the Church. And we believe in a peaceful approach which will not allow us to take up arms."

The old lady reached a hand across the table and laid it on Aletta's. Looking directly into the girl's eyes, she added in soft, consoling tones, "Nor would we ever turn a suspected witch over to any government or church authorities."

"Does my vader know all you have just told me?"

"Your vader knows all I have told you . . . and there is more. But that is enough for now, think you not so?"

Aletta's whole body felt limp, as if she'd been chased from Breda to Antwerp by the great Belgian Lion and had run at last into a secure tower and collapsed into a soft bed of down. Enough for now indeed! Later, she would want to know more. How much would Vader Dirck tell her? And did Tante Lysbet know nothing about these strange, pious, "safe" people who showed such kindness?

"*Ja,* 'tis quite enough," she answered, her facial muscles relaxing into a weak smile offered to her hostess. "And, Oma," she added in halting syllables, "I must ask you to forgive my anger and my hurtful accusations. I did not know."

"You were afraid. Understandably afraid. So would I be. So was I once. But that is for another time . . . when these devilish wars cease, and we may someday speak without fear to reveal who we are and whence we come."

———————

When the evening meal had been cleared away, and candles chased the gathering darkness into the corners of Oma's dingy old house on the edge of Emden, Aletta climbed the steep ladder to her garret bed and struggled with a wide range of strange misgivings and hopes. As at every point of deep confusion, memories of Breda and home beckoned to her troubled heart from ever so far away.

Oh, for Moeder Gretta's broad tiled hearth and open windows to let in the still, damp air of Breda! For the sound of Roland—clear, brazen, rich—announcing the incessant tramping of the sun above a thick blanket of Brabant mist. Brabant! Breda! *The Crane's Nest* on Annastraat and Tante Lysbet and Pieter-Lucas! Pieter-Lucas could help her sort out all the mysteries of this place. If only. . . !

By instinct, she dug beneath the layers of her garments till she touched the dove in her bosom fold and fingered it with ritualistic tenderness. She crawled into her bed, pulled the feather bag around her ears, licked the warm teary drops streaming over her cheeks, and savored their saltiness.

She was nearly nodding off to sleep when from some place not far away she heard the muffled strains of music. On and on they went. Bits and pieces of melody wafted to her ears and defied all attempts to sleep.

At last, enticed and overcome with curiosity, she slipped out of bed, down the ladder, and across the floor in stockinged feet. Guided by light from a tall, thick candle left burning on the table, she crept past Vader and Moeder's bed. All was perfectly still there. Past Oma's cupboard bed and the cooking hearth where a cluster of embers winked at her, she followed the music growing louder, more coherent with each step. She could make out the tune now. Something sad but strong, it was nothing she had ever heard before.

She followed it to the far corner of the huge living room which marked the borders of the house as she knew it. The music came from the other side of the wall behind Hans' cumbersome weaving loom. With her fingers she searched over the rough timbers till they traced the outline of a door so perfectly blended with the wall that she had never noticed it before. Moving quickly to the appropriate place, she found a small leather thong which yielded to her tugging.

The door opened silently into a dimly lighted room, probably as large as the one she came from. Rows of benches filled the space, and people sat on them, facing a small table at the far side of the room.

Aletta guided the door to a soundless closure behind her and stood transfixed, searching with an overawed curiosity. Who were these people? Why were they singing here in the middle of the night? What was this place? Could it be some strange sort of church gathering?

Impossible! Who ever heard of a church in a house?

A chill ran through her body. Indeed she had heard of just such a thing—in Breda. Pieter-Lucas and his family used to go to that awful Calvinist church at Antonis Backeler's house. That was where Hendrick van den Garde had learned to carry a sword into the real church on the market square and cut up Opa's painting.

Could this, too, be such a dreadful place? True, Oma had assured her they were not Calvinists. But what did Aletta know yet about Oma? She was a stranger still, and strangers often lie!

She started to pull on the leather thong that held the door fast behind her so she could return to her bed, when out of the corner of her eye, she spotted Oma and the two granddaughters sitting on a bench down front. Aletta shifted her position a bit so as to see better between the women who filled the left side of the room. Unbelieving, she stared, trying to take in what it was she saw beside Oma on the floor. A sleeping mat, with a body lying on it. Calvinists or whatever, this was a strange thing to find in a church.

The singing stopped, and a man stood to his feet behind the table where a large book lay open beside a flickering lamp. *Hans!* Aletta gasped. What had Oma said about her family? Not Calvinists, but rather simple folk who read the Bible, wasn't it? It began to fall into place.

"We open the Holy Scriptures," he spoke in that warm, firm voice that had both comforted and frightened Aletta so many times during the days she had taken shelter under these strangers' thatch. "We read tonight from the Gospel record of the life of our Lord Jesus Christ: 'Straight away went Jesus and His disciples out of the synagogue and into the house of Simon Peter and Andrew, with James and John. And the mother-in-law of Simon lay with a fever in bed, and they straight away spoke with Him about her. And He came near to her, seized her hand, and raised her up. And the fever left her and she served them.'"

Aletta's heart pounded against the dove lying in the folds of her dress. She knew not what she anticipated or dreaded, but whatever it was, it held her almost too tightly for breath or thought. As if in a dream, she listened to the gentle, bearded weaver read on: "'When, now, the evening was come, and the sun had set, they brought to Him all who were seriously ill and those who were possessed by devils. . . .'"

At the mention of devils, a sharp cry arose from the mat on the floor by Oma. Moeder Gretta! Aletta would recognize that cry at any time. Dear God, what is this? And where is Vader? She, Aletta, must do something, and do it now!

Without a further thought for herself, Aletta dashed through the crowd and to her moeder's side, only to see her vader kneeling on the other side of the mat. Their eyes met, and with hers, the confused girl offered him a questioning accusation.

"All will be well," he said. "Be still, my child." Then, turning to his wife, he took her hand in his and soothed her with his words. "Still, now, Gretta, still. Our God is here."

What is this? How could Vader let them expose Moeder to all these pious strangers in such an unseemly way? Not only had he brought her into this place of great danger, but something told her that Vader had betrayed her, that Oma had lied to her, that Hans had played the pious fraud, and that the *bailiff* and his men indeed waited at the door to cart Moeder Gretta off to the scaffold in the city square. Frantic, Aletta pushed her vader's hand aside and placed her body over her agitated moeder. If Vader wouldn't do it, she had to protect the woman who had given her life.

Vaguely she realized that Hans' smooth voice went on: " 'And He healed many who were seriously ill with many diseases, and many angry spirits He drove out.' " He paused, and the room grew so silent that it was as if all breathing had been suspended. He broke the silence at last. "Brothers and sisters, we have before us one who is sorely afflicted in body and spirit." His tone was so authoritative, yet so compassionate, Aletta felt herself almost believing in the man's sincerity.

"We have brought this tormented woman here tonight," Hans explained, "to present her to the touch of the Christ whose power dwells among us and whose name we invoke. Let us fall on our faces before Him and pray, earnestly seeking His healing touch upon our sister who has so long suffered these afflictions."

Aletta clung to her moeder until Vader spoke. "My child, all is well. Trust these people; trust your vader; trust in God."

He lifted her from her moeder's body, and she found herself enveloped in the arms of Tante Neeltje, who spoke even as Vader Dirck had spoken. "All is well, child Aletta. Trust in God."

Suddenly Oma stood above them, handing to Hans a vial from which he sprinkled out drops of a thick amber liquid onto Moeder Gretta's forehead. A group of men from the congregation gathered around, each laying their hands on the sick woman's body.

Aletta felt smothered by the press of bodies. She looked around the room and saw the strangest sight yet. Every person in the room had knelt down with their cheeks pressed to the floor. On either side of Moeder knelt Vader and Hans, each holding one of her hands in his. Tante Neeltje, too, was kneeling, pulling Aletta to her face.

Nay, but this cannot be right. Deep inside, she resisted even as she knelt there, her eyes open and peering at her moeder, the floor rushes pressing helter-skelter patterns into her warm cheek. In desperation, she wafted one brief prayer heavenward, "Dear God, have mercy on her. Deliver her!"

Then Hans' voice came clear one more time. "Almighty God and Father of all compassion, hear our earnest prayers for this distressed woman in her miserable plight. As Thy Christ touched Peter's mother-in-law and bade the fever leave her, and as He healed the throngs of diseased and possessed near the shores of Galilee, even so, Great God, touch now our oppressed sister and bring her back to new life even as we wait for Thy healing touch. In Jesus' mighty name, we adjure the tormenting spirit to be gone!"

Gretta Engelshofen gave one more sharp cry, followed by an enormous sigh. Aletta lifted her face from the floor and looked at her moeder, expecting to see the gaping mouth and still countenance of a lifeless body. Instead, a soft smile spread across Moeder's face. In the flickering candlelight, her eyes seemed to glow with a steady look of recognition and peace, and her lips moved with the whispered benediction, "Thanks be to God! The curse is over. I'm free!"

Aletta sat back on her knees and stared. She had neither words nor coherent thoughts, only a mass of confusion churning through her mind. What would Tante Lysbet say? Was this the thing she had prepared Aletta to fear? Too dazed to know what she was seeing, she watched Vader lift Moeder by the hand. Then he reached out a hand to her as well. The soft warmth in his eyes said, "Come," and Aletta let him help her to her feet.

"Tante Lysbet did not know this kind of pious persons," Vader whispered to her.

She looked at Moeder, and the woman smiled back at her, then grabbed her hand and said softly, "I'm delivered. The prayers of these people have brought your moeder back."

Even in the dim lamplight, Aletta could see that the wildness was gone. It had been replaced by a gentle peace that she'd never seen on this face before, not even on Moeder's best days.

Together, the three of them left that most unusual gathering. Moeder was leaning lightly on Vader's arm, walking with a sureness of step Aletta had not seen in her since they'd left Antwerp.

Aletta hardly slept for what remained of the memorable night. Feeling as if she'd just witnessed some mysterious enchanted dream, she expected to awaken with the dawn to find everything as it had been the day before. True, the next morning, her moeder was not completely well. But the last remains of her cough had gone. Her head no longer ached, and that vacant stare that had carried her into her own faraway world for as long as Aletta could remember was replaced by warmth and a hint of good-natured wit that matched the sharpness of her chin.

# CHAPTER THIRTEEN

*Breda*

Middle of Grass Month (April), 1567

The Pieter-Lucas van den Garde that rode across the Harbor Bridge into Breda was not the same Pieter-Lucas who had slipped out through the Prison-tower Gate last autumn. He'd gone out a boy—anxious, eager, on a mission of hope. Six months later he returned a man, with all the eagerness and idealism and hope drained out of him.

It seemed so simple, so sure—half a year ago. But Antwerp mocked him, and Oudewater built his hopes more than a score of times. It dashed them, though, with each wagon that arrived at the weigh-house on Guesthousestraat, across from the Halle Bridge and the village market square. He'd seen exactly twenty-five witch weighings. He knew just how many because he'd carved a tiny notch in Blesje's reins for every one and counted them each night.

Finally despairing, certain the Engelshofens had either come and gone before he arrived or had sought out some other haven of refuge, he'd taken to the road. Since just before the first snow, he and Blesje had tromped the roads from Oudewater to Groningen in the far north, from Harlingen on the Zuyder Zee to Enschede in the east and Goederede in Zeeland. Everywhere he went, he drew cartoons that lampooned the Beggars and slipped them into knapsacks and under doors and anchored them in shutters. He did odd jobs in hostels wherever he could to earn his bed and bread. He even tried his hand at drawing portraits for city officials and families and sketches of churches and castles. In the lower right hand corner of every piece he drew, he affixed his unique signature—the figure of the anointing dove with his initials woven in.

Not that he believed in the anointing anymore. How could he? With his own eyes, he'd watched Hendrick van den Garde slice it to shreds in the Great Church.

"But Aletta has to be out there somewhere," he told Blesje at least once a day. "And when she sees one of these signatures, she'll know I'm searching for her. *Ja*, I know it's like drawing a bow in the dark, but it's all I can do."

Nothing ever came of any of it. He found absolutely no tracks, and none of his drawings or paintings brought her to his side. Finally, on a balmy morning approaching noon, he trudged through the streets of Breda, disappointed, thwarted, dragging, angry.

Breda had changed too. He sensed it with his first breath of blossom-laden air. There were the obvious signs. Spring had arrived in full dress, bringing buds to the oaks and birches and alders and to a host of lesser shrubs he'd never bothered to ask names for.

But what he sensed went deeper. An unusual air hovered over the streets as people bustled about their business—a subdued, heavy, almost melancholy air that didn't match the weather. Mingling with the familiar Bredenaars, Pieter-Lucas noted little knots of strangers in Antwerp garb and pairs of soldiers with feathers in their hats and threatening arquebuses at their shoulders.

When he reached the market square and stood before the Great Church, his mind dredged up the hateful image of Hendrick's sneering face and shreds of "The Anointing" strewn across the grave-slab floor. Deep wounds inflicted on his spirit in this ancient, hallowed place opened up and bled. From the pit of his stomach, he felt the stirring of the inner monster that had become his constant companion through the lonely winter months. It sent the word "revenge" echoing again in his ears.

When he turned toward Annastraat and home, the feelings grew no better. He imagined that something stood like an overturned wagon in his pathway. He knew that knee-high weeds would greet him around the doorstoop. Inside, a cold hearth, and next door, an empty bookshop . . .

*Home* indeed! Why had he come back to this place of grievous memories and foreboding fears?

Gradually, as if from a deep fog, he heard a familiar voice calling his name. "Pieter-Lucas! Pieter-Lucas! You're alive—and back!"

He looked up to see his old friend, Yaap, with a grin spread across his mustachioed face. "Had about decided I'd never see you again!" The prince's messenger greeted him with a solid slap on the back.

"Hello, Yaap," Pieter-Lucas responded, trying to put a smile on his own travel-begrimed and unshaven face. "It seems like a lifetime since I left you in Vianen and made my way home."

"It nearly has been, *jongen*. You've been gone so long, I figured you lost your way."

"Lost my way, eh?" Pieter-Lucas sneered. "What do you think I am, some rudderless fishing boat caught in a squall?"

"Oh," Yaap shrugged. Then with a mischievous grin and a jab in Pieter-Lucas' ribs, he explained, "Just thought . . . well, you know, you'd never been any place out of Breda without your personal mounted guide." He thrust his chest out and tilted his nose skyward.

Pieter-Lucas grew defensive. "Look, friend," he said, "Blesje and I have covered the length and breadth of these Lowlands since you and I shared that prison cell in Vianen, and I don't need to account to you for any of it. I'm a seasoned traveler now, do you hear?"

"Oh, I see!" Yaap nodded. "Out casting about on the sea of manhood, eh?" Coming up close he nudged Pieter-Lucas in the shoulder and spoke down on him with a confidential hush, "Did you find her?"

Pieter-Lucas sent him a dagger-glance. "Did you not hear what I said? I don't need to account to you."

The taller man pulled away. "I see." He cleared his throat. "You really should have come home sooner. Lots of excitement in this old city since you left."

Pieter-Lucas chuckled. "I suppose you think I haven't seen excitement? Name me a city, I've been there. Name me a danger, I've been in the middle of it. Did you once say we were on the brink of a war?"

"Congratulations!" Yaap clapped him on the back. "You really have seen the world, haven't you? I guess tales of riots in the streets, shouting matches in the city hall, fiery sermons stirring up rebellion from the pulpits, massive troop recruitment and weapon stocking, threats on Prince Willem's life—these won't impress you anymore, eh?"

"I've seen them all, Yaap. In fact, the only reason I can imagine that I came back was that I kept hoping Breda was still the one place where I wouldn't find such things."

Yaap looked at his younger friend with eyes that seemed to bore clear through. "What if I told you we've had them all here as well?"

"*Nay*, tell me not."

"Did you come here to assume the role of a man of Breda—or to hide?"

Pieter-Lucas looked up swiftly, startled. His gaping mouth made no reply. Yaap pointed his finger in his chest and spoke with punctuated force, "Let me tell you right now, there's no hiding here anymore. Just last month, the day before the Spaniards cut a regiment of ill-prepared Beggars to shreds outside the city walls of Antwerp, our own Aelbrecht the Tailor got all excited and appeared running through this very market square, brandishing a dagger and shouting, 'Death to the Papist Preachers!' "

"Anybody take him seriously?"

"*Nay*, but of course not. But, he was quickly subdued by soldiers. As you can see, we've got plenty of them roaming the streets now. Willem ordered them here months ago to keep order."

"So, it's that bad, eh?"

"Surprise you?"

"Guess it shouldn't. It was, after all, here in Breda's own Great Church that I nearly became a victim of the image-breaking myself. For the rest of my life, I'll carry the scars and the limp in my leg. But if I can't hope here, what is there left to believe in?" Pieter-Lucas' heart was racing, his chest felt tight, and breathing was an effort.

Yaap shrugged. "You have to wonder all right. Prince Willem is in the *Kasteel* right now—that's another long story—getting ready to flee for his life."

"What? The prince is going to leave us? I never thought . . ." Words trailed off into blurred thoughts. Nobody knew better than Pieter-Lucas that the whole country was on the brink of war. But that Willem would flee? That was too much.

"If you've really been to all the places you boast of, I don't have to tell you that King Philip hasn't been enlisting all those Spanish soldiers to string beads. He is famous for his long arms, you know. Even a prince, or maybe especially a prince, knows there's a time to pull in your horns and bide your time till it's safe to come out and attack."

Just then, Roland's resonant voice interrupted their conversation with seventeen long, mellow peals from the tower at the boys' back. Yaap started. "Hey, look," he said, "I got to run another errand for the day. And when I'm through, I've got one more juicy message to deliver—this one for a young man named Pieter-Lucas van den Garde."

"Sure, like I just arrived from nowhere, and you didn't know I was coming, and suddenly you have a message for me. Who'd give you a message for me, anyway?"

"Meet me at the stables after dark," he spoke as he walked away. "Don't know how late I'll be. Wait for me, or you'll be sorry, do you hear?"

"*Ja*, sure," Pieter-Lucas threw the words at his friend's retreating figure. Yaap had already crossed the square and run halfway to the Oat Market by the harbor.

———

"*Ja*, sure," he repeated to himself hours later in the nearly deserted stable. He'd arrived with the first shades of night. How many hours ago that was, he'd lost track. For a while, the old musty building buzzed with a perpetual parade of darting messengers, official-looking strangers, even a handful of Beggars. Then, the activity stopped, the horses settled down for the night, and the stableboy fell asleep, his feet sprawled out before him and his mouth issuing forth an occasional sharp snore.

Pieter-Lucas paced back and forth from one end of the stable to the other, looking in on all the horses, seeing none of them. He shoved his hands into his pockets, bent his head forward till his chin nearly rested on his chest, and dug his heels into the damp straw that squeaked beneath his shoes. Sometime in the night, the air turned blustery and a shower of rain poured onto the roof of the stable. A capricious wind badgered the lanterns that fought to keep back the darkness.

"Not sure what it is about this place," he whispered into Blesje's ear. "But even this old stable has changed. The stalls are all the same; the smell is as horsy as ever." He looked around him. Every hovering ceiling beam, shuttered window, creaky door, and brick on the old wall was inscribed in his memory along with the letters of the alphabet, the days of the week, and his numbers from one to one hundred. None of that had changed. "What is it, Blesje? What makes it feel so different?"

Why did he feel like a spectator on the bridge across the *Kasteel* moat, peering at a long-ago dream, wondering at its not quite realness? With each succeeding pace across the length of the stable, something tugged him farther away. His mind tramped over the meandering countryside of his life, gathering up painful memories that made his heart beat with confusion and anger.

First, he pictured himself kneeling with Opa at the altar in the Chapel of the Holy Ghost and felt the priest's holy water trickling down his scalp. From Opa's lips the word shouted at him, "Wait! Until your day has come . . . *Wait!*" He felt the hope.

Next, he stood in Aletta's tiny garden, certain that the girl he loved stirred just beyond the window, out of reach, out of sight. He felt Dirck Engelshofen's stern eyes glaring at him and heard his foreboding voice. "Wait until the storm has passed, be patient. *Wait!*" He felt the anger.

Then he was sitting beside Yaap in the filth and dimness of Brederode's dungeon, his ankles swollen in irons, unseen vermin skittering through the straw all around him, *waiting* for the Great Beggar to appear and set him free. He felt the pain.

All too slowly that last painful image faded, but the one that replaced it was no brighter. He stood in a twilight street in Antwerp before an empty house, and in his hand he was crushing an old scrap of paper with its tantalizing little inscription: "I PROMISED, I'll *wait!*" He felt the frustration, the panic!

Finally, he was searching the streets and inns and the famous weigh-house of Oudewater for the girl who seemed always, by turns, to tug at his heartstrings, then to slip out of his reach with a calm and steady skill that drove him to the brink of madness. He should have known Dirck Engelshofen would not bring his family to Oudewater. That man always had to do things in his own way, not at all like the rest of the world. In his desperation, Pieter-Lucas had cried out to the leaden skies, "Where is she?" The only answer came in the familiar message that rose and fell from the steady, rhythmic peal of the bell in the church tower. *Wachten! Wachten! Wachten!* Wait! Wait! Wait! Nothing left but despair!

He jerked himself back to the present, where the watchword hadn't changed. Tonight, Yaap kept him *waiting* once more, and for what, he hadn't the slightest notion. At this rate, he'd grow old and die with the stifling word still hanging over him like Hendrick van den Garde's flashing parade knife. He knotted his hands into hard fists and punched them into the air, aimed at all his fine plans that first mocked, then deserted him, always snatched from him just on the threshold of desire.

"Hey there, young friend," Yaap's voice startled him once more, and his friend's flapping cape sent a shower of water spraying Pieter-Lucas from head to toe. He swiveled on his heel in the slippery straw, his lame leg complaining at the hasty change of rotation.

"Finally! I thought you'd deserted me."

"*Ja*, well, I did expect to get back sooner." Yaap swiped the water from his face and shook it from his head.

"Tell me, what goes on here tonight? I never saw these stables so full of people, in and out for the first half of the night."

"Come, you haven't been waiting that long."

"Ever since the sun shut us out. And I don't mind telling you, I'm tired of waiting. If your message is so juicy, why can't you give it to me *now* and at least let me go home to get a couple hours of sleep?"

"Want to take an all-night ride with me in the rain?"

"I've waited all these hours to hear that foolish suggestion?"

"Sounds exciting, doesn't it?"

"Forget it. What you have to say had better be worth the wait or . . ."

"Hold on, *jongen*, hold on. First, I need to know something."

"Such as?"

"Since you've become such a traveler, how would you feel about joining the prince's cause? Running messages for him maybe?"

"What's that got to do with it?"

"Never mind, just answer me, will you?"

Pieter-Lucas hesitated. He had to choose his words with care. He remembered a time when he had jumped at the chance to carry a piece of rolled paper from the stable up to the prince's apartment. He was ten years old then. Could never forget it. But that was back when life was normal, Opa was still alive, Dirck Engelshofen was still his friend, and he and Aletta shared their books and dreams, and . . . And this was the middle of the night and none of the other things were true anymore. Everything he'd tried had failed. All the people he loved had deserted him. Besides, he'd just spent half a year traveling around the country and he was ready for . . . Well, what was he ready for? And could he get it if he knew?

Home wasn't what he expected. So maybe he did need to leave it with all its disturbing memories jabbing at him from every corner. Riding through the countryside carrying messages for Prince Willem just might lead him to the two people he most wanted to find: Hendrick van den Garde to settle a score with, and Aletta to settle down with. Not that traveling had worked before. But what else was there to do?

"I, too, have one question. Will I have to help the Beggars?"

"No more than the prince decides he has to help them so he can win this war and get King Philip out of our cities and our churches. Besides, Brederode's lost a host of battles and destroyed the respect of decent folks. Great braggarts, drunkards, and carousers—the whole bunch. Ha, don't get me started on that one!"

"Not the Great Beggar's devoted follower anymore, eh?"

"Don't dignify the old sot with so grand a title, do you hear? Never again!" He shook his head. "But you sidestep my question. How about running errands for Willem?"

Pieter-Lucas thought a moment. Odd, the way things were going. Back there in that last wayside inn, the day he started for home, he'd already decided that his next move was to offer his services to the prince. If there was anybody left on earth who might show him kindness, it was the prince. He breathed all the way from his toes, straightened to his full height till his eyes met Yaap's, and said, "Well . . . I might be persuaded."

"*Goed.* Then follow me." Yaap was marching toward the door, not even looking back to see whether Pieter-Lucas followed.

"Follow you where? And what about my 'juicy message'?"

Still moving, Yaap answered, "We're going to see the prince."

Pieter-Lucas hurried to catch up with his friend. "What's he got to do with it? Besides, you said he's fleeing!"

"Just hush your mouth and move your feet and you will see."

They were walking side by side now, crossing the drawbridge, answering the guard's questions, passing through the ornate gate. The silence that shrouded the old *Kasteel* ground was broken only by an occasional scream from Willem's blockhouse apartment at the corner next to the bridge across the moat.

"Princess Anna's temper hasn't changed, I hear," Pieter-Lucas said.

"Worse than ever."

They climbed the stairway and hurried across the blue-and-gold tiled pavement of the long open gallery that joined the two towers along the *Kasteel* wall. The spring shower had stopped, and a cloud-scattered sky was lit periodically by a full golden moon that cast its light on them hurrying along past the line of marble colonnades.

Pieter-Lucas remembered a time long ago when he'd walked this gallery in search of Prince Willem, whom he'd found pacing the pavement far into another night pierced by his wife Anna's screams.

Just before they left the gallery and entered the west tower with its spiral stairwell, Yaap stopped short. He moved close to Pieter-Lucas' ear and spoke almost in a whisper, "My juicy message is this, young van den Garde. The prince has been asking for you ever since he arrived a week ago. Gave me instructions to bring you to him as soon as you came home—if, indeed, you did."

"Asking for me?" Yaap could find more imaginary stories to send his feelings soaring, then dash them to the ground with the truth. "Come now. What sort of trap is this?"

"*Jongen*, believe every word of it. The prince has been asking for you ever since his arrival."

"But why for me?"

"Probably needs another messenger."

"Very likely." He laughed. "The woods are full of would-be messengers who'd give anything to run for the prince. And I'm supposed to believe he's been searching for me?"

"If I put in a good word for you, he just might."

"Well, did you?"

"Never mind, just hold your mouth and follow me."

"You mean, just *wait!*"

Neither boy spoke as they wound their way down around the tower stairway, out and down another long hallway. Silence pounded in Pieter-Lucas' ears. The walls he knew so well to be hung with tapestries were barren of all but an occasional mounted torch. Gone were the tables with their statues and vases. The floor, always thick with ornamented carpet, lay stripped of its beauty, and its cold dampness seeped through heavy stockings and shoes and chilled Pieter-Lucas' feet.

"What is this all about?" he whispered to his guide.

"Still . . ."

At the end of the hallway, Yaap stopped before a blank wall. He removed a torch from the side wall and put it into Pieter-Lucas' hand. Then he pulled a knife from his belt and inserted it between two panels of wood, prying one panel till it moved to the right, making an opening barely large enough for the boys to press their bodies through by squatting low, turning sideways, and extending their arms to each side. Yaap closed the panel, and they descended on a simple ladder through a hole in the floor into a damp, cold, earthen cellar.

The room was bare except for one corner where a small table held a helter-skelter array of papers, a silver candleholder with a short piece of well-burned candle, and an inkwell of elaborately carved dark wood with bits of shiny metal inlaid. Behind the table, with his head bent over and his hand busily pushing a long-quilled pen across a piece of paper, sat the Prince of Oranje, Count of Nassau, Catzenellenboghen, Dietz, Vianden, Burgrave of Antwerp; Visount of Besancon; Baron of Breda, Diest, Grimbergh, Arlay, Nozeroy; Lord of Chastelbellin, Lieutenant General of the Netherlands; Governor of Brabant, Holland, Zeeland, Utrecht and, Friesia . . . What, but the gravest of danger, could bring so great a man as this into hiding behind a writing desk in the cellar of his own castle?

Through the years, Pieter-Lucas had seen the prince close up many times, in all kinds of moods. He'd watched him strut around the old *Kasteel*, accompanied by a large retinue of noble friends who laughed and bantered with bravado. At other times, Pieter-Lucas watched Willem come dragging into the stable late at night alone, or with his brother, Ludwig, his shoulders drooping as though carrying the weight of an angry world. One thing never changed, though. Each time, the prince had smiled and spoken kind words to him. Always he asked, "What fine picture have you drawn today, *jongen*?"

The prince had a commanding demeanor, balanced by the warmest brown eyes Pieter-Lucas had ever seen. Tonight, when he lifted his head to greet his visitors, the tired lines that etched his face and made it sag in all the wrong places only seemed to intensify the warmth. When he saw Pieter-Lucas, he smiled as if he'd just discovered a long lost friend.

"*Ah!*, so, you've come home in time."

"Greatly honored that you called for me, Your Grace." Pieter-Lucas bowed slightly. The prince smiled at him with a warmth Pieter-Lucas hadn't seen in anyone's eyes since Aletta bade him goodbye in the birch wood.

Yaap bowed and offered, "I found him on the market square just before the dinner hour and have now finished my errands, that I might bring him to you."

"Well-timed, young man, well-timed." Picking up a pair of folded papers from the pile before him, he handed them to his messenger boy and added, "I have just sealed my last letters, and you may start for Brussels with these as soon as possible."

Yaap took the letters, bowed quickly, and turned to his young companion. "You'll find your way out of here?"

Pieter-Lucas gave the older boy a good-natured scowl and watched him disappear up the ladder. Never before had he stood alone in the presence of this, the greatest man he'd ever known—greatest next to Opa, that is.

"I trust you are well," the prince began. "Yaap tells me you have been gone a long time. On a pilgrimage?" His eyes searched the boy's face.

Pieter-Lucas felt his cheeks flame. "Perhaps a search would be a better word."

"And you met with success?"

He felt warmth building beneath his jacket collar. "I learned many places where the one I seek is not. If that is success, then so be it."

"We must often search a lifetime for those things most precious to us." The older man's voice weighed heavy with a dignified combination of weariness and strength.

After a space of silence, he smiled. "And have you drawn a picture every day along the way?"

"Nearly, *Mijn Heer*."

"Your Opa would be pleased."

Pieter-Lucas squirmed. Finally, realizing the next word must come from his lips, he said dryly, "I hope so."

"Your Opa would also be pleased to know I have a plan to help you."

A plan to what? Did he hear it right?

"In a day or two from now, we are to vacate this ancient family house." The prince was serious. "Yaap has explained to you?"

"He simply mentioned that you flee. For your life? Can that be, even here in Breda?"

"I fear 'tis true. The time has finally come, as I have long expected, that the Prince of Oranje is no longer safe in these Lowlands. I take my household and a retinue of friends collected from across the southern cities, and we go to Dillenburg."

"Your birthplace, *Mijn Heer*?"

"To my birthplace and that of my vader before me and his before him, for more generations than I can guess. 'Tis a lovely place, a fine old castle of the German style, built on a hill such as no Lowlander has ever seen in his own countryside."

"We shall miss you greatly."

Willem was silent and sober for a long moment. "I am no religious scholar, but I recall your Opa once telling me that when God anoints us to do a job, we must sometimes part from those places and persons we love for a time. He said it was something like Jesus who left the river under the watchful eye of the anointing dove. Before He could preach or heal, He had to sojourn in the wilderness. So I, too, must go forth to my wilderness. Before I go, I have a promise to fulfill—one of my more pleasant tasks in preparing for the journey. That is the reason I have called you here to me."

"How could I possibly serve Your Grace in your preparations?"

"'Tis a long story, my boy, much longer than I can tell you tonight. Suffice it to say that I once made a promise to your vader."

"My vader?" What could ever cause such a thing?

"Perhaps no one has ever told you. Long ago, your vader was my favorite stable hand. He had cared for my horse from the first day that I came to Breda from my home in Dillenburg. I was only eleven years old at the time, missing my brothers at home, and needing a companion. A fine, congenial young man, your vader, only a year or two my senior. So like his own vader, your Opa, he was. Though we spent little time together, we grew quite fond of each other. I often felt it a great pity I could not make him a nobleman, so that we might have been free to enjoy each other's company at will."

Hendrick van den Garde, a congenial young stableboy and fond of Prince Willem? Impossible!

"The last time I saw him," the prince went on, "we talked briefly in the stable before I had to return to Brussels. He asked me a startling question. 'If anything happens to me,' he said, 'please promise that you will look as kindly on my son as you have on me.' I wondered then and wonder to this day what strange premonitions prompted such a request. Nevertheless, I promised. And ever since I have tried to be true to my word."

"You have indeed been most kind to me all my life that I can remember." Often the boy had wondered how it was that he'd been given opportunities that other boys of his rank only dreamed about. "Forgive me, my kind prince, but I was not aware, until today, that you had had opportunity to demonstrate that kindness since Hendrick van den Garde left Breda." The words pricked at his throat and trailed off into dead air.

The prince looked half startled. He opened his mouth and closed it again several times before he went on. "All that, to say that in order to make good on my promise, when I leave this place, I will take you along."

"To Dillenburg? With your household?"

"*Ja, jongen*, to Dillenburg with my household. I have need of a seasoned stableboy. Might need another messenger now and again. Your Opa would be pleased to know both my sister and I will be requiring the occasional services of an artist who can help us with a few important works of art much too sensitive to trust to just anyone who can draw a simple picture."

Pieter-Lucas stood speechless. What could this all mean?

Willem went on, "It's sure, I would not dare to leave you here. A ghastly storm is about to break upon the Lowlands. Already King Philip's Duke of Alva is on his way with orders to avenge all the wrongs perpetrated against the crown by rebels and image-breakers. Which means, when he reaches Breda, he will confiscate Hendrick van den Garde's house and goods and put his heirs to the torch."

Hendrick's house and goods and heirs? So, it was determined that he, Pieter-Lucas, peace-loving protector of the Great Church's treasures, was to die for the madness of his vader? He stared at the prince, watching for the slightest flinching of a muscle or twitch of an eyelid. It simply could not be!

The Prince continued, apparently untouched by the boy's scrutinizing look. "If I would fulfill my promise to your beloved vader, I must deliver you from such a fate, now must I not?"

Pieter-Lucas shook his head slowly. "Your Grace, I simply do not understand."

"What is it that puzzles you?"

Pieter-Lucas stood dumb for a long moment. How should he ask the question that burned in his mind? Finally, while his heart raced and his palms dripped moisture, he let it out, one word at a time, never sure how it would fit together in the end. "But first, Hendrick van den Garde did wild and ugly things in the church, things to shame us all. Then he deserted us—his wife nearly ready to go to childbed, where she died because he would not come and sit with her, his city, even you, his prince. What could ever constrain you to keep a promise made to such a man?"

"Nothing, *jongen*. I did not promise Hendrick van den Garde a thing."

"Pardon my dullness, but your words fall on my ears like riddles."

The prince looked down at his desk, then up at the young man trembling before him. Compassion and pain mingled in the long and piercing look that Pieter-Lucas fought to interpret. Something in it wrenched at his heart and drew him closer to his prince than he imagined could ever happen to the son of a common castle guard. Bewildered and comforted all at once, he took refuge in the warmth of the great man's whole being that seemed to fill the room.

"*Jongen*," Willem spoke in measured words, "I see it falls to my lot to say words that only a moeder should reveal. I have no idea how to lift the veil with feminine gentleness, so let me simply say it in the only way that I know how. Has no one ever told you that Hendrick van den Garde is not your vader?"

The boy braced his heart against the shock that rocked him like a fishing boat caught in a violent storm.

"One time I heard it from his own lips. Yaap and I lay fettered to the wall of Lord Brederode's dungeon, falsely accused. Hendrick van den Garde was brought in to identify us, and he claimed only to know who I was and from what 'troublesome family,' but he would not own me as his son. I despised him for lying to me."

"*Nay*, he lied not. He spoke the truth! Your vader—Kees was his name—was the younger brother to Hendrick."

"But I do not remember him . . . I've never heard of him . . . Hendrick is all I've ever known for a vader."

"True enough. A few months after your moeder brought you to the light of day, Kees died suddenly. I was not here at the time, but when I returned after many months, I was told that it all happened quite accidentally."

"You say his name was Kees?" Pieter-Lucas could scarcely believe what he was hearing.

"Kees van den Garde, that was it. No prince ever had a more loyal subject for a friend."

No longer dumb, Pieter-Lucas now had to restrain himself from saying more than was prudent. Resting his hands on the desk between him and his prince, he looked pleadingly into the older man's eyes and asked, "And did he carve 'The Birdseller' on the choir stall seat in the Great Church?"

"As a matter of fact he did. When I learned of his death, I had it installed in the church as a memorial to a true friend."

Pieter-Lucas felt a wave of strange emotions wash over him. Not sure whether to cry or scream, he looked the prince in the eye and said simply, "Thank you."

"I regret that I had to be the bearer of such grave and startling news," the prince apologized.

Already the old monster was churning in Pieter-Lucas' stomach once more and crying out the familiar angry word, "Vengeance! Vengeance on the traitor." With a hurried bow, Pieter-Lucas managed, "Do not grieve, *Mijn Heer*. I shall always be grateful to you. Your words free me far more than I can ever tell." He stopped, then shook his head and added hurriedly, "If you have no other instructions, I shall go home to the house of

Hendrick van den Garde while something remains of this strange and eventful night."

From the foot of the ladder, Pieter-Lucas looked back. "Just one more question, Your Grace. Does Dirck Engelshofen, the bookseller, know the story you told me tonight?"

"That I cannot say. I know not whether he lived here yet in those days, but, even so, scandalous stories haunt neighborhoods and find their way quickly into newcomers' ears."

"Enough. I go now to home. When the time comes, I shall gladly accompany you to Dillenburg to care for your horse, draw whatever pictures you require, run over the countryside carrying your messages . . . provided . . . Oh, may I be so bold as to add a condition to acceptance of such undeserved kindness?"

"What is it you desire?"

" 'Tis only that I might be free to continue my search—for the bookseller's daughter," he said aloud, while the inner voice added, "and for your imposter 'vader' as well."

"She's been my lifelong companion. We made a vow out yonder in your birch wood." He nodded toward the east. "And my heart shall never rest until it is fulfilled."

The prince smiled. "I believe that can be arranged."

"Thank you, Your Grace."

"*Goed*. Then we shall welcome you into our entourage with arms thrown wide."

"I go now. Rest well." Pieter-Lucas nodded his head, the best he could do for a quick bow from the stair ladder.

"Rest well, my son."

*Son*, did he say?

Torn between vengeance, curiosity, and the strange warmth of a promised new identity, he climbed the ladder. Not at all certain whether he was more excited or sad, he headed toward Annastraat for a rendezvous with the memories and trinkets that haunted the deserted place he had once known as home.

# CHAPTER FOURTEEN

*Breda*

Middle of Grass Month (April), 1567

*M*orning's early brush strokes had already streaked the sky with pale tints of rose, lavender, and gold when Pieter-Lucas emerged from the *Kasteel*. He made his way at last to Annastraat. Unbidden, his steps slowed as he passed the corner bookshop where cobwebs hung like curtains in the shutters over the windows. From somewhere behind the bolted door, he imagined he heard the spirit of his beloved calling to him with muffled voice. Empty-hearted, apprehensive, he continued on to the overgrown weeds and cold hearth of *home*.

For the next three days and nights, he worked in a frenzy and slept but little. Propelled by a strange mixture of curiosity, anger, and loneliness, he sifted through a lifetime of memories and possessions in search of valuable treasures to carry with him into the new life that Prince Willem van Oranje had opened up to his wondering imagination.

Above all, he searched for answers and looked at all the familiar objects with newly awakened eyes and a host of questions. Whose house was this, after all—Hendrick's, as he'd always supposed and now found to be the most despicable of ideas, or Kees' before him, in which case Hendrick was doubly villainous? Did this old felt hat really belong to Hendrick—or to Vader Kees before him?

"Kees!" The name sent the blood rushing through Pieter-Lucas' veins. He said it over and over and let the joy explode. Through his imagination ran the constant search for Kees van den Garde—stableboy, friend of Willem van Oranje, loving husband of Moeder Kaatje, and . . . Vader. Strange, how overnight this familiar old word had become warm and comforting and sustaining.

The process also brought forward in his mind a series of unsettling pictures and draped them with a mysterious haze. There was Moeder

Kaatje in tears over a pot of summer vegetables on the hearth. And that feeling of Hendrick's anger smoldering behind a held tongue while Opa taught Pieter-Lucas how to mix the colors on a palette to create a wash of light across a fine landscape. And Hendrick's shrill railings when Moeder dared to protest his orders that they accompany him to the secret meetings in Backeler's house at the end of Boschstraat.

If God was really there—the God Opa used to tell him about—why did He take his real vader away and leave him and Moeder with such a cruel, fiendish imposter? The more he questioned and searched for answers, the more anxious Pieter-Lucas grew to lock the door and run away from this place with all it held of disappointed promises and terror.

He spent every moment possible at the stables in the center of an enormous whir of activity. With eagerness, he took part in all the action—preparing the horses, watching the parade of strangers coming and going with last-minute messages, loading wagons and coaches. And in every corner and familiar furnishing, sound, and smell, he imagined Kees. He now felt a part of this special place more than ever and reveled in the happy wonder it gave to him.

On the afternoon when he learned that they would be departing the next day, he hurried home and stuffed his knapsack till it bulged and strained at the seams and spilled out around the flaps. Each chosen item represented a piece of the old life he could not quite bear to leave behind—two changes of clothes, his woodcarving knife, the metal cup his moeder always filled for him, a brightly enameled vase Aletta admired, Moeder Kaatje's favorite shawl, and her worn leather-bound prayer book which he'd found hidden beneath a stack of bed linens in the old carved chest.

For reasons which he could not fully reconcile with his current anger with God, he held the little book tenderly before he packed it. It felt almost as if it were too holy an object for his fingers to touch, whatever that might mean. One by one, he leafed through the pages, looking, wondering, not able to read the Latin words inscribed there. About midway, the pages came open more easily, and wedged between them he found a miniature canvas with an oil-painted portrait of a young man probably about his own age.

"Hendrick van den Garde!" he said with unbridled disgust. Did Moeder Kaatje really love him enough to preserve his portrait among her treasures? Yanking the picture from the book, he walked to the fireplace and flung it onto the tiny group of embers dying there. Perhaps a fire built with his own hand might silence the unwelcome inner monster that had been his increasingly frequent companion for all these months since his supposed vader had so nearly finished him off in the Great Church.

His heart beat rapidly with a peculiar sense of tortured delight as he watched a thin tongue of reborn flame begin to curl around his vengeful offering. But, all unexpectedly, the eyes in the portrait seemed to reach up to him, pleading as if for mercy. He tried to look away, but they held him. Just as the flames entwined themselves around the border of the picture, Pieter-Lucas thought he saw the lips move and heard an agonizing cry, "How do you know I am not Kees, your real vader?"

Without an eyeblink of hesitation, he reached into the flames and pulled the portrait free. He pressed it to his chest and beat at the flames until they died. Fine, warm, crumbling ashes powdered off around the edges. He smoothed them in his fingers and stared hard at the rescued portrait. "These are not the eyes of Hendrick van den Garde," he mumbled. "How could I have been so mistaken?"

"Forgive me, Vader," he whispered, then tucked the portrait into the folds of his doublet next to the note Aletta had left for him in the shutters of the printshop in Antwerp.

Quickly now, he put Moeder Kaatje's prayer book into his knapsack. He left a pair of dying embers in the hearth and a few crusts of dried bread on the table, along with a burned-out candle beside a Calvinist pamphlet he'd found hidden in an empty box among Hendrick's tools. That should leave no doubt in Alva's mind that Hendrick van den Garde was an image-breaking Calvinist. He chuckled with a peculiar vengeful delight. How could he feel both guilty and so intensely satisfied?

"It is the only way to treat a fiend like Hendrick," he told himself.

Without a backward glance, he shouldered his knapsack, closed the door, and paused at the doorstoop for an instant to savor the memory of Aletta that would always hover there. Then he made his way out the gate and down the street, heading for the edge of town. He had to make one last visit before he could leave this place, perhaps forever.

How long it had been since he'd walked these cobblestones past the Guesthouse Gate and beyond the city wall! Only once had he done it since the death of his anointing. He'd gone to check it all out before he met Aletta in the birch wood and left town in search of Vader Hendrick.

At the Y in the road, he followed to the right on that old familiar path so little traveled that the weeds had nearly hidden the cobblestones. The pathway leading off into the oak trees was only visible because he knew precisely where it ran. A haunting wind sighed through the barely budding branches of the giant trees. The hedge that obscured Opa's secret place grew so wild he never would have found the doorway. In fact, he almost missed it now, but something was not in order.

It stood wide open, held firmly by a profusion of new growth, revealing a gaping hole. Pieter-Lucas shuddered at the nakedness of the sight. Then, with a strange blend of eagerness, caution, and anxiety, he stooped to pass through the doorway and enter the tunnel. He narrowed his eyes to adjust to the darkness, then picked his way with care along the passage, now infested with weeds and filled with mud-oozy puddles of frozen snow and spring rains.

"Who has been here since I last locked you up?" he asked, as if expecting the slimy walls to reverberate with the echoes of the culprit's voice. Instead, they dripped water into the puddles, mocked his fears, and closed in around him.

At the end of the passageway, he dashed up the stairs and stared at what he remembered as Opa's warm, beautiful studio. Where once it had been filled with artistic, nurturing disarray, now the whole scene lay in ruins. Disbelieving, speechless, numb, Pieter-Lucas surveyed the ugly sacrilege.

Smashed paint pots and varnish flasks lay in solid pools of dried, cracked paint. They turned the whole floor into a disorderly palette, sparkling with slivers of glass and broken pottery. Canvases and paintings had been sliced to ribbons and strewn about the room. Remains of paintbrushes had been thrown to the four corners in a shower of splintered handles and plucked-out bristles. Not a pane of the rosette window remained whole, but each served as a jagged pipe for the winds to blow through, creating a mournful symphony of destruction. A layer of cobwebs, dried oak leaves, bird droppings, and dust lay over everything.

The young artist wandered through the debris, still too stunned for words or tears, picking up ribbons and shards of Opa's marvelous life, then casting them down again. He pressed at the pools of paint with his fingers in hopes of finding a few moist drops of soft, colored fluid still capable of bringing life to some canvas.

At last he stood over what had once been the three-legged stool where Opa spent so many happy hours creating the living pictures that had since met with an assassin's sword. The old wooden easel Opa built with his own hands was smashed beyond recognition. Propped up against what remained of the table that once held his paints was a medium-sized canvas.

The wooden frame was broken in several places, leaving the canvas sagging. Across its surface had been scrawled a message in uneven black charcoal letters. A large hole in the center showed that it had been pierced with a knife.

Pieter-Lucas stooped down and read the words: "Opa's paint is spilled out with his blood! Renounce his foolishness and be a man."

"Hendrick van den Garde!" Pieter-Lucas shouted. "Despicable, cruel thief, madman, coward! You came here when you knew no one would challenge your savagery! May your body be consumed slowly, painfully by worms, and may your soul burn in a never-ending hell!"

He spat on the canvas, then snatched it up and drew his own dagger. "If I could not burn Hendrick's memory in his portrait, I shall slice his words to bits!" he snarled.

He inserted his dagger into the hole and cut the insulting message in two pieces. With a combination of rage and smoldering glee, he began to wrench the splintered frame apart at its breaks. He tore it through at the top, then held it at arm's length and searched for the weakest spot in the bottom of the frame. A shaft of late afternoon sun struck the canvas and brought his angry actions to a sudden halt.

He stared and swallowed hard. For beneath the ugly black letters, he now made out a pale, uneventful painting with only hints of color here and there. No work of Hendrick, this.

"How did I not see it sooner?" he muttered. Carefully, tenderly, he brought the two halves back together. His hands trembled.

The moment held a strange air of anticipation. Between the letters of Hendrick's destructive message, Pieter-Lucas examined the dry, desolate dunes and craggy outcroppings of rock covering a sandy-hued canvas. Even the sky hung washed-out and pale yellow. At the far left of the picture stood a lone sun-bleached snag of a tree, without limbs or leaves. Here he scratched at the villainous letters obscuring the topmost branches and found a black, demonic-looking vulture perched.

Wind swept the desertscape in huge sand-laden circles that wound inward, ending in the center, just above the gash Hendrick had made in the canvas. Once more scratching away at the letters, he discovered under the shade of a scrubby grayish green shrub a man in a dirty-white robe kneeling beside a boulder. His brown hair hung in matted strings across his back and around his face, which was covered with his hands.

Pieter-Lucas stared at the painting, a shiver of desolation running along his backbone. Across the top of the canvas, in large, grayish letters, he read, "The Wilderness." What was it Prince Willem had said to him three nights ago about his wilderness? But surely, there was no connection.

Fascinated, he studied the contours of the dunes, the angles of the crags, the hook on the vulture's beak, the swirling of the winds, until his eyes followed the movement to the figure of the man in the center of the dizzying vortex. An arc of tiny, uneven letters outlined the bowed head.

Pieter-Lucas rubbed at the ugly black charcoal, smudging it, continuing on till it paled, giving the painting underneath a grayish cast. In the process, he made out three faintly inscribed words: "The Anointed One."

Those hands. Weren't they the same hands that rested on the head of the little lame girl in "The Healing"? So this was Opa's Healer in a wilderness? Pieter-Lucas tore his eyes away from the Christ in the wilderness and searched the borders of the painting for some clues. At the bottom of the canvas, painted in exquisite calligraphed letters now distorted by the torn canvas and broken frame, he made out the words:

> He whom God anoints to paint His masterpieces
> Must first be wounded,
> Then driven, limping, into life's bleak Wilderness.
> "Take heart," He cries through healing touch
> Of transparent angel wings,
> And sends him forth at last,
> With brushes tied by pierced hands,
> To spread fresh healing colors on the canvases
> Of other men's desert lives.

Scrawled in the corner at the end of the last line, the startled boy read in a well-known handwriting, "By Lucas van den Garde, for grandson, Pieter-Lucas, 1566."

Anointing and wilderness and healing—what did it all mean? And where were the angels? Blinking as if to clear away the swirling sand, he searched the desolate picture and moved it toward a bright patch where sunlight could shine full on its pale, bleak beigeness.

"They have to be here somewhere," he murmured, "near the Christ."

Straining his eyes, he spotted them, partially obscured by Hendrick's letters—filmy, colorless, transparent, with wings like lace covering their bodies. The two ethereal beings hovered near the kneeling Christ. From a tiny shimmering vial in his hand, one poured out drops of oil on Christ's bowed head. Desperate to uncover it all, Pieter-Lucas rubbed at the charcoal again and again, wetting it at times with a dab of spittle and swiping it as clean as possible. Eventually, a simple hand-held harp emerged, being strummed by the second angel.

For a long while, he stood admiring the picture. A stream of tears slid unbidden down his cheeks. Might some angel indeed be hovering near to him in this place made sacred by Opa's presence?

Then softly, insistently, from the far corner high up in the rafters came the cooing of a pair of doves. The spell was broken. Opa had said doves were for anointing, but the anointing had given way to a desert. The presence of doves in this studio but made a mockery of the whole business.

"Fantasy and nonsense," he reprimanded himself. "Out with all this sentimental preoccupation with paintings and angels and anointing doves."

Hurriedly, Pieter-Lucas removed the busted frame from the strange painting, then folded and shoved it into his knapsack along with a single broken-handled paintbrush he had found with bristles still intact. A billowy wind whipped through the shattered rosette windowpanes and blended with the cooing of the doves.

As if spurred on to haste, he rushed past the chaos and through the tunnel, mumbling, "Life is real and cold and hard, and I will make my own way out of the wilderness and into a painter's paradise, with neither anointing nor angels."

He stepped across the threshold, then turned, stooped down again, and shouted toward the studio, "Opa lives on, do you hear me, Hendrick van den Garde? With his paint coursing through my blood, I am more of a man than you will ever think to be!"

# CHAPTER FIFTEEN

*From Breda to Dillenburg*

Late Grass Month (April) and Early Flower Month (May), 1567

*P*ieter-Lucas awoke from a restless sleep determined to put the past behind him. Long enough Hendrick van den Garde had stolen his peace of mind. Beginning today, he would not allow the fiendish imposter to snatch one more moment of his happiness.

Before him lay a journey grand enough to make him the envy of every burgher's son in Breda. Such wondrous sights to see! Traveling in a noble caravan! Lodging in ducal castles along the way! Riding each day just behind the prince, near to his family's coach, often helping Yaap escort the thirteen-year-old Princess Maria! And, wonder of all wonders, the prince himself had offered to let him draw for him—perhaps even paint?

*Ja*, he had every reason to be excited. He intended to make the most of it all.

On the misty morning when the mass of coaches, animals, and people assembled into something that approached an orderly train, Pieter-Lucas groomed and mounted Blesje with genuine enthusiasm. The confusion and excitement of that incredible drama filled him with dreams and visions far greater than he had ever imagined.

Only once did he have to fight off the torments he had sent from his heart the night before. From some distance, he was watching the prince bid farewell to his only son, Philip Willem, a handsome prince several years younger than Pieter-Lucas. Philip Willem's moeder, the prince's first wife, had died when the boy was quite small, and he'd lived most of his life away from Breda. Pieter-Lucas stood at too great a distance from the vader and son to hear what passed between them. But his sensitive imagination filled in the details, the brave attempts of both vader and son to conceal deep emotions, and the last words of a vader's advice to the boy soon to return with his personal steward to his studies at the University of Leuven.

The fleeting picture revived feelings he didn't realize still lingered just beneath the surface of his memory. With fresh pain he recalled the loss of his Opa's vaderly care and the incredible agony of the recent discovery that he had only known an imposter vader.

"Begone!" he ordered the mental intruders. "An important adventure, a matter of life and death awaits."

With increased concentration, he groomed horses, loaded chests of valuable possessions, assisted ladies into their coaches. His final act, helping Maria, prince Willem's daughter to mount her fine chestnut horse and fall into line between himself and Yaap, made him feel almost chivalrous.

Once the journey had begun, many natural wonders caught his attention. Forested rolling hills rose out of the sand dunes and flat pastures of his native Lowlands and reminded him of scenes he had often studied in the fantastic paintings and tapestries that hung in the castle at Breda.

On the day that their pathway began to run along the bank of the Rhine River, Pieter-Lucas exclaimed to Yaap, "Prince Willem was right. No Lowlander could have dreamed the half of these wonders. Even our beloved Rhine River runs more majestically here than at home." Wide and deceptively placid, the ancient river guided their footsteps for days. Here and there, swirling eddies belied the true strength that churned beneath the surface.

Like the Rhine, the mass exodus of Prince Willem's household and endless line of servants, soldiers, and refugees lumbered steadily along. With what seemed to Pieter-Lucas an increasingly slow pace, the coaches groaned over rutted roadways and rattled over cobbled village streets where dense throngs of townsfolk swarmed around them, shoving, shouting, gaping, bowing to the royal personages. Whenever it rained, both coaches and horses slipped about and sometimes bogged in the mire and great puddles of rainwater.

In the beginning, Princess Maria spent much of her time riding beside her father and seemed little inclined to talk when she graced her escorts with her presence. By the third day, Pieter-Lucas grew restless and surly. "If we'd done this trip alone and on foot, we would have been there by now," he complained to Yaap as they rode toward the rear of the line, taking a message from the Prince to the captain of his armed ranks.

"You're right," the older boy agreed. "My horse and I do it in three days of steady riding."

"And you don't have to put up with Princess Anna's petulant howling spells all the way."

From the moment they departed from Breda, the prince's wife, Anna, had poured forth from the family coach an incessant stream of deep-throated howls and hysterical screams. Except when the caravan stopped for the night, the unhappy woman never showed her face but sat huddled in the corner of the coach with her only child, four-year-old Anna. Princess Anna's shared melancholy clouded the whole trip.

Yaap offered a quick retort to Pieter-Lucas' bitter comment. "You think the rest of us enjoy the poor woman's antics?"

"*Nay.*"

"Then just remember, you can't have it all. You can be mighty thankful we didn't leave you back at the castle in Breda."

"I am, I am." Pieter-Lucas gulped.

"Far better to listen to the princess howl for a few hours a day than to face the wrath of the Duke of Alva and end up becoming his torch on the market square."

Pieter-Lucas shuddered.

"Personally," Yaap went on, "I'm thanking my lucky stars I'm not married to the likes of Princess Anna."

Later that afternoon, when the noble lady had been screaming with especial spitefulness, young Princess Maria joined Pieter-Lucas where he rode alone behind the family coach. With surprising openness, she confided to him, "Princess Anna screams because she doesn't want to go to Dillenburg."

"She doesn't?" Pieter-Lucas asked.

"*Nay*, she says it's too plain and dull a place."

"Plain and dull?"

"I fear she is quite ill."

"And you, Your Highness," Pieter-Lucas asked, "do you want to go to Dillenburg?"

"Oh, *ja*, I do!" For the first time, her face brightened. "It's a beautiful old castle on a high hill, with hills all around and trees and magnificent gardens and statues and dogs and a pet monkey."

As she talked on, something in her manner seemed at last untethered. "Besides, Oma lives there, along with Oom Jan and his wife Tante Elizabeth and all their six children." She paused and actually smiled up at Pieter-Lucas before going on as if she feared she might forget somebody. "Then there's Oom Hendrick—he's about your age, I think—and Tante Juliana, and who knows how many other cousins and relatives and noble neighbors' children living there to attend Oma's school. Sometimes Oom Ludwig stays there between journeys around the Lowlands! Of course, Tantes Maria and Anna and Elizabeth and Katarina and Magdalena are all married and live elsewhere with their husbands and children. Oh yes, finally there's Oom Adolph. They say he has gone to live in the court of the king of Denmark."

"Say, but your vader has a great, large family!"

"And have you met them all?"

Pieter-Lucas grinned and shook his curls. "Nay. I've never been to Dillenburg."

"Never? Not even once?"

"Never, not even once. I have only met the members of the family that have come to Breda. Count Ludwig, of course, I've seen and talked to many times. He spent many hours with your vader in the *Kasteel* in Breda. I've even carried messages to them in Ludwig's apartment on the far side of the castle court, near the new chapel."

"And Oma?" Maria's eyes brightened.

"Your Oma, Countess Juliana von Stolberg?" he asked, not waiting for a reply. "A lady of the noblest sort. I remember once, soon after Prince Willem brought Anna as his new bride to live in Breda, the countess came for a visit. I thought she was most austere when I first laid eyes on her."

"My Oma, austere?"

"Well, I was much younger then, and she so tall and straight and sober when she moved about in front of all the people. Then one day I saddled her horse and led it to her in the castle courtyard. She spoke kind words to me, and I saw gentleness in her face, just like I see in the prince, your vader."

"Then she was no more austere?"

"Never again."

"And the others? Did you meet them when they lived in Breda?"

"A stableboy meets everyone who visits his prince. All those that stay for a spell pass through the courtyard many times. I remember Count Hendrick and the Countess Magdalena when they lived there just before the riots last summer. Most of all, I remember their sister, the younger Countess Juliana."

"You do!" Then, before he could answer, she added in a confidential aside, "She is my favorite, you know."

"Oh, *ja*? I suppose she might be my favorite too. You see, she saved my life."

"She saved your life?" The girl's voice registered controlled surprise. "You must tell me about it. I love to hear stories of my *tante's* exploits."

Tell her, indeed. What should he say? That his imposter vader had nearly finished him off in an image-breaking riot and that without Juliana's help he would have died in the Beguinage? Fine story for a refined young lady fresh from the palace of the governess in Brussels.

Slowly, he chose his words, being careful to hedge around the borders of the nasty details. "It happened last summer when I had been in a serious accident," he said. "How your *tante* came to be involved, I never knew. I only know that I awoke one day in the dispensary of the Beguinage to discover this beautiful woman hovering over me with a whole apothecary of miraculous medicinal cures."

"That was my Tante Juliana doing what she does best." Maria could scarcely contain her excitement within the bounds of noble propriety.

"So I had always heard. But until she dressed the wound in my thigh and made me drink some nasty-tasting potions that soothed me in spite of their bitter bite, I did not know how true the rumors were."

"Was that all?"

"What more to say?"

"Did you not feel strange tinglings in your leg and surges of miraculous energy raising you from your sickbed to go out and do battle once more with whatever it was that felled you in the first place?"

Pieter-Lucas chuckled. Except for her ornamented robes, her noble aloofness, and the touch of sharpness in her features, this girl reminded him of Aletta at that age. "*Nay*, I've no such wild tales to tell. Only that from that day onward, I grew steadily better, which was more than all the Beguines could accomplish with their herbs and poultices. My moeder always said 'twas Countess Juliana made me live."

Maria smiled and sighed enormously. Neither of them spoke for a few moments. The sounds of the caravan blended with the subdued liquid roar of the river nearby, creating an almost hypnotic lullaby. Pieter-Lucas looked at Prince Willem riding up ahead, moving steadily along, apparently ignoring the whole performance. What must the prince feel as he plodded on, fleeing for his life to the unending accompaniment of his wife's drunken insults and complaints hurled at his back?

Pieter-Lucas found himself drawn by a feeling of overpowering pity. In the past year or two, he'd watched his prince weighted down with some heavy loads of care and sorrow as he came and went through the stable. But surely, never had he seen his shoulders droop so.

Pieter-Lucas' look turned to a stare, then dissolved into a mental image of Opa's desolate painting of "The Wilderness." The lonely figure dubbed "The Anointed One" sitting beneath the desert shrub in the midst of the swirling sand . . . Could it be? It was a likeness of Prince Willem van Oranje.

And what was that verse at the bottom about the one anointed who must first languish in the wilderness? Could Opa have written this with the prince in his mind? Surely Opa had a prophet's gift. Somehow, he must have actually known what would happen to the prince—and to Pieter-Lucas as well. Pride mingled uneasily with fear. Too much to sort out for now.

One thing he could see and do. Riding with a prince who knew the meaning of more pain than Pieter-Lucas ever dreamt existed in this life, he would make one resolve: Never again would he complain about the pace of this journey or the terrible wailing of a "mad" princess.

Princess Anna's sudden shrill scream from the coach behind them shattered the silence that had accompanied them for some time now. Even Blesje started. Princess Maria guided her horse near to Blesje, leaned as near to Pieter-Lucas' ear as possible, and spoke with wonderful softness, "I must tell you of my plan."

"Are you sure you ought to tell me?" Pieter-Lucas warned her, always fearful that his unbidden association with this special noble household might lead him into some dreadful trap.

Maria ignored his question. A stray shaft of sunlight illuminated a tuft of golden hair protruding from her tight headdress, and her sparkling eyes looked steadily into his. A combination of warmth, excitement, and serious concern beckoned him to listen. "Please promise you will tell no one. I'm not sure my scheme will work, and I do not want my vader's household to laugh at me. Nor would it do for Papa to know and build false hopes only to be dashed."

Never had he been asked to guard a princess' secret. Nor had he the slightest idea of what sort her secret might prove to be. "Nay, but I would have no reason to tell it." His answer felt clumsy, like the gait of a coach on the rutted road. A bit more easily he added, "Only be sure it is proper for you to pass it on to a stableboy before you say a word."

"Stableboy or no, I must tell someone what stirs in my mind. And since you have known my tante's healing touch, none can better appreciate my words."

She sighed, then held her head aloof for a time, as if searching for the right words to couch her thoughts most effectively. At last she leaned once more toward him and said, just above a whisper, "My plan is this. I will ask my Tante Juliana to prepare a cure for the madness of my vader's wife, the Princess Anna." She paused and looked at him, inviting his approval.

"Ah," he responded with a start, "but it is dangerous to call your stepmoeder mad. That she is ill, we must all agree. But mad?"

"Oh!" the girl said, as if to cover the uncontrolled exuberance with which she had spoken. Then her face turned solemn, and she did not look up for a long space. When she recovered, she seemed to choose her words more carefully. "Whatever you call the thing that plagues her, I feel so certain that Tante Juliana can help. Her herbs can do anything, if she puts her mind to it. Think you not that it is true?" she asked.

What herbs in all the world could cure this woman's mad drunkenness and selfish ravings? Especially, if she was as so many believed, simply a wild, unbridled donkey in need of a stern whip. How often Pieter-Lucas had heard the complaint from some visitor coming through the stables. "She reads too many romantic storybooks, drinks too much wine, throws too many costume balls, casts her eyes at too many men."

Yet, he dared not say anything so rude. How could he crush the spirit of a girl with so much hope in her heart? Instead, still hedging and careful not to show overmuch enthusiasm lest he give false hopes, he said, "If half the stories I have heard about Countess Juliana's marvelous apothecary chest are true, your wish may well be granted."

Indeed, if half the stories he had heard were true, then might he also find with this noble *physicke* lady a cure for a truly mad woman—Aletta's Moeder Gretta? In such a case, how could Dirck Engelshofen refuse the hand of his only daughter to the young man who should bear such a cure? The thought set his heart to racing.

Vaguely, Pieter-Lucas realized that Princess Maria was still talking, but he no longer listened. For the deep desire of his heart that had brought him so much pain filled his thoughts at last with the first glimmer of hope he'd known since further back than he could remember.

Princess Maria roused him from his deep thoughts. This time her clear voice was singing a light and hopeful melody. His wilderness, too, had its angel—one little princess who dared to cherish secret hopes.

---

Once Prince Willem's caravan turned from the river toward the rising sun, Pieter-Lucas felt they had entered another world. Each day the hills that had rolled so gently on the western bank of the river seemed to rise higher and stretch, ridge upon ridge, farther and farther until the escalloped purplish horizon on all sides shimmered in a magical haze.

At times the road led up steeply, then down. Often it followed sparkling streams of water that babbled and sprayed over rough beds of rock between gentle hills and grassy meadows carpeted with flowers of every shade of purple, pink, white, blue, red, and gold.

On the morning they left their lodging place in the old city of Siegen, Yaap told Pieter-Lucas, "By noon we should reach the Dill River, which means tonight we lodge in Dillenburg."

"Dillenburg!" Princess Maria, riding now between the two young men, clasped her hands at her breast and smiled. "I can hardly wait!"

"Nor do you have to wait much longer," Pieter-Lucas reassured her.

Cherry and plum trees in full blossom greeted the long caravan as they followed the Dill River on the final stretch of curving, meandering dusty road. Princess Maria chattered continuously about the castle, the monkey, the herb garden, and her cousins, many of whom she had never seen but had memorized their names well enough to recite them without hesitation. Princess Anna, who had screamed all through the morning hours, fell finally into a welcomed sullen silence.

"There it is." Yaap pointed to the vista that opened before them just around a shrubby rock hillock.

"Is he fooling me again?" Pieter-Lucas asked Princess Maria. Would he never learn when to trust his friend's exclamations?

"*Nay*, that's it. Dillenburg! Hurrah!"

Straight ahead, and just across the river, a tiny red-roofed village huddled at the foot of a shrub-covered promontory. Hugging the side of the hill, a simple stone church pointed its spire to the huge castle above. Its dark stone walls and dull green roof blended with the high-rising ramparts that covered the top of the hill.

"Prince Willem's birthplace? His home?" Pieter-Lucas could scarcely believe they'd arrived at last, and he felt completely mystified by the strange feeling that in some way he himself was coming home.

"The Castle of Nassau-Dillenburg," Yaap countered.

"Oh!" Maria squealed her delight.

The imposing fortress that crowned the hill rose up from its broad base as if it had grown there in the course of centuries of sun and rain. In the rays of the afternoon sun, its rough gray stones glowed smooth and golden, its spires glinted like beacons of light, and its blossoming fruit trees ringed the ramparts like a delicate lace ruff.

It seemed to Pieter-Lucas that the lumbering caravan moved more slowly than ever now. They crossed the Dill, then groaned up the hill, sending clouds of dust to mark the steep roadway that led around to the far side of the castle. From above them, a chorus of hunting hounds sounded a welcoming alarm, and a stream of people poured from the castle to meet the travelers on their final approach.

Pieter-Lucas craned his neck to see the top of the fortress walls above him as they entered through an enormous stone gate.

"It's called the Field Tower," Yaap informed him.

"And out there, the herb garden." Princess Maria pointed off to the left, where an ordered arrangement of foliage in muted shades of green, red, purple, white, and gold shimmered in the late afternoon breeze.

"Breda's *Kasteel* was never so huge!" Pieter-Lucas felt himself the size of the mice that haunted the underground storage caverns in the prince's palace in Breda. And Princess Anna called this dull?

To the rhythmless din of excited voices, they passed through a small forecourt under the shade of a spreading linden tree, then rattled across the stagnant moat on a timber drawbridge and found themselves on a broad underground corridor. Passageways led off in all directions.

"Roads up to the various apartments of the old castle," Yaap explained. "Dozens of them." Playing the part of guide that he always seemed ready to assume, he pointed out an assortment of doors he said led into the underground prison cells and casements.

"It's like a whole village all its own, up here above the people's village," Pieter-Lucas exclaimed.

"You haven't seen the half. Look ahead, we're coming out now into the main courtyard."

The corridor climbed steeply and opened into a large cleared space, presided over by a large and colorful display of the coat of arms of the House of Nassau and ringed by stone buildings that rose high as the fortress walls that had dwarfed them all on the other side of the moat. The courtyard swarmed with people, horses, coaches, hunting hounds, and children.

"Makes Breda look like a roadside shrine." Pieter-Lucas whistled and rolled his eyes to take in the looming horizons of his new home. His gaze rested at the doorway to the great hall where Prince Willem had reined in his horse. A row of figures moved toward the coach as the prince dismounted and greeted them. A roundish man with a pointed beard and nose, a high forehead, and mustache like an inverted smile stood with his moeder, a stately grayed woman in simple black velvet gown with a ring of silver keys hanging from the cord around her waist.

"There's Oma," Princess Maria announced, "with Oom Jan beside her, and Tante Elizabeth and Tante Juliana. Oh! Oma! Tante Juliana!"

In the flurry and bustle that followed, Pieter-Lucas and Yaap helped Princess Maria dismount, then moved back, putting a space between themselves and the noble family. They watched brothers and sisters, aunts and uncles and cousins mingle together in a blur of color and a whir of voices.

The prince leaned into his family coach as if coaxing his wife and youngest daughter out to greet the family. But Princess Anna did not emerge. The painful lack of expression on the Prince's face when he descended from the carriage at last spoke of disappointment, resignation, defeat.

The prince had barely begun to present his refugee companions to their noble host and hostess, when a single horseman pounded his way across the cobbles and through the crowds, ignoring all the rest and stopping abruptly before the prince. His hasty dismount and bow were hardly completed before he began to speak in rapid, emotion-charged words.

"Your Grace, Prince Willem, I bring you sad news. Count Brederode has fled to Emden. His men, trying to follow him by ship across the Zuyder Zee, were delivered over to Count Meghen by the treachery of their pilot and were arrested and hanged in the town square of Harlingen. Only the noblemen were spared, taken to Brussels and imprisoned."

A stunned silence brought the blur and whir to a stop. A dark cloud shut out the sunshine. From Prince Willem's family coach rose a curdling howl, and Anna's deranged voice screamed out into the untimely quiet. "It's all over! Brederode's fled! We're lost, undone, condemned! Treacherous husband, cowardly fool! It's all your fault! We're condemned!"

Pieter-Lucas stood beside his horse, trying to grasp what he had just heard. Brederode's men hanged? Brederode's men? Hendrick van den Garde? The two names rang through his brain and roused that strange, wild monster of vengeance that, in recent days, had lain drowsily in the far recesses of his mind. In his calmer moments, if he ever recalled the dreadful force, Pieter-Lucas feared what it might one day lead him to do. But once the monster had been aroused, all fear gave way to a sort of wild anger that controlled him completely—his body, his mind, his raging feelings.

Unaware of any other human presence, totally forgetting where he was, Pieter-Lucas dashed to the side of the messenger. He grabbed him by a sweaty brown sleeve and demanded, "And Hendrick van den Garde, was his body among the hanged?"

"I . . . I know not Hendrick van den Garde," the messenger retorted, pulling his arm free. Sweat poured off his glistening face, down over his unkempt beard, and through the stringy hair matted against his forehead.

Pieter-Lucas felt a panic rising up to stop at nothing. Not thinking what he did, he grasped the messenger's doublet at the throat and shouted, "*Nay*, but I must know. You must tell me."

"Was he one of Count Brederode's Vianen troops?" he cried out.

"*Ja*, hear," Pieter-Lucas gave way to the angry impulses now roaring in his heart and deafening his ears. "Despicable, cruel, violent follower of the Great Beggar." No other subject could cause him to spit his words so forcefully out.

"Then consider him hanged. If he was no nobleman, your man—Hendrick did you say?—did not escape."

Pieter-Lucas stood glaring at the other man for a long moment. Then he loosened his grip and dropped the messenger's arm. As quickly as it came, the anger left, leaving his legs weak and trembling, his hands clammy, and his lips dry. He felt the limp in his left leg more keenly than he'd felt it for many months.

"Sooo . . ." he mumbled, "King Philip's men have gotten me the vengeance." He felt a smile form in the corners of his mouth. His heart began to beat like the roll of summer thunder, and his temples throbbed with a heady rhythm. He clenched his right hand into a tight round fist and watched the flesh of his arm harden and bulge. "Vengeance, at last," he said the word firmly, softly, and felt it warm his whole being.

"Pieter-Lucas, my friend," a soft feminine voice interrupted his heavy thoughts. He looked at Princess Maria standing beside a taller young lady with the familiar smiling face.

"Are you well?" she asked.

Pulling himself up to his full height, he straightened his shoulders and countered, "Very well, thank you." Not in a long, long time had he felt so well indeed. A strange, enormous sensation of unconquerable strength coursed through his body, turning the scene before him fuzzy and removing it oddly from his reach.

As if from some faraway fogbank, he heard the princess say, "Here is my Tante Juliana, the one who saved your life."

"A hearty welcome to you!" Juliana said.

"My pleasure." Pieter-Lucas managed an awkward bow and a smile and pulled himself back to the moment. "Here's hoping my life shall not again need saving while I sojourn at Dillenburg."

"Indeed, that should not be necessary. Instead, I have fine plans for you here."

"For me?"

"For you and your drawing pens."

"My drawing pens?" His knees trembled and the fuzziness dissolved.

"That is, if you care to bring your brushes and canvases and browse with me through my moeder's herb garden," Juliana said. "I've a marvelous plan for a printed herbal with drawings. 'Tis a venture that lies near to my heart. But there is time enough to talk of that later."

Time enough indeed! Pieter-Lucas exerted his best efforts to produce one more convincing smile and told himself that now that vengeance had been won, he should be content to draw and paint for the princess.

"Ja," he offered with dazed lameness. "Plenty of time."

From high in the stone wall of an ancient castle bedroom, a small single window framed the black velvet sky, studded with diamond pricks and a faint crescent of a moon. Pieter-Lucas passed the night on his bed in this ancient Dillenburg room in a turmoil of conflicting thoughts.

So much had happened on this day. So many ideas and challenges had presented themselves for his response. One thought above them all intruded with determined fierceness. Hendrick van den Garde was dead, hanged on a gallows by the shores of the Zuyder Zee! Ugly rebel, senseless heretic, merciless imposter—none ever deserved such a death any more than this vicious murderer. He had seen the glint of murder in the man's eyes that fateful morning in the church.

He should be glad that vengeance had been served! Exceedingly glad! Overjoyed!

What, then, persisted in stirring up discontent and anxiety in him? Was he grieving as if his own vader had been exposed to the elements and shame on those gallows? Surely this was not grief!

"I will rejoice," he said aloud, as if to dismiss the tormenting thoughts.

Once more, he recognized the familiar stirrings of the inner monster baring his fangs in ugly, mocking laughter. "*Nay*, but you shall not rejoice," it taunted, "for you were robbed of the joy of tying the noose around that spiteful neck with your own strong hands!"

"I am no murderer, nor the son of a murderer," he retorted. " 'Tis enough that the deed is done and I will rejoice!"

All night long he fought with his delusions. At times sharp images from the dream that had terrorized him in the Beguinage stabbed at him. Dirck Engelshofen hitting him over the head with that huge book, absconding with Aletta into the storm! Hendrick leering over him with the sharp knife poised above his head! Opa stricken by lightning and sinking into the gaping earth. . . .

He jerked himself awake. "*Nay, nay, nay!*" He beat at his bed with a frustrated fury. "Hendrick van den Garde has been hanged! Juliana's herb garden will yield a cure for Gretta Engelshofen, and I will move on."

He yanked the covers over his head and wailed softly, "Aletta, oh, my Aletta. I shall find you, and you shall be mine!"

From somewhere out in the darkness, a dog howled, and from an apartment on the other side of the Dillenburg grounds came a mournful answer. The familiar wail of Prince Willem's perpetually distressed princess was muffled only slightly by thick, tapestry-clad walls.

A chorus of roosters crowed, the black velvet lightened into a gray sky, then blue. Celestial diamonds faded away. Pieter-Lucas rose from his sleepless bed and shook Yaap awake.

# PART THREE

## The Healing

This flower, whose fragrance tender
With sweetness fills the air,
Dispels with glorious splendor
The darkness everywhere.
True man, yet very God,
From sin and death He saves us
And lightens every load.

*Anonymous fifteenth-century German Christmas carol*

*"A Christmas rose is for healing."*

—Pieter-Lucas

# CHAPTER SIXTEEN

*Emden*

Late in Summer Month (June), 1567

O n the wonderful mornings that followed each winter snowstorm, Aletta loved Emden. The icy-white fairyland outside her windows brought her genuine delight. But with the coming of spring those mornings were rare. For the most part, spring in this far north country was gray, slushy, and drizzly. Still unsure of so much about life in this place, the young refugee girl from Breda grew impatient with the long damp cold that seeped into every chink and crevice of the little harbor city.

Shut up inside Oma's dingy old house, she learned to stay close to the enormous ceramic stove in the corner. She resented the windows and doors always tightly tethered against the fierce winds that blew across the thawing estuary at the mouth of the Ems River. She choked on the close, putrid air and longed to pry open a window.

Ever since that frightening night last fall when Hans prayed over Moeder Gretta, she'd grown steadily better. Yet, at Oma's insistence, the Engelshofen family stayed on through the winter with their kind rescuers. "My patient still needs the herbs and the quiet of this place," their healer woman hostess said. Vader Dirck, as usual, did not argue. Aletta's fear and mistrust of Oma Roza had diminished until she felt free to respect the woman as an expert *physicke* and to learn from her with unfettered eagerness.

By late Flower Month (May), the long cold had begun to wane and a less ambivalent spring promised something better. Dirck Engelshofen finally moved his little family into a tiny house just inside the thick walls of Emden. Oom Johannes' household lived next door, and between them both and the street stood the printshop of Oom Johannes' friend, Gerard.

Every day about midmorning, Aletta returned to Oma's kitchen bearing a gift of freshly harvested garden produce, which she exchanged for the herbs that made her moeder grow stronger daily.

" 'Tis so good to see Moeder bustle about," Aletta told Oma on almost every visit. "The once vacant little eyes now snap with life. Gone are the hollow cries and wild ranting spells."

Yet, for all the good things happening, Aletta struggled with an un-defined restlessness in Emden. The houses didn't look at all like what she'd grown up with, the people of Emden spoke more languages than she dreamed existed, and even Robbin no longer played at home under her supervision. Instead, Oom Johannes kept the boy busy helping Giles in the printshop and learning to read. Her apprenticeship with Oma and the joy of having her moeder in her right mind helped to brighten the daily grind.

With a sudden burst of newness, early Summer Month (June) budded in a dozen shades of green and resounded with the haunting voices of meadowlarks. Deep in her heart, Aletta often ached to go home, to hear the three short taps on her window shutter and look into Pieter-Lucas' big blue eyes. Oh to hear his deepening voice and feel the touch of his hand on hers!

On Sundays, the homesickness grew so intense she had to exert great effort simply to coax herself out of her feather bag. To the call of bells ringing from the tower of the Catholic Church, she went with Vader and the rest of his family and Oom Johannes' household to the big room hid-den away at the back of Hans and Oma's house.

Without statues or paintings or organs or priests or altars, they met here for what they called worship. They knelt on their faces and prayed in silence. They sang hymns about suffering great pain and martyrdom. Then different men of the congregation took turns reading from a big Bible that looked much like the one Vader had brought along from Breda. Either Hans or one of the other men preached a long and tedious sermon.

She was beginning to feel less a stranger amongst these loving, God-fearing people. After all they'd done for her moeder, she could have no doubt they were her friends. Yet deep down underneath the common sense of it all, she feared that no church hidden in a home could ever feel like a real church, and these friends, for all their kindness, could never replace Tante Lysbet and Moeder Kaatje and Pieter-Lucas.

On a Sunday morning in late Summer Month (June), everything in the blooming summer seemed to be calling her back to the Great Church in Breda. Vader was sitting in the chair by the window, waiting for the rest of the family to prepare for the walk to church. Close to tears, Aletta sidled up to him and spoke softly into his ear, "Is this not the day we would celebrate the *Processie* of the Holy Sacrament if we were at home in Breda?"

Visions filled her of long-ago days when Pieter-Lucas took her by the hand and led her to the many wonders of Breda's holy festival. On this Sunday every year, the whole city honored the miraculous healing powers of the tiny host wafer kept in a vial in her grand old church. Aletta had never known anyone who was healed by it, but everyone knew the stories. Thoughts of the bright costumes, colorful Bible story pageants, flashing and sounding trumpets, happy shouts of children, smells, and tastes of festive foods made her yearn to go back!

Vader Dirck looked up at her with an expression that shifted in rapid succession from surprise to tender reflection to panic. "Shh," he said shortly. "In this place, we dare not to speak of popish ways or festivals."

Aletta drew in her breath and answered simply, "So I've seen, Vader. We are not papists while we live in Emden, are we?"

She watched a gentle smile nudging at the corners of his mouth. "Nay, rather, we are counted among the faithful Children of God."

"Is that the name of Hans' church?" She had so often searched for a name, and no one had given her anything better than this. "It doesn't sound like the name of a church."

"They usually do not like to be called by a special name," he said.

Robbin had joined them now. "Are we Anabaptists, Vader?" he asked.

Vader rumpled the boy's hair with his big hand, smiled, and replied with another question, "Where did you hear that name?"

The boy shrugged. "I don't know. Just heard it."

"Well, whoever told you that is probably not one of them. It's a name outsiders like to use," he said quietly. "But most, like Hans and Oma, don't like it."

"Why not?" Aletta asked. "What does it mean? Something to do with baptism?"

"I think that no one knows for sure just what it means," Vader said, standing to his feet and grabbing his hat from the rack by the door, "and these people would rather be known for their love of God than their practice of baptism. And now that our beautiful moeder is ready, we go to the church without a name, to worship the God whose name is the Lord."

All the way to church Robbin chattered continually, and Moeder held his hand and smiled at him and answered his questions. Aletta walked next to her vader and busied herself pondering who these Children of God must be. Surely Vader and Moeder did not belong to them. However, when Robbin asked Vader if we were Anabaptists, he hadn't answered.

Fine, pious people, they all seemed to be. Something about their strong faith in God coaxed Aletta to feel secure with them. No "Eye of God" glared down upon her from the ceiling of their meeting place. In fact, they had no pictures of any kind in their church, nor statues nor colored windows—just cold, barren walls and empty corners and high windows that looked out on the clouds and the occasional patches of blue sky where a gull could be seen now and then.

She had to admit that the words she heard in this strange, unchurch-like room offered a sort of reassurance she wished hard to believe in. And often, in a way she could never explain, she felt as if God was in this church more than any other where she'd ever been. Here He was not the hovering eye, examining her for every evil deed and thought for which He could take some special delight in chastising her. Rather, she envisioned Him standing at the front of the room, sometimes moving among the rows of worshipers. His arms reached out and a warm vaderlike tenderness beckoned them to come and lean into His embrace.

Yet, could she fully trust the people who worshiped here? For all their godly words and kindliness, they also guarded many secrets. They would not talk about their former homes or occupations or the friends and families they had left behind. Oma had told her that they came to Emden as refugees, fleeing from something, even as her family had done. She'd said that if they worshiped in their hometowns as they did here, they would have been imprisoned or hanged.

Aletta didn't understand. These folk were not at all like the Calvinists—destroying images, planning wars. They simply went about their business, helped others in need, and carried a staff in place of a sword. Surely no one could fear such people or mean them harm.

Perhaps it was not so simple as it appeared. Something in the secrets they held from her must account for it all. Did they hide a dark and sinister side that made them the hated enemies of all other religions and forced them to flee here from every corner of the world? Why, then, did the other religions not torment them in this place as they did in other cities?

Today more than ever, Aletta sat through the worship service in her own tightly sealed cocoon. "Great God," she prayed in silence when the congregation all fell on their faces to pray, "please keep us as safe as these friends try to make me feel. Guard us from the pitfalls that haunt their mysterious secrets."

But Aletta felt empty inside. She wondered whether her prayer rose above the rushes on the floor where she prayed it. The service seemed endless. The singing of the hymns, mostly about the suffering of persecuted believers, drew tears from her eyes, and the speaker for the day delivered his sermon in a monotone that allowed her mind to roam freely back to Breda's festivals and to Pieter-Lucas. Just when she thought the worship service had finally come to an end—they'd sung the last song and said the last prayer—an old man with long hair and a full white beard stood by the preaching table and began reading from the Bible once more.

"As Jesus stood on the mountain before He ascended to His Father, He commissioned His disciples to 'Go, then, into the whole world and proclaim the Gospel to the entire creation. Whoever believes and lets himself be baptized shall be saved, but whoever believes not shall be condemned.'"

The man shifted slightly, then raised his head and added his commentary. "We followers of Jesus believe not, as do the papists, in saving grace administered through the sacraments. But we do heed Jesus' words. For if we would call ourselves His followers, we must obey His commands. Hence, we baptize all who have been taught the Gospel of repentance and who believe that their sins have been taken away, not by their own works of holy living, but through the shedding of Christ's sacrificial blood. . . ."

Those who believed their sins were taken away? Aletta suddenly heard the words as if for the first time. Was that the condition for being embraced in those arms she sometimes fancied that Jesus held out to her in this plain sanctuary without images? A parade of all her sins—every disobedience and unkind thought or word—descended on her like a horde of angry soldiers. Frantically she searched the plain bare walls for one simple painting of Christ! If only she could look on His face and find reassurance of the words about His forgiveness.

The walls stared at her, more plain and bare than she had remembered them, and not so much as a flicker of candlelight danced across the heavy ceiling beams on this Sunday morning.

But when she closed her eyes, she saw Christ moving among the people, beckoning with outstretched arms and inviting words. "Come to me, and I will give you rest." How she longed to go, to trust, to be wrapped in His strong embrace. Yet, it seemed as if she held her sins like a large bundle of dirty rags in her arms and heard Him say, "Give them up, my child, so I can hold you tight."

His words only made her grip them the tighter. If only there were a priest to whom she could confess! But to approach Jesus and give her sins directly to Him? The more she struggled the more incapable she seemed of letting them go. Gradually the picture faded, replaced by the warm smile and open arms of Pieter-Lucas.

The old man's voice was droning on, calling her back. ". . . ours is a voluntary baptism of conscious adults, symbolizing and bearing witness before this body of believers of their repentance and faith for the washing away of all sins."

A baptism for adults? What was this strange thing these people believed was so important? She knew she'd been baptized as a newborn back in the Great Church of Breda. Often in desperation, she had clung to that ritual for hope that the hand of God would not strike her dead for her sin of disobeying Vader's orders about Pieter-Lucas and Moeder Kaatje. Now, was she to believe another baptism was needed? Would it relieve her of this awful weight of guilt? Would it free her from the forbidden, yet ever recurring memory of the boy she'd spent a lifetime loving?

*Nay*, but if that was what it meant, did she ever want to have her sins forgiven? She cherished the memory of Pieter-Lucas more than life and breath. How could she allow anything to take it from her? Besides, how could it be a sin to love her childhood sweetheart? To disobey her vader's orders not to see him, *ja*, that must be her only sin. *Ach!* but Vader had commanded her to "forget about him" as well. That she simply was not ready to do.

Suddenly the tight little room grew suffocating under the summer sun that beat down on the heavy thatch roof. Frantically she searched the room. There had to be a way to get out without calling attention to herself. But, no, she was seated squarely in the middle of the women's section, pinned between Moeder on one side and cousin Annie on the other. Nothing would do but to wait it out.

Was this the way a seed pod felt when it had ripened to the point where it was ready to burst and spit its seeds out to the wild and dizzying winds? She squirmed in her seat. "Make haste, Heer Preacher, with your dull goings-on," her heart pleaded. She simply could not sit still any longer.

The patriarch seemed not to be thinking of haste, certainly not of Aletta's restlessness. In his quiet, calm, meandering manner, he went on and on, explaining every detail of what these people believed about this most important institution of baptism. Vaguely aware of each new point in his speech, she suspected that if she'd paid closer attention, she would have learned all about why they rebaptized adults who had been baptized as babies, what the symbolism involved, and how to counter arguments from papists and Calvinists and Lutherans and a dozen other sects against their way of doing things. But what could all such controversies matter to her today? They had nothing to do with her or with Pieter-Lucas.

At last the elderly speaker said, "We have here this morning two believers—a brother with his wife—who come inquiring after baptism.

They have satisfied the brethren of our fellowship that their faith is genuine and their repentance sincere. We invite them to come now." He nodded toward the men's section, where from the far side of the row a man stepped up and walked forward.

"Vader!" Aletta gasped in a spontaneous whisper and clapped a hand over her gaping mouth.

From the corner of her eye, she saw her moeder's sharp glance and heard a subdued, short "shh" escape from a mouth that scarcely moved. Then Gretta Engelshofen, too, stood to her feet and promptly joined her husband.

Together they stood before the old preacher and answered a long list of questions. Aletta could not believe what she heard.

"Do you believe truly that your sins are taken away through faith in the shed blood of Jesus Christ?"

"We believe."

This couldn't be her vader, her moeder.

"Do you desire to walk in the resurrection of Jesus Christ and be buried with Him in death so that you might rise with Him to a new life of repentance from your great sinful ways?"

"We do so desire."

But they had no great sins to repent of!

"Is it your desire by the strength of God the Father, Son, and Holy Spirit to lay aside all old popish and sinful ways?"

"It is our desire."

"And finally, do you promise to henceforth believe and live according to the divine word, and in case you should be negligent, that you will receive brotherly admonition according to the order of Christ in Matthew chapter eighteen for the banning of the unfaithful?"

"We promise."

Vader Dirck, a member of the Children of God? The man who always hid his Bible in Moeder's linen chest, took his family to the Great Church, and never committed himself to anybody for anything at any time? *Nay*, but she must be in a dream!

Vader held Moeder by the elbow and together they knelt on the floor before the table. The preacher picked up a large pitcher and gently poured the water it held first over Vader Dirck's head, then Moeder Gretta's. A group of stately men gathered round them, laying hands on their dripping heads. All fell on their faces to the floor, and Hans prayed a long prayer reciting back to God all the details from the sermon about baptism. When they rose, they shook their hands all around and embraced.

Finally, the congregation sang one more song, and the faithful filed out of the room in sober silence. Never had Aletta felt so alone, so confused, or so homesick.

———

*Gerardus' Drukkery*
Monday evening, Late Summer Month (June), 1567

The last of the workers in Gerardus' printery had gone home for the evening. Dirck Engelshofen sent Robbin on ahead and lingered in the early advancing shadows.

"Run on home, son," he instructed. "Tell your moeder I come soon."

"Can't I stay with you, Vader?" the six-year-old begged. "Please let me stay."

"*Nay*, Robbin." Dirck was firm. "If you go not now, Moeder will worry about us both. I need you to be my messenger. I will not be much longer. Just these few last pages to proof, and I come speedily across the way."

Slowly, a disappointed pout clouding his little face, the boy moved toward the door.

"Watch your step and fall not into a hole between here and there," he warned and watched the door shut solidly behind his son.

Dirck lighted the lamp mounted on the wall just above his head and sighed. "It's been such a long day, the work with these words so tedious, and I wish I could throw it all out and just browse through my old books in *The Crane's Nest*."

How often since he'd fled from that spot so dear to his heart, he'd yearned to go back. The books he brought along were mostly his favorites. But the others? If only he hadn't had to leave so many behind. Were they still hidden safely away in those bolts of fine cloth in Barthelemeus' attic rooms? Dirck shook his head, rubbed it with a vigorous hand, then turned back to the pages before him on the high, wide table.

"An Exposition of the Our Father," he read aloud. It was a sermon penned by a preacher who had since been beheaded for his faith—the last in a collection of sermons Gerardus insisted Dirck must finish before morning. He dipped his pen in the ink and had begun to mark a repeated word when a knock came at the door. Before he could reach it, the door opened and in walked a traveler.

"Dirck, friend," the words burst from obviously eager lips.

"Barthelemeus!" Dirck slid out of the bench and ran to embrace his brother from the academic circle.

"I can't believe I've found you," Barthelemeus said, grasping Dirck by both arms and looking at him with happy wonder.

"What brought you to these far north parts? Business or something life threatening? But here, take a seat," Dirck interrupted himself. The two men found seats before the fireplace where no fire burned.

"*Ach*, Dirck! The story is long and it is not beautiful what has happened to our lovely city. My time has come to flee. I've brought my wife and children, and we stay for a time with her family nearby."

Dirck slapped him on the back and smiled broadly. "Then you will be our neighbor once again. Long live the academic circle of *The Crane's Nest!*"

Barthelemeus shook his head and raised his hand. "Not so eager."

"*Nay?* Why not? I find it a great reason to rejoice."

"Only, Dirck, that I stay here not too long. We hope soon to move on to England."

"England? Whatever would draw you there?"

"Business is good for Lowlanders in England. As you know, I've made several trips there with my wares in recent years. Just now, with all Breda in a ferment, awaiting the soon arrival of the Duke of Alva, I decided the time had come."

The name of the Duke of Alva spoke volumes about the terrors of the future before them all. Sent by King Philip to replace Margriet as his regent, he was known to be as fanatical about enforcing the Inquisition as his king. He was a sharp and ruthless military commander with thousands of hardy, well-disciplined troops.

"Are many people fleeing at this moment?"

"Many are preparing so as to be ready to flee at a moment's notice. You might do worse than to move on to England yourself, Dirck. A fairly large community of Lowland printers of all kinds have fled there to wait out the storm. Can you not see *The Crane's Nest* on a street in the land of your vaders?"

Dirck chuckled at the idea which had often crossed his own mind. "Someday, perhaps. For now, things are quite calm here. The printing goes well. We are blessed with a fellowship of brothers and sisters that have helped us in more ways than you and I have time to talk about. And believe me or not, brother, but my wife has been delivered of the curse that has lain on her these many years, and she and I just yesterday submitted ourselves for believer's baptism."

"*Och!* You talk of miracles, Dirck. Slow down. Your wife was delivered from a curse?"

"That she was," Dirck reassured him.

Barthelemeus smiled. "I seem to recall that Old Meister Laurens always did say her malady was a curse of some sort."

"I know," Dirck said, nodding his head.

"And the two of you argued over that point continually, like dogs worrying an old rag."

"We did," Dirck conceded. "I never could imagine who would have done such a thing to her."

"What changed your mind? Did Gretta finally enlighten you?"

"*Nay*, to be truthful with you, we still have no idea where it came from. Rather, Hans, the weaver-preacher in whose home the Children of God meet, had met with a similar case. We stayed with them in their home when we first came, and his moeder, who is the herbal healer lady of these regions, actually first suggested it. They finally persuaded me to try taking Gretta before the elders. They prayed over her, and she was clearly delivered."

"After all these long years!" Barthelemeus let out a low whistle. "That is the sort of news to put joy in a man's heart."

"Joy like you can't imagine," Dirck agreed. "But now, tell me about Laurens. Where has he fled?"

"Meister Laurens, flee?" Barthelemeus threw his head back and laughed. "That will never happen. You know it as well as I. He is like so many in Breda who have never felt the claws of the king's lion in their flesh. They tell themselves they can always sit and look on as a cat in the top of a birch tree rather than venture out into the dark cold unknown night of exile."

"No one knows that feeling better than I," Dirck recalled.

"In fact, Laurens has sent a letter by my hand—made me solemnly swear I would not fail to deliver it to you."

He reached into his bag and pulled out the paper. "But first, I need to tell you a few things he doesn't explain in his letter, starting with a story to amuse you. Shortly after you left, all Bredenaars awoke one morning to find on their doorstoops copies of *Strong Evidence That People May Have Commemorative Images But May Not Pray to Them*."

"So! The Lutheran didn't need my help, did he?"

"The story doesn't end there."

"What more?"

"Remember Phillip van Marnix?"

"Prince Willem's and Ludwig's friend? The 'noble with the golden pen,' we used to call him in the book business. Did he write a paper too?"

"Indeed he did. No name on it, but his literary fingerprints were all over it. *Of The Images Destroyed In The Netherlands In August 1566* was the title."

Dirck chuckled. "Sounds like him."

"He took every point in the Lutheran tract and answered it with Scripture and gave examples of image-breakings in the Bible as justification for their actions."

"I might have guessed it had I given it some thought. And did he pass his tract out to all the doorstoops as well?"

"That he did! Caused quite a stir and the formation of a visible group of Lutherans in the city."

"Lutherans in Breda? Can't imagine it!" Was Barthelemeus getting carried away?

"Most of us had no idea, either, till these pamphlets were spread over the city. Then, it was like the argument out in the open just drew them all out of the woods."

"Makes you wonder what else might be hiding yet, just waiting for another literary dialogue," Dirck suggested.

Barthelemeus shrugged. "Who knows? I've about decided that most anything can happen anywhere in these days. Does any news at all travel up this far? Have you any idea what's been going on?"

"Ja! With all the merchants, soldiers, and refugees coming and going, we probably hear more than you'd guess."

"Then you no doubt know that Prince Willem took most of his belongings and his household and fled to Dillenburg."

"In Grass Month (April), ja, we have heard, along with rumors that from there he is planning a revolt."

"That may or may not be true. Takes time to determine what's rumor and what's fact, as you know."

Dirck knew it all too well. "Like a thousand Beggars coming from Antwerp turning out to be a fistful."

Barthelemeus cocked his head and pointed a finger directly at him. "But don't forget, they did as much damage as if they'd been a thousand."

"Well . . ." Dirck didn't feel like an argument at the moment.

"Rumors or no, I can tell you this much for certain. The Beggars have declared all-out war. They will win the freedom for all Calvinists to practice their religion alongside the papists—or die trying."

"They don't really think they have a chance, do they?"

"Indeed they do! They've stockpiled the home of Antonis Backeler with arquebuses, halberds, and armor of all kinds. They've already launched forays against Philip's sympathizers all over Flanders and South Brabant."

"No wonder Alva is on his way."

"Ach, but the retaliation has already begun. Philip and the governess keep issuing new ordinances, some of them falsely in the name of Prince

Willem. The city council refuses to enforce any of them, so they've been appointing new city councilors and passing even more repressive ordinances."

"Where will it all stop?"

"On a battlefield somewhere. Or, more likely, a series of bloody battlefields. A good time for you and me to be hiding in our trees." Barthelemeus leaned forward in his chair and dropped his voice nearly to a whisper. "To give you an idea how bad it is, just days before I left, the unthinkable happened. The latest city council actually arrested Pieter van Keulen."

"The goldsmith?" Dirck knew him well. A Calvinist, indeed, but not of the Beggar sort. "Why him? I always said he would be the one influence to keep the rest of them in line."

"They say he was one of the image-breakers."

"*Nay, nay, nay!* Not van Keulen."

"The whole city is in an uproar over it. Even papists who knew the man have been heard to testify that he is a good, peaceful, and righteous man. No one has ever seen or heard him slander or tell a lie or act in any way like a rebel."

Dirck shook his head as if it would remove the words he'd just heard. "If all Calvinists were as godly as Pieter van Keulen, and all papists as godly as Lucas van den Garde, our leaders might never have given birth to the movement of the Children of God. Did they give him no warning so he could flee?"

"What he knew I have no idea. Only that on three or four occasions he had already made ready for flight, the last of these just a week before they took him. As Meister Laurens said, 'He indulged in one catnap too many in the lowest branches of the tree outside the city prison tower.'"

"At least he left no family, his wife being already deceased and no children living in Breda."

"But my wife was concerned for his housekeeper, Lysbet de Vriend. She has on occasion done some work in our household."

"Is she that peasant girl his wife picked up at the orphans' house several years ago? Illiterate, not too bright, she probably is unable to fend for herself with him out of the way."

"But with an amazingly devout spirit, my wife tells me. In fact, it is reported that the girl is capable of reading from her master's Bible."

"I've heard that report too. Sounds a bit hard to believe, but God does stranger things."

"My wife wanted to bring her along with us, but the woman insists it is her duty to stay and attend him faithfully in prison, with food and other necessities. We do wonder what will become of her."

"She should be safe enough," Dirck said. "What about her could pose a threat to Philip or the papists?"

"Strange times, Dirck, strange times."

"I can't believe they'll hold van Keulen for long." Dirck sighed. "Never would I have thought it could happen in Breda."

"Laurens and I have discussed it at length."

"And what sort of conclusion did you reach?"

"We believe the new council members Margriet has recently appointed did this as some sort of example to try to frighten the rest of the city. Which means it may last for a very long time and not end too happily."

Dirck shook his head. "May God have mercy on us all. So far, in these regions we've had nothing more than the usual disagreements between the congregations that seem to thrive in numbers and varieties up here. So far even these have not touched the group that meets in Hans' hidden church. We need to pray much that it stay this way."

Barthelemeus stirred in his chair and handed the Meister's letter to Dirck. "I think I've told you all you need to know before you read this."

Dirck took the letter, eagerly turned it over, and loosened the seal, revealing a full page of Meister Laurens' precisely formed words. "Aloud? Ah *ja*, he says here, 'To be read aloud at the upcoming convening of the most esteemed academic circle.' " Dirck nodded and exchanged smiles with Barthelemeus.

" 'On this lovely afternoon, I sit in my place in *The Crane's Nest*, and I imagine that you two sit with me.'

"You still have access to it? They have not taken it away yet?" Dirck asked.

"The old building still stands as if you had closed up the shutters and put out the fire for a long winter night's sleep," Barthelemeus said. Gesturing with his hands, he went on. "Outside, the crane stands yet on the edge of her nest of chicks that never grow older, and the stone lodges yet in her claw. We guard the key that you left with us and still meet there on occasion."

Dirck shook his head and felt a surge of longing for the old place. Swallowing a lump in his throat, he resumed the reading. " 'Today I face a dilemma of a sort distressingly new to this old schoolmaster, descended from a long line of schoolmasters, none of which to my knowledge ever had to face this same perplexity. I pass it on to you in hopes that as you discuss it between you, you might be given the wisdom to agree with the conclusion I feel constrained to make in the matter.

" 'It appears that Margriet, in her remaining days as governess before the arrival of the Duke of Alva, is desirous of making one last good impression on the king. Hence, she has required of the nobility that all sign an oath of unquestioning loyalty to the Catholic religion and to His Majesty, King Philip.'

"Interesting to see which nobles sign and which refuse," Dirck interjected.

"You can be sure Prince Willem didn't."

"That was probably the drop that made his bucket run over and finally drove him into exile."

"It was indeed!"

Dirck returned to the letter in his hand. " 'But the governess didn't stop with the nobles. Now she brings her oath to Breda, and before the summer is passed, all midwives and schoolmasters will be required to sign it.'

"Midwives and schoolmasters? Curious choice of designations."

"Both having influence on children."

"What other groups are being required to sign?"

"None!"

"What else does Laurens say about this strange oath?"

" 'In our oath we must promise, in addition, never to use heretical books or spread false doctrines.

" 'The standards for judging heresy and false doctrine are not made plain. But I fear with the coming of Alva that a new brand of inquisitors is about to search our books and lessons, brothers. All ideas not totally sanctioned by the pope and king, no matter how subtly expressed, will soon be detected and used to condemn our books and our persons. I only pray they do not find a trail to pursue the seller of the books that still lie on these shelves.'

"Surely we've not left anything there to create danger." Dirck hoped he was right. "Especially since the trail from Breda to Emden is anything but obscure. What will ever happen to Laurens?"

"Read on," Barthelemeus prodded, waving his hands in circular motions.

" 'As for this old schoolmaster, you know my intents and the nature of my devotion to God and to His sacred Word. Hence, it will come as no surprise when I tell you I plan not to sign the oath, not even if Margriet herself should place it before me at the point of a sword. My Prince Willem refused to sign it, can I do otherwise?

" 'Which means, I will not be teaching my schoolboys another year. What I shall do to provide bread and cheese for my wife, God only knows. Perhaps I shall be joining Pieter van Keulen in the tower. I only know I trust in God who does not let His children die of hunger for the bread physical so long as we persevere in faithfulness to consume and break with others the bread spiritual.

" 'Almost I hear your words and will fill my heart with what my memory and imagination supply of the perpetual nourishment of our friendships. Now grace, mercy, and peace be with you both from God our Father and His Lord Jesus Christ. Pray for me, brothers, that God will be gracious.

" 'I leave this place and lock it securely.

" 'Laurens.' "

Both men sat in silence while Dirck folded the letter and wiped a tear from his cheek.

"I fear," Dirck said at last, "that I should not have the courage to act so faithfully."

"Nor I," Barthelemeus added, "which may be the reason we have fled and our dear brother stays behind."

Barthelemeus stood to his feet. "We don't have Meister Laurens here to give us our final word of wisdom and send us on our way. But I must go."

"You will be back, I trust, and we can both imagine that the crane hangs above the doorway."

"Here, Dirck," Barthelemeus said, handing him his large black bag.

"What is it?"

"I brought as many of your books as I could stash away among the bolts of cloth."

Did he hear right? "Blessings on you, a thousand times over. Just before you came here tonight I was thinking of my books and wondering whether they lay yet in the protective covering of your attic."

"I brought all you left with me. Further, Laurens and I went through the others and picked out a few more we felt were not safe to leave for the roaming eyes of the Inquisition. I could not carry them all in one bag, but will bring more on my next visit."

Together, they emptied the books from the bag, and Dirck placed them on the bench beside where he must return to work. It was almost more than he could manage to add each volume to the pile without opening a single cover.

"Now I go," Barthelemeus said at last. He took his bag and stepped out into the darkening evening.

Dirck returned to his proofing table. How would he ever capture his mind again and focus it on the last sermon in the collection? With a mind full of news and a pile of old familiar books at his side, how could it be? How could it be?

# CHAPTER SEVENTEEN

*Emden*

Middle of Harvest Month (August), 1567

*L*ate summer hung heavy with greenery no longer new, goldenrod in fading profusion, and herb gardens going to seed. Mornings and nights grew cooler, days grew shorter, and a few flocks of early migrating birds chattered and honked in their temporary home in the fields along the shores of the Ems Estuary.

For more than a week now, Aletta had awakened each day with fresh memories of this momentous time a year ago. For it was in Harvest month that Pieter-Lucas had paid her that hurried early morning visit enroute to the Great Church. Then came the long days of silent wondering, and finally, that unexpected conversation with Vader Dirck and his stern warning to "dry your tears and put Pieter-Lucas from your mind. . . ."

How life had changed since those devastating words! And how persistent the memories and tears they spawned!

One golden hazy morning, Aletta awoke before the sun had risen, something she hadn't done since summer had arrived with its long days and short nights. In her heart a strange presentiment disturbed her with a feeling she couldn't quite define.

Was it anticipation? Oma had promised that today she would take her, along with her granddaughters, Maartje and Rietje, out into the fields where they would spend the day gathering wild herbs to replenish her dwindling stores. She'd looked forward to this outing for days.

*Nay!* It was an unpleasant feeling that nagged her.

Apprehension, then?

Nothing would come clear except that it seemed certain this day held some events of especial importance. "Control your imagination," she told herself. She turned over and attempted to go back to sleep. Instead, the uneasiness grew both in intensity and vagueness.

Could it have anything to do with Moeder Gretta? Impossible! For weeks now she'd been bright and growing stronger every day. Perhaps Pieter-Lucas was in trouble. She'd felt something like this once before at the time when he was facing his angry vader in the church. The feeling had gone on for as long as he lay in the sickbed in the Beguinage.

Hurriedly Aletta dressed herself and crept out into the single large room her family now called home. She paused outside the cupboard bed where her parents slept and trained her ear intensely. All seemed normal enough—two rhythms of steady breathing. She turned back toward her bed when a sudden loud banging on the door froze her to the floor in midstep.

In an instant Vader Dirck was tumbling from his bed and dashing for the bolted door.

"Help, brother, send your daughter quickly."

It was Hans! "My moeder is very ill," he rushed on, "and she calls for your daughter to come and nurse her."

"Come in, come in," Dirck Engelshofen responded, still sounding a bit dazed from his sudden waking.

Aletta touched him on the arm. "I'm awake, Vader. I go."

He gave her a gentle squeeze and said, "God be with you, my child." To Hans he added, "Keep her as long as you need her."

Aletta slipped out the door with the bearded messenger, patting her pocket to make sure Tante Lysbet's herbal was securely in its place.

They hurried along the slumbering streets, silent as the night that gave way to the rising sun just beyond the far city wall. Through Aletta's mind ran a dozen thoughts, labored memories of all the sick people of Emden she had watched Oma nurse with her herbs. Surely somewhere among these many experiences lay the clues she needed to help the Healer Lady herself back to health and well-being.

At the little house on the water's edge, Hans shoved open the door. Not until they stood inside did he speak. "Praise God, you've come!" He cupped his hand around her elbow and guided her quickly across the room.

Instinctively, she recoiled from his touch. But with Oma in danger, she forced her mind away from her own discomfort.

"What is it that troubles her?" she asked.

"She wails and moans," he whispered, still hurrying her across the floor. "Her face is swollen and red and of exceeding heat to the touch, and she complains of her side, her head, and her leg."

Aletta surveyed the room with one broad sweep of her eyes. "What, no fire, no boiling water?" she asked. Then, "Where are the girls? Have they made no poultices for the swelling? Which herbs have you administered to her?"

"I . . . I know nothing about any of this," Hans stammered. "She's never been like this before. I just awakened to hear her groaning and calling for you, and I left to fetch you before I did another thing. I shall fan the embers into fire and rouse the girls . . . and whatever else you ask."

Aletta caught her breath and held it long. Had she actually given those demanding orders to the man of this house, the preacher, her elder? No, at this moment he was none other than the son of her teacher. A heaviness weighted her spirit—a combination of compassion and confusion in the presence of a duty never before performed.

Aletta stood looking in on the beloved teacher-turned-patient. Her breathing came shallow, her face was puffed and red, her brow wrinkled in obvious discomfort, and she stirred incessantly. "I didn't know I cared so much for this woman," she whispered to herself.

"Great God," Aletta prayed, "for the sake of your dear saintly child, Oma, please hear me and show me what to do."

She touched the burning furrowed forehead. Without opening her eyes, Oma relaxed her brow and spoke with marked effort, her voice weak and quavering. "Aletta . . ."

"Ja, ja, Oma, I'm here." She took the woman's hot limp hand that reached out to her and held the fragile fingers gently.

"Praise God . . . in time."

"Tell me, where shall I begin?"

"My leg," she managed, attempting to pull up the cover and show it to her. "Fell on sharp stone . . . wrapped it . . . Ohhh. . . ." Then she fell silent, slipping into the haze of her searing heat.

Aletta tugged at the feather bag until she uncovered the leg. Midway between ankle and knee it was swollen to twice its normal size, and the skin stretched so tightly over the bulging muscle, she feared it would burst.

She must examine it. She'd seen Oma do such things when she went with her to visit the sick of the hidden church family but had never done it herself. What if she hurt Oma more? As if handling a butterfly with a broken wing, she touched the leg and turned it ever so lightly.

It was as hot as the forehead! Oh, what was that poultice Oma always used to extract heat from a burning leg? Could she find it in the apothecary cupboard?

On the inner side of the leg, the timid novice *physicke* discovered a festering wound about the size of one of the smallest coins she always carried to market. A yellowish watery liquid oozed from the hole. And on the bed nearby lay a tiny crushed leaf stuck to a dried pool of blood in the midst of a length of old linen cloth.

Aletta's mind sprang into action. What was this leaf? And why did it not work? Was it not properly applied? Should she replace it? Could it be she used the wrong herb?

A light touch on her arm brought her suddenly to face Maartje and Rietje. Oma's two miniature replicas, with stray tufts of golden brown hair peeking out beneath their head scarves, stared up at her, their blue eyes wide with questions and brimming with pain.

"Will Oma be all right?"

"Please tell us she won't die."

What now? She could not yet be sure herself, much less make rash promises she might not be able to keep. Aletta looked into the imploring little rosy-cheeked faces and a terrifying thought came to her. Had they watched their own moeder die? Perhaps in this very room . . . this very bed? Was this but one more of the deeply buried secrets to remind her that she did not belong to this mysterious family?

More confused than ever, she fumbled about for words until Hans came to her rescue in his always soothing voice. "We trust in God, who alone knows how many people need our dearly beloved Oma. Her restoration lies in His hands."

The man was standing with one arm on the shoulder of each girl. Surely he was no stranger to prayers for restoration, nor to death in response. What pain must he be trying to hide beneath the surface of his calm composure?

"Yet, if He is to restore Oma, He will do it with our help." Hans addressed his girls with sudden firmness. "Now, Aletta, our *physicke* lady, tell us what we must fetch for you and we will do our part."

What must she do first? She breathed deeply and waited. For what she was not sure—a word from Oma, a bolt of wisdom, perhaps? Most surely, she needed a repeat of that sure commanding spirit she had felt a few short minutes ago. It did not come. She found only enough courage to begin by saying, "Is the fire ready? Have you hot water yet?"

"Ready, Vrouw *Physicke*," Hans replied.

"A large kettle?"

"A large kettle nearly full."

"*Goed*. Then you, Hans, sit here to soothe your moeder when she stirs. Maartje, quickly go to your Oma's garden and pluck a handful of wild thyme. Boil it in the pot on the fire to make a cooling bath. Rietje, bring the candle and come with me to the apothecary. We shall find the herbs to make your Oma well and strong again."

It was working! As she spoke the words she felt the confident spirit return, and incredibly, she seemed to be saying the right things, almost as if they had not passed through her brain but her lips only.

As always, Oma Roza's apothecary closet filled Aletta's nostrils with a feast of delicious aromas, her heart with overwhelming awe, and her imagination with unbridled abandon. It was a paradise of narrow shelves and drawers and bins laden with pottery bottles, pewter boxes, and baskets bearing precious fragrant leaves and seeds and flowers and roots. Bunches of pungent herbs of a dozen sorts hung from the rafters, and a pair of herbal books with yellowed, well-worn pages lay open on the small wooden work counter.

The crowded little room with its single murky window in the roof was Aletta's favorite spot in Emden. Today she entered Oma's "healing sanctuary," as she called it, with a mixture of excitement, apprehension, and terror. Increasingly over the past weeks, Oma had sent her here alone to mix some potion or fetch some ingredient. But the teacher was never far away, always ready with quick instructions.

Rietje, the younger of the two girls, lingered in the doorway and ventured in a quiet voice, "Tante 'letta, you sure it's all right for me to come in?"

"Why not?"

"Oma never allows it."

"Oh?"

"She says I'm still too young."

"And how old might you be?"

Rietje raised her hands, and with both thumbs tucked into her palms, she spread out four fingers of each hand and answered with pride, "I'm eight years old!"

"Well, today I need an eight-year-old assistant for this job. We have to help Oma get well. I can't imagine she would think you are too young for that sort of job, can you?"

"*Nay.*" The girl smiled, smoothed down her white starched apron, and gazed in wondering amazement around the little room.

Aletta wasted no time but began at once turning pages in the herbals until she found a recipe she and Oma had concocted many times. "It says here we need chickweed and violet leaves. Think you that you can find some in the garden, my little helper?"

"I know where they are," Rietje offered.

"Go quickly, then, and bring them back while I prepare the fenugreek and linseed powders."

Maartje had already returned with the thyme leaves and was boiling them with chunks of marshmallow root. When the bath was ready, Hans dipped large cloths in the wild thyme bath and wrung them out so that Aletta and Rietje could bathe Oma's body. Each time the compresses touched her and the fragrant liquid soaked into her feverish skin, she sighed and groaned. Little by little the skin began to sweat, releasing the hot humors that caused her so much grief.

When the leaves of chickweed and violet had softened in their bubbling pot, along with the marshmallow root, Aletta strained them into a paste and mixed a poultice with the fenugreek and linseed powders, all in a base of warmed hog's grease. She applied the concoction to the wound, freshly cleansed by the wild thyme bath, and secured it with a cloth.

Aletta ordered her regiment with a skill she had never dreamed she possessed. Not only the girls moved at her every word, Hans, too, spent the entire day looking in on his moeder and following Aletta's instructions.

"Fetch me an ox tongue from the market."

"Awaken Oma and give her a cup of this hog's fennel tea. Careful, now, to see she is fully awake and takes it only in small sips."

"Answer the knock at the door. Oma may have no visitors today."

All day long Aletta guided the devoted family as they fluttered over Oma, coaxing her body to heal. Together they watched with growing courage as her heat subsided, her swellings diminished, and she complained less and less of pain. In one last effort, Aletta and the girls concocted a tasty ox tongue soup boiled with generous handfuls of borage.

" 'God's cheering-up medicine,' Oma always calls it," she told the girls.

"We know all about borage," Maartje offered. "Oma fills our bowls with it every time we are sad or angry."

"Or whenever we don't want to do what she tells us. She puts it in everything," Rietje explained with exaggerated emphasis.

Finally, just before the rest was done they tossed a few sprigs of chervil into the pot.

"For flavor," Rietje said, mimicking Oma's didactic manner.

"Did your Oma tell you that?"

"*Ja,*" Maartje answered. "Rietje always says what Oma says."

"Good girl. Someday she will be known as the Healer Lady of Emden. But did Oma also tell you that you must not add chervil too soon?" Aletta cautioned.

"*Nay.* Why not?"

"Chervil too long cooked will surely turn the best of soups bitter. So my moeder always says."

"Oh!" Rietje looked astounded, then screwed up her nose and giggled.

"It smells so good, Tante 'letta," Maartje exclaimed.

"It's nearly ready now. We must beat up the white of an egg and mix it with the soup in Oma's cup."

"Whatever for?" Maartje asked. She stuck out her tongue and twisted her mouth and nose into a nasty-taste grimace.

"It's good for soothing the belly so it does not plague her with windiness and pain. Now, Rietje, you set some plates on the table. Maartje, slice some bread and set on the butter. You shall all taste the soup that you have made while I give Oma hers to sip."

Oma was already awake when Aletta parted the bed curtains and approached her. The old lady smiled. Her eyes opened wide for the first time all day. Aletta wiped the sweat from the face that had lost its puffiness and reddish color and again showed the wrinkles of her years the way they all knew her.

"Your granddaughters helped me to prepare a pot of fine ox tongue soup," Aletta said. As best she could with the cup of soup in one hand, she settled herself and her layers of skirts on the edge of the bed. "We hope you like it, Oma."

"You put borage in it?"

"*Ja*, Oma, with a touch of chervil."

"And the white of an egg?"

"*Ja, ja.* I believe that was all?"

Slowly, deliberately, the graying head nodded and a smile curved her lips.

Aletta dribbled the soup into the parched mouth one spoonful at a time and watched her swallow. Between sips, Oma smiled her approval.

"Delicious," she exclaimed at one point.

"You're looking better," Aletta offered. "The last time I changed the poultice on your leg, the wound had given up its angry scowl and a bit of its extra size."

"Praise be to God, I am feeling much better."

"You frightened us with your hotness and your swollen leg."

"And myself as well. You're a fine *physicke*, my child. So like an assistant I once had. I never thought I'd find another. God has prepared you, anointed you . . ."

" 'Tis only that you, Oma, are such a good teacher," she stammered. "I simply found your recipes and could not forget the things I've watched you do to bring healing to your patients all over Emden."

"I pray you, take care that you never make the kind of trial I made yesterday, do you hear me?"

"What trial, Oma?"

"That little crushed leaf—did you find it in the cloth tied to my leg?"

"I saw a crushed leaf in the cloth indeed, but I had no idea what it was."

"An herb called all-heale. I bought it once at a market square. The huckster who sold it to me recited a long list of wonder-working claims for it. He said that it had been known to heal deeply ulcerated wounds long given up by the best of *physickes*."

"Know you of anyone else who has used it with success?"

"*Nay*, none."

"Then why, Oma? You always told me . . ."

"I know, I know, my child. That is why I feared to use it on a patient before I had tried it on my own self."

"Oh, Oma, what dangers you put yourself in! What would we ever have done without you?"

"If no one had ever risked, what would we know of the healing properties of any of our herbs? 'Tis a part of the calling of a healer, my child."

The old lady finished her soup, then grasped Aletta's hand and said, "Tonight you may go home and rest with your family. With Hans and the girls, I shall be fine. You've taught them well."

"If you are to be fine, 'tis time now to close your eyes and sleep once more." Aletta pressed the woman's hand to her own lips, then tucked it under the covers, wiped the last remains of the soup from her wrinkled face, and let herself down to the floor.

"Sleep well," she whispered and paused long enough to assure herself that all was in order. Oma smiled, closed her heavy eyelids, and promptly slept in peaceful, steady quietness.

Aletta turned from the bed to find Hans standing behind her. "Ah!" she started.

For an uncomfortable moment, the man said nothing, just looked down at her. The gentle warmth of his eyes terrified her. She looked at the floor and heard him say, "Only God knows how often I give Him thanks for the goodness He has brought to us in this house through the coming of your vader and his family to Emden."

Panic gripped her in the chest, the panic this man's nearness always precipitated. So different from the peaceful sense of protection she felt when Pieter-Lucas stood by her side. Involuntarily, she edged away slightly. Feeling oddly aloof from her own voice, she listened to it stammer with a labored politeness that masked her fright. "Very kind of you, thank you." Clearly, she was no longer the *physicke* in charge. Hans had once more assumed his threatening position as the man of the house, the preacher, her elder—and that something else she feared more with each encounter.

He stood with his hands behind his back, ignoring her discomfort, and continued his speech. "My moeder has so long prayed for you to come and learn the herbal arts from her. So many of our people here need her expertise and God's touch through her herbs. You cannot know how blessed of God you are to be called to wear her mantle." He paused, shifted, and moved his hands into a clasped position before him.

Blessed? Indeed! So it seemed every time she worked with the herbs. So it seemed when she enjoyed Oma's presence and laughter and wisdom. Even in the young girls' chatter and companionship she found pleasure. But what sort of blessing was it when this man's hovering attentions must ever go with it?

Fighting to distance herself from him again, Aletta spoke in short, nervous syllables. "Oma rests. Her leg and head are better. I think you do not need me more this day. I go to home for now."

Hans raised his hand and opened his mouth, but Aletta did not stop talking. "If she awakens, give her more hog's fennel tea. If the heat returns, bathe her in wild thyme and dress her wound with a fresh poultice. Let her not throw off her covers. I shall be back tomorrow, early."

Continuing to ignore the man's attempts to interrupt, and without looking directly at him again, she brushed across the room to where the girls cleaned up dirty dishes and scrubbed the long wooden table.

"Must you go to home already, Tante 'letta?" Maartje asked.

"Not yet, please," begged Rietje.

Aletta smiled and rested her hand on Rietje's head. "Oma has in you two darlings the very best *physickes* in Emden. How much you have learned this day. Tomorrow I shall return, and together we shall learn what next to do for a patient whose heat has been consumed and whose wound is no longer angry."

She hugged them, one in each arm, bade them "Good night, rest well," then donned her cloak, secured her scarf, and went for the door.

Hans waited for her there. "I . . . I . . ." he stammered, opening and closing his mouth several times before he managed to speak. "I thank you for your expert services."

"And I you, for your assistance. Good evening."

With half a bow, he opened the door and let her out into the early evening fresh sea air.

———

A vigorous wind was whipping the water into noisy slaps against the sides of the few boats scattered along the harbor wall at the end of the street. It had also stirred up huge piles of white billowy clouds in the heavens. Aletta moved dreamily through the streets of Emden, ignoring the people who swarmed around her. She passed through the city gates, on beyond the group of houses where her family lived, and out into the field where Oma would have brought her today to gather herbs if all had gone as planned. A light filmy haze hovered over the harbor, the city, the wheat fields ready for harvest. The marshes throbbed with the steady chanting of a migratory feathered choir.

She seated herself on a large boulder beside a narrow beaten pathway and gazed upward at a pair of black-headed gray gulls soaring and dipping through the summer sky. The sun tipped their wings with silver, and the patches of blue sky behind them seemed to say they had some regal purpose in God's magnificent creation.

Something in the unhindered abandon of this special pair of gulls gave her hope that someday she, too, would know the freedom to dip and soar with the one young man to whom she had promised her heart's devotion. Pieter-Lucas, her Pieter-Lucas! How she yearned for him! How could she go on without even knowing where he was or when or whether he would ever find her in this lonely, isolated place?

"Great God," she prayed, "carry my voice to Pieter-Lucas and lead him to my side. We made a vow. A vow, Great God. Does that not matter to you whose eyes look down on all we do and say?"

Aletta sat on her stone remembering pleasant days of long ago and trying to forget Hans' gentle but frightening eyes and Vader Dirck's stern words of a year ago that had caused so much grief. She watched the sky turn from blue to pink to a dazzling gold. The sun slid down between the billowing clouds and hovered just above the estuary on the far horizon. Numberless flocks of birds chattered in the fields just beyond her, filling the twilight air with a mesmerizing din.

Where her mind was when she first became aware that her vader had joined her, she never could remember. The golden sky had darkened into gray, but the world was still dusky light all about. How long had he stood there? Did he speak? Or did he simply look on, perhaps reluctant to intrude into her sacred meditative sanctuary?

When she saw him, she wondered at the total lack of panic or joy that she felt.

"My child," he spoke, his voice rising, then dropping off into a profound pause.

"How did you know to find me here?"

"I only knew. I understand your adventure as a *physicke* went well."

"You went to Oma's in search of me?"

"And to see how the old lady fared. I heard many kind and grateful words about you, Aletta. Words to make a vader proud."

" 'Twas Oma's tried and proven recipes, and the eager assistance of her granddaughters did the work."

He cleared his throat and walked a bit away then back. She did not look up but felt him staring down at her.

"Why did you leave so soon?"

"My duty for the day was done, Oma slept, and . . ."

"What more? Why did you not return directly home?"

Aletta dug her toe into the loose pavement of crushed shells and tiny gravel. Still not looking up, she answered at last, "My thoughts called me here to be alone."

"Thoughts about the herbs and your obvious aptitude for the healing arts? Or thoughts of Oma and her weaver-preacher son?"

Startled, Aletta looked up. He still stared down on her. "Why ask you such a question?" she asked.

In the waning light of a day reluctant to be gone, Vader Dirck's figure stood like a towering silhouette. He knelt down on the path beside his daughter and studied the ground in silence for a long while before he answered.

"Hans is a fine and upright man—a godly and humble man, you know."

"I know." Who could ever question that?

"Never will he become wealthy, and as a leader in the brotherhood of the Children of God, his life will always be—ja, and always has been—in danger—his and all his family with him."

"How so, Vader?"

"You know the story of his wife, do you not?"

She shook her head.

"She died at Hans' side in a filthy prison where they both were held captive, and for nothing more than the capital sin of being rebaptized. Only by God's miracle did he escape, bringing what remained of his family here to a safety that lasts perhaps only for the moment."

"Why do you tell me all this?" Little tremors began to quiver in the pit of her stomach. Her imagination sketched the first shadowy lines of a picture she did not care to see.

"Because you need to know it if . . ." His voice slid away like the sun over its horizon.

"If what, Vader? Oma tells me that who they are and whence they come is secret information to be guarded. It's almost as if to tell too much would endanger their lives."

"You're right, my child," he said.

"Then, why do you tell me? How did you learn it?"

Vader Dirck took a long deep breath, laid his hand on her arm, and answered slowly, "Hans told me, and you need to know it as well, because . . . well, because he put to me a question which I cannot answer without your help."

"My help? Vader, you know it all."

"*Nay*, not all. For weeks, now, since he first talked with me, I have struggled to know how I must ask you. An hour ago, he put it to me once again."

Aletta swallowed back a flood of tears that arose in her throat. The picture Vader Dirck was sketching grew frighteningly clear.

"What must you ask me?" She did not really want to hear.

"It's this way, Aletta," he said at last. "Hans the weaver-preacher has asked my permission to give you special instruction in order to prepare you for believer's baptism."

"Prepare me for believer's baptism? Why me?" She shuddered at the thought of so much close contact with this uncomfortably friendly man.

Vader looked helpless; no answer came from his lips.

"I do not even know that I will ever want to be rebaptized," she went on. "What is Hans thinking—that now that you and Moeder have been baptized, I must do the same simply to unite the family? That sounds not like what I hear him and the others preach."

"*Nay*, child, of course that is not the reason."

"Vader, I am still young. You and Moeder have only just now submitted to baptism. If you could wait so long, why must I proceed before I fully understand the reason for it?"

Vader Dirck cleared his throat three times before he said, "Your moeder's people were all Children of God; she grew up with their ways and ideas in the early days when many of them lived in Antwerp."

"She did? And you, too, Vader?"

"I too believed quite young."

"Why were you not baptized then?"

"In those days and in that group, the elders considered young people not yet thirty years of age not to be ready for baptism. From then until now, we have not lived in another community of these Children of God."

Aletta stared at her vader in silence for a long space, letting her mind adjust to the surprising revelations she had just received. He did not return her gaze but seemed to be watching the sunlight fade into twilight gray.

"Do you mean to tell me, Vader," Aletta spoke at last, "that for all the years you went to the Great Church and took your children there, you let the priests baptize them into the Holy Catholic Church and teach them all the things you disagreed with? Yet, you were no papist in heart?"

Vader Dirck spoke uneasily, never looking her way. "Almost, you speak the truth."

"Almost? What is not true?"

He looked at her then, took her hands in his, and spoke haltingly, "Just one thing you never knew." He paused and cleared his throat before going on. "No priest has ever baptized you, child."

She gasped, pulling her hands free to cover her mouth. "I've never been baptized, Vader?"

"Never. When you were first born, your moeder was ill and we postponed the event. Then finally, we made a trip to Antwerp to stay with family for some months. Our friends in Breda assumed we'd had you baptized in Antwerp, and we never had to do it. We did the same when Robbin was born."

So that was why the "Eye of God" always scowled down on her from the ceiling of the Great Church in Breda. Yet, the man in Hans' church had said it was because she carried around that dirty load of unforgiven sins, the ones she could not quite give over yet.

"But, Vader, I thought unbaptized children lived in constant danger of . . ."

"Of what?"

"I never knew what the danger was, only that one dare not go through life without baptism. Every time I felt the 'Eye of God' scowling down on me, I trusted my baptism to keep me safe from whatever God would do to naughty children who hadn't been baptized."

Vader shook his head and his eyes brimmed with pity. "My dear child, 'tis not baptism protects you from the wrath of God."

"What then?"

"The forgiveness of your sins."

"For what purpose, then, is the baptism?"

"It follows belief and forgiveness as a witness to the world that you are now forgiven and ready to live or to die for your faith."

"If this is so, Vader, why did you not tell your children about it before now?"

"I tried. You will remember that I read to you and taught you to read from the Bible and from the books in *The Crane's Nest*. I truly believed you had heard enough to make it clear. I had not realized that the power of a man-made painting on a ceiling could speak so much louder than the words I read to you."

"But, Vader, every week you took us into the Great Church. We thought you were a faithful papist, and you never told us that some things were right to believe and others not. How could you do that?"

"You ask a hard question," Vader said, pausing before he went on. "You must understand, child, that there are many in Breda who, if they had a choice, would not practice the religion of the papists."

"Why have they no choice?"

"Our churches all belong to the Catholic religion. Our Catholic king and the laws that shape our lives will allow none other. If we would worship in public, we must do so as papists. We who call ourselves the Children of God have learned to practice godliness in all places and our religion in private if we would avoid the executioner's sword. For the few things I did teach you, I could have been swiftly imprisoned if the local priests had known."

"What about Tante Lysbet? Did you not fear for her to see our private practice of religion, since she lived beneath our thatch?"

"Tante Lysbet knew all along. If the truth were told, one reason she came to live with us was that she might have access to our Bible and our books. Many of the works of Menno Simons and the others lay hidden away in her attic room. There were others, too, who came to *The Crane's Nest* to read the books and discuss the new ideas." She watched him clasp and unclasp his hands uneasily, then look her full in the face, and add, "No man lies in greater danger than a bookseller, my child. No man!"

Aletta felt a strange mixture of awe, disappointment, and excitement churning within her. "How can that be, Vader?" she asked. Was it possible that at last he might be ready to give her answers to the questions she had so long asked in vain?

"When I was about your age," he began, "I watched a friend die in the public square of Antwerp. William Tyndale was his name. They burned him at the stake for believing much the same as we do and for translating the Bible into the English language so others could come to the same sort of faith. As I stood there choking in the smoke, feeling the warmth of the flames, listening to Mr. Tyndale's final prayer and cries of anguish, I determined that I would be wiser than he. I would pursue great caution."

"Oh, Vader," she said, slipping her arm around his shoulder, wishing for a way to hug away these awful memories.

"Just remember this," he concluded. "A bookseller with an anointing of God to peddle books that will free men from the shackles of tradition must first save his own head if he would be alive to sell his books." He sounded as if the last of his spirit had drained from him.

Aletta stared at the ground, unable to speak, unable to cry, unable to believe the words she had just heard. So much that she had wondered all her life began to make sense now.

"Vader," she said at last, "please urge me not to prepare now for this new baptism. I am not sure about forgiveness and am not yet ready to die for a faith I may not even possess. Can you not see this?"

Vader sighed, then spoke hesitatingly, sliding into each word. "I do see, my child. I will never urge you, for the way is hard, and I shall always be as cautious for my children as I have been for myself. One day God will urge you as He did me. You must not refuse Him."

"*Nay*, that I shall not do. But since you are not urging me, am I to believe my baptism at this time is Hans' wish?"

"If you must know . . ." He paused as if searching for an easy way to say some hard thing.

"If you must have my answer for Hans," she responded, "then I must know the true question."

"*Ja*, I see that you must know it all." He paused. "Hans knows that only when you have been baptized can he gain permission from the elders to ask for one thing he wants very dearly—your hand . . . in marriage."

It was not all of her imagination, then. The uneasiness she had always felt in Hans' too-warm, hovering presence had not been without good reason.

"Oh, Vader, Vader." She drew into a tight ball, embracing herself to keep him at a distance. "*Nay, nay, nay*, Vader. I cannot, not even for the godly, goodly Hans. Ask me not to do such a thing. I beg of you, ask me not."

When he spoke again, Aletta heard in his voice deep tones of the sort that spring from a bleeding heart. "You know that the man and his moeder have been more than gracious to our family. They sheltered us for so long, and his moeder nursed Moeder Gretta back to health. He has taught us all such marvelous words from God's Holy Book. And he is a kind and loving man."

"I know, Vader. All that I know. I respect the man and have learned much from him about God and His ways. I have even come to love his family nearly as my own. I owe so much to Oma. She trains me to carry on the herbal healing in the brotherhood when she is no longer able. Maartje and Rietje are charming and sweet and capable. But . . . but . . ."

"Is it that you object to a man as old as he, a man already with daughters to raise?"

"Nay, Vader, that is not it."

"What then?"

"I simply cannot give my heart to Hans or to any other suitor. It is already given. I made a vow, and I must keep it."

"A vow? Why, that is a popish notion and has absolutely no binding effect."

"I know that, Vader." She offered no further explanation. Yet, she could never forget the lure of such a welcome doctrine. Nobody ever longed more than she to extricate herself from Moeder Kaatje's old and popish vow that threatened to destroy her dreams.

"When you become a Child of God, you, too, will be freed from bondage to vows."

"The vow of which I speak has naught to do with popishness nor any other sort of religion, nor do I have any desire to be freed from it."

"What then?"

"'Tis simply that my heart has always belonged to Pieter-Lucas van den Garde. I vowed to wait for him, no matter how long, until you would approve."

Dirck Engelshofen looked up with a start. Jumping to his feet, he paced along the pathway. The crunch of crushed shells beneath his feet filled the evening for what seemed a long forever. Finally, he said, "I see. You are not a child anymore, Aletta. You are telling me that your love goes deeper than some childish affection for the little friend from next door."

Aletta reached out to him, and he pulled her to her feet. "Oh, Vader, Vader, Vader," she cried out. "So long I've wanted to unburden my heart to you. One long year ago you gave to me an order I could not obey. 'Forget about Pieter-Lucas,' you said. It was impossible. I met with him only once more, but that was the day I vowed to wait for him. Daily, after he left Breda in search of his vader Hendrick, I visited his moeder in the Beguinage until she died—she and her newborn daughter.

"In spite of all you said, never have I forgotten him or ceased dreaming of him or longing for him. I've suffered greatly the condemnations of an evil conscience for my sin of disobedience to your command. For all I know, God can never forgive me or save me from the terrors of eternal judgment. But be that as it may, believe me, I can do no other."

Vader Dirck didn't say a word but opened his arms wide. She melted into them and sobbed till her whole body shook.

"Can you ever forgive me, Vader?"

"If you can forgive me," Vader murmured, his cheek resting on her head. "It was too much I asked of you. I had no idea . . . no idea." For a long while he held her close and let her weep.

When her weeping had subsided, she held him by the flaps of his doublet and asked, "Vader, do you mean to say it is no longer a sin for me to think of Pieter-Lucas?"

He answered slowly, as if thinking each word into existence with a struggle. "*Nay*, child, it is no sin to think of him, but I must wonder how possible it is that you shall ever see him again."

"Torment me not with such questions," she begged. "God only knows where and when, but I know I shall see him again."

He sighed and smoothed back the damp strands of hair from her face. "Have you any idea where he hangs his cap and lays his curly head at night? Or under whose table he shoves his feet at mealtime?"

"Not any."

"Or have you any inkling of what new wild disgraces Hendrick van den Garde has planned and executed in the name of his strange brand of religion?"

Aletta swallowed down an uneasy lump rising in her throat. "Probably only Hendrick knows the answer to that question. Is it not sufficient to know he lives not in Emden, and if he did no one here would know either him or Pieter-Lucas? Oh, Vader, can you not see that everything has changed since we last talked about this back on Pieter-Lucas' doorstoop?"

He shook his head. "Everything has changed and nothing has changed. So much you do not know. So much I never told you . . ."

"Indeed, you've always treated me like some fragile festival doll with an empty head."

"*Nay*, that was never the idea."

"Why, then, have you refused to talk to me about so many of the things that matter—things that have changed our lives? When we left Breda so hurriedly in the night, I wanted to beg the reason, but you had closed the door to your ears and your heart. The same when we left Antwerp. It was as if you thought I could not understand. Instead you left me always to wonder, to grieve, to fear what strange new thing would overtake us in the night."

"These many years I've simply tried to hold you close, not wanting you to bear burdens too heavy for such young shoulders. When you were still an infant, I promised God I would protect you from all pain and harm. That was my only purpose."

He took her in his arms and smoothed her head with his big hands. "Aletta, my brave and beautiful daughter, I had to shield you, to give you as much joy in your childhood as possible. Even now, it pains me more deeply than I can say to open your young, innocent eyes to these dreadful truths."

"*Nay*, let it not give you pain, Vader. Your words are the healing herbs that purge my mind of its deep dark questions."

She pulled herself from his embrace, held his arms in her hands, and looked up into his face. "Tell me," she pleaded, "what do you really know about my Pieter-Lucas since we left Breda?"

"I've heard absolutely nothing! Only that King Philip's Duke of Alva sets about even now to confiscate the lands of the image-breakers and to execute both them and their families."

"They wouldn't touch Pieter-Lucas, Vader."

"He belonged to the household of a wild image-breaker. If he stayed in Breda, when Alva arrived . . . there is no chance . . ."

"He lives yet, Vader, I know it. And we shall find each other one day."

"How can you be so sure?"

"We made a vow before the God of heaven, and He wrote it in His book. I simply know it shall be."

Dirck Engelshofen sighed. "How long shall you wait?"

"I'll wait a lifetime if need be."

"And if he comes not ever?"

"Then, I marry not ever." Visions of the Beguinage and Kaatje van den Garde's stiffening body flashed through her mind. And if Pieter-Lucas should choose his moeder's vow over their own, she would also marry never! Until this moment, Aletta had not allowed her mind to run so far. Now that she had done so, she felt her heart would break beyond repair.

The last glow of evening light had turned into the near blackness of a late summer night, and the birds had ceased their noisy concert when Dirck Engelshofen and his daughter started home in a shared silence. They neared the old city wall before Dirck spoke again, picking up the conversation as if no pauses had occurred.

"Meanwhile, the kind and gentle Hans, the lonely widower, needs a wife to stand by him in the mission to which God has called him. How can I let you reject this worthy man as your suitor? What, pray tell, shall I say to him?"

"Tell him the truth, Vader. Truth is like a bitter herb. No matter how it stings, it is the only thing that can bring light and healing and relief. If Hans is a man of God, he will swallow it."

The words came out too smoothly, as if she'd practiced them for months. But inside, she sensed a growing fear of what difficult truth the days ahead might bring.

"*Ja*," he said with an air of resignation. He patted his daughter's hand and added, "In the end, we must trust God to do what is best for us all."

"Thank you, Vader." Aletta breathed the words softly.

"And if God decides it's best not to bring Pieter-Lucas back to you?"

"You have my answer, Vader. I have no other!"

They walked on in silence. At the printshop gate, Aletta stopped, grabbed her vader's arm, and spoke again. "I want you to know that I have learned in these weeks to put my trust in the God of Hans and you and Moeder. But I am not yet ready for baptism."

"That I can see." His words were as gentle as the sighing of a summer breeze in Breda.

"One thing more," she ventured. "As you have forgiven me my sin of disobedience, is it possible that my Heavenly Father will also forgive all the other sins I carry on my conscience?"

Vader smiled. "Possible? More than that. He eagerly waits for you to ask."

"Even without the help of a priest as confessor?"

"Without the help of any man as confessor."

Aletta leaned her head against her vader's chest and prayed aloud, "My Heavenly Father, will you forgive?"

The great burden that had weighted her heart for so long lifted, and a gentle peace settled in its stead.

"The guilt is gone, Vader," she said. "The 'Eye of God' is smiling."

"And His voice is saying, 'Thy sins are forgiven thee.'"

"I hear it, Vader, I hear it."

# Chapter Eighteen

*Emden*

Middle of Harvest Month (August), 1567

*A*letta passed an interminable night struggling with a volley of urgent questions that refused either to be answered or to go away.

How was Oma? Did the fever leave her in peace as it had when she parted from her at sundown? Or had it returned to torment? What surprises would the new day force upon them all?

How could she walk into that house and pass under the kindly, yet aggrieved gaze of the man who had done nothing but good to her and her moeder? The man who deserved a devoted and loving wife to hold his hand, cook his meals, praise his sermons, moeder his daughters . . . and nurse his moeder? The pious man she could neither love nor marry?

When at length the first shades of morning light seeped in around the edges of her bed curtains, they terrified the girl. Already she heard someone stirring in the kitchen.

She yanked the feather bag over her head and squeezed her eyes together till the crinkled skin around the corners ached. She fancied that somehow holding her eyes tightly closed enabled her to suspend all unwanted thoughts as well. If only she could stay this way forever, like the fairy tale she once heard about the princess who fell asleep and naught could break the spell until her loving prince arrived and kissed her awake.

It was not her loving prince that brought her back to reality. Rather, the noisy whispered voice of Robbin at the corner of her curtain.

"Sissy, be you awake?"

She squinted one eye open just far enough to see her brother's pudgy fist curling round the edge of the curtain. Above and behind it just a trifle appeared a familiar little peachy nose, then two round open eyes of dancing blue, and a broad forehead with a crop of unbrushed, straw-colored curls falling toward the nose. In spite of herself, Aletta smiled.

If she could not be a princess in the embrace of a magic sleep, perhaps she could at least pretend she had awakened to quieter days in Breda. Days when Moeder was not too very ill, Tante Lysbet watched the fires, Vader tended his bookshop, and Robbin had come to coax big sister out of bed before Pieter-Lucas would arrive on his way to the *Kasteel* stables.

Acting on an old impulse, she sprang out from beneath her covers, snapped her brother's chubby hand in one of her bigger slender ones, and pressed the fingers of her other hand warningly to her lips.

"Silence, young man, or I shall drag you to my web and tether you fast till Vader decides to have mercy on you."

The boy was all over her bed now, his curls bouncing with each movement, his face wreathed in smiles, his laughter filling the sleeping cupboard. With both arms, he pounced on her, then rocked back on his knees and grew quiet. A quizzical expression spread across his cherry cheeks and lit his eyes with a tantalizing fire.

"Sissy. . ." He slid into the word and ended it with a suspended question mark.

"*Ja, jongen*, what is it?" The magic of the moment made her feel like a child again. How long it had been since life had allowed her this privilege, she could not remember.

Robbin hesitated, his expression unchanging. "I have a secret," he said at last, unable to conceal a childish delight.

"Tell me," she prodded.

"You must promise not to tell anyone I told you this." He waited for her response.

"If it needs not to be told, why should I tell it?"

"You promise?"

"Of course, just tell me."

"I saw Pieter-Lucas yesterday."

"You what?" Aletta raised her hands, opened her mouth, and stared.

"I saw our friend Pieter-Lucas yesterday. You know, the boy that used to live next door to us."

"*Ja, ja*, I know who you mean, but where did you see him, and how can you be so sure, and does Vader know about this?" Questions rolled off her lips like apples from a basket, each one bumping against the other. She felt her mouth still gaping and her heart at a standstill.

"I was having my reading lesson. I heard Oom Johannes talking with a stranger in the front room of the printshop. The other voice sounded like somebody I knew—not somebody that belongs in this place—but I wasn't sure who it was. I wanted to run out to see, but I had to stay in my place. Vader gets very upset with me when I leave my lessons. When

I heard the door slam shut, I looked through the window and saw him walk down the street. I didn't see his face, just his back. It had to be Pieter-Lucas. That was his voice, I just know it. Besides, he had that funny hat on his head and those baggy britches. You know, like Pieter-Lucas always wears."

Aletta grabbed her brother by both shoulders. "Robbin, are you sure? I mean, how could Pieter-Lucas ever come all the way to this strange, wild country and walk into the bookshop where Vader and Oom Johannes work? You'd better not be playing games with me, *jongen*."

Robbin wriggled free from her grip and settled himself once more on his knees. With his fingers, he worked at the feathers inside Aletta's bag, moving them in every which direction. "*Nay*, I play no games. I know, Sissy."

"How do you know?"

"His hair was long and yellow and curly, and he walked funny. You know!" He concluded on a note of exasperation, his hands twisted into a knot and his face contorted into a grimace.

"He limped with the left leg?"

"*Ja*, I guess."

Aletta felt the fire go out of her bones and leave her trembling. How could this be? "Where is he now?"

Robbin shrugged, leaning his head to the left, his mouth turned down into an undecorated arch.

"Didn't you run after him? Talk to him? Ask Oom Johannes?"

"*Nay*, I told you I couldn't leave," he defended.

"Then how will we ever find him?" Aletta felt panic rising.

"He'll be back."

"How do you know that?"

"He said so."

"When?"

"On his way out the door. I heard him."

"I mean when will he be back?"

Once more the boy shrugged, then scooted over the edge of the cupboard and disappeared beyond the borders of Aletta's dreamworld. For an instant, he poked his head back in between the curtains, his bright eyes snapping but serious, and whispered, "Remember, don't tell Vader. He doesn't like it when I don't pay attention to my reading lessons." The boy scampered off.

Unnumbered thoughts tumbled through Aletta's mind now as she hastened to dress and begin her day. In one way, she found it no easier than before to face her inevitable visit to the house of Hans. But if indeed

Pieter-Lucas was somewhere about in Emden, surely she would find him, and Vader would come to her aid. How could he possibly insist on giving her to Hans once he actually saw Pieter-Lucas again? Unless, of course, Pieter-Lucas had decided to honor Moeder Kaatje's vow. *Nay,* but that could never happen. Excitement enticed her pounding heart beyond the fringes of her dread.

Tantalizing pictures filled her mind—pictures of Pieter-Lucas striding across a green field or bounding across an arched canal bridge toward her, grabbing her in his arms and never, never again letting her go.

But what if Robbin was mistaken? Since when did she dare pin her hopes on the whimsical apparitions reported by a six-year-old? But Robbin knew Pieter-Lucas so well. Besides, he had said he walked funny. It had to be true.

"Great God, whose eye no longer glowers at me from the ceiling," she prayed, "it was before you that Pieter-Lucas and I made our vow. Before your holy altar in the Great Church, Opa commissioned Pieter-Lucas to take care of me. It must be so!"

---

By the time Aletta emerged from her cupboard bed and washed her face and brushed her hair, she found Moeder busy packing her basket with freshly harvested carrots and onions. Something bright and fresh and almost lilting filled Aletta with hope. As if possessed by an old habit she'd begun to ignore since they came to Emden, today she took especial care with her hair. Each little ringlet must hang at its precisely appointed angle from beneath the plain white headdress she had learned to wear in this place of exile.

"Did you rest well, child?" Vader asked her.

Aletta turned her head ever so slightly, just enough to avoid his gaze. She did not answer immediately. "The night was long, Vader," she said at last. "And morning brought ample sunshine." Then turning to her moeder, she asked, "You pack Oma's basket so early today, Moeder?"

"You must go early to call on your patient." She made a protective nest of curly kale leaves on top of the vegetables and laid in a collection of hen's eggs, then covered it all with a clean white cloth. "You will need these things when you go."

"Of course." Regardless of all the dreams of Pieter-Lucas, her fearful encounter with Hans would not take wings and fly away.

Moeder spoke again, "I thought I would go along with you today. What think you of that idea?"

Aletta caught at her breath. "Oh, will you? Nothing could cheer my patient better than to see the glowing face of one of her own patients now returned to robustious health through her expert skills." Nor could anything do more to calm her own apprehensions than to have Moeder Gretta's company.

"Me go too? Me go too?" Jumping up and down, Robbin tugged at Aletta's skirt.

Aletta ran her fingers through the boy's bouncing curls. "I think you need to stay with your studies and duties at the printshop. Besides, a sickroom is no place for a schoolboy who has not yet learned to read the herbals."

"Aawh!" His lips drooped into a pout and he turned toward his vader. "Vader, please . . ."

Dirck Engelshofen wagged his head and his long index finger in unison. "No, please, son. We men have other matters to attend to."

The boy's eyes brightened and he stood before his vader, hands clasped into a begging position. "But maybe Aletta will need an errand boy. Someone to run to the market . . . and watch for danger. . . ?"

"*Nay, nay, nay!* The answer will remain for a thousand times, *Nay!*" Vader's voice, even at its sternest, could never sound threatening, and Robbin refused to accept the finality of his words. Once more, he looked into Aletta's eyes with pleading. Aletta smiled, patted him on the shoulder, and said, "That's a good boy. Who knows what exciting new adventures may befall you in the printshop today?"

Robbin nodded his head, not looking up.

Aletta stooped down to his level, lifted his chin with her right index finger and said softly, "Promise me that you will do your lessons well and keep your eyes open to see what sort of things that you can learn." She winked at him with her right eye.

"I promise, Sissy." The boy managed a lopsided wink in return, then threw his arms around his sister's neck and whispered into her ear, "When Pieter-Lucas comes, I'll grab him fast and drag him all the way to you at Oma's house—even if Vader gets angry. You'll see."

---

A cold fog hung over the little city. Moeder anchored the handle of her market basket securely into the crook of her elbow to guard her morning offering. She and Aletta tramped side by side through the wakening streets of Emden. They passed scarcely a word between them. Walking with Moeder usually went this way. Even her journey back to wholeness of mind had not made this quiet, self-contained woman talkative.

Today Aletta did not care. Her own distracted mind flitted up and down every street and alleyway, and her eyes caught at each moving figure. Could it be her Pieter-Lucas? Where did he lodge? How would he find her?

A wind coming in off the estuary whipped at them as they rounded the last corner and headed down the uneven paving stones along the old harbor. Activity ruled this place, and Aletta looked up and down the lines of fishermen preparing their boats for the day's venture, searching for a sign of Pieter-Lucas. As always, a number of older men stood in little knots or lounged on wooden benches up against the houses along the harbor. Smoking their long ceramic pipes, they busied themselves by doing the idle things men too old to work always do to pass the time— watching the younger men at work and talking about days gone by.

Three houses down from Oma's, Aletta's heart sagged. What if Robbin was mistaken? Maybe Pieter-Lucas was nowhere near Emden.

Vaguely she realized that she and Moeder Gretta were passing by a group of men who were neither fishermen nor honorable elder men. Appearing unkempt and drab, they were wearing ragged, ashen-gray clothes and plain felt hats on their heads. At their sides hung large leather pouches, wooden beggar's bowls, and long shiny swords. Such groups of Beggars were not an uncommon sight on the corners and in the dark alleys of Emden. Brederode, the Great Beggar, himself, had even been in town for a time at the beginning of the summer.

As usual, Aletta simply looked past the ragtag bunch this morning in search of someone truly important. But Moeder gave a sudden gasp, stiffened, and quickened her gait, rushing Aletta along. A fresh tension jabbed at Aletta's already jittery mind.

"It's all right, Moeder," Aletta tried to reassure her.

The agitated woman seemed not to hear. Instead she grabbed Aletta by the arm and pulled her on to Oma's. She knocked on the door and cast frantic glances back over her shoulder at the Beggars.

When at last the door opened and Hans stood before them smiling and whispering to them to come in, Aletta felt a strengthening detachment from the pain she had so dreaded from this encounter. "Moeder decided she felt well enough to join me today," she announced.

"I am sure my moeder will be much cheered to see you, too, Vrouw Engelshofen. You look weary. Please, won't you have a seat by the fire?" He took her by the elbow and guided her across the room.

"Gladly," Moeder Gretta answered and moved in that direction. Aletta followed her and noted with concern that she seemed to hold her head as she sat down.

"Are you all right, Moeder?"

She nodded, rested her hand for an instant on her daughter's arm, and gave her a distant half smile. "A spot of rest will restore me."

"Hans already has a fire burning in the fireplace," Aletta said, "and water boils in the kettle. I shall soon bring you a cup of soothing tea."

The activity of preparing the tea provided a welcome accompaniment to conversation. "How is Oma?" she asked. "Did she rest well?"

"She awakened a time or two in the night, and I gave to her each time a cup of hog's fennel tea."

"Did her fever return?"

"*Nay*, thank God. I looked in on her wound and left its dressing for the morning light."

"And for the *physicke* to attend to!" Aletta laughed lightly without looking in his direction. Then she turned toward Oma's bed and said, "I trust our nursing services shall not be so urgently required as yesterday. The girls—they are not up and about?" Aletta asked.

"Shortly," Hans said.

Aletta had barely poured the hot water over the leaves of mint for Moeder's tea when Hans approached from behind. "While the tea steeps and before my moeder and the girls awaken," he said, "I beg of you to look at something strange." The tone of his voice combined concern with eagerness.

On the table before Aletta lay a pair of papers with rolled up edges. One sheet contained a letter written in a delicate hand. Finely formed letters flowed across the page in a text of words Aletta could not understand. The other was filled with an elaborate drawing of some sort of plant.

"Like a page from an herbal!" she exclaimed.

"So it appears," Hans agreed.

"Where did you get these?" Aletta felt her pulse quicken.

Hans took his place on the bench opposite her and explained, "It was a most curious thing. They were brought last night, just about sunset, by a young man who knocked at the door."

"No one you knew?"

"I'd never seen him before. A pleasant-looking young man, he was, dressed as if he'd come from the south."

"What did he want?" Excitement rippled through her body.

"It seems he was a servant of a noble lady, and he was traveling through Emden on some sort of business. He said he was looking for a woman who was reported to be the Herbal Healer of Friesland."

"Is that not our Oma?" Aletta asked.

"Indeed, she must be the one."

Aletta's heart beat wildly with questions she desperately wanted to ask. Wears he baggy britches and an old felt cap? Do his long blond curls hang down his back? Does he limp on the left leg? "Careful, careful, ask not too much too quickly," she warned herself.

Suppressing the eagerness that tugged at her, she asked, "Tell me, what did this stranger seek from Oma?"

"He would not say much. Only that he desired to make a secret request for an herbal elixir that she might be able to provide. It seems he has a friend in need of it."

"Then why the drawing and the letter?"

"He said they bore his credentials. I know not how, but supposedly if my moeder is the healer lady he seeks, it will all make sense to her."

Aletta bent over the paper of text and traced the meticulous letters. "The words are in no language I have ever read, but I can make out the signature. Juliana, Countess van Nassau."

"Juliana, Countess van Nassau?" Hans echoed. "Moeder of Prince Willem van Oranje-Nassau."

"Or it may be his sister by the same name," Aletta corrected. Things began to spin together in a whirl of dizzying colors. "Juliana, the prince's sister, is her moeder's finest herbal student. She saved my friend, Pieter-Lucas, from a nearly mortal wound with her herbal cures." As the name rolled off her tongue, she felt her legs go weak.

She reached for the other sheet and held it reverently in trembling hands. Hans hurried to her side and examined it over her shoulder. His breath felt warm against her forehead. "Beautifully done," he said. "Do you recognize the title inscribed above the drawing?"

Aletta read slowly, thoughtfully, making out the letters as she went. "*Helleborus niger verus.* I know it well—the black hellebore. Tante Lysbet called it the Christmas Rose, and it grew in the Beguinage. As a purgation, it is a powerful herb for curing the mad and furious, the dull and heavy persons. Oma uses it yet for Moeder Gretta. Most excellent for patients molested with persistent cases of black choler or deep melancholy."

"That explains the verse at the bottom."

"Lo, how a rose upspringing," Aletta found herself singing the words of the old familiar Christmas hymn.

> "On tender root has grown:
> A Rose by prophet's singing
> To all the world made known.
> It came a flower bright,
> Amid the cold of winter,
> When half-spent was the night."

"I see you know the words well." She felt Hans' hovering presence press against her chest.

Fed by a growing frenzy, Aletta scrutinized the drawing. Surely it must be Pieter-Lucas' work. There had to be some clue, perhaps his signature. She held the paper closer to the lamp still flickering on the table. It was his style—just the way he always drew plants. She recognized the strokes of the drawing pen and imagined his hand etching each fine line, each broad shading. Her hungry eyes followed the stems, the blossoms, the fruits hanging from each stem. Somewhere in a bud or stem or leaf or tendril, he had to leave a vague tracing of his initials. It was his way.

Then she saw it! Deep in the heart of a tangled ball of root hairs, her straining eyes made out the faint motif of a hovering dove. Its outstretched wings held the perfectly excuted initials, PLvdG. Only one artist on earth would draw a dove in this way, and who else would put it in the roots of a Christmas rose?

Aletta clasped the drawing to her breast. She closed her eyes and felt warm saltiness flowing over her hot cheeks. A kind of recklessness possessed her. She simply had to know more.

Without looking at the man nearby, she blurted out, "Did he limp?"

"Who . . . what. . . ?" Hans stammered.

"The stranger! Did he limp?"

"Why . . . now that you ask, I believe he did."

"And carried he an arched scar across his right cheek?"

She looked up and saw pain in the man's eyes. He nodded slowly.

"To you, he is no stranger, is he?"

Aletta turned away, bowed her head, and sighed. Ah, but she had asked too much. Almost in a whisper, she answered, "*Nay*." Never had the simple word had to be coaxed from her lips with such intense difficulty.

At length Hans spoke in a heavy tone, "Perhaps the healer lady this young man seeks is my moeder's assistant."

Moeder Gretta, whose tea was past ready, had fallen asleep in her chair. Hans' two daughters were stirring about the room, and Oma was calling from her bed on the south wall. Aletta rushed to her patient's side.

# Chapter Nineteen

*Emden*

Middle of Harvest Month (August), 1567

*T*he *Black Swan Inn* lay tucked up into the far corner of Emden where a stretch of city wall running east and west curved and ran north and south. Pieter-Lucas van den Garde chose it simply because Yaap had told him it was the best Emden had to offer. The fact that it was as remote as one could get from the center of the city gave him hope that he might find in it a haven where he could rest after a long and disappointing day.

From the day he and Yaap had set out from Dillenburg—how many weeks ago was that now?—it seemed that all the stars in the heavens were lined up against him. He'd set out with such high hopes and dreams. For weeks before he left, over and over he'd fancied the story of their journey in glowing colors and with undaunted enthusiasm.

He and Yaap would ride into some tiny village carrying Pieter-Lucas' drawings made with great care in Juliana's herb garden. They'd walk into the local bookshop and show a couple of sample drawings and make inquiry about an herbal *physicke*. Then when the printer would ask, "And how do I know you are to be trusted, young man?" he'd produce that impressive letter from Juliana. The man would read it and bow. "Ah, Juliana Countess van Nassau has sent you. Why, but of course, we do indeed have such a *physicke* as you seek living in yonder street. Step right this way."

He would take them to the woman who would gladly give them her secret elixir, even with the recipe, for who could withhold the most secret of recipes from the great Juliana?

Further, in some mysterious way his little dove signatures on all the drawings he would pass around to printers and herbalists would bring about the seemingly impossible. They would lead him, at last, to Aletta and her family in the hidden village where they had fled for refuge. Of course Dirck Engelshofen would play the aloof adversary when confronted. But Pieter-Lucas would immediately present him with his two cherished bits of amazing evidence.

"Hendrick van den Garde is not really my vader," he would say with triumph. "What's more, the villain has been hanged on the shores of the wild Zuyder Zee."

How he loved to practice reciting the shocking news and imagining the man's reactions. While the stunned man would stroke his beard and look back and forth between him and Aletta, Pieter-Lucas would produce his latest cartoon, drawn with precision to lampoon the Beggars. Like nothing else, these masterpieces would reveal what disgusting rascals the Beggars all were. Dirck Engelshofen would be nearly bowled over at this point.

Then, quickly, lest the man have time to reconsider, Pieter-Lucas would whip out his final proof—the tried and proven secret recipe. He would assure Dirck that it was absolutely guaranteed to bring healing to Moeder Gretta.

Dirck Engelshofen would then shake him by the hand and smile a broad welcome, maybe even call him son and put his hand into the hand of Aletta. She would look up at him with those adoring eyes, and they would marry with great pomp and ride off to Leyden as Opa had promised. There he would learn to paint and they would live happily till the sun would set on their lives.

How many times he'd relived the dream, each time refining it a bit here and there until it filled him with the most fantastic anticipation imaginable.

And how many times it had mocked him.

No printer he found seemed impressed by his drawings—neither the cartoons nor the herbs. Amazingly, almost none of them had heard of Juliana, Countess van Nassau, and none knew any old ladies with secret elixirs for curing persistent madness.

Never did a sign of Aletta or her family surface, not even a tale of Moeder Gretta's noisy madness. In one place, Pieter-Lucas and Yaap had been nearly captured by a regiment of Spanish soldiers getting ready to pillage some unguarded village. In another, they had hit upon a nest of Beggars who claimed to be survivors of the great hanging where Hendrick met his end. They refused to believe he and Yaap were messengers of Prince Willem. They robbed them of their money and nearly absconded with their horses and victuals as well. If they'd uncovered Pieter-Lucas' precious cartoons, no doubt they would have ended all of both boys' dreams in an instant.

Only in Leeuwarden had they found anything as they expected. Ludwig van Nassau, Prince Willem's brother, was indeed where they were told he would be. They gave him a message from Prince Willem and he, in turn, sent them to Emden, where he was quite certain lived an elderly woman known as the Healer of East Friesland. "If anyone has such a recipe," Ludwig said, "surely this is the woman."

He provided them with fresh provisions, and for a time Pieter-Lucas almost had hope. Then, the first day back on the road, Yaap's horse was frightened by a passing coach and threw him to the cobblestones. Yaap's leg was broken, and he had to stay behind in the care of some loyal followers of Willem and Ludwig.

Almost, he'd given up his search at this point. But Yaap reminded him that if he quit now he might ruin his last real chance to find Aletta. "Go on, do you hear?" he had urged. "You don't need me."

"But what about you?"

"What makes you think I need you here? If I live until you return, well. If not, I'll not have ended my life in hindering you on your quest."

"Of course you'll live," Pieter-Lucas mocked his friend for one more exaggerated statement.

"Then, what are you waiting for, *jongen*?" He'd waved him away with such vigor that he strained his leg and turned his face into a painful scowl.

Cautious enthusiasm spurred Pieter-Lucas on, and indeed, at first it did seem as though there might be hope. He located the inn without difficulty or incident and tethered his horse. The innkeeper seemed more than willing to give him the information he sought.

"Printers? We've a lot of them in this place, my boy. Which one you looking for? The recognized official one, the questionable Calvinist ones, or the—ahem"—he cupped a chubby, grimy hand around his whiskered mouth and finished in a rough whisper—"the illegal Anabaptist press?"

Pieter-Lucas threw him a perplexed question mark. "I . . . I don't know," he stammered.

"I'll tell you where they all are . . . You pick . . ." The innkeeper followed with a volley of detailed directions to half a dozen printers spread over the city.

"I've been told there is a healer lady living in this city. Is that so?"

"Oh *ja, ja*. The Healer Lady of East Friesland. In the greatest of luck, you are, do you hear? She lives a short walk from here. You'll soon be thanking your lucky stars you beat a pathway to the lodgings of *The Black Swan*."

Almost it seemed too good to be real. And so it turned out to be. The printers, again as everywhere else in his journey, didn't care an apple about his drawings. Nor did they know who Juliana was. And when he found the house where the healer woman lived, he learned she lay sick in bed herself and could not see him.

Her son met him at the door and invited him to return. Of course he'd heard this answer before. Always, when he did go back, the door would be slammed in his face more firmly than anywhere else. But this man at least had a kind and honest face.

Pieter-Lucas yanked off his jacket, tucked his knapsack carefully into his bed, blew out his light, and stretched out for a good night's rest. "I'll close my eyes and forget it all for a few hours. Maybe morning's light will put a different color on things."

He had hardly closed his eyes, however, when the quiet was shattered by loud, boisterous noises rising from the tavern on the ground floor. For a while, they seemed simply to be the pleasant sounds of revelry. Had he not been traveling alone in a land so far from home and familiar things, and had his day not gone so badly, he might have been happy for a bit of revelry himself.

Then, just after the city bellman had called out the hour, and Pieter-Lucas had grown accustomed to the sounds which had nearly lulled him to sleep, the mood of the carousers changed. A loud banging of doors was followed by angry voices that grew more intense and more angry by the moment. Where was the proprietor of this place? How could he sleep through such hubbub? Surely he must care about the reputation of his house. The storm of anger worsened until he sensed his very safety was in danger.

At last the noisy intruders began clumping up the long stairs. If Pieter-Lucas thought this would signal peace, he was soon to discover the great error of his expectations. For they all climbed up to the attic floor above him, where, in the room directly over his head, they continued their hostilities. Added to the angry shouts and thunderous steps, Pieter-Lucas heard clashes of metal against metal.

"A duel!" he cried.

Then one enormous, shuddering thud shook the room. Pieter-Lucas stared at the ceiling aghast, half expecting to see a hole open up and human limbs come dangling through.

"Enough! Where is the proprietor?"

Pieter-Lucas bolted for his door. He unfastened the latch, pulled the heavy door open with a grating screech, and looked out to see the proprietor clambering up the stairs. He carried a candle in one hand, a big stick in the other, and was closely followed by his wife, her arms loaded with linens and a big pitcher. He heard a mad dash of feet toward the outside wall, then a long moment of silence—deathly, heavy, ominous silence.

Next, a progression of scurrying sounds and soft voices interspersed with heavy moans seemed to come from a spot directly above him. One more door banged shut and all died down again. Pieter-Lucas prepared to sleep.

Instead, a chorus of new sounds tormented him. Persistent winds sweeping down from the North Sea howled and whistled around the corner of the building. From somewhere out beyond, a windmill creaked in rhythm with the wind. From the room above, he heard an occasional moan, then a soothing voice. When for the second time in this long night he thought he might find the coveted oblivion of sleep, a raucous horn sounded in the street below and a voice called out,

> "Loving Sirs, lett me say to you,
> The clock twelve hath strucken now,
> Looke to your fyer and your light,
> That no mischance befall this night."

Too late to prevent mischances in this place. Pieter-Lucas crawled beneath his feather bag and pulled it close over his ears. "*Nay, nay,*" he scolded himself aloud, "listen not to one thing more. Go away, wind in the dark skies, moans in the attic above, and bellman in the streets below. Come sleep, merciful, numbing sleep." Pounding his fist into the sleeping mat beneath his restless body, he vowed, "With the first rays of morning light, I leave this place. Nothing but misfortune awaits me here."

The next thing Pieter-Lucas knew, he heard a loud banging on his door. He pried open his eyes and staggered across the room in a narrow wedge of subdued daylight filtering through the opaque window.

"Quickly, quickly!" Shouts from the other side of the door turned his fingers into thumbs all struggling with the bolt and latch.

"*Ja, ja,*" he retorted. "I come."

He freed the door at last and looked out on the distraught face of the proprietor. "Hurry, *jongen*, go get the healer lady and bring her here. I've got a tenant dying upstairs, above your very head."

"But the healer is sick abed herself. . . ."

"Then drag her out."

"But . . ."

"Then bring her son . . . her assistant . . . Bring somebody NOW! Can't have it said I let a regular tenant die in my rooms. Go!"

The proprietor grabbed Pieter-Lucas by the arm and dragged him from the room, then shoved him toward the stairs. Pieter-Lucas stumbled down the stairs to the tune of the man's mumbling voice, "Oh, my wife, you nearly let him die! Oh me!"

Not till Pieter-Lucas stepped out into the fogginess of an Emden summer morning did he begin to awaken. Was this another dream? Was he running through these streets for naught? He thrust his hands through tousled hair. Didn't even get his hat . . . or jacket. He had no idea who was dying or why. Was someone injured in the duel last night? Or was it just a fever?

"Brr . . ." He shivered, then moved from a fast gait into a running jog as he darted down the long street that issued from the front door of *The Black Swan*. He took the second street on the right and raced past the market square and the weigh-house. Already folks were gathering, setting up their stalls for the day's business. Sprinting past the harbor, he saw that the fishing boats and their owners had already set sail for the day. How late was it, anyway?

"I must have slept, after all," he told himself with a start.

Now, which house was it? They were all so plain and alike. One, two, three from the corner . . . Pieter-Lucas knocked two short, sharp knocks and waited. He ought to be impatient for an answer. A man lay dying in the inn! Must be the same man that moaned along with the wind last night. But whoever was he, anyway? After all, men died in inns every day, and why should he, Pieter-Lucas van den Garde, give a thought to it? He rumpled his hair, entangling his fingers in the unbrushed curls.

The door opened and the healer's son with the thick dark beard answered once again. This time, though, a cloud veiled those penetrating eyes and the man spoke hesitantly, "Uh . . . good morning, *jongen*, you've come early."

"I have indeed," he said, squirming under the disapproving gaze. Just as he suspected, the man had no intention of helping him. "I didn't plan it so." The words fell out clumsily, and Pieter-Lucas' discomfort grew in the presence of this stranger. "You see, the proprietor of *The Black Swan Inn* has sent me. He needs the services of your healer lady."

"I'm sorry, but my moeder has just awakened and is not yet able to get up and nurse another in need. What is the problem?"

Was this man an inquisitor? How much did he dare to tell him? He really had nothing to lose. "The innkeeper says one of his tenants is dying."

"Dying? From an injury? A wound? A fever?"

"I know only that the proprietor awakened me rudely and insisted I bring someone to help. Are you your moeder's assistant?"

"*Nay*, healing of bodies is not my business." He chuckled a little.

"Can you send me to another?"

"Wait here." The man motioned him inside the house. Pieter-Lucas stepped across the threshold and pulled the door shut behind him, holding tightly to the latch. He watched his host scurry across the darkish room and through a small curtained doorway. For what seemed forever, he clung to the door latch and looked about him in the large dimly lit room where bunches of herbs hung from the beams all around. On one side of the room, two girls chattered and giggled and busied themselves over the fire of the large open hearth. Across the room, beside an enormous ceramic stove of the kind he'd seen only in this part of the country, an older woman sat dozing by the fire, an occasional snore escaping from her bowed head. A strange aroma filled his nostrils, much like the herbs Tante Lysbet used to brew for Moeder Gretta. Oh, to be back in Breda with . . . But *nay*, a man lay dying in the inn. When would the healer's son come out of that room? He stared at the doorway where he'd seen him disappear.

When finally the man reappeared, he carried a large plain case. A young woman followed, going directly to a cupboard bed on the far wall. The man thrust the case into Pieter-Lucas' hand. "The young lady who is apprentice to my moeder has consented to go with you," he said. "You may carry the apothecary chest." He cleared his throat nervously, then spoke as if trying to appear threatening, something for which he was obviously not adept. "Only take care that you treat her with propriety, *jongen*, and return her promptly when the job is done."

Taken aback, Pieter-Lucas defended himself. "I may look a bit disheveled since I was roused from a dead sleep and thrust out into the streets. But I am accustomed to treating young ladies with respect."

"She may be only an apprentice, but you can safely trust . . ."

Pieter-Lucas heard no more. The young woman had turned her face in his direction. He gasped and held his breath. *Aletta!* He blinked in the dim light and stared hard. Could it be?

At the same time she looked straight toward him and stopped short, bringing her hands quickly over her mouth. "Pieter-Lucas," she gasped. "It's you, it's you!"

"Aletta, my Little One," he called back.

In his fondest dreams about their meeting, the frustrated lover had not imagined his Aletta to be more beautiful than he saw her now. Like the long-searched-for angel in "The Wilderness," she swept across the room toward him, her skirts swishing over the floor with a familiar rhythm, her curls hanging with the same precision he remembered, the perfect figure of all that was pleasing and warm. His head spun, his heart whirred, he had to restrain himself to keep from grabbing her and disappearing out the door, over the countryside . . .

She smiled directly into his heart with that special smile she always reserved just for him. "You've come. Praise be to God, I knew you would."

Then she stopped short, and in a flurry of excitement she faced the man of the house and asked, "Hans, is this the stranger who came yesterday to your door?"

"The very one," he said evenly.

"As you say, he is no stranger. This is my Pieter-Lucas." She turned now toward the stove across the room and shouted, "Moeder, Moeder, look who's here!" Turning back to Pieter-Lucas again, she said, "Moeder Gretta is well again, and you must meet Oma and the girls and . . ."

"And," the bearded man interrupted with a sober voice, "your friend came here to say a man is dying in the inn."

"Ja . . . ja." The words jerked Pieter-Lucas back to his senses. "A man is dying in the inn. We must go!"

Aletta shouted back over her shoulder, "Don't forget to dress Oma's wound, girls, and give her the hog's fennel tea in sips." She went to her moeder, patted the awakened woman on the hand, and said, "All will be well, Moeder. We shall return as soon as possible."

She moved toward the door and nodded toward the bearded man who stood between her and Pieter-Lucas with an unconvincing smile. "Pray us Godspeed, Hans," she begged.

"I shall," he mumbled. Stiffly he moved aside and let them pass.

Pieter-Lucas held open the door and breathed in pure euphoria. His beloved in warm flesh-and-blood presence rustled past him and out into the world. With one hand he carried the apothecary chest, and the other he shoved resolutely into a pocket lest it get away and grab his love around the waist.

"Am I really awake? I mean, nobody told me you were here. I was routed out of bed to call the healer lady. If I'd known you were the one"— he remembered his hair and clothes rumpled from unshed sleep—"I'd have combed the tangles from my hair, washed the sleep from my eyes, grabbed my cap and jacket . . . Oh, Aletta, my love, my love . . ." The phrase rolled off his tongue like silken gold. How long he'd waited to say it for her listening ears!

"What does that matter? You've finally come." She spoke through rose petal lips with an awed hush that melted the young man's heart and stirred up an intense inner passion. Had he not been carrying the apothecary, he would have been unable to restrain himself a second longer.

"Can anything ever matter again, now that I've found you?" he asked.

Nothing must intrude to mar this moment given to them for drinking at the bubbling well of happiness. Words of any kind seemed unnecessary. Even the man dying in the inn faded far away from thought. Their feet floated over the cobblestones and their heads soared and dipped with the free-flying gulls. The dismal fog lifted and dissipated into the blue heavens above them.

"I fear there is one thing that does matter," Aletta said, her head drooping suddenly.

"*Nay*, nothing could possibly matter. We are together. What more?"

"Moeder's Kaatje's vow, Pieter-Lucas."

A sharp pain pricked at his heart. "She told you, then?"

"She told me just before she died. She charged me to be sure her daughter kept the vow for her. Since I am her only daughter . . ."

"Say no more," Pieter-Lucas interrupted. "That was Moeder Kaatje's vow, not mine, nor yours!"

They were standing before the huge old doors of *The Black Swan Inn*. Pieter-Lucas pulled his hand from his pocket and reached out to seal her lips with his forefinger. Then he lifted her chin till their eyes met and held each other in an irresistible gaze. "We, too, have made a vow," he said at last.

"You mean. . . ?"

"And God wrote it in His book."

"Oh, Pieter-Lucas!" Her eyes told him she agreed.

---

The instant the young pair set foot in the inn, the spell of warmth and exhilaration was savagely attacked. The proprietor awaited them, his protruding belly draped with a dingy white apron, his balding forehead partially exposed with strings of thin graying hair straggling out beneath the brim of a dark felt tam.

"This is the healer lady?" He bellowed without a greeting.

"As I told you, she's sick abed," Pieter-Lucas retorted, "but she sent her assistant." A feeling of pride swelled in his breast.

The stout little man looked Aletta over, a frown puckering his brow and pulling hard at the lower corners of his mouth. All the while he groused to himself and cast looks of doubt at her like miniature daggers.

What right did he have to look at her so? Pieter-Lucas bristled and moved closer to Aletta. If only he could carry her off in his arms to safety. His heart ached, being so near and yet so very, very far!

The proprietor opened his mouth as if to say something, then swallowed his words. Finally he turned around and headed for the stairs. "Follow me," he ordered with a gruff mumble.

They complied, moving across the room, up one flight of creaking wooden stairs, then down a dingy hallway. Stopping at the foot of a ladder leading to the attic, the old man said, "Just want to warn you. This is no job for a delicate stomach. Surprised the old guy's lasted so long. My wife sat with him through the night listenin' to his moans, washin' out the wound, and wipin' up the oozin' blood. If he weren't a regular tenant, I would've left him to his fate."

He scrambled up the ladder, grousing, "Contemptible, quarreling Beggars! Knew I shouldn't have let them in here last night."

"Beggars?" Pieter-Lucas exploded. "So that's what all the ruckus was about last night while I tried to get some sleep?"

"Contemptible villains, all of them!" The proprietor seemed to have only one line.

Pieter-Lucas felt a shiver trip down his spine and a hard knot punch at his stomach. Ever since he'd gone to Dillenburg he'd heard dozens of reasons why a servant of Willem van Oranje was expected to treat these uncivilized men like respectable soldiers. "Crude as they are, they're still the only hope for saving the Lowlands from tyranny!" He'd heard the line so many times he'd even been tempted to believe it a time or two.

But this late morning, standing in the dim light of the shaggy-ceilinged attic room of *The Black Swan Inn* was not one of those times. One look at the miserable, shriveled heap of a man still lying on the floor, no doubt in the same spot where his assailant had felled him, and Pieter-Lucas could see he, too, was a Beggar. *Despicable scum!*

Aletta was already kneeling at the man's side. Pieter-Lucas stood aloof, watching her with a growing mixture of wonder, admiration, and the urge to snatch her away and protect her from whatever harm he felt surely would come to her from touching a Beggar. Strangely, she acted as calm as if she were attending to Prince Willem himself. Did that go with being an herbal healer? Juliana was the same, he remembered.

"What have you done for the angry knife wound in this shoulder?" the gentle nursemaid asked the proprietor's wife.

"Even a Beggar is human, you know, and deserves a quiet way to die," the woman said defensively.

"What are you talking about? This man's no Beggar," the proprietor interrupted. "A respectable, longtime tenant, that's all."

"Look for yourself," the woman challenged. "No matter how respectable the tenant, when he comes wearing all these trappings, the whole world knows he is a Beggar."

"What trappings?" the proprietor challenged.

"See the bowl around his neck?" she demanded. "And this Beggar's penny in his hat? Now, get out of the way."

She turned her attention back to Aletta and went on, "Anyway, as I was trying to say, I did my best."

"I know, I know," Aletta said. "Only, please tell me what you did."

With hesitation she began, "First I used a shepherd's purse bath to stop the bleeding. It bled somethin' awful. Never saw the likes. Can you believe these ruffians had a duel goin' on up here? And in our room!"

"Hush, woman," her husband interrupted again. "Just answer the girl's questions, never mind the embellishments." To himself he mumbled, "My tenant a Beggar? Nay, I don't believe it."

"I see you wrapped him in a feather bag," Aletta prodded. "Wise woman you are."

"Had to keep the chill from sending him into Hades. Tried all the things I know to do. Even sliced some onions and laid them over the wound. But he's burning now with a heat. I've no more ideas."

"Fine work, Vrouw. The man can surely thank you for saving his life."

Before the woman finished reciting her efforts, Aletta had already opened her apothecary and begun to remove glass bottles and little pouches of powders and spoons for stirring. She dispensed instructions like a real herbalist. She sent the proprietor and his wife to fetch a fresh pitcher of water, a clean basin, and a supply of cloths for bandages. Then, handing the woman a cloth pouch, she added, "And prepare a cup of this goldenrod tea for chasing away the fever."

Pieter-Lucas stood looking down, his hands in his pockets. He wrestled with a host of new emotions surging through him. More and more, one feeling overpowered the rest. He could scarcely believe the subtle changes in his Aletta since they had parted that afternoon so long ago in the birch wood of Breda. What was it exactly? Something strange, but comforting and wonderful. Never had he felt so proud!

As soon as the proprietor and his wife left the room, the young herbalist folded her hands in her sloping lap, bowed her head, and began to weep. Pieter-Lucas heard the sobs and fell to his knees beside her. He took her quickly in his arms. How warm and soft she felt!

"What is it, my love?" he whispered. An hour ago when he'd found her, he'd felt so certain nothing in the world could mar their happiness. "I never should have brought you to this wretched place."

She shook her head and protested. " 'Tis a part of the plan."

"What plan?"

She did not answer, only wept.

Beside himself, he begged, "Please do not weep, Little One. I'll take you away. You need not finish this ugly work."

She touched his hand and lifted her eyes to his. He felt an odd discomfort under the pressure of her gaze. Compassion combined with disappointment, pain, and disbelief in that long, unflinching look. What power this new Aletta had!

" 'Tis God's plan put us here, Pieter-Lucas—God's plan."

God's plan, indeed! "And does this God forever plan that we live only with pain and waste our energies on troublesome Beggars?"

"Stop, Pieter-Lucas. Look at this man."

He could bring himself to do no more than toss a glance at the ragtag old creature lying at his feet without movement or color. "Dead already?" Almost he hoped it might be so.

"*Nay*. Just look . . . really look, and tell me what you see."

Pieter-Lucas swallowed the lump of revulsion that welled up in his throat and searched the pale wrinkled face with its high broad forehead and long sharp nose. The dark hair, unkempt mustache, and scraggly beard were all heavily laced with ribbons of gray and had grown so wildly that they nearly obscured the face. He looked at Aletta. She returned his look without a smile and let the tears course freely down her cheeks. "What am I searching for?" he asked again.

"You recognize him not?"

"Should I? All Beggars look alike."

Aletta lifted the man's head into the distorted block of daylight coming through the single window in the ceiling. She shoved the wild hair back from the leathery face. Suddenly the man groaned and stirred, and for an instant he opened his eyes. In their unsteady, filmy gaze, Pieter-Lucas saw the thing that set this man apart from every Beggar on earth. The angry madness was gone from the man's eyes, leaving the fever's redness burning around the edges. But their steely grayness told the story.

"Hendrick van den Garde? How. . . ?" Pieter-Lucas pulled away and braced himself against the fierce flow of energy that surged through every part of his body. The man's eyes flickered, his facial muscles twitched, and his lips moved ever so slightly.

"Impossible! Hendrick van den Garde was hanged on the shores of the Zuyder Zee."

"Hanged? Oh, Pieter-Lucas, how dreadful!"

"He was supposed to be in the regiment of Brederode's men who were caught fleeing the country."

"You weren't there?"

"*Nay!* A messenger brought word to Prince Willem in Dillenburg where we had just arrived from Breda. Oh, but I was so sure. . . . He *had* to be among the hanged, I counted on it. . . ."

Just when he'd grasped his fondest dreams in one hand, before he'd had the chance to see Dirck Engelshofen, to tell him the good news and produce the evidences that would set him free to have and to hold his beloved . . . Just when life was about to begin for real, this . . . this . . . despicable enemy had to reappear and put the final sword to it all. Why, why, why?

Pieter-Lucas leaned back away from the body. In his heart he heard the now familiar voice of vengeance once more.

"Revenge," it cried. "You have the last word after all. Your enemy's life lies in your hands. You only need to take away your beloved with her healing herbs, and he will die. You will tell the world you did all you could but it was too late. None will ever know better. The world will rejoice at the riddance of one more nasty Beggar, and you will be satisfied with your revenge!"

Pieter-Lucas pushed himself to his feet. "Quick now!" he urged himself. "Heed the voice and finish this just design before your heart destroys your nerve." He grasped Aletta by the arm and coaxed, "Come with me, away from here, my love, before your Vader Dirck finds Hendrick van den Garde still living and snatches you once more from my arms."

She looked up at him, wild confusion darkening her fair face. "Pieter-Lucas, how can you say such a thing?"

"If we linger, what's to save us? Come. . . !"

"But your vader's life lies in our hands, and you would forfeit it for our happiness?" She wrenched her arm from his grip.

"This man is not my vader," he retorted.

"But he is. You said so yourself."

"Hendrick van den Garde is not my vader!" The words stormed out of his lips and left him quivering inside.

Aletta gasped, "Pieter-Lucas, what has possessed you?"

Pieter-Lucas stood staring at the young woman beside the fevered heap of human flesh and bones on the floor. A vicious storm tore at his emotions. On the one hand, the wild voice of vengeance screamed in his ears. With quiet persistence, his conscience responded, "Be gentle with her, *jongen*. Don't stab the heart you love."

Overcome by the tender passion of a long-frustrated suitor, he stooped at last and spoke more gently. "Aletta, you've a kind and loving healer's heart. But I cannot let it keep us apart any longer. 'Twould take an hour to tell you all I've learned since last we parted. But this is neither the time nor place. Just believe me, it is true. Hendrick van den Garde is not my vader."

"Wherever did you get such a wild notion?" she demanded.

"Prince Willem van Oranje told it to me."

"The Prince Willem van Oranje, Lord of Breda?" She shook her head and stared into his eyes.

"The very one."

She took his hand in hers and ventured slowly, "If Willem van Oranje said it, it must be so no matter how absurd it sounds. And if it be so, then go to the kitchen and speed up the proprietor's wife that we might get on with the job before my vader arrives and we have to explain. Why waste your anger and revenge on this man, whoever he be?"

"Because whether he's my vader or not, he is Hendrick van den Garde, that's why," Pieter-Lucas retorted in a voice and manner far more frantic than gentle. "This man smashed more of my dreams than you ever knew about. I once had a nightmare about him while I lay ill in the Beguinage. He pursued me throughout and finally stood over me with his knife poised at my heart." He grasped her by the shoulders and looked into her eyes, searching for the core of her being. "Can you not understand," he challenged, "he will always threaten us and our happiness . . . unless I strike now while the sword lies in my sheath?"

Aletta's expression mingled shock and disbelief with pain and compassion so intense Pieter-Lucas could no longer resist the urge to gather her in his arms. If only she would go with him away! For an instant her body yielded to his embrace, then she pulled free, trembling.

"Remember," she pleaded, "that day long ago in the Great Church before the altar of the Holy Ghost, when your Opa led us to 'The Anointing' and the priest poured his holy anointing water over both you and your Opa?"

He hung his head and remembered it all as if the water still trickled down his forehead. "Anointed for what? To paint pictures for some pack of Beggars to mutilate and shred into ribbons?"

"*Nay*, Pieter-Lucas. Did you never understand what Opa was trying to tell you? 'You are anointed to bring healing in a world that is killing itself with hatred and ugliness.'"

"So many ear-tickling words for the inspiration of an idealistic child! I'm a man now, Aletta. In more ways than you'll ever know, I've learned that real life's not like that at all."

Aletta gasped. "Your Opa was no liar, Pieter-Lucas."

"*Nay*, he did not intentionally lie. He only had the misfortune never to fully understand that life given to childish dreams of anointings turns into a dry and arid wilderness. He knew enough about it to paint such a place, all filled with whirling, stinging sand and weakness and thirst. But

I have wandered in that wilderness for a long and lonely year. And I've learned that we must take the sword in our own hands and heal ourselves." He stopped and listened to the hollow echo of his words. They left him disappointed and drained.

"*Nay*, Pieter-Lucas, *nay*." The voice was Aletta's now. "We cannot heal ourselves with a sword. Rather, when we are faithful to the healing God has anointed us to do, He will give us reason to go on—and protect our vows as well."

"The anointing is dead, Aletta. This imposter that you nurse once sliced it to shreds in the church. The anointing is dead." Each time he repeated the words, they seemed less convincing.

"Can't you see it, Pieter-Lucas? Hendrick van den Garde destroyed nothing more than the painting." The authority in her challenge stung at him and beckoned him at once. "Your anointing was a gift from God. As Opa said, 'It can never be taken from you, unless you fail to use it to heal others.'"

Aletta reached into the folds of her dress and pulled out a familiar little object—the blood-spattered, painted dove he'd long since given up hope of seeing again. She pressed it into the big hand that had first given it to her, then turned and began to unwrap her patient's festering wound.

"Great and merciful God," Pieter-Lucas heard the words escape her lips, "bless these herbs we are about to apply and bring the healing for which you have anointed our fingers."

Herbs *we* are about to apply? *Our* fingers anointed?

Pieter-Lucas stared, first at the battle-worn relic in his hand with its shredded edges now worn smooth, then at the beautiful and devoted young woman at his side. He slipped his arm around her shoulders and whispered, "Aletta, my Little One, you have become Aletta, the Healer Woman. A healer not only of shattered bodies but of wounded spirits of men both young and old!"

A strange urge seemed irresistibly to overpower him. He bowed his head and, fingering the dove, heard himself saying, "Great and merciful God, give *us* strength to do what is right. . . ."

He clambered to his feet and slipped out of the attic room and down the creaking stairs. "Why is the proprietor's wife taking so long to brew that cup of tea?" he mumbled all the way.

# CHAPTER TWENTY

*Emden*

Middle of Harvest Month (August), 1567

*T*he tea was not yet ready, so Pieter-Lucas carried up the water and fresh linens and could not resist the urge to stop and watch the wonderful healer woman at work. Could this angelic creature with the tender touch and calm, quiet spirit really be his own Aletta?

"Please, Pieter-Lucas, go tell the proprietor's wife I must have the tea *now* if my patient is to live."

The urgency in Aletta's voice roused Pieter-Lucas from his adoring reverie. "I go once more," he said. He clambered down the ladder and ran for the stairs. "God help us if Vader Dirck finds us trying to spare this despicable man's life," he mumbled to himself all the way.

He had reached the proprietor's wife by the hearth, and she had just laid the little copper kettle of life-giving brew in his hands when he heard the front door of the inn burst open and a woman's hysterical voice pierce the air.

"Where is my daughter?"

Pieter-Lucas caught passing sight of a distraught woman dashing into the room with a man trailing behind.

The proprietor rushed to the unexpected guests and shouted back, "How should I know?"

"I told you it was a trap, my husband. *Ach, ach, ach!* Great God, have mercy on us all!"

A man's muffled voice murmured beneath the jabs of hysteria. "Easy, my wife, easy. Pardon her, please, kind keeper of the inn. My wife is not well . . . that is, she . . . she . . . Come, come, my wife."

Pieter-Lucas had placed one foot on the long stairwell that led to the floors above when he recognized the voices. Dirck and Gretta Engelshofen had come! "Make haste, *jongen*." He urged himself up the stairs. "Escape! But careful . . . spill not the tea."

He had almost reached the doorway when Gretta's shrill words darted from the background and caught him by the heels. "There he is, husband, there he is . . ." she called out, "the *jongen* who absconded with her. Stop that abductor!"

Pieter-Lucas dodged into the hallway and ran for the ladder. From below, a confusion of shouting and mad scuffling followed his hasty retreat. By the time he had reached the attic room, he knew they were close behind like a pack of wild hounds closing in on a frightened hare.

"Aletta, Aletta," he gasped. "Your parents have come."

"Did Vader see you?"

"They both saw me, and your moeder is howling with madness."

"*Nay*, that cannot be. Moeder is no longer mad."

"Just listen to her screams."

"But she has been healed."

"Healed?"

Aletta glanced toward the ladder, then motioned Pieter-Lucas to the floor. "Here," she ordered, "you give our patient the tea. Make sure he is at least in part awake before you pour it into his throat. I go to Moeder Gretta. She'll be calm when she sees my face, and I shall keep her away from here."

It was too late. By the time Pieter-Lucas had dropped to the floor and Aletta had moved Hendrick's head into his lap, he spotted Gretta Engelshofen's closely capped head emerging over the horizon of the floor. Recoiling from the enforced closeness of his contact with the man, he poured a cup of goldenrod tea into the cup and watched in disbelief.

"Where has the scoundrel taken my child?" the woman exclaimed between the shoves and grunts that hoisted her little body up and over and into the room. Dirck and the grumbling proprietor came close behind.

So she was healed, was she? Pieter-Lucas shook his head and narrowed his vision of the proceedings to a skeptical squint.

Almost before he'd planted his feet on the floor, the proprietor began dashing about, waving his arms frantically, and jabbering nonstop about his faithful tenant and his own impeccable record as an innkeeper and threatening to call the bailiff to evict this crazed woman.

Gretta, Dirck, and Aletta all ignored him as if he were part of the permanent furniture of the room. Gretta had hardly found her balance and squinted her eyes into seeing in the darkness, when she spotted her daughter and cried out, "Aletta, are you safe? Precious baby, God protect you."

Dirck reached for her, but she shoved him away, threw herself into Aletta's arms, and commenced to weep.

"Now, now, Moeder, all is fine." The young woman did not raise her voice or let it race. "'Twas no scoundrel led me away from Oma Roza's house, Moeder Gretta, but Pieter-Lucas, our dear lifelong friend who brought me here."

Gretta stopped crying and stared around the room. She looked at Pieter-Lucas and back at Aletta, her jaw hanging, a look of silent wonder speaking volumes.

Aletta added, "You see, we are safe and on a mission of mercy to an injured man."

"What man?" Gretta demanded.

At this point the proprietor interjected with an air of saucy triumph, "I told you there was a real injured man here. You thought it was a trick. Well, here is your evidence. . . ." He rattled on, pointing toward the patient on the floor.

Pieter-Lucas felt a strange protective impulse well up within him. Dirck Engelshofen must not recognize Aletta's patient. "*Nay, Nay,* Heer proprietor, have a care, stand back," he warned.

Acting on impulse, he curved his body around the sick man's head, creating a shield between him and the frenzied proprietor, the frantic woman, and her husband, whose eyes Pieter-Lucas could feel boring into him already. Who could ever have convinced him that he would one day try to protect Hendrick van den Garde from anything or anybody—from Dirck Engelshofen, of all men on earth?

Ignoring Pieter-Lucas' pleas for caution, the proprietor grabbed him by the shoulder and yanked. Pieter-Lucas resisted, but the man persisted and in the process upset the pot of tea and began trampling Aletta's fragile apothecary preparations.

"Stop, old man, stop it," Dirck Engelshofen ordered and stepped in to restrain him. "We believe you. It is clear to see a man lies here in great brokenness of body. Let my daughter do the duty you called her here to do. Stand back, stand back."

Stunned, the proprietor straightened and stood staring at Dirck Engelshofen.

Suddenly Pieter-Lucas felt Hendrick van den Garde's body stirring next to his breast. He watched the dark eyes open and the fevered lips crack and move. He grabbed the cup of tea which had narrowly escaped the angry proprietor's rampage and prepared to pour it into the patient's mouth. But before he would drink, Hendrick uttered one desperate, bone-chilling cry, "Great God, have mercy!"

Silence fell across the dark shaggy-beamed room. Hendrick van den Garde reached for the cup with his parched lips. He drank like a ravenous desert traveler, then fell back into the protective cradle of Pieter-Lucas' arms. The rhythm of his breathing told them all that once more he slept. The proprietor backed away, padded toward the ladder, and slunk off over the edge of the room. Dirck Engelshofen paced the length of the room and back again while Gretta clung to Aletta in a pool of weak sunlight in the middle of the floor.

She stared at the man on the floor and began to shrink back into the shadows. Then, without a warning, she grabbed her head in her hands, let out a pitiful shriek, and crumpled to the floor. Her husband rushed to her and Pieter-Lucas strained to see and hear the sudden shuffling about.

"I am fine now." The woman's voice came clear at last. Dirck and Aletta helped her to her feet. She took four short steps toward the patient and Pieter-Lucas until she stood directly over them. With an expression of profound pity, she continued looking at the unconscious man and said calmly, "That man on the floor once placed a curse on me and turned me into the mad Gretta you've all known. And the very sight of his Beggar friends near Oma's house nearly drove me mad again this day."

"What makes you say such a thing?" Dirck Engelshofen asked. "You have never seen this man before."

"Ah, but I have. He speaks with the voice of Hendrick van den Garde."

"Hendrick van den Garde?" Dirck stooped quickly to the side of the injured man and stared into his placid face. "Hendrick van den Garde, indeed." He rose to his feet and his eyes met those of Pieter-Lucas. The two men exchanged a flash of bewilderment.

He laid his hand on his wife's shoulder and said, "I don't understand. Hendrick van den Garde never did you any harm." His rebuke had no teeth, only perplexity.

"Ah, but he did," the now-calm woman protested simply.

"You never told me such a thing." His tone was as indignant as his words.

"I never told anyone because I was not sure what happened myself," she said. "For all these long years, I've held in my mind a confused jumble of memories from that awful day when Hendrick fought with his half brother on the bank of the moat beside the *Kasteel* stables—the day young Kees van den Garde fell into the water and died."

"Kees van den Garde fell into the water and died?" Pieter-Lucas blurted the question. Resting Hendrick's head on the floor, he stood to his feet, thrust his hand into his bosom, and pulled out the tiny portrait he'd salvaged from his mother's prayer book. With an eagerness that made his heart race, he handed it now to Aletta's mother. "The man in this portrait, is he the Kees you speak of?"

Gretta took the miniature canvas in her slender fingers. Pieter-Lucas watched her face. A look of pleasant recognition set it aglow. "Ja, ja. Oh, ja! Kees van den Garde was such a good man," she said with admiration. "He loved so to carve with his little knife. Left his mark in the Great Church, he did."

" 'The Birdseller!' " he said eagerly. "My Opa showed it to me."

Gretta's face was awash with a dreaming puzzled expression. "Your vader used to say again and again that no van den Garde would ever be free from an artist's prison cage. Your Opa scolded him for it many times, but he never seemed quite to believe otherwise."

Pieter-Lucas stared long at the portrait in his hand before putting it gently back into its place in his doublet.

"If only I could have saved Kees from Hendrick's ill will," Gretta said, near the verge of tears.

"Do you mean Hendrick shoved my vader into the water?"

She wrinkled her forehead and rubbed it distractedly. "I . . . I do not know for sure," she stammered.

Pieter-Lucas felt a violent throbbing drumming in his chest. A tumbling array of angry faces, blood, Beggar's chants, and biting dungeon chains swirled through his brain. Leering over him, he fancied Hendrick's shiny parade knife pointed straight at the spot over his heart where he had hidden the portrait. Impulsively, he grabbed the woman by both arms and demanded, "Hendrick killed my vader, didn't he?"

Gretta hung her head, wept, and nodded ever so slightly. "Perhaps."

"But didn't you see it?"

"I saw something . . ." She hesitated, stopping with an open-mouthed pause.

"What did you see?" he demanded.

"I . . . I . . ." Her wary eyes moved from Pieter-Lucas to Dirck to Aletta and back to Pieter-Lucas.

Dirck put his arm around his wife's waist and challenged the boy, "Take care, young man. She will tell us what she wants us to know."

"It's all right," she said evenly. "For years I've struggled to remember just how it was. Not until God's people prayed for me in the assembly room at our friends' house and dear old Oma and her Hans cared for me with such long and tender patience did I regain enough soundness of mind to bring it back. Even now, not all is perfectly clear."

Pieter-Lucas released his grip on the woman's arms. "Then you must tell me, what part is clear? I have to know!"

"It happened so," she began. "I was heavy with you, child." She nodded toward Aletta. "On a late afternoon as I passed by the stables on my way home from market I heard Hendrick shouting at his brother. A tragic premonition gripped me. Even you, my child, stopped still in my womb and did not move again until that evening when you were born. I had long known something tragic would one day happen between those two half brothers."

Dirck spoke up now. "There had always been trouble between them."

"Why so?" Pieter-Lucas asked.

"Well, you see, Hendrick was not your Opa's son," Dirck replied.

"Hendrick was not Opa's son?"

"*Nay*, Hendrick was fathered by a lusty castle guard before your Oma's marriage."

"How. . . ?" Pieter-Lucas felt the blood rising in his face and a knot forming in his stomach.

Dirck Engelshofen explained. "Your Opa, who loved your Oma with a deepest possible affection, married her immediately. But while from the beginning he treated Hendrick as his own son, the boy both envied and despised Kees."

"How so?" Pieter-Lucas asked.

"Kees was obviously a child after his vader's own heart—one more artist trapped with the name van den Garde but with no desire to join in the ranks of the *Kasteel* guard."

Pieter-Lucas felt the knot in his stomach tighten with each new sentence. "Despicable, nasty, heathen wretch!" He spat the words at the man he had so recently tried to protect. With great effort he restrained his feet from kicking the crumpled man he so detested across the room, down the stairway, and out of his life once and for all. But, *nay*, first he must hear the rest of the story.

Gretta picked up the account where her husband had left it. "One thing Hendrick envied of Kees more than any other—the love of your moeder, Kaatje. After you were born, Pieter-Lucas, it seemed more than Hendrick could endure. It was as if he simply must have Kaatje for himself. We all saw his intentions—all, that is, except your moeder."

"She was taken in by him? How could she trust him?"

"God only knows the answer to that. Immediately when Kees died, she sold all her possessions and took you, *jongen*, to live in the Beguinage. She even claimed she made some private vows in the church on Christmas morning, the very day Tante Lysbet first came to stay with me. Soon, however, she tired of so cloistered a life. No doubt she found it difficult to keep a small son in the Beguinage. And Hendrick, playing the ever present charmer, plied her with smooth words and gentle promises. In short time she allowed him to woo her away from her private vows with God and into public ones with Hendrick."

"Did no one warn her?"

"Many of her friends tried. Willfully oblivious to her danger, she would only say, 'A Beguine takes no binding vows.' She never understood."

Almost beside himself with rage, Pieter-Lucas arranged and rearranged the patterns and colors of each new revelation on the canvas of his mind. The mysterious pieces of the picture his moeder had begun to paint for him from her deathbed seemed at last to fit. Only one scene remained detached, alone on the sketch pad.

"But you have yet to tell me exactly what you saw when the two brothers fought behind the stables." He must place this scene, too, on the canvas.

"I can try. Neither of the men saw me, and from my obscured vantage point behind a huge linden tree—the one originally planted to mark the corner of the old Beguinage before it was moved to Annastraat—I could not be certain what I saw."

"But you did see my vader killed?" The boy was growing impatient with the calm and detailed recitation.

"It looked to me as if Hendrick shoved Kees hard against the brick wall, and then the younger man cried out and splashed into the moat. I screamed and Hendrick fled, yelling out as he ran, 'Curses on you.' When I did not hear Kees swimming to safety, I rushed to the spot as quickly as possible—I was foolish enough to fancy I could rescue him. But already his body had disappeared into the icy waters with only a line of bubbles to suggest the spot. Terrified, I fled, and by the time I reached home, the pains had begun in my belly. Aletta was born that night, and from that time I could not remember how it had all happened."

"Hendrick van den Garde was never tried for his deed?" Pieter-Lucas felt the familiar cry for revenge stirring about in his heart once more.

"Hendrick convinced the whole city—even your moeder—that he had tried in vain to rescue his brother."

Dirck held his wife close. "If only you had told me . . ."

"*Ach*, but I feared Hendrick van den Garde's ill temper. Besides, from the day Aletta was born, I was already having headaches off and on, and every time I thought about it, I became confused. Maybe Hendrick had told the truth and it was an accident. After all, I had not seen it really . . . and each day the scene grew more and more unclear."

By now the woman was weeping once more, and Aletta tried to quiet her. "Sit down and be still, Moeder. That is enough."

Pieter-Lucas looked at the man beneath his feet. So, just as he had begun to suspect, it was not the Calvinists who taught Hendrick van den Garde violence. Rather, it was he who taught them instead. Gone were the protective urges he'd felt so briefly. In their place, the inner voice taunted, "You listened to Aletta's advice and spared your vader's murderer!"

He clenched his fists. An irresistible urge to strike out at the pitiful-looking creature swept over him. *Do it now, jongen, before you lose your nerve.* Exhilarated by the energies that fed his anger, Pieter-Lucas fancied himself all alone with the helpless wounded man and yielded his whole being to the dreams he had nurtured and the opportunity he had sought so long.

He dropped to his knees beside Hendrick, murmuring with pent-up delight, "Murderer!" He spread his fingers cagelike and went for the man's neck. The sinewy cords felt dry and leathery in his grasp and he braced himself to tighten his fingers slowly. For one long waiting moment, he stroked the inner monster now purring with incredible satisfaction and savored the revenge that grew stronger with each rise and fall of Hendrik's heaving chest.

He began to squeeze. His fingers felt the warmth and steady pulse of life under his control. Suddenly, from some far corner he heard another voice calling to him as if through a deep midnight mist. "You are no murderer."

Involuntarily, he felt his grip slacken. A cold sweat broke out all over his body. It trickled down his arms through the long blond hairs on the back of his hands and onto his victim's neck. The inner monster's voice came through only faintly in choking gasps. "Finish . . . the . . . job!"

Unnerved, trembling, he tried once more to fix his grip. But his fingers slipped with the sweat, and a wave of nausea swept over him. Just then, a pair of strong arms tackled him around his chest and pulled him tumbling to the floor. Startled, he heard his assailant saying in his ear, "You are no Beggar, nor the son of a Beggar."

Dirck Engelshofen said that? Pieter-Lucas struggled against the older man to a sitting position. Grabbing him by the doublet flaps, he demanded, "You knew all along that I was no Beggar, didn't you?"

"Of course."

"And . . . you knew Hendrick van den Garde was not my vader."

"I knew it better than you."

"How, then, could you accuse me of being a Beggar and the son of a

Beggar?" Pieter-Lucas felt fire in his bones and his eyes and a strength in his arms he did not know he possessed.

"I called you neither a Beggar nor the son of a Beggar!" Dirck Engelshofen protested.

"*Nay*, but you did."

"I see that you heard me not well. I only said that for that time of trouble, I dared not allow my daughter to associate with any member of an image-breaker's household. I was careful not to call you the son of a Beggar."

Pieter-Lucas tightened his grip on Dirck's doublet flaps and fought to stay his body from trembling. But the older man obviously trembled as well. "So," Pieter-Lucas said with a sneer, "no matter how innocent I was, you found me guilty enough by association to send me away from your threshold to wander these long months in frantic search of the love of my life?"

"I only tried to save *The Crane's Nest*, my family . . ."

"Your reputation!" Pieter-Lucas interrupted. "Cowardly crane! You dropped the stone so quietly that no one heard you." He spat out the accusation and left it hanging in the short distance between them.

A groan escaped from Hendrick on the floor nearby, and Pieter-Lucas felt Gretta's hand tugging at his. Without a word, she put his hand into Aletta's. Then, taking her husband by one hand and Aletta by the other, she pulled them all to their knees beside Hendrick van den Garde's sleeping form.

"This is no time for accusations and explanations," she said. "God's book tells us to 'be toward each other friendly, merciful, forgiving, even as God in Christ has granted forgiveness to us.' 'Tis His message for this sacred moment."

What was so sacred about it? Only the soft hand of his beloved lying intertwined in his fingers kept Pieter-Lucas from bolting free. But Gretta Engelshofen had only begun.

"Ever since God restored my mind and filled my heart with so many good things in the fellowship of the brothers and sisters in this place," she said, "I have longed for this opportunity, but never thought that it could be."

She bowed her head and closed her eyes, and Pieter-Lucas, squirming, still sweating and breathing heavily, heard from her lips an astounding prayer.

"Almighty God," she began "who hast forgiven me so much, Thou hast put it into my heart to forgive this man the evil which he has done against not only me and my family, but against our dear Pieter-Lucas here and his family, most of whom have already passed on into Thy heavenly arms. We implore Thee to forgive Hendrick van den Garde for the blindness of his heart that has not allowed him to know the greatness of the evil he has done. Touch Thou also his body and restore him to full health, that he may be given from the abundance of Thy mercy one more opportunity to seek Thy forgiveness and do Thy bidding for the remainder of his mortal life. In the name and through the finished work of Thy Son Jesus Christ, Amen."

Gretta laid a hand on Hendrick van den Garde's and gave it a gentle squeeze.

How could she? Pieter-Lucas shuddered. But the answer was ringing in his ears. "Almighty God . . . Thou hast put it in my heart to forgive . . . as God has forgiven us. . . ."

This God Gretta just talked to, the God who puts forgiveness in people's hearts, was he not the same God Opa Lucas had loved and taught Pieter-Lucas to revere? The God who anointed him to paint? Could He be real, after all?

Great and merciful God! A stunned Pieter-Lucas heard the words move through his mind, winging their way heavenward. Could such a God also put it into his heart to want to forgive the murderer of his vader? From a dark, distant corner of his mind he heard the faint voice of his inner monster whimpering, "You vowed never to forgive."

How long he stayed on his knees wrestling with the enticements of revenge he had no idea. When at last he looked up, he saw through misting eyes that Aletta had taken her place as *physicke* again. He watched her fingers search the man's wound and prepare and apply a fresh dressing. He felt a new kind of urge tugging at his heart. Was he actually beginning to care what happened to this miserable wretch? Impossible!

"Be still," he addressed the monster. The tormenting words shriveled and sank out of his reach.

The sensation of some magnetic presence drew his gaze upward till he found himself staring into the eyes of Dirck Engelshofen. The last time he had searched those gray eyes they'd glinted with hard steel. Now they brimmed with kindness and warmth.

Before he knew what was happening, Pieter-Lucas was on his feet. Dirck Engelshofen laid a hand on his shoulder and said, "When I chose to save my family, I let fear destroy my powers of reason. I had no idea you loved my daughter so much. Can you forgive me?"

Pieter-Lucas blinked his eyes as if to clear away a heavy mist that hung over the scene before him, so filled with surprising revelations and strange new emotions. Minutes ago, he had asked Opa's God to put it in his heart to forgive Hendrick van den Garde the sin of murder. How could he not now forgive Dirck Engelshofen, whose only offense against him lay in a strong desire to protect his family? He looked the older man squarely in the eye and said, "What's to forgive? You were simply protecting the love of my life and bringing her into the safety of this place."

With firm arms, the two men embraced. Pieter-Lucas heard the older man say, "Thank you, son."

Son? Did Dirck Engelshofen really call him son? A thrill ran through the young man, setting him aflame with unabashed passion. Holding firmly to the arm that had just embraced him, he pleaded, "Tell me, since the danger is now past, how soon may I claim your daughter for my bride?"

Aletta's vader gasped, then opened and closed his mouth. "Why . . . well . . . that depends," he stammered, at last.

"Depends on what?" Pieter-Lucas felt the blood rising to warm his face, and he stared at the man before him like a cat eyeing a mouse attempting to escape.

Dirck Engelshofen shifted nervously and did not look directly at him as he cleared his throat, then edged cautiously into his answer. "There are two things the suitor of my daughter must promise before we can begin to consider his proposal."

"What two things?" he shot back the query.

"First, that you will not tote a sword for Prince Willem, or any other." He glanced up and paused, his eyes insisting on a reply.

Pieter-Lucas spread both hands in open palms toward Aletta's vader and spoke with calculated control, "My hands were made for sticks of charcoal and the paintbrush. Paint runs in my blood. One day my Opa's words may come true, and I shall spend my life painting." He pointed to Hendrick and added, "That man on the floor at our feet is the last van den Garde to carry a prince's sword."

The boy rubbed his hands together, moved a bit closer, and asked, "What was the other promise?"

"Second," Dirck Engelshofen said with more obvious ease, "you must cease roaming around the countryside." He lowered his head slightly in Pieter-Lucas' direction and added with a mock severity, "You know, a man must teach his restless feet to be still if he would take care of a wife."

Pieter-Lucas laughed. "I will not set a foot outside of Emden until I do so with my wife duly betrothed and by my side—as soon as I can locate, in Emden, some means of livelihood for sustaining her."

Dirck Engelshofen appeared deep in thought for a moment, then said deliberately, "I know of no one who will pay you a *styver* to paint a picture in this north country. But I did hear the owner of our printshop recently bemoan the fact that he had not been able to locate a trustworthy cartoonist."

Pieter-Lucas sucked in his breath to feed the wild visions that darted through his mind. "Is it possible that I might be considered?"

Still maintaining his sober composure, the older man pursed his lips and nodded. "I will speak to him for you."

"Then it is agreed that we may marry soon?"

"As soon as proper arrangements can be made." With a chuckle and a sweep of his arm in the direction of Aletta, Dirck Engelshofen added, "Provided my daughter will say *ja*."

Aletta jumped up quickly and wrapped her vader in a spontaneous hug. "Thank you, Vader, thank you!"

Then, turning to Pieter-Lucas, she laid her hand on his and whispered through broadly smiling lips, "Your anointing is not dead, Pieter-Lucas!"

He enfolded both her hands and pressed them to his chest. "Nor are the vows we made in the birch wood!"

# EPILOGUE

*Emden*

Christmas Day, 1567

*A*letta padded across the single room she and her family called home and stopped at the frost-etched window. Stretching up onto her tiptoes, she blew gently on the windowpane until a tiny ragged-edged hole appeared in the icy pattern. She peered through and sucked in the cool, moist air excitedly.

"Emden has donned her finest pure white fairyland dress," she exclaimed.

"God Almighty is smiling upon our celebration!" Moeder Gretta's words startled her from behind.

"Even on Christmas day?" Aletta asked.

" 'Tis your betrothal day. That is enough reason."

Aletta felt her moeder's gentle hand resting warm and reassuring on her shoulder. With her nose pressed against the window, Aletta mused, "Our pious friends that gather in Hans' hidden church may reject Christmas as an unholy pagan tradition, but they seem eager enough to come together to witness the betrothal of the bookseller's daughter to the printer's new cartoonist, Christmas day or not."

She turned slightly from the window to address her moeder. "Think you not, Moeder, that God must chuckle with delight because we celebrate this day?"

A soft gasp escaped from the older woman. "Hush, child," she whispered, then clamped her hand over her mouth. In the dim gray of early dawn, Aletta watched a playful grin break out around her moeder's fingers and a mischievous light dance in the narrow eyes. She squeezed her hand, then turned for one more hurried peek out into the enchanted world.

Instantly she spotted Pieter-Lucas through her peephole in the ice. All thoughts of Moeder and Christmas controversies fled. Entranced, she watched him move across a blanket of new-fallen snow toward their house nestled in the far corner of the printshop courtyard. He walked with great, ravenous strides. His breath trailed him in long vapory streamers, and she imagined she could see the broad dimpled smile and sparkling blue eyes. She felt her own face turn to smiles, her palms moisten, and her heart pound a wild and rapid rhythm. Breathless, she stared at the young man as he drew nearer. He rapped on the door with his characteristic three short, brisk knocks.

Vader sauntered across the room, drew the bolt, and opened to him. "A good morning to you, *jongen*," he said in surprise. "I didn't expect to see you so soon—nor here. I thought we were to meet at Hans' house after the summoning of the church bells." Vader did not invite him in but left him standing on the doorstoop while the frigid air seeped in through the gaping doorway.

"I know, I know."

Aletta detected an eager flutter in the familiar voice and longed to rush to his side. But not today. She must wait for her vader to say *ja*.

"I came early to beg your leave to borrow your daughter." Pieter-Lucas sounded breathless with eagerness.

"Borrow my daughter?"

"Just for a short spell. I'll have her back in plenty of time."

"A most irregular request on your betrothal day. Very shortly now, the bells of the Catholic Church will call their worshipers to holiday mass, and our friends will also hasten on their way to our celebration. What, my son, could be so urgent that it cannot wait?"

How hardly Aletta resisted the urge to peek around the corner of the doorway. She knew Pieter-Lucas must be rubbing his hands together in the cold and shifting from foot to foot. What could possibly have brought him here at this hour on this day?

"I've discovered something special I must show to her. It's just behind the printshop. You can even watch us from your window as we go."

"Before the betrothal?"

Why must he be so hard to convince? "We'll not be long!"

Aletta heard the pleading in his tone and ached to go to him. A tingle of excitement tugged her slowly along the wall toward the door. Gradually she crept on until she laid a hand on her vader's arm. When he looked down at her, she found she could not speak. Only with her eyes she begged, "Please, Vader!" He glanced up at Moeder and back. Aletta held her breath and watched as his expression shifted from uncertain perplexity to vaderly affection. Then he leaned in her direction and kissed her on the forehead. Turning to Pieter-Lucas, he said simply, "You may take her and go."

"Oh, Vader," she cried. Then grabbing her cape and slipping her feet into the street shoes resting by the door, she scurried over the threshold and warmed to the nearness of the man with whom she was soon to exchange public vows of her intention to marry.

"Only be sure you return," Vader called after them, "at the first pealing of the bells, do you hear?"

"At the first pealing of the bells," Pieter-Lucas repeated, "we shall return."

As if in an enchanted dream, Aletta snuggled close to him and together they crunched their way across the courtyard. Midway, Aletta stopped abruptly and spread one cloaked arm in a wide arc to take in all the scene around them.

"Oh, Pieter-Lucas, look," she exclaimed. "The whole city sparkles as if it has chosen to rejoice with us!"

She drew the heavy hood of her cape tightly around her head to keep the dampness from her white starched cap and her rows of ringlet curls. The frosty air bit her cheeks and nipped at her nose. What a glorious morning to be at last a woman in company with the young man for whom she had vowed so long ago to wait.

"None can rejoice half so much as you and I!" he said, giving her arm a squeeze.

The voice she'd known since she could toddle around her vader's bookshop back in Breda had deepened. The hands that had led her through the streets to many a festival and carved her a hundred little animals from wood had grown broad and manly. The profusion of straw-colored curls still framed his fair face beneath the old brown felt cap, but his chin now grew the whiskers of manhood. His blue eyes still sparkled at her and laughed and sometimes scolded as they had done for all the years.

"Come, Little One," he urged.

She hoped he would always call her by that name. She yielded her elbow to his protective care and let him lead her to a secluded spot behind the slumbering printshop. They stopped before a rounded mound, where he stooped and brushed the snow away from a perfect clump of white-petaled, purple-veined flowers.

He plucked off a blossom and laid it in her hand. Then, with a finger beneath her chin, he held her gaze as if savoring all the rich sweetness of the adoration she offered. "To my Christmas Rose," he whispered through beckoning lips.

She shielded the blossom against her breast and leaned into his open arms, pressing hard against him. With his nose he pushed back the hood of her cape and caressed her head with his lips. No spot on earth could be more safe, more warm, more ecstatic. Must she ever leave it again?

With steaming breath that wafted like incense on the frosty air, he spoke at last.

" 'This flower, whose fragrance tender,
With sweetness fills the air,
Dispels with glorious splendor
The darkness everywhere.'

"No more skillful words could I find to describe you if I searched the whole world over a hundred times," he concluded.

An air of wonder made his voice seem to float and stirred something in her heart so deep and powerful and altogether pleasant that she thought she could hold no more. She lifted her head and feasted her gaze on his fine masculine features. Something deep within her melted under the look of pure and penetrating love that lit up his entire countenance.

"Oh, my strong and wonderful love," she said in a rapturous half whisper, "such beautiful words! Only they can never apply to me."

He smiled and pulled her head to him again. With nimble fingers he tousled the curls that framed her cap. "*Nay*, but they could not apply better. The Christmas rose is for healing, you know. And 'twas you who healed the gaping wounds of my lonely heart."

Still protecting the flower, she pushed against his chest with one hand and said as gently as she knew how, "There is more to the poem, you know."

"Oh?" he started. "Maybe a couple of lines but nothing of any importance."

She cleared her throat, looked shyly up into his puzzled face, and answered, "I fear the three little lines you have omitted hold the key that will forever disqualify me for the honor you seem so eager to bestow."

"Impossible!" he protested.

She watched a strange combination of curiosity and perplexity move across the face she loved more dearly than life itself. Must she go on, break the spell that held them in its glorious captivity? Perhaps she should say no more, simply accept his glowing words. After all, this was their betrothal day.

"What do the other lines say?" he demanded.

"Another time," she suggested.

"*Nay*, we go no further till I hear it all. I must know what could possibly steal from you the honor of your title."

Hesitating, she offered him a reassuring smile on upturned lips and recited the words carefully.

" 'True man, yet very God,
From sin and death He saves us
And lightens every load.' "

A wondering look lit up Pieter-Lucas' rosy-cheeked face. "Which means?" he asked.

"Tante Lysbet always said it meant that the Christ child was the Christmas rose, sent to heal us from the madness of our many sins."

"Tante Lysbet! What did she have to do with it?"

"Do you not remember, Pieter-Lucas?"

"Remember what?"

"Tante Lysbet sang the words of this song to Robbin and me every Christmas morning." She let the warm memory shape her lips into a delicious smile and lifted her frosty cheeks. "It was a hymn composed by a distant cousin of her moeder's. Surely I told you that when I taught the song to you."

"You never taught it to me."

"Then where did you learn the words?"

"I inscribed the first stanza of this same verse on the drawing I left with Hans."

"I recognized them well, Pieter-Lucas. But if I did not teach them to you, then how did you come by them?"

The young man shook his head. "You won't believe me. In fact, the story is so strange, I'm not sure I believe it myself."

"Tell me," she begged.

"Well, if you must know, they were handed to me by a dark, shrouded personage on the doorstoop of my house in Breda. Pretty mysterious!"

He stopped short and his face broke into a grin, as if he'd just made some momentous discovery. "Wait a minute. You said Tante Lysbet sang it?"

"*Ja!*" What was so strange about that?

He lifted his head to the sky and laughed. "So that's who the Wilderness Angel was. Why did I never think of it?"

"Wilderness Angel? What are you talking about?"

"Oh, put it from your pretty mind," he said. " 'Tis a long story—for another day, my love."

Charmed by his hearty laughter, she twirled the creamy blossom in her fingers and looked up into the wonderful blue eyes hovering over her. "Did you ever doubt we'd come to this day?" she asked.

"Never—and always!" He pushed back her curls and framed her face with his hands. His smile reached to her soul and held her immobile.

"I only wish this could be our wedding day," she said.

"No more than I," he countered.

Disappointment pushed against her heart, creating a desperate urge to apologize. "I had no idea Vader's 'arrangements' would include all these months of preparing for baptism with Hans."

"Nor did I," he admitted. "If I had, I might have carried you off on my steed and settled it all in a hidden chapel somewhere the very night your vader gave me his word."

She brightened. "Why didn't you when you found out?"

He enfolded her with his arms, held her tenderly, and spoke in deep, somber tones, "When he first told me, I was sorely tempted. But then I looked into his eyes and saw something that brought me to a sudden halt."

"What did you see?" she asked.

"I saw the warm, protective love of a devout Child of God vader who could never marry off his beloved daughter till he knew both she and the man she was marrying were fully instructed converts. In that moment, I knew I loved you too much to do it."

"You loved me too much?"

"I loved you too much to take you away and make you disobey your vader."

For a long cozy moment, she reveled in the warmth of his arms and mulled over his words. He broke the silence without letting go the embrace.

"I think you have no idea," he said just above a whisper, "how great a treasure is a vader's love."

"Oh, Pieter-Lucas, you are so wise. God alone knows how much I need you."

He unwrapped his arms from about her and held her shoulders in his big hands. "God also knows it won't be much longer until our wedding day. The New Year is almost here." She heard the sparkle return, and saw it in his face. "Besides, I think we had to wait until Hendrick van den Garde left Emden."

"I suppose," she sighed. "A pity he never recognized you."

"I'm glad enough he didn't. He could have caused a lot of trouble for us both, you know."

"I do know. It's just that our healing work failed."

"Why do you say that?"

"It didn't bring back his mind, Pieter-Lucas."

"You saved his life, Healer Lady. That was all you were called to do.

More important, in the process, you saved my life and gave me back my anointing. Without you there in the attic of *The Black Swan Inn*, I would have killed that old man, then died of a mortal wound from my own guilt."

"Oh, Pieter-Lucas, how dreadful that would have been!"

With a twinkle in his eye he said, "That's why God gave you to me."

"Why?"

He lay a restraining finger across her lips before he answered. "To be my flesh-and-blood Christmas rose, that's why."

Aletta smiled with pursed lips, then tucked the blossom under her cape and into the bosom of her dress. She raised her face expectantly, and he met it with a cold nose and warm honeyed lips.

From the distant street, the church bells called their insistent invitation. Slowly, reluctantly, Aletta pulled herself free and chuckled softly. "The bells are calling," she said.

"I know," he sighed. "We promised your vader!"

"Besides," she announced, "the celebration cannot begin without the bookseller's daughter and the printer's cartoonist."

# ACKNOWLEDGMENTS

To all who encouraged, facilitated, taught, critiqued, and prayed me through this project, my deepest thanks:

Mother, for begging God to make creative use of my stubbornness and for glowing as I read each new chapter to you. Walt, for listening to my excited ramblings about Dutch history for thirty years. Martha, Tim, and Mary Jane, for being your mother's great cheerleaders and your spouses, Ted, Helen, and Don, for joining in.

Louk, Gerry, and Henriette, for teaching me your language. Han and Willeke, for offering resources, hospitality, and linguistic expertise. John and Anna Kay, for making contacts and unearthing facts in Breda. Brum and Ge, for newspaper clippings and the reminder that the biography of Willem van Oranje must be the biography of the God of Willem van Oranje.

Dr. Lewis Spitz, for bibliographies, addresses, and advice. Reference librarians, especially Karen, Mary, and Linda in Sunnyvale, and Frank Brechka at the University of California at Berkeley. Professor de Vries, for introducing me to Berkeley's extensive collection of Dutch history. Marjorie, for accompanying me on the research treks to UCB. The Institute for Historical Study, for accepting me as a historian, then teaching me how to be one.

A voluminous list of men and women with names like Motley, Guicciardini, Rien, Wedgewood, Beenakker, Mulder, and van Braght, for writing the piles of books that crowd my office and provide raw materials for creating *The Dove and the Rose*.

All the professionals who helped me on my research trip to Europe in 1985: Mr. Wolf, retired librarian from the Dutch Royal Military Academy housed in Willem's old *Kasteel* in Breda, for a valuable tour and that treasured chunk of blue-and-gold tile Willem once walked on. General-Major Leeflang, then governor of the Academy, with your wife, for inviting us into your apartment where Willem had lived four hundred years before. Mr. Van Boven, city archivist, for selling me your extra copy of the book, *Breda in the First Outbreak of Revolt, 1545–1569,* one of the most valuable books in my library. Queen Beatrix and archivist, B. Woelderink, for allowing me to peruse your Royal Archives in the Hague and hold your multigreat-grandmother Juliana's letters in my hand and feel the sealing wax still intact. Mr. Wijbenga, Delft historian, for a copy of an incredibly detailed chronology of Willem's life. Dr. Bremmer, minister and House of Orange historian, for the interview and books. Mr. Schmidt, keeper of the Museum of Oranje-Nassau in Dillenberg, for letting me copy Juliana's biography. Dr. Heinhold Fast, Mennonite minister and historian in Emden, for entertaining us, feeding us in the old Friese style, and letting us peruse your books. Marc Laenen, Conservator of the Open Air Museum in Bokrijk, Belgium, for giving us a fascinating appointment at nine P.M.! Martine Bergmans, for showing us all the remnants of the sixteenth century in Antwerp, then being a faithful pen pal ever since.

The many who taught me to write—especially fiction (Helene Barnhart, Louise Vernon, James Hall, Carole Gift Page, Lissa Halls Johnson, Lee Roddy, Donna Fletcher Crow) and poetry (Lucille Gardner, David Earl McDaniel, and Luci Shaw). LaVonne Neff, Carole Gift Page, and Till Fell, for reading my early chapters and suggesting improvements. Robin, Henreitte, Anne, Hank, Ted, Bettie Lou, Beth, Hans (born and raised in Breda), and Willeke, for reading the entire manuscript and giving me valuable feedback. Every member of the "Parts of Speech" critique group who has gathered around my Dutch dining table in the past ten years, for your loving encouragement and honest criticisms of what's become "our" book. Especially Barbara and Bi, who stayed with me from beginning to end and are already knee-deep into Book Two.

Les Stobbe, editor, friend, now agent, for reading the book with an enthusiasm you shared with the editors at Bethany House. The Bethany team—Steve Laube and Carol Johnson for believing in the book and Sharon Asmus for sharing my vision and for helping me improve it with a kind and godly spirit. Jack and Lance and all the rest, most of whose names I've never heard, for a job well done.

Finally, to all my family, friends, colleagues, and church family, for praying so persistently, I say, "*Hartelijk bedankt!*" (Hearty thanks!)